"You wished to see me, my lord?"

He swung round and looked at her. He thought: She knows. She is as much aware of this as I. She longs for me as I do for her.

He hesitated. "I . . . have thought a great deal about you, Lady Swynford."

She did not express surprise. She merely said quietly: "Yes, my lord."

"I wonder . . . if you had thought of me."

"The father of my charges . . ."

He took her by the shoulders suddenly. "I think," he said quietly, "you understand."

She held back her head. He saw the long white throat. He had never seen such white skin. He looked at her ripe lips and then suddenly he seized her. He heard her laugh softly and there was complete harmony between them.

PASSAGE TO PONTEFRACT

JEAN PLAIDY

FAWCETT CREST • NEW YORK

A Fawcett Crest Book
Published by Ballantine Books

Library of Congress Catalog Card Number: 82-7645

ISBN 0-449-20265-8

This edition published by arrangement with G. P. Putnam's Sons

Manufactured in the United States of America

First Ballantine Books Edition: September 1984

CONTENTS

BIBLIOGRAPHY

Armitage-Smith, Sydney	*John of Gaunt*
Aubrey, William Hickman Smith	*National and Domestic History of England*
Bryant, Arthur	*The Medieval Foundation*
Cammidge, John	*The Black Prince, an Historical Pageant*
Chute, Marchette	*Geoffrey Chaucer of England*
Collins, Arthur	*Life of the Black Prince and the History of John of Gaunt*
Costain, Thomas B.	*The Last Plantagenets*
	The Pageant of England 1377–1485
Coulton, G.G.	*Chaucer and His England*
Davis, J. D. Griffith	*King Henry IV*
Davis, W. W. C.	*England Under the Angevins*
Froissart, Sir John	*The Chronicles of England, France, Spain, etc.*
Green, John Richard	*History of England*
Guizot, M. Translated by Robert Black	*History of France*
Howard, Sir Robert	*The History of the Reigns of Edward III and Richard II*
Hutchison, Harold F.	*The Hollow Crown: A Life of Richard II*
Hume, David	*History of England from the Invasion of Julius Caesar to the Revolution*
Mathew, Gervase	*The Court of Richard II*
Ramsay, Sir James of Banff	*The Genesis of Lancaster, 2 vols*
	English Society in the Middle Ages
Stenton, D. M.	*The Dictionary of National Biography*
Stephen, Sir Leslie and Lee, Sir Sidney	*Lives of the Queens of England*
Strickland, Agnes	
Wade, John	*British History*

THE PLANTAGENETS

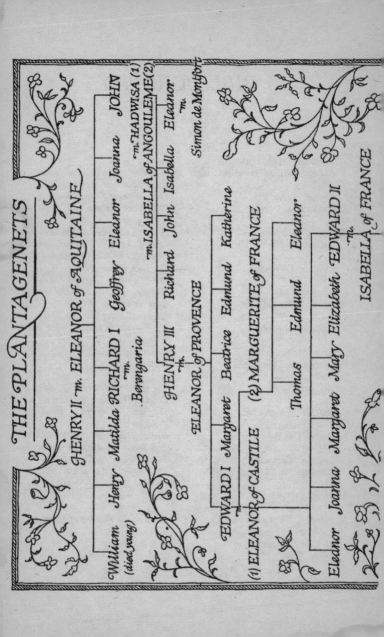

HENRY II _m._ ELEANOR _of_ AQUITAINE

William (died young) — Henry — Matilda — RICHARD I _m._ Berengaria — Geoffrey — Eleanor — Joanna — JOHN _m._ HADWISA (1) _m._ ISABELLA _of_ ANGOULEME (2)

HENRY III _m._ ELEANOR _of_ PROVENCE — Richard — John — Isabella — Eleanor _m._ Simon de Montfort

EDWARD I _m._ (1) ELEANOR _of_ CASTILE — (2) MARGUERITE _of_ FRANCE — Margaret — Beatrice — Edmund — Katherine

Eleanor — Joanna — Margaret — Mary — Elizabeth — EDWARD II _m._ ISABELLA _of_ FRANCE — Thomas — Edmund — Eleanor

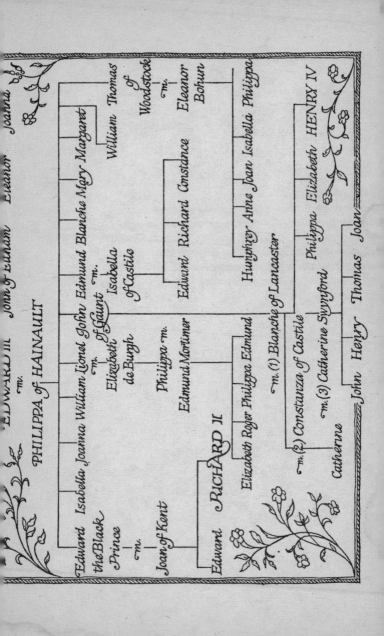

PART ONE

JOHN OF GAUNT

THE BIRTH OF THE BOYS

LONDON WAS IN a festive mood on that glorious May day. There was little the citizens liked better than a royal occasion and this promised to be one of the most splendid the capital had ever seen. The King loved display—the more magnificent the better. It was one of his endearing qualities. A weakness perhaps but a lovable one indulged in by a man who was said to be the greatest warrior in Christendom and whose reputation was as illustrious as that of his grandfather, great Edward, the first of that name.

Three days earlier the King's son—he who was known as John of Gaunt because he had been born to Edward and good Queen Philippa in the Flemish town of Ghent and the English despising foreign tongues found Gaunt came more easily to the tongue than Ghent—had in Reading been married to Blanche, the daughter of the Duke of Lancaster.

All would agree that the union of two handsome young people was a matter for celebration particularly as they were both royal, for Blanche was descended from the Plantagenet tree even as John was; and the parents of both bride and groom were revered throughout the country.

Henry of Lancaster, the bride's father, was known in England—and in Europe too—as Good Duke Henry, the perfect knight. He was chivalrous at all times, generous to his enemies, loyal to his friends, a deeply religious man, and his grandfather had been Edmund the second, son of Henry the Third.

As for the bridegroom's parents they were beloved by

the people as few monarchs had been before them. Their subjects must be proud of this tall handsome King whom many said was the image of his grandfather and only slightly less tall than that Edward Longshanks whose reputation had been enhanced by memory. This Edward had all the Plantagenet good looks—the abundant fair hair, the straight nose, the flashing blue eyes, the fine physique. Moreover he had brought stability to the country and such was his popularity that it had been forgotten that the glories of Crécy and Poitiers had been paid for not only with blood but with taxes wrung from the people, and that the acquisition of the throne of France was no nearer than it had been at the beginning of the war. He had married Philippa of Hainault of whose benevolence the people had been made aware and even in his marriage he had shown his good sense. Philippa might be over plump and show signs of continuous childbearing and be scarcely a beauty, but her fresh rosiness was comely and her expression one of gentle goodwill. She had on several occasions been known to plead with the King to show mercy, for he like most of his race was possessed of a temper which could be violent when provoked; and for this quality she had been deeply respected. She was womanly; she was virtuous; and she was known as Good Queen Philippa.

Their devotion to each other had been an example to the nation, and if there had been rumours of late that the King was not quite the faithful husband it had, in the past, been generally believed he was, such suggestions were forgotten when the royal pair appeared together.

London was delighted with its ruler; and all wise rulers knew that the approval of the capital city was essential to their security. Yes, they loved this King who could give a good account of himself in the jousts in which he so liked to indulge, and they enjoyed seeing him glittering with the jewels with which he so loved to adorn his handsome person.

Not only had he restored the prestige to England which it had lost during the previous disastrous reign of his weak

4

effeminate father, he had sired sons—all handsome and the eldest, as was fitting, was one whose fame had spread far and wide and already showed signs of being as great as his father and grandfather—another Edward, known throughout the country as the Black Prince.

So on this occasion of the marriage of the King's son, London determined to honour its sovereign. There was noise and bustle everywhere. From the gables of the houses women chatted to each other, discussing the merits of the bride and groom. People crowded into the streets; they lived most of their lives out of doors when the weather permitted, for they liked to escape from the closed-in darkness of the little houses huddled closely together, and regarded them only as shelters against the cold and places in which to eat and sleep. Celebrations such as this one made the highlights of their lives.

May Day had just passed. Then they had danced round the maypole welcoming the summer; they had decorated it with the wild flowers growing outside the city walls by the Strand which connected the City of London with Westminster and where lay the houses of the nobility, their gardens lapped by the river—the City's great highway along which craft of many descriptions plied back and forth at all hours of the day and night. They had festooned their doorways with flowers; and had even hung little glass lamps among the blossoms. After dark the effect had enchanted all who beheld it.

That was May Day. But this was an even greater occasion, for it had been announced that there was to be a great joust and that champions had come forward to hold London against all challengers. There was an air of mystery about this for none knew who those champions were; but all declared that there had never been, nor ever would be, a celebration to match this which honoured the marriage of the King's son, John of Gaunt, to the Lady Blanche of Lancaster, daughter of Good Duke Henry.

The pavilions were being erected. In these the knights would don their armour and await the summons to come forth and fight. Some were glorious indeed, made of silk and velvet; but the mystery was stressed because on the grandest of these pavilions were there no mottoes, no shield of arms to identify those who would occupy them. This reminded the people that the defenders of London were the mysterious knights who had come forward to serve the City at this glorious time.

Stands were being erected for the nobility. It would be a glorious sight. The King would be present. A royal occasion indeed. It was no wonder that hours before the tournament was due to begin people should be converging on the City. From Clerkenwell and Holborn they came, from St. John's Wood and Hampstead. They slept in the meadows of Marylebone and dabbled their feet in the Paddington brooks.

Even the sombre Tower, that grim Norman fortress, brooding over the scene seemed less menacing on this day and no one thought of the dark deeds which had gone on behind those grey walls. Rather they looked towards Westminster and the magnificent Savoy Palace on the Strand. The Savoy was the home of Duke Henry now and had passed through the hands of many owners; it had been built by the notorious Simon de Montfort who had married King Henry's sister and had come near to ruling England himself. But when he had been subdued King Henry the Third had presented the house to his wife's uncle Peter, the Earl of Savoy, and it had been known as the Savoy ever since. He in his turn gave it to a priory and it was from this priory that Queen Eleanor had bought it as a suitable residence for her second son Edmund, Earl of Lancaster and that was how it had come into the family.

Close to the City but outside its walls the joust would be held and already the people were waiting there. Cheeky apprentices, like boys let out of school, were chatting to the milkmaids; ploughmen, prelates, merchants—men and women of all ranks—had come to see the pageantry.

*   *   *

Excitement was intense. The joust had begun. The Queen and her ladies sat watching. With her was the young bride. Blanche was as beautiful as she had been proclaimed to be. Her long fair hair was loose about her shoulders; her skin was delicately white, her eyes deep blue. She was eighteen years old. People gazed at her with interest. Tall, slender, almost delicate she looked so young and tender beside the corpulent Philippa.

The people cheered themselves hoarse for the ladies. But they waited for the King and they waited in vain.

But there was little time for speculation for the challengers had come forward and the defenders were riding out to meet them—twenty-four knights led by five of the tallest men in the field. For a few moments the silence was intense. Then the trumpets were sounding and the heralds had come forward announcing that the tournament was about to begin. The heralds ran from the fields as the horses came pounding in. There was fierce excitement in the sound of the crash of steel against steel, in the shine of shields and lances as the sun caught them, in the battle cries of the noble knights. The Londoners looked on in utter fascination and their attention was focused on the men who had taken upon themselves the task of defending London. Who were they? The crowd thrilled with delight for the challengers were no match for them.

In due course their victory was complete. London had been bravely and skilfully defended against all comers, as it always had been and always would be.

Now the great moment had come. The mysterious defenders must uncover and show themselves. They rode into the centre of the field—those five tall men who had led the defending team.

One rode a little ahead of the others and when he lifted his visor there was no mistaking the thick fair hair, the blue eyes, the handsome Plantagenet features.

'The King!' The people went wild with joy. What greater compliment could he have paid his City than to place himself at the head of its defenders. They might have

7

guessed whose face was beneath that visor for he had not been beside the Queen in her loge. It was a game that kings loved to play when they were sure of the loyalty of their people. It was Edward's way of telling them that his City of London was dear to his heart and that he would defend it with all his might.

'Long live the King.' The cheers that rent the air could have been heard from the Tower to the village of Knightsbridge.

The second knight had ridden up. He had removed his visor and the crowd was now almost hysterical with joy for there was no mistaking that handsome face either. It was so like that of the King. More austere perhaps but as handsome, the great military hero Edward, heir to the throne, who had won his spurs at Crécy and was the hero of Poitiers, who a few years previously had led his royal captive, the King of France, through the streets of London and lodged him in the Palace of the Savoy. Edward, acclaimed throughout the world as the soldier whom none could equal. The Black Prince himself.

And he too was here to defend London!

The third knight was even taller than the King and the Black Prince. He was not so well known as they were but that he was a Plantagenet there was no doubt—the same colouring, the same handsome features and his outstanding height proclaimed him as a son of the King.

'Long live Lionel Duke of Clarence, Earl of Ulster, defender of London against all comers.'

How they revelled in the disclosures. They were not surprised however when the next defender was revealed as John of Gaunt, the bridegroom. A special cheer for him because it was due to his wedding that the joust was taking place. All eyes turned to the little bride seated so demurely beside the Queen; she was flushed with what must have been pride and happiness. What a handsome pair they were. Only great Edward could have sired such splendid sons.

What rejoicing there was. What better gesture could the King have made.

There was not a more popular man in London that day than the King of England.

When the feasting was at an end and the King and the Queen could retire to their apartments Philippa looked forward to a cosy talk with her husband. Philippa was ever ready to cast aside her rank. She had been brought up in a happy home which by the standards of royalty was homely. She cared more deeply for the happiness of her family than for their military glory or the possessions they might acquire. She had always deplored Edward's obsession with the crown of France.

Often she wished that Edward were merely a nobleman without the responsibilities of state though she knew of course that he would not have wished for that.

She liked to spend most of the time they could be together in discussing family affairs, and what occupied her mind now was her eldest son.

'Seeing John so happily married to dear Blanche has made me think more than ever about Edward,' she said.

The King nodded. Edward's future was not a new subject.

'He is twenty-nine years old,' went on the Queen.

'I well remember the day he was born,' said the King. 'What rejoicing there was! It was like you to give me such a son . . . our first born. Do you remember how the people stood about in the streets and how they would go wild with joy at a glimpse of him?'

'I shall never forget their joy. And they still love him. He has their devotion even as you have.'

The King took her hand and kissed it. 'You have brought me great happiness, my dear. It was the best day of my life when I came to Hainault and set eyes on you. I loved you then and I love you now.' He added with fervour: 'There has never been any to take your place in my heart.'

Even as he spoke he was thinking of his meeting with the Countess of Salisbury who would always be to him the most beautiful and desirable woman he had ever seen. Love had come to him so suddenly that it had over-

whelmed him and to the astonishment of his followers, for
hitherto he had been a faithful husband, he had made every
attempt to persuade the fair countess to become his mistress.
The situation was even more deplorable because she was
the wife of William de Montacute, one of his greatest
friends who was at the time a prisoner of the French, taken
in fighting for Edward's cause. It was a serious blot on his
honour, and even though the Countess had been too virtuous to submit to his lust, his conscience was sorely troubled.
Whenever he remembered that occasion he was particularly tender towards Philippa and made a point of protesting his eternal fidelity. Dear homely Philippa, who must
never know how near he had come to betraying her!

Philippa gave him her pleasant smile. She loved him
dearly. She had always been aware of her lack of allure
and had never ceased to marvel that Edward had loved her
as he did. She knew of course that great beauties like the
Countess of Salisbury must tempt him from time to time.
Rumours reached her. But she had decided to ignore
them. She longed for peace in her home. She was the Queen.
Edward was her husband. She must always be his first
consideration, and he and her children were her life.

But the occasion of John's marriage must make her
think with apprehension of her eldest son, for he was ten
years older than John and still a bachelor. Lionel who was
eight years younger than Edward was married. A wife had
been found for that second son when he was little more
than a baby, and a very good match it had been, according
to the King, for the bride although six years Lionel's
senior was a great heiress. Elizabeth de Burgh had brought
him Ulster and he now bore the title of Earl of Ulster as
well as Duke of Clarence, and Elizabeth's vast inheritance
was in his hands. He was happy, which pleased Philippa
as much as his wealth. Lionel was an easy-going young
man, pleasure-loving, far less serious than his brothers
Edward and John. He was the tallest in a tall family and
the handsomest. It had been said that there was not a man
in England who could compare with Lionel in good looks.

In between Edward and Lionel there had been the girls,

Isabella and Joanna, and little William who had died; and after John there had been Edmund, who had distinguished himself at the tournament this day; and after Edmund little Blanche who had lived but a short time. Mary and Margaret, her two darling girls, had followed; then another William who had died. An unlucky name for the family, William. And lastly Thomas, the youngest of the brood. None could say she had not done her duty as a mother.

Isabella, the eldest daughter, was headstrong and her father's favourite, spoilt, wilful, flaunting the fact that she could with a little wheedling always get her own way with the King. Philippa was uneasy thinking of her eldest daughter's future; she had constantly tried to restrain the King in his inability to stop spoiling her. But the greatest sadness had come to her through Blanche and her two Williams and Joanna. Joanna had died in Loremo, a small town near Bordeaux, when she was on her way to marry Pedro of Castile. Poor child! It seemed now that she had been fortunate to die, even horribly as she did of the plague, for Pedro who had earned the name of The Cruel would have been a fearful husband for such a gentle creature. She heard that his mistress commanded him and he was her absolute slave, and that he had murdered the wife he had eventually married and had strangled his bastard brother in addition to countless crimes of cruelty. Never again, Philippa had vowed to Edward, should a child of theirs be sent out to marry a bridegroom of whom they knew nothing except that he possessed a great title.

Edward always soothed her. He loved his children even as she did; he wanted them to be happy; but he must be mindful of the demands of state. He never stressed this though with Philippa, and he knew that in the case of his daughters he would always be lenient.

Lionel married, John married, and what of Edward?

'It is not,' said the Queen, 'that he does not like feminine society.'

She frowned. She was thinking of the King's father who had been devoted to the handsome young men on whom he

11

showered wealth and titles. No, there was nothing like that about Edward. He was entirely a man.

'He just feels disinclined to marry,' replied the King.

'But he is the heir to the throne! He should have sons by now.'

'You know, my dear, it is no use trying to tell Edward what he should do. He will do what he wills.'

'We have self-willed children, Edward. Isabella does what she wants with you.'

'Isabella. She is a minx.' His face softened. He loves this daughter more than anyone on earth I do believe, thought Philippa. She was not jealous, only pleased that their daughter should mean so much to him. But she did feel that the girl was becoming more and more unmanageable. However, the concern at the moment was not with Isabella but Edward.

'A minx yes, but it is Edward who is the greatest importance. It is no use speaking to him, I suppose . . .'

The King shook his head. 'Edward will go his own way. He knows the importance of marriage. He knows the people expect it. See how they applauded John's marriage. How much more so would they applaud the marriage of our heir. But he will go his own way. He will marry when he wishes and whom he wishes. You know Edward.'

The King's eyes were glazed with memory. That son of his who had filled him with pride from the minute he could walk. Isabella he loved the most. Well, she was a girl and he was very susceptible to feminine charms, but he was rarely so proud as when he rode out with his first-born beside him.

Crécy where the boy won his spurs! What a great day! And he had been ready—nay eager—to pass over the triumph to his son. Fifteen-year-old Edward. He had risked the boy's life then; had left him to fight his way out of trouble while his urgent prayer was 'Oh God, let the boy earn his spurs this day.' And valiantly had young Edward done so, proclaiming himself as a warrior at that tender age. And more recently Poitiers when against great odds he had won a decisive victory and captured the King of

France himself. How like Edward to let his father first know of the victory by sending him the French King's helmet!

A son to warm the heart of any King. England would be safe with this Edward to govern it. It was only in this matter of marriage that he was a disappointment. Twenty-nine and unmarried! Moreover he was a soldier and soldiers, even the greatest of them, could never be sure when they might meet a violent end.

'I sometimes think,' went on the Queen, 'that his heart is with Joan of Kent.'

The King flinched. Joan was another of those women with whom, had the opportunity offered, he would have dallied. Joan was quite different from the Countess of Salisbury. She was beautiful and she had something else—a provocation, some quality which was a constant invitation to the opposite sex. There had been a time when it seemed that the Prince of Wales would marry Joan.

Even so, faced with this provocative creature, Edward had been severely tempted—which would have been even more sinful than a liaison with the Countess of Salisbury. *She* was the wife of his best friend. Joan might have been the wife of his son.

They called her the Fair Maid of Kent. Fair she was without question and her father was Edmund of Woodstock, Earl of Kent, who had been the youngest son of Edward the First, so she was of royal descent.

In those days it had seemed that there could be no obstacle to her marriage with the Prince of Wales except that of consanguinity and that was a matter which could always be overcome by an obliging Pope.

'I often wonder what went wrong,' continued the Queen. 'I am sure Joan was fond of Edward and she is not the sort to say no to a crown. Yet . . .'

Philippa would never understand. Joan was ambitious. Joan was not averse to Edward; but Edward was too slow and Joan was not of a nature to stand by and wait. Her warm passionate nature demanded fulfilment and such a beauty had no lack of suitors. She had been affianced to

13

William Montacute, son of the fair Countess, but in the meantime Thomas Holland had managed to seduce her. There had had to be a hurried wedding and that was the end of the hope of a marriage for Joan with the Prince of Wales.

The King was thoughtful. He would have been a little uneasy perhaps if his son had married a woman whom he so much admired. It would have been very disturbing to have temptation so close and what if he were to succumb to it! He shuddered at the thought. It would be like incest. No, it was as well to have that temptress removed from his orbit. Even so there had been certain rumours. No one would ever forget that occasion when Joan had dropped her garter in the dance and he had picked it up. He could still remember the looks on the faces of those about him; he had fancied he heard a titter. He had faced them all with his comment which had now become well known: 'Evil be to him who evil thinks.' He had honoured the garter; he had attached it to his own knee and he had made it the symbol of chivalry.

'Well, my dear,' he said, 'it is no use thinking of Joan of Kent. Let us hope that someone suitable to his rank will lure him from this bachelor's state which he seems to find so pleasant. He must realize that he should marry for the sake of the country. Perhaps I should speak to him after all.'

The Queen shook her head. 'Perhaps it is better not. This constant questioning of the matter may well stiffen his resistance.'

'As always you are wise, my dearest. We will wait awhile and hope.'

'Perhaps the happiness of John and Blanche will decide him.'

'We must hope for that.' The King frowned. Then he said: 'There is Lionel and his little daughter. There is John . . . We do not lack sons, Philippa.'

'Edward was made to be King,' replied Philippa firmly. 'He is a young man yet. One day I know he will marry. He will have strong stalwart sons even as we have had.'

'Amen to that,' replied the King. 'And now enough of these children of ours. We are not so old ourselves that we should not give a thought to our own wellbeing.'

Philippa smiled. He could still be the impatient lover. It was an achievement really. She could scarcely have believed it would be possible if he had not again and again given her proof of it.

The bridegroom was uneasy because he had a duty to perform and it was a secret one.

He was delighted by his marriage. Blanche was enchanting. He had long heard of her beauty, though he did know that a bride's charm was invariably measured by the size of her fortune, but this was not so in the case of Blanche. With her long fair hair and her very white skin and that air of vulnerability, she was irresistible and that she was a great heiress was just an additional attraction. Moreover had she not been rich and of such noble birth she would never have been chosen for him. He could not complain. He was in love with her already. It was a different sort of love from that he had had for Marie St. Hilaire and he was deeply aware of the difference. It did not mean that he loved either of them the less. Blanche was the romantic lady, the kind of whom poets sang; Marie was the earthy mistress who knew how to satisfy him, how to soothe him, at all times. She did not complain. She understood that a man in his position could only come to her rarely. She knew that no great titles would come her way. Yet she had given him a deep and satisfying love.

He had talked to her as he never talked to anyone except Isolda Newman. Isolda—that staunch Flemish woman who had been his nurse—was a mother to him. It was to Isolda that he could reveal his innermost thoughts—even more so than to Marie, for Marie would never have understood entirely. Isolda did. He was aware in his Flemish nurse of a similar resentment which he himself felt.

When he was a little boy she had called him her little

king and it had been a secret name for she had never used it before others.

Once she had said: ' 'Twas a pity you were not the first. What a King you would have made.'

He had been quite young when he had begun to feel the resentment because he was the fourth son. Edward and Lionel came before him. Young William had died. He had seen the adulation given to his brother Edward, the great Black Prince. When they had ridden out together people scarcely looked at him, and he had been very conscious of being only the little brother, while the people always shouted for the mighty Black Prince.

Lionel did not mind being the second son. Good-natured, lazy, stretching his long legs before him, stroking his handsome face, Lionel shrugged his shoulders. Lionel did not want to rule a kingdom. 'Rather you than me,' he had said to Edward. 'I would not be in your boots, brother. Go on living, there's a good fellow. Produce as many healthy sons as our parents did. Make sure that there is no way for me to come to the throne.'

How differently John felt! When he saw the crown his fingers itched to take it. He often thought: there are Edward and Lionel before me. And Lionel does not want it. What if . . .

He dismissed such thoughts. He was fond of his eldest brother. When he was a boy he had thought he was some sort of God and had joined in the general worship. But Edward was now twenty-nine years of age and he did not show any desire to marry; he was a fighter and one who liked to be in the forefront of the battle. If he did not marry; if he did not produce an heir; if he were killed in combat, there would only be Lionel before him. It was true Lionel had a four-year-old daughter Philippa—named for her grandmother the Queen— but a girl.

He must not think of these things. He could imagine the horror of his parents if they knew he did. He had a beautiful wife; passionately he wanted sons. It might well be that one day his son . . .

No, he must stop. There was an important matter to

settle. He must see Marie. He must explain to her. He wondered if she had been among the spectators at the joust. Poor Marie, how had she felt to see the fair Blanche seated beside the Queen, to see him go forward and take her hand and kiss it fondly and ride with her into Westminster?

Blanche and he must have sons. It might well be that already she was with child. He hoped so. She seemed over fragile for much childbearing—unlike his mother—stolid, firm, Flemish wide-hipped, ample-bosomed, born for motherhood.

He must slip out of the palace unnoticed. It was well that he was not as easily recognized as his father and elder brothers were—for while the visage of the Black Prince was well known throughout the land, Lionel's excessive height made it impossible for him to remain incognito. John himself was tall but not as tall as his brothers; his hair was less fair being more of a tawny shade; he was clearly Plantagenet, but the cast of features did appear here and there in the land, due no doubt to the lustiness of some of his ancestors.

He left the palace alone and made his way towards the City. Riding along the Strand past the noble palaces he saw the Savoy towering above the rest and he thought exultantly, one day that might well be mine. It belonged to his father-in-law and Blanche with her sister Matilda was his heir.

It was a pity that Blanche had a sister—and an elder one at that. Never mind the fortune was vast and when Duke Henry died it must pass to his daughters.

His fair bride could bring him more than her beauty.

He made his way into the City and rode along by the Water of Walbrook which came from its source in the heights of Hampstead and Highbury and flowed through swampy Moorfields to empty itself into the Thames. He came to a house near St. Mildred's Church close to Bucklersbury and here he paused. He rode through an arch at the side of the house and as he entered a courtyard a man ran out to make a sweeping bow. John dismounted and the man took his horse. He pushed open a door in the courtyard and was in the house.

Marie was waiting for him. She did not rush into his arms as was her custom. She stood back waiting for him to give some sign of what was expected of her. It was her indication that she realized there was a marked change in their relationship.

He thought: She was at the joust. She saw Blanche there . . .

He caught her hands and kissed her passionately.

'Oh my lord . . .' she murmured.

They went together into the room with the leaded windows that looked out on the courtyard. How often had he been here and found solace with Marie. It had been a satisfying relationship. He was not a promiscuous man. He had had one mistress at a time and Marie had held that position for more than two years. She was older than he was but he had been very young when he had first come to her.

They did not go to her bed as they would have done had this been an ordinary occasion. Marie was aware of this. She had set out on a table wine and the wine cakes she liked to bake for him. She knew that he had come to talk.

'You were in the crowd?' he asked.

She nodded. 'I saw your bride. She is very beautiful. She looks . . . kind and good.'

'Yes,' he answered. 'I know she is.'

'You will love her well and she will love you.'

'Marie,' he said. 'I am sorry. It had to be.'

She smiled bravely. 'I always knew it would be thus. I never forgot that you were the King's son and some day there would be a bride for you. Sometimes I thought that might not be the end.'

'It must be the end,' he said.

She nodded. 'I knew you would wish it so.'

'I could not deceive her,' he said.

'I understand.'

'Dearest Marie, you have always understood. It is not

that I do not love you. I shall for ever be grateful to you . . .'

'You owe me no gratitude,' she answered. 'It was my pleasure to give and to take as it was yours. Suffice it that we have been happy together.'

'It is a new life. I shall be sailing for France with my father ere long.'

'So she, too, will be alone.'

'It is the way our lives go. I must not stay. They will miss me.'

'She will miss you,' she murmured.

'Marie. Before I go. The child . . .'

She rose. 'She is sleeping.'

'Let me see her.'

She led the way into a room, where lying on a pallet was a child a little over a year old.

'How lovely she is,' he said.

'She has a look of you. The same tawny hair . . . the blue eyes. I shall have her to remind me.'

'She shall never want. Nor shall you.'

'I know it,' said Marie. 'She must never want, because she is your daughter.'

'You may trust me to make all arrangements. It is to assure you of this that I came.'

He knelt by the pallet and bending kissed the child. She smiled in her sleep.

They went back to the table; he drank a little of the wine and ate one of the wine cakes. He explained what arrangements would be made for her and the child.

Then he took his farewell. They stood facing each other, both deeply moved. She had meant so much to him; he had trusted her. Here in the dark room when he had lain beside her after making love he had talked of his dreams, of how he resented being born the fourth son instead of the first, of how he longed to be a king. He could talk to Marie as freely as he could talk to Isolda and no one else. 'I have the blood of kings in my veins,' he had said. 'I was born to rule, but born too late.'

And she listened as Isolda had listened; and she commiserated and soothed him and understood.

It was over now. They had always known it must be some day. Once he had thought Marie would always be there in his life and so she would have been if they had married him to anyone but Blanche.

Blanche filled his thoughts. There was something in her which appealed to his manhood. Soft and white and vulnerable. That was it. Heiress as she was, stem of a royal tree, she needed to be protected.

He said goodbye to Marie and he chided himself because he felt less sad than he should. Marie and her child should always be cared for. But he was in love with Blanche.

Those summer days passed delightfully for the young married pair. Each day it seemed they were more and more in love. The King and the Queen watched with pleasure and continued to sigh because the Prince of Wales still avoided the same happy state.

It was with great joy that Blanche at length discovered that she was pregnant.

John was exultant. In an unguarded moment he cried, 'If this child is a boy, he may one day be King of England.'

Blanche was a little shaken. 'Oh, my dear husband, there are many before him.'

'Many,' agreed John. 'But who can see into the future?'

She said nothing, but she knew of his great ambition and it gave her a certain apprehension. She accepted the fact that he was bold and ambitious but her father had taught her that duty and honour were greater blessings than titles and lands and she knew her father was right. There had been a strong bond between them, because she supposed she was the only child who was near him, Matilda being far away.

She prayed each night that her child would be a boy, for she could not bear to disappoint her husband.

In October of that year John went to France with his father. The truce which had been made two years before with the capture of the King of France was coming to an end as the Dauphin of France refused to recognize the treaty his father had agreed to in captivity it was clear that Edward would have to attempt to enforce it. Preparations had been going on during the summer months and the King, in accordance with the custom at such times, had made a tour of the holy shrines accompanied by members of his family with their households.

The great cavalcade made its way through the country and it was cheered wherever it went. The people were certain that great Edward could not fail and soon these wretched wars with France would be over and Edward would attain the crown which for so long he had made such determined efforts to get. It was true all had thought the war was over when the King of France had ridden into England with his captor the Black Prince; but now it seemed there was a wicked Dauphin who was determined to cling to the crown for himself.

So it was war again.

In the household of Lionel and his wife Elizabeth was a young man who interested Blanche. He was about the same age as her husband—bright-eyed, intelligent; seeming different from other pages. He was in favour with Elizabeth and Lionel and looked quite elegant in his parti-coloured breeches of red and black—the fashionable colours at the moment. He even had a silk paltok, the new kind of coat which was very elegant.

Blanche would find his eyes on her whenever he was near. She was amused and asked him why he stared at her.

He told her that he had never in his life seen anyone as beautiful as she was.

Such a comment might have been impertinent from one in his lowly position but it was given with an air of dignity and Blanche graciously accepted it.

She asked her sister-in-law who the young page was and Elizabeth laughed and said, 'Oh, he is an interesting boy. He writes clever verses. Both Lionel and I encourage him.

He is the son of a vintner who distinguished himself in the wars. His name of Geoffrey Chaucer.'

Blanche found herself watching for the young man and she always had a smile for him when they met.

His admiration gratified her. There were plenty to admire her of course, but there was something rather unusual about the young page.

In due course the army left and Blanche must say farewell to her husband.

The Queen was sad. She hated these wars. 'Would to God the King had never got it into his head that he had a claim to the throne of France,' she confided to Blanche. 'How much happier we should all be if there were not this continual fighting. I never sleep peacefully when the King is away because when he is he is always engaged in battle. My dear Blanche, you will condole with me for alas, John is with him.'

They were great friends and had been all Blanche's life for Blanche had spent a large part of her early life in Philippa's household. Children loved the Queen; she was the natural mother and even those who were not her own children had a share of her affection.

'When they go away,' Philippa mourned, 'we can never be sure when they will come back. It may be a year or more.'

'I hope by the time John returns that our child will be born and oh how fervently I hope that it will be a boy.'

'My dear child, you must not hope too much. It is better to wait patiently and see what God sends you. If it is a girl don't fret. You are both so young. You have time to get boys.'

'John longs for a boy.'

'John would. I sometimes think he is the most ambitious of my sons. And Lionel is the happiest because he is content with his lot. He was born in Antwerp. You see his father had started the war against France even then and I was with him. Oh this war, will it never end! But let us talk of happier things than war. I trust you are resting when you feel tired. I have some fine silk which I will give you for some of the baby's garments.'

The company of Queen Philippa was certainly comforting. Blanche needed that comfort when her child was born, for the longed-for son was denied her. It was a little girl they brought and laid in her arms.

For herself she would have been content. But she thought what John's disappointment would be when he heard that she had not given him the boy he longed for.

Blanche wanted to call her Philippa after the Queen and Philippa was delighted that the child should be so named.

By May of the next year the army had returned to England. There was talk of a divine interference which had changed the King's attitude towards France. He had marched to Paris and believed that victory was close. The French had offered terms for peace which Edward would not accept. He had continued to ravage the country and was so doing when suddenly a terrible storm of hail, lightning and thunder had descended upon him. Rumour had it that six thousand men and horses had been killed by the elements which had only abated when the King had lifted his arms to Heaven and sworn that if God would stop pouring his wrath from the Heavens he would accept the terms for peace which the French were offering. It was like a miracle, said rumour. The storm had ceased, and Edward prepared to return to England. King Jean of France was released after four years of imprisonment and Edward declared he would accept the ransom which had been offered.

'Peace for a while,' said the Queen. 'We must be grateful for it even though it may not last.'

So home came the warriors and when John of Gaunt was introduced to his little daughter, he hid the chagrin he felt on account of her sex. His delight in his marriage persisted, and it was not long before Blanche was pregnant once more and this time John was convinced that they would have a boy.

Great was his joy when a boy was born to them.

'Let us call him John after his father,' said Blanche. So John the child became.

Alas, fate was cruel. Only a few weeks after his birth the child sickened and all the efforts of the royal physicians could not save him.

John lapsed into gloom and even Blanche found it difficult to rouse him from his melancholy.

'We shall have a boy,' she assured him. 'I know it. I shall not rest content until I have given you the son you long for.'

He kissed her and tried to hide his disappointment.

Fate had been unkind to him, he thought. First giving him an overweening ambition and making him the fourth son and then giving him a daughter and when a son was born to him taking the child away.

But fate was full of tricks and that year was to bring great change into his life.

Some years before a terrible pestilence had swept through Europe enveloping England. Thousands had died of it and it had been spoken of with dread even after it no longer raged.

Very few who developed the plague ever survived. When it attacked, a discolored swelling would be perceived under the armpits. These would be followed very quickly by more swellings and in a few hours the sufferer would be dead. So infectious was the plague that it could be caught by coming near to the body of someone who had died by it. It had spread through the country like a hurricane, impoverishing it, wiping out the population in its thousands. It was only when ships had ceased to call at the ports and grass grew among the cobbles of the streets that it had subsided and then had come the terrible reckoning, when there were few left to till the fields and to carry on the country's business.

The Black Death would be talked of until the end of time.

And now it had returned.

However something had been learned from the previous visitation. The plague had struck its cruellest blows in the towns where people lived close together, and those who could left them for the country. A careful watch was made so that no people from abroad should enter the country if there had been plague on their ships.

John and Blanche were with the court at Windsor when the news was brought. Blanche could not believe it was true. She was stunned by her grief. Her father Duke Henry of Lancaster had taken the sickness and died.

John tried to comfort her. He knew how devoted she had been to her father, but all the time he was thinking: Lancaster is dead. The richest man next to the King, and his daughters are his heirs. That vast fortune will be divided between Blanche and Matilda.

He, the impecunious fourth son of a King, would be one of the richest men in the Kingdom, and riches meant power. Was this Fate's way of compensating him for the loss of his son?

He could not talk of this to Blanche. It would shock her beyond belief. Dear Blanche! She was good and noble and he loved her dearly, but she did not understand ambition and particularly his.

Marie would have understood as would one other—Isolda.

He had always cared for Isolda. He had made sure that she would be well provided for. He had kept her in the household. It was strange that an ambitious man should find comfort with an old Flemish woman. But she understood him; she had nurtured him; perhaps it was she who had first sown the seeds in the heart of her little king.

'My dear one,' she said when he called on her, 'your father-in-law is dead. Your wife will be a very rich woman now.'

'She shares with her sister. When I think of what would be hers if she were an only child . .'

Isolda laughed. 'It is like you to want it all. And rightly so. If I had my way everything you ask should be yours.'

'Everyone is not as kind to me as you are, Isolda.'

'You were always my little king. And the Lady Blanche must share. It is a pity. But still there will be great riches for you. What of his title? Duke of Lancaster eh.'

'That would die with him. There will be the earldom though.'

'And I doubt not if it came your way your father would make a duke of you.'

'There is Matilda. She is the elder.'

'A pity . . . a pity . . . And a lady who will claim to the last penny I doubt not.'

'I think Matilda will want all that is hers.'

'But she has no heirs, my king.'

John shook his head.

'Who knows . . .' said Isolda.

'It is strange so soon after the death of my son . . .'

'Fate will be good to you. I promise you. I can see the crown there . . . I always have.'

'Is it true, Isolda, that you have the powers?'

She laughed. 'Those of us who have them are never sure. It is only the charlatans who know so much and invent so much more. But in my heart and in my bones I know there is a crown and it is close to you.'

'Perhaps a son . . .'

'You will have a son. A great son. I promise you.'

She took his hand and kissed it. 'I shall watch and pray and work for you.'

'God bless you, Isolda. May all my dreams and hopes come to naught if I ever forsake you.'

She comforted him, Isolda did. She was the only one to whom he dared open his heart.

The greatest blow of all to John's schemes fell that very year when his father-in-law's death had made him one of the richest men in the country.

Joan of Kent returned to England. Joan, who had scandalized the court by her frivolous behaviour in living with Sir Thomas Holland while she was betrothed to the Earl of Salisbury, had become a widow.

Joan was beautiful. In her youth she had been known as the Fair Maid of Kent. The Black Prince had been enamoured of her but in such a desultory way that it had obviously rendered the Fair Maid so impatient that she had turned elsewhere. She was voluptuous and flighty, she liked to be the centre of admiration and of course she had once had hopes of marrying the Prince and being the next Queen of England.

This would have been acceptable because she was royal, her father being Edmund of Woodstock, Earl of Kent and the son of Edward the First.

But Joan had married Sir Thomas Holland and had sons by him. Holland had done well by the marriage. He seemed contented with Joan as a wife as she did with him as a husband, and Holland had recently assumed the title of Earl of Kent which had come through his wife. He had been made governor of the Fort of Creyk and the pair had lived very happily in Normandy. Now he was dead and Joan with her boys had come to England.

She was thirty-three years of age—young enough of course to marry again. She was still beautiful, though she had lost her willowy figure and was a plump matron now, but it seemed she was as fascinating as ever.

John received the news from the Queen who was half delighted, half apprehensive.

'Your brother has married,' she told John. 'It has surprised us all.'

'Married. Which . . . brother?'

'Edward of course. I think he was always attracted by her and now she has overcome his objections to marriage and it has already taken place in secret if you please.'

'My dear lady mother, pray tell me of whom you speak.'

'I speak of the Prince of Wales and his wife of Kent.'

'Joan! She is so recently widowed.'

'I know but she was never one to let the grass grow under her feet.'

'I thought there was talk of her marrying Sir Bernard de Brocas, that knight of Gascony. He is deeply enamoured of her, I believe, and it seemed most suitable.'

'Suitable indeed but not good enough for Joan. Edward approached her about de Brocas and she made it very clear that she would take none but himself and then he realized that that was what he wanted and was the reason for his remaining unmarried all this time. They are deeply in love.'

'And what says the King?'

'He was uneasy at first. He thinks Joan over flighty and of course—though pray God it will be many years yet—she will be the next Queen of England.'

John was silent. Dreams were disintegrating before his eyes. They will have children, he thought. She has already shown herself fertile with Holland. There will be her sons to stand between me and the crown. And first Edward himself. Who would have believed that life could deal him such blows! After making him a rich man it had then made well nigh impossible the greatest dream of all.

There was nothing to do but accept the position. The Black Prince was married at last and to his sweetheart of years ago. Neither of them was in their first youth but there were a few years ahead for childbearing. How could fate be so cruel!

Of course there was some delay. But Joan and the Prince snapped their fingers at ceremonies. At least Joan did and Edward followed her. But in due course the papal dispensation arrived and in October the espousals were celebrated at Lambeth by the Archbishop of Canterbury. That Christmas Joan and Edward entertained the entire royal family at their home in Berkhamsted; and the people from the surrounding country joined in the festivities. It was a great occasion, the marriage of the Black Prince, which was all the more to be enjoyed because it had been delayed so long.

After Christmas great preparations were afoot for the Prince and his family to leave for France. The King had made him Prince of Aquitaine and Gascony and he was to set out with his wife and entourage for Bordeaux.

During that very month when Edward and Joan sailed for Bordeaux, Matilda, Blanche's sister, arrived in England to take possession of her inheritance.

She had not been more than a few weeks in England when she caught the plague and within a day or so was dead.

Blanche was now her father's sole heiress and the entire Lancastrian fortune, by courtesy of her marriage, was in the hands of John of Gaunt.

He reflected with Isolda on the strangeness of fate which seemed determined to shower blessings on him with one hand and take them away with the other.

So there he was rich beyond his dreams but his path to the throne it seemed blocked for ever by Edward's marriage to the lusty Joan.

He considered the situation with Isolda. Joan was two years older than her husband; but she had already borne five children and could bear Edward sons. Once she did that—one or two boys . . . that would be the death knell of his hopes.

'The greatest man in the kingdom . . .' crooned Isolda.

'Next to the King and my brother of Wales. There is also Lionel.'

He was in possession of the earldom of Richmond, of Derby, Leicester and of course Lancaster. His father, delighted at the turn of events, rejoicing in his foresight in arranging the match with Blanche of Lancaster, decided to make him a Duke, and one dull November day John knelt before his father and was girded with the sword, and the cap was set on his head while he was proclaimed a Duke— Duke of Lancaster.

More than ever he longed for a son but when Blanche was next brought to bed, she was delivered of a daughter. He could have wept with mortification, though he kept his disappointment from Blanche.

They called the girl Elizabeth and he loved her even as he loved her elder sister Philippa, but he went on longing for a boy.

His bitterness was great when the news came from Aquitaine that Joan had produced a fine boy. There was great rejoicing throughout the court and the country. It was fitting that the Black Prince should give the country an heir

29

who would be exactly like himself. They christened the boy Edward. There was a feeling that that was a kingly name. People forgot that there had been one Edward—the Second— who had been slightly less than kingly. The Prince was there to step into his father's shoes, already loved and revered by the people—and he had not disappointed them. There was another Edward and a little one in his cradle to grow up in the light of his father's wisdom—a little king in the making.

John curbed his disappointment. He would have hated Blanche to know his feelings. His love for her was idealized, as was hers for him.

He could talk to Isolda about the new turn of events, but she continued to look wise—almost as though she were some soothsayer who could see into the future. He half believed that she feigned this for his pleasure; but some-times he felt that she had some insight and she continued to insist that there was a crown close to him.

Blanche was once more pregnant. So was Joan of Kent.

The King was in close conversation with his son and on the table before him lay letters from Bordeaux.

'Your brother is eager that you should join him,' said Edward, 'and I am sure when you know the reason you will be eager to do so. The King of Castile is at Bordeaux.'

John knew that there was trouble in Castile, because Henry of Trastamare, Pedro's bastard brother, had for some time believed he had a right to the throne and would rule better than Pedro.

'Henry of Trastamare now reigns in Castile and Pedro is asking our help to regain his throne,' went on the King.

'Is it any quarrel of ours?' asked John.

'Your brother believes and I with him that it is no good thing for bastards to depose legitimate heirs. Moreover Pedro has promised to make little Edward King of Galicia and to reward well those who help him.'

'If he can be trusted that seems fair enough.'

'I am sure your brother agrees with that. He asks that

30

you join him there. My dear son, it is my wish that you make preparations to leave without delay.'

John bowed his head. He was not averse to the adventure and it was true that legitimate sons could not stand aside and allow bastards to triumph. It was a dangerous precedent.

Blanche was apprehensive when he told her he must prepare to leave, but as the Queen pointed out to her women in their positions must learn to accept these separations.

Bravely Blanche said her farewells. 'And when you come back,' she added, 'I trust I shall have a fine son to show you.'

'We'll have him yet,' replied John. 'Never fear. Isolda swears it and she is a wise woman.'

So he left her and sailed for Brittany and when he reached the shores of that country, a message awaited him from his brother.

'On the morning of Twelfth Day Joan bore me another son. The child was born in the Abbey of Bordeaux. A boy. God be praised. A brother for little Edward. Truly I am pleased in my marriage. There is great rejoicing here at the coming of Richard of Bordeaux.'

John ground his teeth in envy. Another boy. Another to stand between him and the throne.

Whatever Isolda said fate was mocking him.

Blanche had decided that her child should be born in the Lancastrian castle of Bolingbroke. This had been one of her father's castles which was now in the hands of her husband. She had always had a fancy for the place although many of the servants believed that it was haunted. A very strange kind of ghost was this one. It was said to be the spirit of some tormented soul which took the shape of a hare which had been seen running through the castle and some swore they had been thrown by it as it passed swiftly between their legs.

Blanche remembered her father's telling how a pantler

of the castle who had once tripped while carrying wine had blamed the hare, but it seemed more likely that he had been indulging too freely in the cellars.

There was an old story that once some bold spirits had gathered together a pack of hounds to hunt the hare. They had pursued it through the rooms of the castle down the spiral staircases to the cellars. Then the hounds had come dashing out, mad to escape, their hair on end, their eyes wild and none of them would enter the castle again.

In all her sojourns at the castle Blanche had never seen the hare and as the fancy had come to her to visit Bolingbroke, hither she had come and decided that it should be the birthplace of her child.

Here she awaited the event and thought constantly of John, praying to God and the saints to bring him safely through the battle.

She sent for Isolda who was a great comfort to her, for she believed that Isolda had some rare gift of looking into the future. Isolda was sure that her beloved John was coming home safely. She was sure too that this time there was going to be a healthy boy.

So while the winter days grew a little longer and the signs of spring increased with passing time, Blanche waited at the Castle of Bolingbroke for the birth of her child.

On the battle field of Nájara the Black Prince with his brother John of Gaunt was ready to fight the cause of Pedro of Castile.

Against them was the army of Henry of Trastamare. 'This day,' the Prince had said to Pedro, 'we shall decide whether or not you are to have your throne.'

He had begun to doubt Pedro. Henry of Trastamare had written to him in a manner which seemed frank and plausible. Pedro was known throughout Castile as The Cruel. He had shed much innocent blood. Legitimate he might be but Castile suffered under him and the people of Castile would be overjoyed to see him deposed. The great Black Prince had no notion of the man he was dealing with. If he really knew Pedro the Cruel he would recognize him as a false friend.

'Ha,' said the Prince, 'it is clear that Bastard Henry has no stomach for the conflict. The battle is as good as won.'

So they rode forward and there was not a man in Henry of Trastamare's ranks who was not aware that that military legend the Black Prince came against them and in their hearts they knew that the hero of Crécy and Poitiers was undefeatable.

They saw him there, at the head of his army, his black armour making him easily identifiable.

From the moment they heard his shout: 'Advance, banner in the name of God and St. George. And God defend our right!' the result was a foregone conclusion. All knew that the Black Prince was the greatest soldier in the world next to his father and his great-grandfather; and the former was growing old and the latter was dead. He had gathered under his banner the flower of English chivalry and there was not a man who did not regard it as the greatest honour to serve under him.

The battle was over. Henry of Trastamare had fled the field. The Black Prince had given Pedro the Cruel his kingdom. He had shown the world that even for a King of questionable worth he would fight rather than a bastard should usurp his right.

They rode back to Bordeaux. The Black Prince looked weary as John had never seen him look before. There was a faint yellowish tinge in his usually fresh-coloured face.

'You are unwell, Edward,' said John.

'I confess to certain disorders,' admitted Edward. 'Of late I have been aware of them. I pray you do not mention this to Joan. She would have me in bed and be acting the nurse to me.'

John nodded but he thought, Joan will have only to look at you, brother, to see that all is not well.

When they reached the castle, there were letters from England.

Great waves of exultation swept over John.

Blanche had been safely delivered of a son.

She had christened him Henry. 'Henry of Bolingbroke, they are calling him, for, my husband, I decided that he should be born in our castle of that name. He is well formed, lusty, perfect in every way. I long to show him to you.'

A son, Henry of Bolingbroke! Born three months after Richard of Bordeaux.

It was the greater victory.

At last . . . a son.

CATHERINE SWYNFORD

Queen Philippa, *suffering* as she was from a dropsical complaint, was scarcely able to move. Her women helped her from her bed to her chair where she would sit with her needlework and dream of the past.

She was always delighted to see members of her family, and that included her daughter-in-law Blanche of Lancaster who contrived to spend much time with her.

During this year the Queen had come to Windsor Castle, one of her favourite residences and there she found it expedient to remain for the progress from palace to palace was too exhausting to be undertaken unless there was some important reason why she should do so.

In spite of her sufferings she was amiable and was always interested in the activities of those around her, ready to share in their triumphs and commiserate in their tribulations.

Blanche was a great favourite with her. There was a similarity in their characters. They were both capable of deep affection; and ready to forget themselves in their service to the loved one. Neither of them was of a complaining nature. They did mention however when their husbands were absent that they missed them, but both of them accepted these partings philosophically and the similarity of their lives was an added factor which drew them closer together.

Philippa would sit with her women at one end of the apartment stitching at garments for the poor or working on an altar cloth while Blanche sat close beside her where they could talk intimately. Philippa's hands would be busy and so would Blanche's. The Queen had never approved of idleness.

It pleased her very much to know that Blanche was pregnant once more.

'It is good that John is home again,' she said. 'I trust my dear that it will be long ere he has to go to war again. I'll swear you are hoping for another boy.'

'It is what John wants.'

'Your young Henry is a rascal I'll be bound.'

Blanche's face betrayed her pride and joy in her only son.

'My lady, I know all mothers think their children are the best in the world, but Henry . . .'

'Henry really is the most beautiful and clever child that ever was born.' The Queen smiled. 'I understand, dear Blanche. I was so with mine. Every one of them filled me with wonder. If you could have seen Edward as a baby! Of course he was the first-born. And Lionel. He was big from the start. And dear John. Such an imperious young gentleman. Then Edmund and Thomas. And the girls of course. They were just as dear to me. I had my sadness. Death has taken its toll. But when I look at my fine sons I can rejoice. Oh, Blanche, if you are as happy in your family as I am in mine you will be a fortunate woman. But we must remember that while God gives with one hand, He takes away with the other; and He has always his reason for doing so and that, dear daughter, we must accept.'

Blanche bowed her head in agreement. She had lost the dear little boy she had borne, but now that she had her Henry she had ceased to grieve so deeply, although she believed she would never forget.

She was sure Philippa would always remember those children she had lost. Her greatest blow had been the deaths of her two daughters some years before, Mary and Margaret who had died within a few weeks of each other. She had never been quite the same since.

But she must not think of death now with the new life stirring within her.

'This matter of Castile,' the Queen was saying, 'would seem to have been satisfactorily resolved. Pedro will have much to thank my sons for. He owes his crown to Edward and John.'

'It was a glorious battle John tells me.' Blanche frowned a little. Could any battle which meant death to many be called glorious? She did not think so and she knew Philippa would agree with her. If she mentioned this to John he would have smiled at her indulgently, amused at her woman's sensibilities.

'Aye,' added Philippa. 'Pedro the rightful King back on his throne. I hear news from Joan though that Edward returned from the battle in poor health. She is alarmed for him. She has changed since her marriage. She was such a flighty girl. Capable of any indiscretions I am sure. But she seems to be a good wife to Edward and they have those two dear boys.'

'It is good for young Edward to have a little brother.'

'It is always good for kings to have several sons, and Edward will of course be King of England one day. I always rejoiced because he was so worthy, right from the time of his boyhood. But in battle one never knows what may befall and it is good to have others who could step forward in case of disaster.'

Blanche was thinking: John believed that. John had hoped . . . but his hopes had been dispersed because of the birth of those two boys to the Black Prince.

As they were speaking a woman had entered the room. Blanche had seen her at court once or twice and had on each occasion been very much aware of her. She was tall and had a flamboyant somewhat coarse kind of good looks. There was a boldness about her which Blanche found decidedly unattractive.

Instead of joining the women at the other end of the chamber she came to the Queen and bowing to her and to Blanche she took a seat beside them.

Blanche was startled. Surely it was the duty of the

woman first to wait until she was summoned to the Queen's side and to sit only when she had been given permission to do so.

She waited for the Queen to dismiss her but Philippa did no such thing.

The woman took up the piece of needlework on which they were working.

'It grows apace,' she said. 'My Lady Blanche is a rival to the Queen . . . with her needle.'

'You like the colours, Alice?' asked the Queen.

'They are a little sombre, my lady.'

'Ah, you like the bright colours.'

' 'Tis a weakness of mine. What thinks Lady Blanche?'

Blanche was astounded. She could not understand why the Queen endured such insolence.

She said coldly: 'I like those well which the Queen has chosen.'

She noticed that a ring of rubies and diamonds glittered on the woman's hand. Who was she? wondered Blanche.

'Alice,' said the Queen, 'I wish you would join the ladies and tell them they are dismissed. I wish to be alone with the Duchess of Lancaster.'

The woman nodded but made no haste to rise and it was some minutes before she sauntered to the other end of the room. There she laughed with the women for a while and Blanche noticed that they seemed somewhat sycophantish towards her. At length they went out together.

Blanche said: 'Who is that woman?'

'She is one of the bedchamber women.'

'She seems to give herself airs . . .'

'Oh . . . that is her way.'

Blanche was astonished. The Queen was friendly to those around her; she had never stressed her rank or behaved in an imperious manner but there had been a certain dignity about her which prevented people from abusing her gentleness. Blanche had never before seen her so subdued by one of her subjects.

There were many questions which Blanche wanted to

ask, but she could tell from the Queen's manner that it was not a subject she wished discussed.

That there was some mystery about this woman was clear. She would ask John if he knew what it was. The incident had been extremely unpleasant and Blanche felt faintly depressed. It had obviously had the same effect on the Queen and the intimacy between them had become clouded.

Blanche took her leave soon afterwards and made her way to her own apartments in the castle. As she did so she heard the clatter of horses' hoofs below and looking from a window she saw the King with a group of attendants in the courtyard below. Among them was John.

The sight of the King shocked her a little. He had aged considerably since she had last seen him. But perhaps she was comparing him with John who looked so robust and well.

The King had dismounted. He was standing in the courtyard saying something to one of the knights. He looked up suddenly. For a moment Blanche thought he was looking at her, but she soon realized that his gaze had gone beyond her. She saw the expression on his face. It alarmed her faintly. She could describe it as lustful.

Then she heard the sound of laughter. A window had been opened and a woman was leaning out. She was obviously the one at whom the King had been looking.

Some signal passed between them.

Blanche understood a great deal in that moment, for the woman was that Alice of the Queen's bedchamber whose insolence towards Philippa had been so thinly veiled.

When she was alone with John she could not stop herself from referring to what she had seen.

'I know the woman of whom you speak,' he said. 'The whole court is talking of her. She has bewitched the King.'

'It seems impossible!' cried Blanche.

John took her hands and smiled at her tenderly.

'It is difficult for you to understand, my dearest,' he said. 'The King will always be devoted to the Queen.'

'Yet he allows this woman to insult her!'

'I am sure he would not allow that. But you see, my dear, the Queen can no longer be a wife to the King . . .'

'She *is* his wife. She has been his wife for many years . . .'

'She can no longer share his bed. That dropsical complaint of hers has immobilized her to such an extent that she can no longer live a normal life. This woman . . . you would not understand but she flaunts her sex at him . . . She is one of those women who . . .'

He looked at her helplessly. 'Dearest Blanche,' he went on, 'try not to think of this. It is unfortunate that the King should not have chosen a different mistress—if mistress he must have, and all worldly men and women would understand that, my love. It is unfortunate that this is the one who should appeal to him.'

'So this bedchamber woman is his mistress.'

'It would seem so.'

'And for this reason she flaunts her position before the Queen. She was wearing a valuable ring.'

'She is fond of fine things and the King delights to give them to her. I suppose he had to have a mistress but that it should be Alice Perrers . . .'

'I could not bear it if I were the Queen.'

John put his arms about her and then releasing her held her face in his hands.'

'I promise you,' he said, 'that you shall never find yourself in such a position. You and I will be faithful unto each other until death divides us.'

She clung to him. 'Oh John, dearest husband, do not talk of death. You cannot know how I suffer when you go away to war.'

'Never fear. It will not be easy for my enemies to rid themselves of me. I shall continue to live for you, my Blanche, and our children. How is that young lion Henry faring today? And you look a little tired.' He touched her stomach gently. 'You must take care of that little one. He will soon be with us.'

'I shall pray for a boy,' said Blanche, 'and that he shall be exactly like his father.'

She felt a little better. The obvious devotion of her husband, so affectionately expressed, wiped away the unpleasantness which had been planted in her mind by Alice Perrers.

A few days later news came to Windsor which brought such sorrow to the King and the Queen that they were drawn very close together and it seemed that Alice Perrers would be like a meteor shooting across the sky—to startle everyone with its brilliance and then drop to oblivion. The King scarcely left the Queen's side and the tragedy visibly aged them both.

It was so unexpected.

It was not so many years before when Lionel, their second son, had come back from Ireland—which he had inherited through his wife who had died some years before—declaring that he had enough of the place and would remain in England.

Philippa who loved to have her family around her was delighted that he should be back with them. Easy-going Lionel who asked nothing more than that life should flow comfortably around him was a good companion. He was so pleasant to be with. He never asked for grants and lands and privileges. He was righ enough through his widow, of course; but he was unlike the rest of the family inasmuch as he lacked that overwhelming ambition which Philippa sensed strongest of all in her son John.

He had but one daughter of his marriage with Elizabeth, Philippa; and it was natural that he should marry again.

It so happened that the Visconti of Milan was looking for a suitable bridegroom for his beautiful and only daughter Violante. Negotiations were set in progress and after some time Lionel went to Milan to marry Violante. First though he had settled the future of his daughter Philippa by marrying her to Edmund de Mortimer, the Earl of March.

Then with suitable pomp he had set out and in due course had been married in Milan Cathedral to the beautiful and rich daughter of Galeazzo Visconti of Milan.

Blanche knew that John had not been very pleased by the marriage. She could read his thoughts. He still hankered for the crown, even though he had an elder brother and that brother, the ever popular Black Prince, had two sons, another Edward and young Richard of Bordeaux. She wished that she could curb those ambitious thoughts of his. But she knew she never would. They were part of his nature.

Naturally when Lionel, that other brother who would rightfully claim the crown if some disaster removed the Black Prince and his family, married again he was depressed. A young and beautiful wife, the warm sun of Italy, the pleasure-loving Lionel who indulged himself on every occasion, surely it would not be long before he fathered a child who would be yet another to stand between John and his desire.

Violante and Lionel were married and so great was the rejoicing in Milan that the festivities went on for weeks. That, John had said, will suit Lionel very well. His father-in-law Galeazzo was delighted with him, it seemed. The alliance with the English royal family was something he had set his heart on, and all seemed to be going well in Milan.

And then had come the shattering news.

Lionel was dead.

In the midst of the feasting he had become sick and although at first no one had taken his indisposition very seriously it had rapidly grown worse and a few days after it had begun he was dead.

The Queen could not believe the news when it was brought to her.

Lionel—the tallest of them all, the one who liked so much to enjoy life—dead. It could not be.

She and the King spent hours together trying to console each other.

It was too cruel a blow. Lionel was the seventh of her children to die. Two little Williams and Blanche had died at birth and that was less heart-breaking than losing them when they were grown up. Joanna had died of the plague on her journey to marry Pedro of Castile and Mary and Margaret had died of some mysterious ailments in their teens. The Queen had never recovered from that. And now Lionel, hale and hearty Lionel, was cut off like that in the flower of his youth.

She was old and sick and she knew—although she tried to pretend she did not—that Edward, who through the many years of their marriage had always kept up the show of being a faithful husband, and she believed he had been almost entirely so, was now unable to hide his lascivious longing for an insolent bedchamber woman.

All that she had borne and now here was the most cruel blow of all. One of her beloved sons was struck down by a cruel fate.

Edward sat beside her. He held her hand. He was not thinking of Alice now. Desperately he sought some comfort for himself and Philippa.

When John brought the news of his brother's death to Blanche she could see that in spite of his tragic expression a certain triumph gleamed in his eyes and she knew that he was thinking: Lionel dead. One obstacle to the throne removed.

Then Blanche shivered with apprehension and fear for the future.

She went to her nursery and picked up the little Henry who was some eighteen months old now—lusty, bright-eyed, beginning to take notice of everything around him.

John joined her there. He could not keep away from the nursery and although he loved his girls all his hopes were centred on this boy.

She watched him take the child in his arms.

'And what have you been doing today, Henry of Boling-broke?' he asked playfully.

She saw the dreams there . . . dreams for the boy.

There was the usual outcry about poison and Lionel's father-in-law was suspected of taking his life. But, as John pointed out, there was no reason why Galeazzo would do so for the death of Lionel was the end of his ambitions for his daughter and Milan.

No, Lionel had indulged himself too freely with the food of the country; he had been unaccustomed to its strangeness and to the heat of that country; he had succumbed to that dysentery which often attacked travellers abroad and in his case it had been fatal.

He was buried first at Pavia but he had asked in his will that his remains should lie in the convent of the Austin Friars at Clare in Suffolk so they were brought there and placed beside those of his first wife.

In the midst of this morning Blanche gave birth to a son.

John was delighted with the boy and he was named after his father.

Alas, poor little John lived only for a few days.

Blanche was desolate. In spite of all her care the child was gone.

She was a great deal with the Queen and they tried to comfort each other.

'We must be brave,' said Philippa, 'you have your daughter and your boy Henry. I have my dear Edward, my John, Edmund and Thomas left to me as well as my daughter Isabella. We must be thankful for what is left of us.'

It was clear however that the shock of her son's death and the knowledge that Edward was drifting away from her had cast a heavy shadow over the Queen.

It was in the royal household that Blanche again encountered the young poet, Geoffrey Chaucer.

The Queen had taken an interest in him because he had married one of her bedchamber women, Philippa de Roet. 'A good girl,' the Queen had said, 'perhaps over zealous. Given to bustling and taking much on herself. But reliable and honest. A good wife I think for Geoffrey. Lionel thought highly of him. He has written some pleasing verses.'

Because Lionel had thought highly of Geoffrey and had enjoyed his poetry and given him a stipend which was more than he would have earned as an ordinary page, the poet was now taken into the royal household.

It was a pleasure for the Queen to know that her bedchamber woman, Philippa de Roet, was married. She gave rich presents to the pair and took a personal interest in them. Philippa Chaucer continued to serve in the bedchamber and Geoffrey was often summoned to the Queen's presence to read his poetry to her.

She talked to Blanche of the girl who was a much pleasanter subject than that other bedchamber woman, Alice Perrers.

'She will make Geoffrey a good wife. He needs someone who is practical to look after him. He is a dreamer that young man, but he writes well and his verses are thought very highly of. The King enjoys them. Lionel was delighted with them. Dear Lionel, he would have wanted us to find a place for Geoffrey.'

'I have noticed him.'

The Queen laughed. 'And he has noticed you. When your name is mentioned he all but falls on his knees in worship. He admires you, Blanche, oh in the most respectful way.' The Queen went on, 'I felt a certain responsibility to Philippa de Roet. Her father was a good servant to me. He came over from Hainault to join me. He would wish to see his daughter settled in life, which she will be with young Chaucer. The King will give him a pension, I am sure. He has promised me to see to it.'

'They are a fortunate young pair to have won your interest, my lady.'

'I did feel I must do what I could for de Roet's girl. He was a good and honest servant. She has a sister who has recently married . . . rather well. I think, for someone in her position. Philippa was telling me about it. This sister Catherine is something of a beauty I gather. In any case she has managed to attract Sir Hugh Swynford. John will know him. He is one of his men and I believe was with him in Gascony recently. However this girl Catherine was clever enough to get him to marry her and it *was* clever of her because she has no fortune. De Roet left nothing. That is why I feel I must do what I can.'

'At least you have only to concern yourself with one daughter since the other knew how to take care of herself.'

'Catherine is Lady Swynford—a fact which pleases her sister mightily. Mistress Chaucer does not sound so well in her ears as Lady Swynford. I tell her, you have married a poet, my child. Your husband's verses may well live on after we are all dead and gone when the world may have forgotten a country squire and his wife. Dear Philippa de Roet. I think she is a little impatient with her husband's verses.'

'I should like to see the girl.'

'My dear Blanche, you shall. I shall have her wait on me this day. She shall sit there with the ladies and work on the garments we are making for the poor. I always feel happy when we are working on those garments although I love to embroider in bright colours. I think of the poor often, Blanche, particularly now that I am old and tired and ill. I think of what a happy life I have had and how some of them live in misery and poverty . . .'

'Happiness and riches do not necessarily go hand in hand,' said Blanche.

'You speak wisely, dear child. I hope you will be as happy in your marriage as I have been . . . until . . .'

The Queen stopped abruptly and Blanche bent her head low over her work that Philippa might not see the flush which had arisen to her cheeks.

That afternoon Philippa Chaucer was in attendance and Blanche was able to study the sturdy young woman who had married the poet. The marriage would have been arranged for them and neither partner would have chosen the other; and it occurred to her that they could well be an incongruous pair.

She and the Queen talked of her children as they so often did.

The girls were of an age now when they needed a governess and she was looking for a suitable person. She must have someone who loved children. There was little Henry too. He was becoming the terror of the nursery. Blanche wanted someone who would be able to teach the children a little and at the same time take charge of them in a motherly way. She did not want the usual high-born governante.

'I know exactly what you mean,' said the Queen. 'You want someone who will show that devotion to them which Isolda Newman gave to John.'

Blanche agreed that was what she was looking for.

'We will look for someone and I am sure we shall find the right person.'

It was a few days later when the Queen asked Blanche to come to her apartments. She was in bed and looking very tired. She told Blanche that she had been too weary to rise that day.

'But let us not talk of my dreary ailments. There are more interesting subjects. Philippa Chaucer has been to me with a request. She said quite candidly that she had over-heard our conversation when she was stitching with the ladies and she wishes to put forward the name of her sister as governess to the children.'

'Philippa Chaucer's sister. That would be interesting.'

'I have told Philippa that I will lay the matter before you. Philippa is eager for her sister to be part of Court life. She says it is no place for her tucked away in Lincolnshire. Swynford's estate is not a large one, and Philippa says her sister lives like a farmer's wife. I wonder what you feel about this.'

Blanche said: 'I should like to see this Catherine Swynford. She may well be just the one I need. Moreover I should like to do something for the Chaucers.'

'I thought you might,' said the Queen. 'I will tell Philippa to send her to you.'

A few moments later Philippa herself entered with a posset for the Queen.

Blanche wondered whether she had been listening to the

conversation and had timed her entry that there might be no delay in sending for her sister. There was that about Philippa Chaucer which suggested a resourcefulness and a determination to arrange the fortunes of her family.

'Ah, Philippa,' said the Queen, 'we have been speaking of you, the Duchess and I.'

'The Queen has told me of your sister,' said Blanche. 'You may tell her to come and see me.'

Philippa flushed with pleasure as she made a deep curtsey and murmured her gratitude.

The Queen took the posset and when Philippa had gone she said, 'They bring me these things. I drink them to please them. But there is no remedy for what ails me, Blanche.'

Blanche took the Queen's hands and kissed them in a rush of affection. 'You must not lose hope, dear lady. So many of us need you.'

When she had first seen Catherine Swynford, Blanche had been startled by her appearance. Catherine was a strikingly attractive woman and far younger than Blanche had imagined her. She had been thinking of another Philippa— rather square, sturdy, not unattractive in a fresh and countrylike way, a homely woman, motherly, perhaps a little forceful like her sister, the sort who would know how to gain immediate obedience from the children.

Instead of that here was Catherine. Tall, slender, about eighteen years of age—abundant hair with more than a hint of red in it, long greenish eyes fringed with lashes the blackness of which contrasted arrestingly with her white skin. The short nose was provocative and the full lips suggested a certain sensuality. Quite a disturbing young woman.

Blanche hesitated. She felt a little bewildered simply because the girl was so different from what she had been imagining her to be.

Catherine told her in a charming cultured voice that she had spent some six years in the convent at Sheppey.

'The Queen arranged for me to go there,' she said. 'She has been very good to my family.' Blanche bowed her head in acknowledgement of the Queen's goodness.

'My mother was French and my sister and I lived with her in Picardy while my father was at the wars. My father was herald to King Edward and knighted by him for bravery on the field.'

'The Queen has told me something of this. He died, did he not?'

'He was killed on the battlefield . . . fighting for King Edward.'

The girl lifted her head high. She was one who would not wish for charity. Doubtless she thought any service the Queen had given her and her sister had been earned with their father's life.

'The plague struck our household,' went on Catherine, 'and only my sister and I survived. We were brought to England and taken to the Queen. I was very ill and none thought I should survive so I was sent to the convent to be nursed by the nuns and my sister Philippa was found a place in the Queen's household.'

'And when you left the convent?'

'I came to see my sister and Sir Hugh Swynford was at Court. He saw me . . . and very soon we were married.'

'So you made a good match, Lady Swynford.'

'It was called so, my lady.'

'And you want to leave your country home and come to Court?'

'My husband is in France serving the King. Our estate is very small and we have few retainers. Yes, my lady, I do wish to leave the country and come to Court.'

'Very well,' said Blanche. 'I will send for the children and you shall see how you like them . . . and they like you.'

She sat still, with great dignity, confident that the children would like her.

They came into the room—Philippa eight years old and very much aware that she was the eldest; Elizabeth four years younger but already showing signs of a somewhat tempestuous nature and Henry who was not yet two years old in the charge of his nurse.

'My dears,' said Blanche to the two girls, 'this is Lady Swynford who would like to be your governess.'

Elizabeth ran forward and stood looking up at Catherine. Philippa remained still watching her silently.

Catherine held out her hand. Elizabeth took it. Then Catherine knelt so that her face was on a level with the little girl's.

'I hope you will like me well enough,' said Catherine.

Philippa came forward and took her sister's hand.

'I like her,' said Elizabeth.

Philippa said nothing but there was approval in her silence.

Then young Henry finding that he was not the centre of attraction made them all aware of his displeasure in his usual lusty fashion.

'He is a spoilt boy,' said Philippa to Catherine.

Catherine went to Henry and picked him up in her arms.

They looked steadily at each other and then Henry's face broke into a beautiful smile.

It was clear that he, like his sisters, had taken a fancy to the beautiful new governess.

Catherine Swynford is an enchantress, thought Blanche.

There was bad news from Bordeaux. The health of the Black Prince so seriously affected at the battle of Nájara, far from improving, was steadily growing worse. Moreover Pedro of Castile had shown himself to be a dishonourable ally. He had kept none of his promises.

Edward had remained in Valladolid for some weeks during the hottest of the weather while he was waiting for the payment due to him for coming to Pedro's aid, but Pedro had made constant excuses. Dysentery had struck the army and many had died of it. The Prince himself had been badly affected and some had even suggested that Pedro might have bribed one of his spies to poison him.

Pedro's reputation being what it was, this seemed a possibility.

The fact was that it had been a mistake to help Pedro back to his throne for he was a worthless ally and it would have been better to have left his bastard brother in control.

Because of his health Edward needed his brother's help. He wanted John to come to France for he feared that Charles of France would take advantage of the situation so John must make preparations to come out at once.

John consulted with his father. The King was showing signs of his age. He had never recovered from the shock of Lionel's death and he was worried about reports of Edward's health. He was tormented too by Alice Perrers for while he deplored his infidelity to the Queen he could not resist Alice.

'You must leave us, John,' said the King. 'Edward needs you. I should like you to tell me exactly how he is. I fear Joan is over anxious. She has always seen Edward so strong and healthy. She is afraid because he has this unfortunate illness. It will pass, I feel sure. But see for yourself, John, and tell me the truth. Alas, my son, you must once more leave your sweet wife. I know what it means to be torn from the side of one's wife and children . . .'

Poor old man, thought John, he was over anxious to tell people what a good husband he was now that he was so no longer.

'I will prepare at once to leave for Bordeaux,' he said. 'And rest assured, I will let you know exactly how I find things there.'

He sought out Blanche. She would be sad because of the coming parting, but she would understand, of course, that it must be so.

Her women told him that she was with the Queen.

Ah yes, he thought. Poor mother. She could not last long now. Every time he saw her he was aware of the change in her. She had lost the healthy rosy colour which had been with her all her life until the last year or so. Now there was an unhealthy yellowish tinge to her skin; and the dropsy was growing to such an extent that she could scarcely move at all.

He went to the nursery. He hated to say goodbye to his children. It gave him such complete joy to gloat over the sturdy Henry. What a little man he was already! Just such another as I was, thought John. His eyes taking in everything, his hands eager to grasp all within his reach. My son. What is in store for you? I wonder. Could it be . . . a crown?

There was a young woman in the nursery. She turned, startled, as he entered.

The children ran to him; Philippa giving a grave curtsey, Elizabeth trying to do the same and abandoning the effort to catch at his knees. Henry was not to be outdone. He staggered towards his father.

'My dearest daughters . . . my little son . . .' He embraced them and all the time he was aware of the young woman watching him.

Holding the children against him, he looked over their heads to her.

She swept a curtsey to the floor. She remained there for a few seconds, gracefully poised with her dark red skirts about her. He noticed the bodice laced across a rather full bosom; her thick red hair hung in plaits one of which fell over her shoulder. The brilliant green eyes edged with incredibly dark lashes regarded him with interest. He felt a great excitement grip him.

He signed to her to rise and come forward.

Now he could see that she was more startling when close. Her skin was soft and white as milk—a deep contrast to the flaming hair and the black eyelashes, green eyes and red lips.

'You are . . .' he began.

Philippa said shrilly: 'She is Catherine . . . our new governess. Our father is a great great lord, Catherine.'

Elizabeth said: 'Yes, a great great lord, greater than the King.'

'Hush hush,' said John smiling. 'You see my daughters

have a high opinion of me. I believe the Duchess mentioned you.'

'I am Catherine Swynford, my lord. My husband is in your service.'

'Swnford,' he murmured. And he thought: That oaf. And this glorious creature. He went on: 'Sir Hugh. Yes, he has served with me. He is in France now, I believe.'

'Yes, my lord. He is in France.'

'And you are here to care for my children. I am pleased at that, Lady Swynford.''

She bowed her head, and when she raised it her eyes were brilliant. It was almost as though some message passed between them.

He turned to the children, but he hardly noticed them. He was so deeply aware of her.

He left the nursery because he felt a need to get away.

He went to his apartments and said that he would be alone until the Duchess returned from her visit to the Queen.

He kept thinking of the governess. Catherine Swynford, he murmured. Ridiculous name. And married to Hugh! He supposed he was worthy enough but he was uncouth and she . . . she was a magnificent creature, there was no question of that.

It was absurd to have allowed her to make such an impression on him. Had he not seen attractive women in his life before! But never one quite like this woman. What was it? Beauty certainly. But he had known many beautiful women. Many would say she was not as beautiful as Blanche his wife. Blanche was a poet's beauty. Young Chaucer was aware of that. Aloof, to be admired from afar. Not so this Catherine Swynford. One would not wish to remain far from her. There must be an urge in all men when they beheld her to take her . . . to possess her . . . even those who were most satisfactorily married . . .

This was ridiculous. He had not felt like this before. He was not by nature a promiscuous man. And yet in the presence of the governess he had felt an almost irresistible urge to throw aside those standards to which, since his marriage to Blanche, he had strictly adhered.

When Blanche came into the apartment, he rose quickly, took her hands and held her in his arms. He was reminded momentarily of his father playing the uxorious husband after one of his sessions with Alice Perrers.

'My dearest,' he said, 'what is it? You look sad.'

'It is the Queen,' she replied. 'I fear she grows worse; every time I see her there is a change.'

'If only they could find some cure.'

'She is fretting . . . about the King . . .'

'That horrible woman. How I hate her! I believe she flaunts her newly acquired jewels before my mother.'

'And the Queen is too gentle, too eager not to hurt the King to complain about her.'

John spoke fiercely against Alice Perrers. He had never hated her so much as at this moment.

He led Blanche to a window-seat and they sat there together, his arm about her. 'I have to go away, Blanche.'

She turned to him and buried her face against him.

'I fear so, my love,' he went on. 'Edward needs me and my father thinks I should go.'

Blanche said nothing.

'Perhaps it will not be for long,' he went on.

'You will be fighting.'

'There is always fighting. It is a man's lot, it seems.'

'When must you go?'

'As soon as I am prepared.'

She was silent and he said slowly: 'I went to the nursery and saw the new governess.'

'What thought you of her?'

'That the children looked well and as full of high spirits as ever.'

'They are in good health, I thank God. But I meant what thought you of Catherine Swynford?'

He hesitated.

'You do not like her?' she asked quickly.

'I am not sure. I had not thought she would be so young.'

'She is serious minded.'

'I was thinking that Swynford's wife would be different. When he comes back to England she could be sent back to the country, I suppose.'

'I am sorry you do not like her. The children are fond of her already.'

'I would not say I did not like her. I thought she might be . . . perhaps a little flighty.'

'Men's eyes follow her. She is good looking and . . . something more . . .'

'Perhaps,' he said.

'The Queen is pleased at the appointment. She remembers the girl's father. Philippa Chaucer is her sister, you know.'

'It is a pity she is not more like Philippa Chaucer.'

'The children seem very fond of her. I notice they like pretty people around them. Henry is already devoted to her.'

'I hope that is not an indication of events to come.'

'You mean . . .'

'I hope he will not be too obsessed with pretty women.'

'I dare swear our son will be a normal man. In any case he is already fond of Catherine Swynford. Of course if you would like me to send her away . . .'

'Oh no, no. Give the woman a chance. I cannot judge her. I was in the nursery only for a few minutes. We have to think of my departure. Would you like me to take letters from you to Joan?'

He was glad to be alone, and although he tried to dismiss Catherine Swynford from his mind her face kept presenting itself to him.

That night he dreamed that he awakened and saw her standing by his bed, her red hair loose and her red lips smiling. She came in beside him and he put his arms about her.

She said in that dream: 'This has to be. You know it, John of Gaunt and so do I, Catherine Swynford.'

A disturbing dream and it showed clearly what effect she had had on him.

He was almost glad that he was going away.

Before he left there was more news from his brother.

Pedro had become so unpopular in Castile where he was known as The Cruel that his half-brother, Henry of Trastamare, had been welcomed back by the people and when he had returned he had confronted Pedro and stabbed him to death.

Nothing had been gained by the English from the battle of Nájara, that resounding victory which had seemed so glorious. Many English soldiers had died of dysentery and it seemed that the health of the Black Prince was impaired for ever; the money Pedro had promised to pay the English armies would never be paid now; Biscay which was to be the Prince's reward for his help had not come into his hands and if he wanted it he would have to fight a fresh battle for it.

It was disaster.

And the King of France was rubbing his hands with glee.

Yes, the Black Prince needed his brother John who must take his leave of his devoted wife, of his anxious father and his ailing mother.

'I shall be back ere long,' John promised Blanche. And he thought: I wonder if, when I return, Catherine Swynford will still be in the nurseries?

The Queen knew that she was dying. Steadily over the last two years she had become more enfeebled. Her body was now so swollen with dropsy that it was a burden to her and she could feel no great sorrow at leaving a world which had lost its charm for her.

As she lay in bed she thought of the past when she had been so happy. So vividly that it seemed like only yesterday did she recall the day Edward's envoys had come to Hainault to choose a bride for him and how fearful she had been that they might select one of her sisters. And how they had laughed when he told her that he warned his ambassadors that it would be more than their lives were worth to bring him any but Philippa. So happy they had been, so much in love—a boy and a girl no more. And when they grew up, the love between them grew stronger and they had had a wonderful family to prove it to the world.

Happy days—but past. So many of the children dead and herself nothing but a mass of unwanted flesh that encumbered her like a prison from which she longed to escape.

Life was ironical. Some lived too long. Others were taken before they had had a chance to live at all. Oh my sweet Joanna, dying of plague in a foreign land. My dear Lionel who left us in the prime of his manhood. Mary and Margaret smitten down so suddenly. And all the little babies.

Such tragedies! And yet such joys! That was life; and none could escape what fate had in store be they kings or queens.

There was little time left.

She said to those about her bed: 'It is time to send for the King.'

He came at once, hurrying into her apartment and throwing himself on his knees by her bed. Edward, her King. Instead of the ageing man he had become, she saw the bright-eyed flaxen-haired boy, so handsome, so vital, a leader in every way.

Oh it was sad that youth must fade, that ideals be lost, that will o' the wisps must be pursued when the wise know they can only lead to danger. It was sad that lives must be spent in making war in hopeless causes.

Oh my Edward, she thought, if only you had been content to be but King of England. Why did you have to fight these hopeless battles for a crown which could never be yours?

But it was all over . . . for her. Death was calling her away. She had played her part in the drama. She must leave it to others to finish.

'Philippa . . . my love . . . my Queen . . .'

His voice seemed to be coming to her from over the years.

She said: 'We have been happy together, husband.'

'Happy,' he echoed. 'So happy . . .'

There were tears in his eyes, tears of remorse. She was dying. He might have remained faithful to the very end. Yet he had seen that witch Alice and had been tempted, and unable to resist.

'Philippa,' he murmured, 'you must not go. You must not leave me. How can I live without you?'

She smiled and did not answer him.

Her youngest son, Thomas, had come to her bedside. Such a boy, she thought sadly. He will need his mother yet. He was only fourteen years old.

'Edward,' she said, 'care for Thomas.'

'I will care for our son, my dearest.'

'I must speak to you, Edward. I have three requests.'

'They shall be granted, dear lady. Only name them.'

All she wanted was that he should see that her obligations were fulfilled—all the gifts and legacies for her servants paid.

'And when you die, Edward, I would that you should lie beside me in the cloisters of Westminster Abbey.'

'It shall be. It shall be.'

She was fast failing and William of Wykeham, the Bishop of Winchester, had arrived at her bedside.

She asked to be left alone with the Bishop for a short while and her wish was granted. At the time there was thought to be nothing strange in this. It was natural that she should want to confess her sins and be alone with the Bishop before she died. But it was to be remembered later and then seemed to be of great significance.

The King came back to the chamber of death and knelt beside her bed. She placed her hand in his and thus she died.

Blanche had left the children at Windsor in the care of Catherine Swynford and had set out for Bolingbroke Castle.

In due course they should all follow her there. Blanche had felt a need to be alone for a while where she might mourn in solitude for the dead Queen.

Philippa had been almost a mother to her; she had loved her dearly. Nothing would be quite the same without her to confide in; there would be no more of those calm judgments to be given, that innocence which was closer to wisdom than most men of the world possess.

Yes, thought Blanche, she had done with life. She had lived long and happily—at least she had been happy until illness had affected her, and it was only of late that there had been an Alice Perrers in her life.

Riding through the countryside she was shocked when one of her servants said they must not enter a certain village.

'No, my lady, there are red crosses on the doors. The plague is with us again.'

She said then they must change their route to Bolingbroke. The plague would not survive in the fresh country air.

They continued their journey and at length came to the castle of Bolingbroke which would always be one of her favourite castles because little Henry had been born there and she could never think of the place without remembering the joy of coming out of her exhaustion to hear the glad news that she had given birth to a boy.

Bolingbroke lay before them—looking less grim than usual because of the September sunshine.

She rode into the courtyard. Grooms came running forward to take the horses. She alighted and went into the castle.

She was tired and made her way straight to her apartments and had food brought to her there. In the morning she would make plans for the children to come to her. She was glad to think of them in the care of Catherine Swynford. She was sorry that John had seemed to take a dislike to her. It could only be because he had imagined someone homely like the good Philippa Chaucer.

She ate a little and was soon asleep.

When she awoke next morning a sudden foreboding came to her. She could hear no sounds of activity in the

59

castle. She arose and went into the antechamber where her personal attendants should be sleeping.

The room was empty.

Puzzled she went out to the head of the great staircase and looked down into the hall. A group of serving men and women stood there, strangely whispering.

They stopped when they saw her and stood as though turned to stone, gazing at her.

'What means this?' she demanded.

One of the stewards stepped to the foot of the stairs.

'My lady, two of the serving-men have been stricken. They are in the castle . . . now. We do not know what we should do.'

'Stricken,' she echoed. 'The . . . plague?'

' 'Tis so, my lady.'

'Have any of you been near them?'

'Yes, my lady.'

She stood looking down on them and as she did so she saw one of the women creep into a corner and lie there.

'A red cross must be put at the castle gates,' she said. 'No one must go out. No one must come in. We must wait awhile.'

There was a deep silence in the hall. Then it was broken by the sound of someone sobbing in another part of the castle.

The plague had come to Bolingbroke.

Death was in the castle.

Blanche thought: 'Thank God the children are not here.'

Three days had passed and she knew that several were already dead.

'We must pray,' she had said; and they had prayed; but they all remembered that when the plague entered a dwelling be it cottage or castle there was little hope of survival for its inhabitants.

On the fourth day Blanche discovered the fatal swelling under her arms. In the space of a few hours the loathsome spots began to appear.

Oh God, she thought. This is the end then.

She lay on her bed and when one of her women came in she called to her 'Go away. You must not enter this room.'

The girl understood at once and shrank away in horror.

Blanche lay back on her bed. She was fast losing consciousness. She thought she saw the phantom hare close to her bed. He appeared, did he not, when death had come to Bolingbroke.

He has come for me, she thought. Oh John, I am leaving this life and you are not beside me to say farewell. Where are you, dearest husband? What of my children? My girls . . . my baby Henry. Dear children, you will have no mother now . . .

This was not the way in which a great lady should die . . . her husband far away, her servants afraid to come to her bedside. But this was the plague, that cruel scourge which took its victims where it would. Cottage or castle, it cared nothing for that. But it was merciful in one way. Its victims did not suffer long.

The news was carried through the castle.

The Lady Blanche is dead.

THE LOVERS

WHEN THE BLACK Prince returned to Bordeaux after his victory at Nájara his wife Joan was greatly disturbed by his appearance.

She knew that that long stay in the heat of Valladolid had affected many of his followers and there had been deaths from dysentery; but the Prince had always been a strong man, one who was able to take the rigours of battle as they came and throw off any ill effects they might leave. She remembered the recent death of Lionel in Italy and this did nothing to ease her anxiety.

'Now you are home I shall look after you,' she announced. 'There shall be no more going off to battle until you are well.'

The Prince smiled at her fondly. Joan had never behaved in a royal manner. She was a woman who would go her own way. It was a relief to know that she was there and that he could comfortably allow her to tell him what must be done until he was ready to go off again.

He should retire to his bed, said Joan. No, she would hear no protests. She knew the very posset to cure him. At least they must be thankful that this wretched matter was at an end. It had been a folly from the start to finish.

His servants smiled to see the great Black Prince ordered by his wife but they knew his nature. If he had made up his mind at that moment to leave the castle and take up arms no one—not even the masterful Joan—would have been able to stop him.

'You should have been a commander in my armies, Jeanette,' he told her fondly.

'My lord, I *am* the commander in our castle.'

That made him smile.

'I am happy to be home with you and the children,' he told her.

'Then you must prove your words by not going off again to fight senseless battles for ungrateful people.'

'A waste, Jeanette . . . a waste of blood and money . . .'

'And squandering of health. But enough of that. I'll soon have you well again.'

She kept him to his bed and none might see him without her permission. The Prince was happy to lie back comfortably and allow her to rule him. The comfort of his bed, the assurance of her devotion, these were what he needed.

A ruler must have his failures, and what seemed the greatest triumph could in time be seen to have been an empty victory. So with Nájara.

Joan was right. If she had her way, there would be no battles. She would say: 'You are the King's eldest son. One day England will be yours and our little Edward will follow you. Be content with that. In any case it is one man's work to govern England.'

His mother had felt the same, only she did not say it as forcefully as Joan did. He was sure that John's wife Blanche would have agreed with them. It was a woman's outlook.

There were times like this when he wondered whether they were right. How far had they advanced with the war in France? How much nearer to the French crown was his father than when the whole matter had started?

No farther after years of struggle, bloodshed and squandering of treasure! And if this ambition had never come to his father, if he had never decided that he had a claim to the crown of France . . .

This was no way for a soldier to think, particularly one who was reckoned to be the greatest soldier in Christendom. Jeanette's influence, he thought wryly.

And there she was standing by his bed with yet another of her potions.

'I believe you are a witch,' he said. 'You want to keep me to my bed so that I can never leave you.'

Joan laughed. She had the gayest laughter he had ever heard.

'You put ideas into my head, my Prince. Ever since the day I forced you to marry me I have been wondering how I could keep you at my side.'

'Jeanette,' he said softly. 'Oh Jeanette, did you have to use much force?'

'You know full well,' she retorted. 'We could have been married years ago but for you.'

'You were dallying with Salisbury and Holland then.'

'Only in the hope of arousing some jealousy in your sluggish breast.'

'Was that indeed the truth?'

'You know it. You were for me and I for you but I could not ask you, could I? Some foolish law says that it is the man who must ask for the hand of the lady not she for his. It is a law that should be changed. When you are King, my love, that must be your first consideration.'

'I doubt my parliament would be much impressed with my rule. Moreover there are women who decide to take matters into their own hands no matter what the custom.'

'Some have that wit and boldness.'

'Like my own Jeanette.'

'You were cruel to attempt to persuade me to take that man de Brocas.'

'I never meant you to.'

'In your cowardly way you forced me to tell you I would marry no one but the greatest knight in the world and there was no doubt who that was, was there? My lord, I know your courage is great on the battlefield but you were a coward in very truth when it came to the lists of love.'

'My Jeanette I never thought you would look my way.'

'As my eyes were fixed in your direction for many years that is a poor excuse. But no matter, thanks to your resourceful wife the matter was solved though belatedly and now you have at last—through none of your own effort—been brought to where you belong . . . and that, my lord, is in my care.'

'God bless you, Jeanette,' he said. 'Often I thank Him for you.'

'And I thank Him for you,' she replied more soberly. She went on briskly, 'The task of the moment is to have you well again and I warn you, my Prince, that you are not leaving this roof until you are.'

'I would I could stay with you every day of my life.'

'Untrue,' she said. 'You are a soldier . . . the greatest in the world they tell me. You long to lead your men into battle. It is in your blood. But not when you are sick. That is when I take command.'

'As you say, my general. Tell me what has been happening here in Bordeaux?'

'Pedro's girls are still here.'

'Constanza and Isabella. What will become of them?'

'Constanza has become a rather ambitious girl for as you know, since the death of her sister Beatrice she has become the elder and the heiress to the throne. Now do not look excited! I have made up my mind that whatever grows out of this, Constanza is going to fight her own battles. Now, a happier subject and one which is really our concern. Your sons are clamouring to see you. ''Where is our father?'' they constantly ask. When I tell them that you are resting after the battle they cannot believe that you would need to rest. I am going to bring them to see you. Lie still and they shall come to your chamber.'

'Jeanette.' He caught her hand. 'I like it not that they should see me thus.'

'They will not know how ill you are. I have promised them they shall come. I will bring them myself.'

In a few moments she had returned, a boy on either side of her.

Edward the elder was about six years old, Richard three years younger.

Edward tore his hand from his mother's and ran to his father, climbing on to the bed and embracing him.

'My son, my son . . .' The Prince looked at the eager

little face glowing with health and high spirits. 'Would you throttle me then?'

'No,' cried Edward, 'only love you.'

'And how are you, my son? How have you been faring? Tell me how far you can shoot an arrow . . . I hear good news from your horsemaster.'

'I am very good, Father. I have to be because I am the son of the Black Prince. That's you,' he added almost conspiratorially. 'And did you know you are the greatest soldier the world has ever known?'

'That's what they tell you, is it?'

Edward nodded vigorously and Joan said: 'Richard is here, too.'

She brought the younger boy forward. He did not look as robust as his brother although he was tall for his age—in fact almost as tall as his brother. His long fair curls shaded a face which was almost feminine in its beauty. Young Richard had all the good looks of his Plantagenet ancestors, but he certainly lacked that sturdiness which Edward had undoubtedly inherited.

There was a reproach in Joan's voice. She was constantly warning her husband that he paid too much attention to his elder son and she feared that little Richard might notice this. She herself was inclined to lavish more affection on the younger boy, to make up, she told herself, for true mother that she was she must give more care to the weaker of the two. She loved young Edward but as the Prince doted on that boy, she made Richard her favourite.

Young Edward allowed himself to be put aside with a certain lack of grace while Richard came forward.

The Prince laid his hand on the fair head and said: 'Well, my son, and how fare you?'

'Well, my lord, I thank you.'

Grave, dignified, and with a certain grace, this boy seemed intelligent beyond his years. The Prince knew from his wife that Richard's prowess was with his books rather than in outdoor exercise. Joan seemed to think that was something to be applauded, but the Prince would have preferred it to be the other way round.

It was well that Edward was the first-born. He was going to make a good king. He would be trained for that, just as the King had trained him, so should young Edward be brought up. It was good for a boy who was destined to rule a great kingdom to become aware of it from an early age and prepare himself.

'His tutors give good accounts of him,' said Joan proudly. 'I am going to have some of his exercises brought to you.'

'Richard is still on the leading reign,' said young Edward scornfully.

'So were you when you were a few years younger,' retorted his mother. 'Richard sits his horse gracefully as a knight should.'

'I am better . . .' began Edward.

'Now,' said their mother, 'you may sit on the bed . . . one on either side and talk to your father for a few moments. Then you shall go to your apartments and tomorrow, if you are good, you may see him again.'

The Prince was amused at their ready obedience. There was no doubt that Joan ruled the household.

She herself took them away at the appointed time and, although there were protests from young Edward that he wanted to stay longer, Joan was adamant.

'You must obey your mother,' said the Prince. Joan was smiling at him, well pleased with the life her boldness in proposing marriage to the Black Prince had brought to them all.

When John of Gaunt reached Bordeaux he too was amazed at the ill health of his brother. He had known that during the campaign for Castile Edward had been afflicted by the malady which had attacked so many men in the army, but he had expected him to throw it off with the ease which seemed natural for one of his strength.

He wondered whether Joan was thinking, as he was, of Lionel, who had not so long before died of a similar disease. However, within a few weeks, under the assiduous care of Joan, the Prince's health did begin to improve a little.

He was delighted to see John; and their younger brother Edmund had also arrived at the castle.

Edmund of Langley, fifth son of the King, was so called because he had been born in King's Langley in Hertfordshire. Like his brother he was tall and handsome, and resembled Lionel in the temperament inasmuch as he appeared to be devoid of that ambition which the two elder brothers shared, Edward perhaps naturally as he was the eldest son and heir to the throne and John overwhelmingly because he had so narrowly missed all that he most desired.

It had never worried Edmund that there were several between him and the crown. He did not seek the anxieties of state in any case. He much preferred a life of ease and comfort—good food, good wine and a certain dalliance with the ladies.

Being his father's son, of course, he must indulge in the family occupation which was battle. He accepted that, as he accepted everything else; and because he was the most handsome member of the family—now that Lionel was dead—and was easy-going, never giving himself royal airs, he was immensely popular and often achieved through the loyalty of his followers a success which a sterner leader might have had to work hard to achieve.

He hoped there would be some good hawking and hunting and that too much time would not be given to the war.

John discussed with Edmund the state of their elder brother's health. It seemed a little better, he pointed out, but he knew this form of dysentery. It was weakening the Prince and there were days when he seemed to have a complete relapse. Even Joan's care was not working as well as it should.

'Consider the position,' said John. 'Our father has aged considerably since our mother's death.'

'He is a changed man,' agreed Edmund. 'I wish he would carry on his business with Alice Perrers in a more private manner. He positively flaunts his relationship with the woman and it is not as if she is a high-born lady.'

'The flaunting is part of the price she demands for her favour. She wants the whole of England to know that she is his leman. They say that men of rank are afraid to offend her. But it was not of her I wished to speak. Our father cannot live long. And what think you of our brother's chance of returning to health?'

'By God's teeth, brother, what do you suggest?'

'I pray to Him that it will not be so. But if our father dies and Edward were to follow him, this child, his eldest son, would be our King. A boy, nothing more . . .'

'You are thinking of a Regency.'

'It might come to that.' John looked searchingly at Edmund. 'We should have to stand together to protect our brother's son.'

'He would be our rightful King and we could do no other.'

'We must stand together. But I pray God that it may never come to pass.'

Edmund avoided meeting his brother's eyes. A thought flashed into his mind. It was: 'You mean you pray God that it might.'

He dismissed it at once. That was unfair. They were a united family. They had been brought up in affection by loving parents. They had always been taught that they must stand together. The family was supreme and if one was in need all the others must go to that one's aid.

No, he was misjudging his brother and he was ashamed of himself.

But they had always known that the most ambitious member of the family was John of Gaunt.

At the Court of the Black Prince there were two young ladies. They were very interested to meet the new arrivals.

They were beautiful in the exotic way of Spanish ladies— quite different from the pale noble beauty of Blanche or that overwhelming sensual beauty of Catherine Swynford which John even now had been unable to forget.

They were interesting of course because they were the daughters of Pedro.

Constanza was the elder of the two girls. She was a determined young woman and it was clear that she was trying to find some champion who would restore the throne of Castile to her for she considered she was the rightful heir.

John listened attentively to her. Edmund, too, was drawn into their conferences. He was rather attracted by Constanza's younger sister, Isabella, but of course he could not enter into a light love affair with a girl of such position, so he gave himself up to a little harmless dalliance while John discussed the state of affairs with the elder sister.

'I would gladly marry the man who would win my throne for me,' said Constanza.

John watched her thoughtfully. Yes, she was right. She had a claim. There had been an elder sister Beatrice who had gone into a convent and had died there, so that Constanza, now the eldest child of Pedro the Cruel, could claim the throne if she could oust the usurper.

He wondered whether she would find someone to help her. Some ambitious man might, for the sake of the title of King, he supposed. It would be a good gamble, and a throne was an ever enticing goal.

While he talked with her the children came riding in—sturdy Edward, delicate Richard and with them their two half-brothers, those noisy Holland young men, the result of Joan's misalliance with Sir Thomas Holland. The elder Holland must be about twenty years old, the other two years younger; but there was no doubt that the little boys looked up to their brothers and the Hollands made the most of it.

John's eyes rested on young Edward. A King to be, and another Edward. That seemed to be a name the people loved. Whereas John . . . They should never have named him John because people still remembered that wicked ancestor of his, the King John who had made the signing of Magna Carta necessary.

He turned away from the window. He was beginning to think that he would never wear a crown.

A few days later, news came from England. He could not believe it. Blanche dead . . . of plague at Bolingbroke, that castle which they had both loved so much since it was the birthplace of their son.

He was stunned. He thought of her gentleness, her nobility. He was bowed down with grief.

He must leave at once for England. Edward would understand that he must go.

That the plague should have struck her down! All that beauty made loathsome by the fearful enemy which stalked the towns and villages of the world in search of victims. Blanche . . . not beautiful, noble Blanche!

Downstairs he could hear the sounds of music. The musicians were practicing for the evening. Joan was anxious to fill the castle with rejoicing because she was sure that the Black Prince was recovering from his sickness.

Constanza and Isabella would be there.

Constanza who wanted a husband to help her gain the throne of Castile.

That husband would be King of Castile.

Blanche had been buried near the High Altar in St. Paul's, and John had ordered that a magnificent alabaster tomb be erected on which was an effigy of his wife.

He was overwhelmed by his sadness. He had loved her dearly, and he was ashamed of the fact that there were two women who would come into his mind even while he mourned for her. One was Constanza, the heiress of Castile, the other was Catherine Swynford, the wife of his squire Sir Hugh who was with one of the armies in France. One promised a crown, the other such sensual delight as he felt he had never known yet.

But nevertheless he mourned for Blanche. He knew that there would never be one who loved him so devotedly, so selflessly, as Blanche had. Blanche would always be enshrined in his heart—the most beautiful of ladies, the most

71

perfect of wives, the mother of his children, his beloved daughters and the one he loved about all others because in him was enshrined his ambition—Henry of Bolingbroke.

Geoffrey Chaucer had presented himself to him. He was deeply affected. Once John had laughed at Chaucer's devotion to Blanche. He had teased her saying that the little poet loved her and it was well that his devotion was of the soul and not of the body otherwise he would have been jealous and have cut off the head of the presumptuous fellow.

As it was he had been amused and liked the poet for it.

He received him with friendliness and was touched when Chaucer produced what he called his Book of the Duchess.

John read it with emotion. It extolled the beauty and virtue of Blanche, setting it down in such a way that would immortalize her. It told of his own love for the incomparable Blanche.

He was deeply moved to read those words:

> 'My lady bright
> Which I have loved with all my might
> Is from me dead.'

Those simple words, which Chaucer in his poet's sensitivity had attributed to him, putting himself in his place no doubt, writing what he would have felt had he been John of Gaunt, conveyed so much more than flowery speech could have done. Chaucer had gone on:

> 'Alas, of death, what aileth thee
> That thou wouldst not have taken me
> When that thou took my lady sweet
> That was so fair, so fresh, so free
> So good that men may well it see
> Of all goodness she had no mete.'

He would not forget Chaucer, nor his wife . . . nor his sister-in-law.

He must go to the children. Poor motherless ones. They would be bowed down with sorrow.

It was his duty to go to them.

They were installed in the Palace of the Savoy in the care of their governess, and it was with strange emotions that he made his way there. He was wondering how he would find his children; they were over young perhaps to realize what this meant. Their governess would have talked to them.

Their governess! He was not really thinking of his children, he found, but of their governess.

He sent for them and waited for their arrival, his heart beating fast. He wondered what she would look like now. Perhaps she had grown over fat; some of these women did when they came to the palace. Perhaps he had endowed her, in his imaginings, with qualities she did not possess. She had become a kind of dream woman, a fantasy possessed of charms beyond all human knowledge.

The door had opened. Philippa came in. She ran to him and threw herself into his arms.

'My child, my child,' he said overcome with emotion.

Then there was Elizabeth. His younger daughter was six years old now, old enough to mourn.

'She went to Bolingbroke and we were to join her there. We never saw her again.' Philippa was looking at him sternly as though there was some explanation that he could give.

'Alas of death what aileth thee . . .' he thought. Why take Blanche . . . dear good Blanche, who had never harmed anyone and who was so sadly missed?

'And where is your brother?'

'Catherine told us to come first. She will bring him when you have seen us. He is only three you know.'

As if he needed to be reminded!

'Does the boy miss his mother?'

'Not as we do. He forgets sometimes that she is dead. He says he will show her something and that makes us cry and then he says "Oh, she is dead. I forgot." He does not know what it means. He thinks she has gone away for a while . . . like going to Kenilworth . . . or Windsor or somewhere like that.'

'And you, my darling daughters, you know what this sadness means?'

'It means she will never come back again,' said Philippa seriously.

'It is fate, my daughters. It is life. It is something we must accept. It happens to us all . . . in time.'

Elizabeth looked alarmed. 'You are not going to die too?' she asked.

'Oh no, no, my daughter. Not for years I think.'

'If you did,' said Elizabeth, 'we should be real orphans! Who would look after us then? The Queen couldn't. She is dead too.'

'I know,' said Philippa. 'We would go and live with our cousins in France. Henry is the same age as cousin Richard.'

'My children, my children, I am not going to die. There is no need to wonder what will become of you for I am here and while I am you will always be my concern. Ah . . . here is my son.'

They had come into the room. He was holding her hand. John scarcely saw the boy. He could see nothing but her.

No. He had not exaggerated. It was there . . . the voluptuous overwhelming attractiveness . . . just as he had imagined it.

She curtsied to him. Henry made a little bow . . . obviously taught by her.

'Rise, Lady Swynford,' he heard himself say. 'I see you have taken good care of my children. Henry . . .'

Henry ran forward and threw himself at his father's knees.

He lifted him up. The boy glowed with health. 'That was a fine bow you gave me,' said John.

'Catherine said I must,' replied Henry.

'Catherine did . . .' He repeated her name. He glanced at her. She smiled and again that understanding passed between them.

'Lord Henry grows apace, my lord,' she said. 'You will be delighted with his progress.'

'I'm getting bigger every day,' boasted Henry. 'I shall soon be bigger than you . . . bigger than the King. Bigger than everybody.'

'I see you have given my son a fine opinion of himself,' he said.

She answered: 'My lord, I believe he was born with that and it was his birth that gave it to him, not I.'

He put the boy down. 'I am well pleased with your care of the children, Lady Swynford.'

'Then I am happy,' she answered softly.

He asked her questions as to their progress. Philippa and Elizabeth kept butting in with the answers; but he was not really listening. He was thinking of her all the time and the dreams he had had of her. She had never been so alluring, so exciting in those dreams as she was in reality.

She took the children away and he stood looking out of the window on to the river at the craft that was plying its way from Westminster to the Tower.

Then he made his way to his bedchamber. There he said to one of his pages: 'I wish to speak again with Lady Swynford. There is much I have to say to her regarding the care of my children.'

It was the first time he had ever thought it necessary to explain his motives to a servant.

She scratched at the door and he called: 'Enter.'

He was looking out of the window and he did not turn. He found that he was trembling with excitement.

She was standing close behind him. 'You wished to see me, my lord?'

He swung round and looked at her. He thought: She knows. She is as much aware of this as I. She longs for me as I do for her.

He hesitated. 'I . . . have thought a great deal about you, Lady Swynford.'

She did not express surprise. She merely said quietly: 'Yes, my lord.'

'I wonder . . . if you had thought of me.'

'The father of my charges . . .'

75

He took her by the shoulders suddenly. 'I think,' he said quietly, 'you understand.'

She held back her head. He saw the long white throat. He had never seen such white skin. He looked at her ripe lips and then suddenly he had seized her. He heard her laugh softly and there was complete harmony between them.

They lay on his bed. They both seemed bewildered by what had happened and yet each was aware of its inevitability.

He took a lock of her thick reddish hair and twisted it about his fingers. 'I have thought of you ever since I first saw you,' he told her. 'What did you do to me on that first occasion?'

'I did nothing,' she answered. 'I merely was myself and you were yourself . . . and that was enough for us both.'

'I have never felt thus before . . .'

'Nor I.'

'There has never been such perfect union . . . We were as one, Catherine. Did you sense that?'

'Yes, yes, my lord. I knew it would be so.'

He held her close to him. In that moment of bliss he thought: We must always be together. I would marry her . . . The thought came quickly: She is the wife of Hugh Swynford . . . and with it relief. The son of the King could not marry a governess!

He thrust such thoughts from his mind and dwelt on her perfection. Her sensual beauty, that perfect body which responded unfailingly to his own; her soft musical voice; her complete abandonment to the act of love. She was a rare woman. She was his from the moment he had set eyes on her.

She told him now that she must go. She would be missed. She was right of course. What had happened had been so sudden and so overwhelming and for those moments neither of them had thought of anything but the slaking of their passion. There would be prying eyes in the castle. She was a woman with a husband overseas; he was a man who was mourning the death of his wife.

> 'Alas of death, what aileth thee
> That thou would not have taken me . . .'

Those were the words Chaucer had put into his mouth, and when he had read them he had felt deeply moved; and yet here he was, with Blanche so recently dead, sporting in the very bed which he had shared with her.

But this was Catherine. There was no one like Catherine. He had never experienced anything like this emotion she aroused in him, this heady intoxication which made him oblivious of everything else but his need of her.

'Tonight,' he said.

'I shall come to you,' she promised.

He had to be satisfied with that and reluctantly he let her slip out of his arms.

When she had gone he lay for a long time thinking of her.

He was all impatience for the night.

They lay beside each other, limp, exhausted by the force of their passion.

He knew so little of her except that she was the most desirable woman in the world. She knew much more about him, naturally. He had wondered about Hugh Swynford and she told him that the marriage had been arranged for her and she had been a reluctant bride. Everyone had told her that she was fortunate to find a titled land-owning husband; she had felt herself less fortunate.

'He's an uncouth fellow,' muttered John. 'A good soldier but I shudder to think of you together.'

'As I do.'

'And there have been others?'

'No. I left my convent and almost immediately was married. I am not a woman to break my vows . . . easily.'

He believed her.

'I would you had never married Swynford,' he said. 'I would you had come to me straight from the convent.'

She was silent.

There was a certain pride in her, he knew. She was the daughter of a Flemish knight even though his knighthood had been bestowed on the battlefield and he had died soon after receiving it. Her mother had been a sturdy country woman of Picardy who had brought up her children in a fitting manner; and when Catherine had become an orphan she had received some education at the hands of the nuns of Sheppey.

He wished that she was unmarried; that she was some princess who would be considered a reasonable wife for him. Yes, his feelings were so strong that he could think of marriage. He had never seen Marie again, though he had made sure that she and their daughter were well cared for. In spite of his ambitions he was a man who was capable of love. He had loved Marie; he had revered Blanche; he had thought himself fortunate to possess such a bride. Yet this feeling he had for Catherine Swynford was entirely different. It was wild, passionate, sensuous in the extreme and yet he knew that tender love was stirring in him too.

If she had been some great heiress . . . Constanza of Castile for instance . . . what joy that would be.

But she was not. She was merely the wife of that uncouth squire, Hugh Swynford. If she had not been . . . what temptation she would have put in his way.

That was his feeling for Catherine. When he was with her it overwhelmed him; he would have been ready to offer her anything.

He was surprised to learn that she had had two children by Swynford—Thomas and Blanche.

'Do you not long for them?' he wanted to know.

Yes, there were times when she did. But she had the satisfaction of knowing that they were well cared for in the country.

He said no more of them. He feared she might wish to return to them.

'How grateful I am to your sister Philippa,' he said. 'But for her we might never have met. Where is she now?'

'She is still in the Queen's household, but she will have to go, of course.'

'Bring her here. Let her be of our household. Would that please you, Catherine?'

'It is good of you, my lord.'

'Philippa did so much for us, we must do something for her.'

He was wondering if he could do something for her children also. He would of course. But he would have to think carefully of that.

'Catherine,' he said, 'I never dreamed there was a woman in the whole world who could please me as you do.'

THE CASTILIAN MARRIAGE

JOHN RODE OUT to Windsor and presented himself to the King.

The sight of his father shocked him. Edward's character seemed to have changed completely since the death of the Queen. He now had no reason to hide his relationship with Alice Perrers and the signs of debauchery were marked on his face. The blue eyes once so bright were dull and there were deep shadows under them; the strong mouth had slackened.

By God, thought John, he looks what he has become—an old lecher.

Alice sat beside him. It is true then, thought John, she scarcely lets him out of her sight. He is quite unbalanced. He must be to allow a woman like that to share in his councils with his ministers—and all because she insists! How could a man like his father—great Edward, hero of Crécy, sink so low. And all because of this woman!

But although Edward had prided himself on being a faithful husband who deplored promiscuity at his Court there had always been a latent sensuality in him which was straining to emerge. There had been rumours about his efforts to seduce the Countess of Salisbury; it had even been said that he had cast his eyes on Joan of Kent and there was that incident of the garter to suggest it might be true. Now it seemed, that since he had become a widower he had convinced himself that there was no need to conceal this side of his nature and it had broken free of restraint. Alice Perrers no doubt had determined that it should be so.

He bowed to his father, then to Alice.

She inclined her head and smiled at him, almost triumphantly as though to say: I know you don't think I should be here but here I am and here I stay.

On her finger was a magnificent ruby ring which he recognized as his mother's. So it had come to that. She was now in possession of the Queen's jewellery.

She saw his eyes on the ring and she lifted her hand to her face that he might see it better—a triumphant insolent gesture.

'Welcome, my son,' said the King. 'It is a sad return for you to find dear Blanche no more.'

John was aware of Alice's mocking glance. It was almost as though she knew of his encounter with Catherine.

'I could not believe it when I heard,' he said. 'I was overcome with grief.'

'She was a fine woman and a good wife to you. I was glad to see you so satisfactorily settled.'

'It *was* a fine marriage,' put in Alice. 'Look what it brought my lord. It made him the richest man in the kingdom next to you . . . my King.'

John would have liked to order her out of his presence but the King was smiling fatuously. He patted Alice's hand.

'Yes, yes,' he said, 'a good marriage. It makes it all the more sad that the plague took her. And I hear disturbing news of Edward.'

'He suffered after Nájara,' said John. 'He never seemed to recover his old rude health. Joan cossets him and orders him . . . and he accepts it.'

'A man needs a woman to look after him,' put in Alice, smiling beningly at the King.

'Alice speaks truth there,' agreed Edward.

John felt sickened. He could scarcely believe that this was his father. If he must have the woman, let him keep her in the bedchamber. How could he have her here sitting beside him flaunting the Queen's jewels. He was completely bemused by her. She did what she would with him.

Why? Why? She was a woman of no breeding. Fit only for the beds of serving men. And the King . . . Great Edward . . . Oh, it was unbelievable! And yet he recognized that inherent sensuality. Alice had it. Catherine had it. My God, he thought. It makes slaves of us all whoever we be.

'Edward wants you to go out again,' went on the King. 'He says the King of France is bent on a conquest of Aquitaine. He has heard that the Dukes of Anjou and Berry are assembling two armies for the attack. Edward is sick. Joan does not wish him to go to war.'

'Joan would not be able to prevent him if Aquitaine were attacked.'

'I know it well. But I want you to go out there, John. I want you to leave as soon as you can muster an army. What can you raise?'

'I could attempt to get together four hundred men at arms and, say, four thousand archers.'

'Do it, John. Would to God I could go with you. Affairs in England . . .'

Alice looked at him and smiled provocatively.

'You're a minx,' said the King.

John turned away impatiently.

'Have I offended the Duke of Lancaster?' asked Alice mockingly.

'Nonsense, my dear. John is delighted with one who is so good to me.'

'My lord,' said John, 'I have much with which to occupy myself if I am to raise this army in good time. I pray you give me leave to go about my business.'

'Go, John. Go. I expect to hear good news of you.'

As he left Alice's laughter echoed in his ears.

How could a great man become a slave of his passion? he thought. It made him none the more easy in his mind because he could understand the King's feeling for his siren.

The Black Prince was at Cognac awaiting John's arrival.
He was coming with a big force. Four hundred men at
arms and four thousand archers should give them what
they needed.

The Prince was fighting off one of those debilitating
attacks of dysentery which were occurring with alarming
frequency. Joan had been against his coming. 'Leave it to
the others,' she had said. 'You have done your part. You
have earned a rest.' He could not heed her though. Battle
was in his blood and he could see that if he was not there
these possessions in France, so vital to England, could slip
away.

The King of France was naturally taking advantage of
the situation and must be rejoicing in the disability of the
Black Prince.

But John would come with his army and they would
stand together. He felt uneasy about John. He had always
known of his brother's ambition. He had now brought with
him a commission that such places of Aquitaine which
gave their allegiance to the King of England should be
received into favour. He, John, would be the arbiter, in the
absence of the Black Prince. Was John trying to take over
Aquitaine from his brother?

No, it was reasonable enough. Edward was ailing. There
were times when even in camp he was too weak to rise
from his bed.

He must not be suspicious of his own brother; and yet
the anxieties would not be entirely dismissed.

He felt old and ill and disillusioned. His life was battle.
He had been bred to it; and since his father had laid claim
to the throne of France he had been dedicated to that goal.
He himself would one day be King of England and King of
France. He must not forget that. And he must make those
thrones safe for little Edward.

Thinking of his son gave him heart. As fine a boy as he
had ever seen. Joan scolded him and said he spoilt his
eldest son. She was always trying to push Richard forward.

Richard was a good boy, it seemed, but he was not like his elder brother. Never mind. They would have a scholar in the family. It did not matter as long as they had the kingly Edward as the first-born.

He was depressed nevertheless. He had heard only recently of the death of Sir John Chandos. Beloved friend of his childhood who had been close to him ever since. Chandos had saved his life at Poitiers and he had been rewarded with the manor of Kirkton in Lincolnshire, but nothing could be adequate reward for what he had done. Chandos once said that he had the reward which meant most to him—the Prince's lifelong friendship.

And now Chandos was dead—killed in battle. Edward mourned him deeply and could not forget him. He had died—this good friend—in his service, killed not far from Poitiers and buried at Mortemer.

To lose such a friend left a scar on his memory which would never heal.

And here he was, himself so sick that at times he thought his end was near.

It was a depressing outlook. He could only thank God for the devotion of Joan and the good health of his son.

As he lay in his tent, exhausted by the ride and determined not to take to his litter until it was absolutely necessary, news came to him that Jean de Cros, the Bishop of Limoges whom Edward had regarded as his friend, had surrendered the town to the French.

Limoges! To have let the French in. The man was a traitor. A raging fury possessed the Prince.

'By God,' he cried, 'he shall suffer for this. Traitor that he is. Why should traitors such as this man live while great men like Chandos are cut down in the flower of their manhood?'

Never had any of his men seen him so overcome by fury.

'Not a moment shall be lost,' he cried. 'We shall leave without delay for Limoges.'

*   *   *

Nor did his fury abate as he rode out with John of Gaunt beside him.

'We shall have the town in a matter of days and then, by God, we shall see what happens to traitors.'

John was amazed by his brother's fury. Towns had surrendered to the enemy before. Sometimes it was a wise thing to do if it could save bloodshed and destruction, and the Prince, who was not naturally a violent man, should understand this.

But on this occasion his anger persisted and it did not abate. All through the six-day siege he was like a man possessed with one motive in life—revenge on Limoges.

At length, the city could hold out no longer. The moment had come.

The Black Prince, hitherto famous for his chivalry towards a fallen enemy, screamed in his rage: 'Let no one in that town live. Put them all to the sword.'

'Women and children, my lord?'

'All. All!' screamed the Prince.

'But, my lord . . .'

'By God. Did you not hear me? Do your duty or it will be the worse for you.'

What had happened to this man, this noble Black Prince whose name was associated with all that was glorious in military matters?

He had changed. He was a tyrant. He called for blood. He wanted vengeance. The very name Limoges sent him white with fury.

The Bishop was captured.

'Bring him to me,' shouted the Prince. 'I will show him what happens to traitors.'

His brother was beside him. 'Edward . . . I would speak with you alone . . .'

He turned on John—this brother who had always sought honours, who had married Blanche of Lancaster, inherited her estates and become the richest man in England under the King.

John was humble now . . . appealing. 'A word, Edward . . . just a word.'

They were alone in the tent.

'Edward,' said John, 'we must have a care. This is a man of the Church. We could bring down the wrath of the Pope on us if harm befell him.'

'You would plead for this traitor!'

'Traitor he may be, but he is a Bishop. Edward, I beg of you. You have had your revenge on Limoges and I tell you this, it may well be in time that you will regret this act. But for the sake of England and our armies do not harm the Bishop.'

The Prince put his hand to his head. John took him by the arm and made him sit down.

'You are sick, Edward,' he said. 'You are overwrought. I beg of you take care.'

The Prince was silent for a few moments. Then he said: 'I pass the traitor Bishop over to you.'

John was greatly relieved.

The Bishop was made his prisoner.

The army encamped outside Limoges and the Black Prince stood watching the black smoke of the devastated town rising to the sky. He fancied he could hear the cries of murdered people as his men went from street to street carrying out his orders—not a man, woman or child to remain.

Now that he had shown everyone what it meant to defy the Black Prince, a calm had settled on him.

With it came the terrible realization that he would hear the cries of the people of Limoges for the rest of his life.

They carried him in his litter. It was useless to attempt to sit his horse. He was sick and he had to face that fact.

They rested awhile at Cognac where he hoped he might recover sufficiently to continue with the army, but it was clear that this was not to be.

There was only one alternative. He must return to Bordeaux.

When he arrived Joan, horrified at his appearance, insisted that he stay in his bed; moreover she sent for the doctors and told them that she wanted to know the truth and why it was that her husband, hitherto so strong, had become a victim to this recurring sickness.

The verdict was that he had endured too many hardships on the battlefield over many years and that he should not return to such conditions until he was completely recovered.

'My lady,' they said, 'he should return to England. There he should retire to the country and live quietly until his health is restored. It is our considered opinion that this is the only way to prevent his illness growing worse.'

That decided Joan. She would hear no protests.

'My dear,' said the Prince, 'what will become of Aquitaine if I go home?'

'My dear,' she retorted, 'you are worth a thousand Aquitaines.'

'I am not sure that anyone else would agree with that.'

'I have never greatly cared for the opinions of others. We are going home.'

She was delighted. It was what she had always wanted. She had made the Court of Aquitaine one of the most brilliant in Europe. Wandering musicians had always been well received at the castle; poets flourished there; it was delightful in the evening when the trestle tables had been cleared of food and taken away and songs of love and chivalry were sung.

But alas the Prince was so seldom there—he was always away winning some glorious battle which never seemed to bring the war any nearer to an end. How much better it would have been if he had remained at home.

Joan could have been happy in Bordeaux if it were not for this senseless fighting.

But even though she loved the climate which was softer than that of England and the fertile country with its colourful flowers, she had often felt a longing for her native land, and if she could go home and take her husband and her boys with her and have them completely under her care she would be happy.

Edward's health was an anxiety but she was convinced that if she could keep him at home and look after him herself and there was no more of this senseless going to war he would become robust again. That would mean more argument of course but she would face that when it came. The important task now was to restore him to health.

So there was the bustle of imminent departure in the castle.

Joan explained to the little boys who were very excited at the prospect of a journey with their parents.

They listened attentively. Edward wanted to know what would happen to his falcon and his horse.

'My darling,' said Joan, 'you will have many falcons and horses in England.'

'May I take my books?' asked Richard.

'We shall see, my love.'

'Shall we see the King?' asked Edward.

'I am sure he will want to see you.'

'He is our grandfather,' said Richard.

'And he has my name,' added Edward proudly. 'The King is Edward, my father is Edward and so am I. Edward is a King's name.'

'So is Richard, is it not, my lady? There was a King Richard. He was very brave.'

'There was only one Richard but there have been three Edwards,' said Edward scornfully, 'and my father will be the fourth and I the fifth.'

They heard talk these boys, thought Joan uneasily. So young Edward already knew that he was destined for a throne. She would rather he had not heard of this. Edward had said: 'You want to keep them babies for ever just as you want to keep me under your wing. You're like a mother hen.'

She supposed she was. Yet she had wanted to marry the heir to the throne—not just because he was the heir, of course; but she had been pleased at the prospect of becoming Queen. Now she was more mature she could visualize the anxieties of kingship. When one was young and inexperienced one thought only of those ceremonial moments when the ruler appeared all powerful, all glorious, but there was another side to the picture.

She said sternly to little Edward: 'That will not be for many many years.'

'What shall I be?' asked Richard.

'You will be my little son.'

'He won't always be your *little* son,' Edward pointed out.

'To me he will,' said Joan.

She put her arms about him and held him tightly. She felt his thin body and wished he would put on a little more flesh to be more like his robust brother.

Edward started to pull his brother away. He was a little jealous of her preference for Richard although it was clear that he himself was his father's favourite.

Joan felt Edward's hands which seemed to her over hot.

She touched his forehead. That was also very hot. There was a flush on the boy's cheeks too, and she noticed that his eyes seemed unusually bright.

'Do you feel hot, Edward?' she asked.

He considered. 'A little,' he replied.

She ruffled his hair and laughed at him. She was, as the Prince said, like an old hen with her brood.

She left the boys and went to her husband. He was lying on his bed rather restlessly. His eyes were closed and he appeared to be sleeping.

As she went close to him she heard him murmuring. He was saying something about Limoges.

She sat down by the bed and took his hand.

'All is well, Edward. I am here. You are in your bed here with me beside you.'

'Jeanette,' he said.

'Your own Jeanette,' she replied.

'How long have you been there?'

'I have just come in to see how you are.'

'I was dreaming,' he said, and she felt him shiver.

'I know. You must forget it. It's over now.'

'I cannot think what possessed me. Some devil I think.'

'It was the fever.'

89

'Those people . . . innocent people . . . I would have had the Bishop's head if John had not restrained me.'

'It is done with, Edward. It is this war that goes on and on. We are all heartily tired of it.'

'That must not be until we have the crown of France.'

She sighed. 'Well, you are going to be away from it for a while. We shall rest in peace in Berkhamsted while I nurse you back to health.'

'I wish I had never gone to Limoges . . .'

'Stop thinking of Limoges. It is over now.'

'Never before in all my life have I done such a thing. It will be remembered against me. I shall never be known for my chivalry again.'

'You had to take the town. You had to show them. You spared the old Bishop did you not? Enough of Limoges. Let me tell you how excited the children are. Edward wants to see his grandfather.'

'I am wondering what we shall find at Court. John says that woman openly flaunts her influence over the King.'

'These tales are always exaggerated.'

'It is hard to believe that my father could behave thus.'

'People are always behaving in a way which it is hard to believe, which shows that we don't know each other very well. Perhaps we don't know ourselves.'

'No. Limoges . . .'

'Enough of Limoges. I am going to bring the children to see you. Edward wants to know which of the horses and falcons are going with us.'

The Prince smiled.

'You would like to see them, my love?' she went on.

He nodded.

'I will bring them myself.'

When she went to the nurseries she was met by a solemn-faced attendant.

'The Lord Edward is unwell, my lady,' she was told. 'One of the women has gone in search of you. He seems to have a high fever.'

*   *   *

It had happened so suddenly. A few days before he had been full of health and high spirits and now he lay there limp and exhausted by the struggle to stay alive.

The Prince had risen from his bed. He was as one demented. What could have happened? How could God be so cruel as to take this beloved child from him?

Even Joan could not deceive herself or him. He saw the terrible fear in her eyes.

'There is hope yet,' said the doctors. But there was no hope.

They sat beside his bed—the Prince on one side, Joan on the other. The child sensed their presence and was comforted by it.

'Father . . .' he whispered.

'I am here, my son.'

Little Edward smiled, while Joan bent and kissed the hand which lay in hers.

'You will soon be well, my darling. We shall go to England. There you shall have a new falcon.'

The child smiled slowly.

They continued to sit by his bedside.

The doctors hovered.

'Is there nothing . . . nothing to be done?' demanded the Prince.

The doctors shook their heads sorrowfully.

There was nothing to be done then but to sit there while that young life ebbed away.

The Prince was inconsolable. He paced his bedchamber; he sat on his bed and buried his face in his hands.

'My son, my son,' he mourned. 'How could this be?'

Then in his mind he heard the cries of women and children being put to the sword. Mothers, fathers had lost their children. They had loved them as he had loved Edward and he had destroyed them.

It is retribution, he thought. Oh my God, why did You not guide me? Why did You let me betray my chivalry?

The fever was on me . . . I was a changed man. I know it. You know it . . . yet You punish me like this.

Joan came to him. 'It is no use, Edward,' she said. 'Nothing we do or say can bring him back.'

'But why . . . why . . . ? It seems so senseless.'

'Many things are senseless in this world, I fear.'

'This child . . . I cherished him so.'

'Too much,' she said. 'Too much.'

'You loved him too.'

'He was my son. I loved him and his brother. You still have a son, Edward.'

'I fear for him.'

'He is strong and healthy.'

'Edward was stronger and healthier.'

'Nothing shall happen to Richard.'

'How can we know what punishment God will mete out to us?'

'We will have more sons, Edward. As many as your father has.'

'I am a sick man.'

'When we are in England you will grow strong again. I promise you, Edward, in England life will be good. We have suffered this terrible tragedy but it is over now. We have our little Richard. We will have more sons. Edward, look forward, my love. Put the past behind you.'

He turned to her and clung to her as though he were a child.

She could offer him some comfort. She was the only one in the world who could.

She made him lie on his bed and later she brought Richard to him.

The little boy looked bewildered. He was only four years old and he could not quite understand what had happened to his brother.

His mother had tried to explain. Edward had gone away. He had gone to Heaven.

'Am I going too?' he had wanted to know.

'Not for years and years.'

'If Edward goes I want to go.'

'No, dearest, you are going to stay with me and your father. But you have to learn quickly now. It is different being without a brother.'

He was not altogether displeased. He sensed that Edward's departure had made him more important. He noticed the change in people's attitude towards him. He had become of some consequence in a subtle way.

His father was seated on a chair in his bedchamber he held out his hand when Richard entered.

Richard put his hand in his father's.

'You are my heir now, Richard,' said the Prince. 'Do you know what that means?'

Richard was not quite sure. He said: 'It is because Edward has gone to Heaven.'

The Prince was too moved to speak for a moment and so was Joan. She was thinking how young and vulnerable her little son was and of the great weight of responsibility which would be put on his shoulders. She pictured a crown on those fair curls and the thought made her apprehensive. It was because the child was Richard, her youngest. He had always seemed to her frail and delicate and thus vulnerable.

'Yes,' said the Prince at length. 'That is the reason. You will have to learn quickly.'

'Richard learns very quickly,' said Joan. 'His tutor says so.'

'You are a good boy with your books but now, my son, you must be good at all things. You will have to learn to be brave and daring. You will have to excel at the joust.'

'That is for later,' said Joan. 'Never fear, Richard, you are going to surprise everyone with your skill.'

'Am I?' asked Richard.

'Of course you are, my darling. You have to be to your father all that Edward was.'

'May God bless you,' said the Prince.

'Always,' added his mother.

Then she took her son by the hand and led him away.

*   *   *

The Prince realized that Joan was right. He must not dwell on the past. He must forget the sack and massacre of Limoges; he must not brood on the fact that he had lost his elder son who had seemed to him a perfect king in the making. He must look to the future. He must plan ahead.

Richard was now the heir to the throne and very special tuition must be given to him. A boy who already at his tender age preferred to pore over books rather than be out in the fresh air practising riding and manly sports needed to be turned in the direction he must go. It was all very well when he was a second son. Book learning was not a bad thing for second sons. They might go into the church. It was always good to have a member of the family in some high office. But all that was changed. Richard was now in the direct line of succession. Providing events took their natural course Richard would one day be King of England.

Two tasks lay ahead. First to train Richard and secondly to go back to England, regain his health and beget more sons.

He sent for two men whom he trusted completely—Sir Guichard d'Angle and Sir Simon Burley.

Guichard d'Angle had the reputation of being a perfect knight. He was skilled in the arts of chivalry. He had won distinction for his military prowess. He would be a perfect tutor for young Richard.

As for Sir Simon Burley he was a man whom the Prince esteemed more than any other since death had deprived him of the friendship of Sir John Chandos. Sir Simon had fought bravely with King Edward in France and in due course had entered the service of the Black Prince. He had been present at Nájara and later he was taken prisoner near Lusignan much to the grief of the Prince who had sought an early opportunity of bringing about an exchange of prisoners when Sir Simon had been returned to his service.

Such tried and trusted servants should always be appreciated by rulers and the Prince had never been one to forget those who served him well.

Simon was an ideal choice, for besides being a great

soldier he was also a man of culture, a lover of literature and music.

The Prince explained what he required of these two men.

'Now that Richard is my heir,' he said, 'there must be some change in his education. He must be brought up in such a way that when the time comes he will be prepared to face his responsibilities.'

Sir Guichard said: 'There are many years before the boy would be called upon to do that.'

'I hope that may be so,' said the Prince, 'for we are going to need time. He is such a child so far and his mother has been over-lenient with him.'

'He is a bright child, my lord. He loves his books and that never harmed anyone.'

The Prince was pleased. It was like Simon to speak up and say what he meant even though he might be disagreeing with his master.

'I want him to be learned,' said the Prince, 'but outdoor exercise must not be neglected.'

'It shall be so,' said Sir Guichard.

'Thank you, my lords,' said the Prince. 'Now we must prepare to leave for England which we shall do within the week.'

The knights bowed and retired.

It was a cold January day when the party set sail for England.

Richard was excited. Sir Simon had explained to him that now that Edward was dead he, Richard, could one day be King of England. There was his grandfather who was the King but a very old man; then there was his father; and after him came Richard himself.

'It will be many years yet,' said Simon, 'but a king is different from other people. He has to learn how to be a king and that is not an easy thing to learn.'

'How does a king learn to be one?'

'He must first of all be unselfish.'

'Is my grandfather unselfish?'

'Your grandfather always thought first of serving his country. That is why he has been a great king.'

'Is he not a great king now?'

'What makes you say that?'

'You said he has been a great king.'

This boy is too sharp, thought Sir Simon.

'I should have said your grandfather is a great king.'

Richard was satisfied.

'What shall I have to do?' he asked.

'What you are told.'

'I always had to do that. So what is the difference?'

Sir Simon smiled and came to the conclusion that it was better to let matters take their course.

There lay the cog in the harbour. It was flying the flag which was his father's. The Black Prince! When he had first heard the name Richard had thought it was something terrifying—like a nightmare, a great dog with slavering jaws trying to get into the nursery, a priest in long dark robes who was trying to catch him to punish him, something shadowy and grotesque . . . a strange shape that haunted him in dreams and made him cry out so that Edward had said he was a baby. And then the Black Prince turned out to be only his father, who was always kind to him although he loved Edward better. Edward had boasted of it. '*I* am the first-born. *I* am the one who is going to be King.'

Perhaps Edward had boasted too much and God was displeased. Richard had gathered that God could rather easily be displeased. In any case Edward had gone to Heaven and Richard had moved up. He was the important one now.

And he was going on that big ship to sail on the sea—as soon as the waves ceased to pound the shore so. He was going to see his grandfather and live in England and be brought up to be a king.

It was an exciting prospect.

He went on board with his mother and father. He noticed that they did not like him to be too far from them; he fancied they were afraid that God might send someone to snatch him away and take him to Heaven to join his brother there.

He wondered vaguely about Heaven. Perhaps he would like to go there and join Edward. Edward had always been boasting about how much cleverer he was than Richard, how he could ride better and jump and run. No, he preferred England to Heaven. He had a notion that he would be far more important in England than he would in Heaven.

It was interesting to be on board. Sir Simon was close to him and he plied him with questions. He wanted to know everything about the ship. Sir Simon always answered his questions. He liked an interest to be taken in everything.

His father and mother went below to lie down, for the sea was wild. The captain said it was going to be a rough journey.

Sir Simon looked at Richard and said: 'Will you face the elements or would you like to go below and lie down?'

Richard was a little afraid but he felt that he was expected to say that he would remain on deck with Simon so he did so.

It *was* a terrifying journey. The water washed over the deck. He was wet and cold but Simon remained on deck and so Richard was with him.

'If your stomach's strong enough fresh air is the best thing in seas like this,' Sir Simon told him.

His hand grasped firmly in that of Simon he watched the pounding seas and when they had left the Bay of Biscay behind them and had turned into the English Channel the wild winds abated a little.

'Here is the coast of England, my lord.'

Richard stared at it. It was very green, he noticed, and there came to him then an overwhelming pride because this was the country his grandfather ruled and his father would rule one day . . . and far far ahead he himself would reign over it.

*   *   *

They dropped anchor in Southampton Harbour. It was very cold and there was snow on the ground. Even so a crowd of people stood on the shore watching their arrival.

Richard was now beside his mother who was supervising the men who were carrying the litter. That was for his father. The rough sea voyage had not suited him and he was too sick to walk.

He had wanted to but Joan had said he was going to do no such thing. She had made him see that it would not do for the people to see a poor sick man stagger ashore. It was far more fitting that he should be carried in his litter.

'It is a very cold place,' said Richard to Simon.

'That's because it is winter. You wait until the summer comes, and the spring will soon be here. Then the trees will be covered in buds and the birds go wild with joy. The spring is never anywhere else as it is in England.'

Richard looked up at the dark sky and the royal banners which fluttered rather dismally, damp as they were.

When his father's litter appeared the people cheered enthusiastically and there were cries of: 'Long live the Black Prince.'

His father waved his hand in acknowledgement of the cheers.

'You'll keep well now you've come home, my lord,' shouted one man. 'God bless you.'

It was clear that the people here loved his father very much.

Now he came ashore holding his mother's hand. The people looked at him and then suddenly a loud cheer went up.

'Long live the little Prince. Long live Richard of Bordeaux.'

His spirits were suddenly lifted. He felt a wave of ecstatic happiness pass over him.

They loved him too. He had never heard anything that thrilled him so much as the cheers of the crowd.

Suddenly he was glad that Edward was in Heaven—for he knew that if Edward had been here he would have been the one they cheered. He was glad that he had come to

England. He was glad that one day he would be King of this land. He loved it from that moment because it belonged to him and one day he would be its King.

John of Gaunt watched the cog sail away with an emotion which it was not easy to analyse. The death of his nephew had stunned him almost as much as it had the boy's parents, but for a different reason.

One of the heirs to the throne had been removed at a sudden stroke. Of course there was another to step into his place—that delicate fair-haired boy who, one imagined, would have been the one to go if any.

It was an exciting prospect which lay now before him. His father was ageing fast and his pursuit of Alice Perrers could not be good for his health; his brother the Black Prince was very sick; then there was this child, Richard of Bordeaux. Lionel had a daughter who had been married to the Earl of March; there would be some who would say she came before John of Gaunt. But a girl . . . and Richard a child . . . Sometimes he thought it an exciting prospect; at others it depressed him.

In the meantime here he was in Aquitaine—his brother's lieutenant. It might well be that his brother would never be well enough to return and his future lay here on the continent.

Often he thought of Catherine. He could send for her, perhaps. But could he? The governess of his children, the wife of one of his squires who was serving now in the army!

Life was full of promise yet it was only promise. He wanted fulfilment.

First he must arrange the funeral of his nephew. Joan had wanted it to take place after they had left partly because she had been eager to get Edward home to England and partly because she feared that to attend it would bring such overpowering grief to the Prince that it would impair his health further.

It was a ceremonial occasion but those who would have felt real grief were no longer there.

No sooner was it over than news was brought to him that Montpoint in Périgord had surrendered to the French. He must therefore set out to regain the place. This occupied him for several weeks and it was not until the end of February that he had regained the town.

When he returned to Bordeaux it was clear to him and to everyone else that his heart was not in the task which had been assigned to him. He was holding Aquitaine for Edward. He wanted to rule in his own right not through another.

His brother, Edmund of Langley, joined him at Bordeaux and there also were Constanza and Isabella, the two daughters of Pedro the Cruel.

The spring had come. The weather was warm and the two brothers rode out to hunt or merely to enjoy the countryside with the two young women.

Constanza was serious minded. Her great object was to break out of exile and regain the crown of Castile which she declared was hers by right.

'And so it is,' agreed John, 'and so should it be yours. This bastard Henry should be deposed and you should be welcomed back.'

'He will never leave unless he is forced to,' said Constanza. 'If only I had the money to raise an army . . . I think the people would be with me. Surely they would wish to see the legitimate heir on the throne.'

John pondered this. He had been playing with the idea of suggesting to his father and his brother that the Salic law be established in England. It existed in France. That was why Edward was having to fight for the crown. The crown of France came to him through his mother but because of this law he had been set aside. That was what the war was about. John was now thinking of Lionel's daughter, Philippa, who unless the Salic law was introduced would come after Richard and before him in the claim to the English throne.

He realized that this law would be considered illogical and there was no hope of its being introduced in England when the very recognition of such a law would render null and void Edward's claim to the throne of France.

So therefore as he saw it there was ageing Edward who could not last more than two or three years at the most; the Black Prince whose recurring sickness suggested he too might not be long for this world; then there was this four-year-old boy, Richard, rather delicate and in any case little more than a baby. Then Philippa, daughter of Lionel, married to the Earl of March who no doubt had his ambitions. These were the ones who stood in line before John of Gaunt.

It could well be that the crown would never come his way. He had never won the popularity the Black Prince had enjoyed. He was not the great warrior that his brother had always been. He was not enamoured of war; he preferred to use the cunning moves of statecraft which were far less costly. The people were foolish; they never understood that such as he was would be so much better for the prosperity of the country than these great warriors whose aim was always to win glory in battle.

His great-grandfather had been a great king but he had wasted men and money in fighting the Scots—and what good had that brought England? His father had been obsessed by the French wars and what good was that bringing England? How much better it would have been to hold what he possessed in France—which needed continual watchfulness to be held—and to forget this wild dream of taking the crown of France. No, John of Gaunt would be a different kind of king if ever that glorious day came.

But how could it . . . with so many to stand between him and his ambition? The people would never accept him. They would be bemused by the sight of this pretty fair-haired boy or young Philippa—a Queen. They were ridiculously sentimental and they had never really taken to John of Gaunt. For one thing he had not been born in England. His brother Edward was Edward of Woodstock. They called him that sometimes. Edward the Black Prince. A magic name, and they would support his son however young he was. The crown of England seemed a long way from John of Gaunt.

But there was another crown which he might win.

Constanza had shown very clearly that she would be ready to marry the man who would help her win her heritage.

Constanza could make him King of Castile.

He talked the matter over with Edmund.

'Constanza is determined to regain the crown of Castile,' he said. 'Methinks she looks to us, brother.'

'I am sure she does.'

'I have been thinking, Edmund, that I should like to be the King of Castile.'

Edmund clasped his brother's hand.

'There is nothing that would please me more, brother, than to see you Constanza's husband. We should be near each other for the rest of our lives, for I have decided I shall marry Isabella.'

'The younger sister . . .!' began John, and Edmund laughed.

'I am not ambitious as you are, John. I would be quite content to spend the rest of my days in a pleasant Court given over to the enjoyment of living, of which I declare, there is too little in our lives.'

John nodded. Edmund was easy-going, pleasure-loving, Lionel all over again. Good-natured, generous, loving music and poetry, Edmund had no great love of battle. It was unfortunate to be a son of the Plantagenets and to have this kind of temperament because there must always be a certain amount of fighting to be done. Men such as his father would have been horrified if Edmund had told him that he preferred to live quietly in some little Court surrounded by troubadours and poets rather than to fight to enhance the family's prestige and gain new possessions.

John understood Edmund's attitude; he did not share it by any means. He wanted the possessions and he would fight for them but he preferred to win them by other means—he would never be a great general like his father and elder brother. The battle for him was the means to an end; he had no joy in it for its own sake as these military heroes had.

'I have not absolutely decided yet,' he said. 'I want to think about it.'

'But why not, John? Constanza is an attractive woman. Moreover you want to be a king. That's your chance.'

'I know,' said John. He could not explain that he did not want Constanza. He wanted Catherine Swynford. Even Edmund, who would have understood in some measure, would have laughed. Sons of kings did not marry governesses. Besides the woman had a husband already.

I am foolish to think of her, thought John, and yet . . . The fact was he could not stop thinking of her. He knew that as soon as he returned to England he would seek her out. He would have to be with her. He would not be able to keep his liaison secret from Constanza. How could one plan to marry one woman while one was thinking constantly of another?

What nonsense this was! Of course he must marry Constanza, and when he returned to England this feeling towards Catherine might have changed. It was long since he had seen her. Why was he hesitating? How could he marry Catherine? She had a husband. Could he be like David in placing Uriah the Hittite in the forefront of the battle?

Be reasonable, he admonished himself. Be sensible. Marry Constanza.

He sought her out without delay lest he should change his mind.

'Constanza,' he said. 'If you marry me I will fight to regain your crown.'

Her joy was reflected in her face. She held out her hands and he seized them.

He drew her to him and kissed her.

He felt nothing for her, only a great sickness of heart because she was not Catherine.

*   *   *

It was springtime when the two brothers returned to England with their brides.

John and Constanza went to the Palace of the Savoy, riding through the streets and the people came out to see them.

There were mild cheers for the King and Queen of Castile as they were calling themselves.

Along by the river they rode and into the palace which had delighted John ever since it had come into his possession through his marriage to Blanche. Now he was thinking not so much of the grandeur of that magnificent pile of stones as to what he would find within.

Constanza was amused at his eagerness. She thought it was to see his children. It was not that he would not be delighted to see how they had grown during his absence; but what put that flush in his cheeks and shine in his eyes was the prospect of seeing Catherine again.

In the great hall those who served him in the palace were lined up to greet him and pay homage to the new Duchess of Lancaster who was also the self-styled Queen of Castile; and there were his children. He dared not look just yet at the tall graceful woman who stood holding young Henry's hand.

Philippa had grown almost beyond recognition. Elizabeth too. And young Henry was a sturdy five-year-old.

John lifted his eyes from the children and looked at Catherine. She smiled serenely.

He felt a great impulse then to take her in his arms, to hold her to him . . . there before them all. She knew it and her smile was confident. Nothing could change the overwhelming attraction between them. Certainly not this dark-eyed bride from Castile.

'And how are my son and daughters?' asked John.

He was not looking at her but at the children but he was seeing her—the soft skin, the thick red hair which sprang so vitally from the smooth white forehead. He knew the texture of that skin and he longed to touch it.

'We have seen the King,' said Philippa.

'Alice Perrers was with him,' added Elizabeth; she was more outspoken than her sister.

'Hush,' said Philippa. 'We are not supposed to talk of her.'

'Must you talk of others when your father has just returned? And what has my son to say for himself?'

Henry told his father that he went hunting last week. 'We caught a fine deer.'

'Nothing has changed much since I have been away,' said John. 'You must meet the new Duchess. Constanza . . .'

The children were presented to their stepmother. The girls regarded her with suspicion, young Henry with interest.

'May I present to you, Lady Swynford, their governess?'

Catherine curtseyed and Constanza gave her a cold nod.

Then John with Henry's hand in his and the girls on the other side of him passed on.

At the earliest possible moment he sent for her.

When she came to his apartments, he was shaking with emotion.

'I wished to see you, Lady Swynford, to hear from your lips how my children have fared during my absence.'

'All is well with them, my lord,' she answered calmly. 'They are in good health, as you see, and progress at their lessons. Henry's riding masters will give you a good account of his conduct I am sure . . .'

He was not listening. He was watching her intently.

'I have longed to see you,' he said quietly. 'You have changed little. It has been so long.'

She lowered her eyes.

'I must see you . . . alone . . . where we can be together.'

She lifted her eyes to his. 'Is it possible, my lord, now?'

Of course it had been different before. Blanche had been dead. He was a widower then. Now he was just returned with a new bride.

'I married for state reasons,' he said. And was amazed at himself. Why should he, the son of the King, explain his reasons to a governess?

'Yes,' she answered. 'I know it.'

'You have a husband,' he said, as though excusing

himself for not marrying her. What did she do to him? She made a different man of him. She unnerved him; she bewitched him. He believed that had she been free he would have married *her*.

If he had what bliss that would have been. No subterfuge, they could have been together night and day.

'I must see you,' he said.

'When, my lord?'

'You must come to my bedchamber.'

'And the Duchess?'

'I know not . . . but I will arrange something . . . I must. I yearn for you. I have ever since I left. There is no one like you, Catherine, no one . . . seeing you again, I know.'

She answered: 'I know too.'

'Then we must . . .'

'But how, my lord? It will not be easy.'

'But it must be. It *must*.'

She was right when she said it was not easy, but he contrived it. He had to. There was a small room in a part of the palace which was infrequently used. They met there.

There was a bed on which they made ecstatic love.

He thought of Constanza and the necessity to get her with child. He wished he had never let his ambition lead him into this marriage. The King of Castile. It was an empty title. It was one which Henry of Trastamare would never allow him to have.

It had been a reckless marriage. He should have remained free.

Suppose he had done so. Suppose Hugh Swynford died . . . Soldiers did die. They died like flies in hot countries. If it was not in battle it was in the fight with disease. Suppose he had married Catherine. How beautiful she would have looked in the robes of a duchess! How proud he would have been, and all the time they would have been together.

What mad dreams to come to an ambitious man. H could imagine the astonished fury of his father and of Edward. Edmund and Thomas would have been amused, though they did not count.

But he had married Constanza; he had become the King of Castile—and it might be a title that had some meaning some day; and these were wild foolish dreams which came to him only because he was in the thrall of an enchantress.

She was whispering to him now. 'It will be necessary to be very careful.'

'Careful. How can I be careful? I betray my feelings for you all the time.'

'Yes,' she said, 'you do.'

'Then what am I to do?'

'Go to Castile?' she suggested.

'Wherever I go,' he said, 'there must you be. I will not be without you so long again.'

And he lay there, knowing that his absence would be noticed; that hers would be too.

Surely it was only necessary to see them together to recognize this flame of passion which seemed as though it would consume them both.

THE BLACK PRINCE

THE BLACK PRINCE came up from Berkhamsted to confer with the King. The Prince's health had improved a little since his return to England but the periodic bouts of fever remained and when they came they were as debilitating as ever. He would lie in his bed frustrated and bitter. He had never really recovered from the death of his elder son and he worried continuously about Richard's future.

At this time he was in one of his more healthy bouts and in spite of Joan's attempts to dissuade him he insisted on going to Windsor.

The sight of the King shocked him as it did each time he saw him. Edward was growing a little more feeble every day, a little more doting on the ubiquitous Alice, and the image of the great King who had won the love and admiration of his people was becoming more and more dimmed.

The Prince thought: If he goes on like this the people will depose him. How much longer will they tolerate Alice Perrers? She behaves as though she is his chief minister and some inspired statesman instead of a rapacious woman, a harpy, just clinging to him for what she can get.

At the moment Aquitaine was the Prince's concern.

'I should never have left,' he said. 'John has made a great mistake.'

'Well, he is King of Castile now.'

'King of Castile,' said the Prince contemptuously. 'An empty title! How near is he to ever becoming the true King of Castile? What has this marriage done but brought Henry of Trastamare and the King of France closer together? They are allies now. Far from John's reigning over Castile we shall find the French taking Poitou and Saintonge.'

'You take too gloomy a view, my lord,' said Alice.

The Prince felt ready to explode with fury. He deliberately ignored her and turned to his father. 'It will be necessary to prepare ourselves. I can assure you that an attack will come before long. The French are not going to lose this advantage. I should have stayed.'

'You were in no fit state to stay,' said the King. 'You are recovering now. You must wait until you are well.'

'Yes,' said the Prince bitterly, 'wait until the French have robbed us of everything we possess. We must act without delay.'

'The King will not go to France,' said Alice sharply.

'That is for the King to decide, Madam,' retorted the Prince coldly. 'My lord,' he continued, turning to the King, 'this is a matter of great importance. I think we should discuss it in private.'

'We are in private, Edward,' said the King.

The Prince raised his eyebrows and looked at Alice.

'Alice is always with me. She understands what it is all about, do you not, Alice my love?'

'I understand because it concerns you, my King,' replied Alice smiling at him.

He is becoming senile, thought the Prince. What is going to happen? The French triumphant; myself sick; John, clever as he is, not a man to lead victorious armies, the King losing his wits and robbed of his strength by a harpy whose only thought is to feather her nest while the old man lives; my son Edward dead and a frail child all I have left! Oh God, what is happening to England? But a few years ago this great country was one of the most powerful in the world, ruled over by an able man. How in a few short years could God bring us so low!

I must regain my health. I must hold the Kingdom together before it is completely lost.

'Then if we must discuss these matters vital to our

country's survival thus, I will send for John, for he should partake in our discussions.'

'Yes, do send for John,' said the King.

'I hope he is enjoying his marriage,' put in Alice rather maliciously. 'Our King of Castile should be rather pleased with himself. There are rumours . . .'

The Prince gave an abrupt bow to the King and walked out of the chamber. If his father forgot the required etiquette so would he. He would not stand and listen to that low-born creature discuss his brother.

He rode to London and made his way to the Savoy Palace where he knew he would find John.

John was surprised to see him and declared that he was delighted that his health had obviously improved.

'It is useless to attempt to talk to the King with that woman beside him,' said the Prince impatiently. 'I would not have believed this possible if I had not seen it with my own eyes.'

'She seems to do what she will with him.'

'The country will be ruined if this goes on. That marriage of yours was not very clever.'

'I begin to see it now.'

'What do you suppose the French will do? Make an alliance with Henry of Trastamare obviously. That is clear. You have no chance of winning Castile.'

'I can see it will be a difficult task.'

'And you will not achieve it by staying here in England.'

John's heart sank. He had been foolish. There was no need to have married Constanza. He had allowed himself to believe that there would have been a quick conquest. He might have known that Henry of Trastamare would not be so easily disposed of; and clearly the French would take advantage of the situation. More fighting. More leaving Catherine.

He had been seduced by the glitter of a crown.

The Prince went on: 'If I but had my strength again! I should never have left Aquitaine. If I had stayed . . .'

He paused in frustration.

'What is done is done,' said John. 'Let us go on from there.'

'That makes sense,' replied the Prince. 'We must make plans to send out a fleet to Rochelle without delay.'

The Prince's health seemed to improve as he busied himself with the urgent work of preparing a fleet to sail to France.

He did not intend to go with it. Joan was determined to stop him and with his health in such a precarious state he had to agree that he might be a liability rather than of use.

The Earl of Pembroke should lead the fleet and they would set out as soon as weather permitted for Rochelle. In the meantime the Prince would gather together more men and arms ready to support the landing when it had taken place.

Pembroke set out in June. A few weeks later the disastrous news reached England that the fleet had been intercepted by the Spaniards, and scarcely a ship had been able to limp back to England. So many lives lost, so much treasure squandered!

The Black Prince was in despair. He went to the King and cried: 'God has deserted us and I am not surprised.'

The King did rouse himself a little, and took his mind from the new jewels he was having made for Alice to think of the implication of this defeat.

'Would you lose everything we possess in France while you dally with your leman?' shouted the Prince. 'I tell you this, my lord, if you persist in you indifference to your crown there will soon be nothing to give your mistress.'

'You should remember that you speak to your King,' retorted the King.

'I remember I speak to my father who was once a great King,' answered the Black Prince.

The King was shaken. It was true. He thought briefly of the glorious days. This son of his, of whom he had always been so proud and still was, was right of course. There must be a return to the old days of greatness. They were losing France and the Prince was hinting that if they continued thus they could lose England.

He roused himself. Alice's jewels would have to wait. He would explain to her. She would not want him to lose his crown. He must tell her to try not to anger the Black Prince. She must be reminded that he would be the next King of England.

'You are right, Edward,' said the King. 'We must act promptly. We must muster another fleet. We have to reach Rochelle.'

The Prince clasped his father's hand.

'If you can be as you once were, my lord,' he said, 'and if I can but keep my health, none will dare come against us.'

A few days later news came that the French had overrun Poitou and Saintogne.

The Black Prince had renewed his energies. He was urging on his father and brothers the need for immediate action. The King himself was aware of the danger and it seemed as though he was returning to his old vigour. Even Alice Perrers could not divert him from the purpose in hand.

But as the preparations went on the Black Prince's health began to fail again. Joan urged him to take to his bed but he would not listen to her.

'No, Joan,' he insisted, 'this matter is of the utmost urgency. The crown of England itself is in jeopardy. I have to hold it . . . for Richard.'

Joan knew that it was useless to protest. Frantic with anxiety she watched her husband leave.

'I shall soon be back again.'

He did come back, sooner than she had expected. The weather was so bad that it was impossible for the ships to land on French soil; and while they were attempting to, the town of Rochelle surrendered. That of Thouars waited in vain for relief but when it failed to come the city gates were thrown open and French invaders moved in.

It was a disastrous defeat. The fleet returned to England having achieved nothing.

The Black Prince was in no state to continue making war. John had been right. He should never have attempted to go. His presence had made no difference because the fleet had been unable to land. All that had happened was that the fever had returned and after every bout he was a little weaker.

Gloom settled over the Court and the country. Alice only could arouse the King from his lethargy. He seemed to be telling himself that he must lose all that he had fought so hard to gain, that God did not favour his claim and had sent Alice to divert him from war and spend his energies in other directions. The Black Prince raged and fumed but he could only do it from a sick bed.

John of Gaunt realized that efforts would have to be made to hold the French possessions and that it would be his lot to try to save them.

Constanza had become pregnant and was pleased about this. She was aware that he had a mistress in the household and that she was the governess to his children by Blanche of Lancaster, but was not really grieved by the discovery, although some of her women thought she should be and should dismiss the brazen red-haired creature. Constanza shrugged her shoulders. She had not married John of Gaunt for love. He had seemed to her the means of winning back for her the throne to which she believed she had a right, and she still did not give up hope of doing so. If he would fight for her crown—and he would if the opportunity arose because it would be his crown too—she would be satisfied.

They had made a show of living together; this child she was to bear was proof of that. She did not object to his having a mistress and Catherine Swynford was a very different kind of woman from Alice Perrers. Catherine had been well brought up in a convent; she had some education; she never attempted to exploit her position. No, Constanza did not greatly object to Catherine Swynford.

It was good to have children, thought John, and he was glad that Constanza was pregnant. His marriage could have been far more inconvenient, and there was always the chance of winning the crown of Castile.

Now of course he would have to return to France as the

Black Prince could not go. Nor could the King. So the task would fall to John. He would have to cross those turbulent waters which had proved so recently to be on the side of the enemy. He would have to hold what was left, but for whom . . . for the King, for the Black Prince, for young Richard?

He did not want to leave England. He hated leaving Catherine for the more they were together, the greater was his need of her.

Then news came to him that among those who had been wounded in the force which had been left to stand against the French was Hugh Swynford. He would tell her the news when she came to his bedchamber. She came to him openly now, for it was impossible to keep their relationship a secret. However much they had tried there were certain to be some who noticed it; and it seemed to them both that it was better to be an open fact than a clandestine one to be whispered about and giggled over in corners.

They both told each other that they were neither of them ashamed. So it was common knowledge throughout the Court that Catherine Swynford was the mistress of John of Gaunt.

Well, the King was sporting with Alice Perrers, but the Black Prince upheld the honour of the family. He was the faithful husband, the hero of the people and he had a son to follow him. Now and then the people had a glimpse of the fair-haired boy who was growing up to be tall and handsome; and when they did they cheered him wildly.

Everything would be all right, said the people, while the Black Prince was with them.

When Catherine was alone with him John immediately told her of the news about Hugh.

'He is lying sick and in need of nursing close to Bordeaux.'

'Poor Hugh,' she said. 'He will be most unhappy. He is not the sort of man who is blessed with patience. He cannot occupy himself unless it is with horses and fighting.'

'He is very badly wounded indeed, I believe,' said

John. 'An idea has come to me. Perhaps you should go out to nurse him.'

'You . . . you would send me to him. Does that mean . . . ?'

'It means that if you were in France, so should I be and the sea would not separate us.' He had become excited. 'Listen, my love. I shall have to leave England soon. I have little heart for this coming campaign, but I must go since my father cannot go, nor can my brother. Even he must realize he is too sick for more campaigns. I must leave for France. My spirits would be lifted indeed if when I arrived there I should find you . . . waiting for me.'

She shared his excitement. She must go. She must nurse Hugh. Often she suffered great remorse on his account. She had something to tell John. She had not wished to mention it until she was sure, but now there could be no doubt.

'I am going to have your child,' she said.

A wild joy came over him. It was a delight which he had not felt at the prospect of Constanza's legitimate child.

'I am so happy,' she told him. 'I had always feared the day would come when you would no longer be with me. I could not hope that you would go on loving me.'

'You talk nonsense, Catherine, and that is not like you. I shall love you till the day I die.'

'Perhaps,' she answered. 'And I shall have your child. How I shall love it. How I shall cherish it.'

'I too,' he replied fervently. 'Now let us plan. You will go on ahead of me. It is impossible for you to travel with the armies. Oh, my Catherine, this has changed everything. I dreaded journeying to France. Now there is all the difference in the world for when I arrive there I shall find you awaiting me.'

John, assiduous in his care for Catherine, had arranged for her to travel almost royally. She had women to attend her and one of these was a midwife, for John was very anxious, even though it was some months before the child was due, that nothing should go wrong.

Philippa and Elizabeth had been aware that there was some unusual relationship between their father and their governess, and that this gave an importance to Catherine. They were very fond of her; and Elizabeth, who was more precocious although four years younger than her sister, was adept at listening to the gossip of serving men and women. Catherine was a sort of wife of their father she gathered, though not a real one. They had a stepmother, the Queen of Castile, of whom they saw very little; they much preferred Catherine.

And now they heard that she was going away from them. She had a husband it seemed, who was the father of young Thomas and Blanche whom they had seen now and then. And now Catherine was going away and someone else would teach them and be constantly in their company. It was rather mysterious and disturbing. Henry was reduced to tears at the prospect. But nothing they did could keep her; and in due course Catherine was ready to depart.

Now they must say goodbye to their father for he was going away too. He was going to fight the wicked French who would not give their grandfather the crown which really belonged to him.

It was all somewhat mystifying but as the weeks passed they became accustomed to being without Catherine and soon Henry could not remember what she looked like.

It was a long and tortuous journey across France. In the first place it had been necessary to wait for a favourable wind; and then they must be very careful not to venture near those places where there might be danger of meeting the French.

Catherine began to realize that it had not been over zealous of John to send a midwife with them.

She was far gone in pregnancy when they reached Bordeaux and she wondered what she would say to Hugh when she came face to face with him. He might well have heard of her relationship with the Duke of Lancaster in which case he might not be surprised to see her so heavily pregnant.

Poor Hugh! Did he regret their marriage? If he recovered perhaps John would advance him in some way. She would ask him. Not that that would compensate him for the wrong they had done him. It was possible that he had had a few mistresses, for he was not the sort of man to resist the call of the flesh. A sorry business, she thought; and but for the existence of Thomas and Blanche she would have wished the marriage had never taken place. The children always stirred feelings of guilt in her but this wild all-consuming passion between herself and John had been such as to set aside all other considerations.

By the time she reached Bordeaux Hugh was dead, and she could not help feeling relieved, dreading their meeting as she had. His servant told her that he had suffered greatly from his wounds and finally they had become so inflamed that his flesh began to mortify.

He had been buried hastily because of his putrefying flesh and it was feared that her journey had been in vain. Orders had been received from the Duke of Lancaster that her child should be born in Beaufort Castle in Anjou where preparations had been made for her, so there was nothing to do but continue her journey which she did.

She arrived at Beaufort Castle in time for her child to be born.

It was a boy and she called him John after his father.

It was not long after the birth that John came to the castle. His delight in their son was great. A perfect boy, he said. How like her to give him a boy. Constanza's child was a girl. She had called the child Catherine, which seemed a little ironical since it was the name of her husband's mistress.

'It must mean that she does not revile me for taking your love,' said Catherine.

'It means that she is quite indifferent to what happens to me . . . or to you. She wanted me to fight for her crown.

117

She still does and she is hoping that I shall win it for her one day. That is her only concern.'

It was a comfort to Catherine. She had no desire to live in anything but peace with her lover's wife.

So they were together again if only briefly and they must make the most of the time; he visited her whenever it was possible. It had been a piece of good fortune that had given her a reason for coming to France.

But he must tear himself away from her for he had been appointed Captain General of the armies with three thousand men at arms and eight thousand archers as well as other troops under his command.

It might have been that he was unlucky in war; it might have been that his heart was not in the fight; it was very likely that he longed to be in Beaufort Castle; in any case his campaign was far from successful. He marched through Artois and Champagne to Troyes and into Burgundy and Bourbonnois to the mountains of Auvergne. The winter had come and it was severe; it was hard to find food for the soldiers. He had to keep on the move and at the end of December he arrived at Bordeaux. The campaign had been disastrous. His losses had been great and nothing was achieved.

He was utterly depressed until a messenger came from Beaufort with a letter from Catherine with news of herself and little John. She was pregnant once more and she was longing for the birth of their second child.

How he yearned to be with her. He must see her.

There was nothing to be done, he assured himself, during the winter months. So he rode to Beaufort and he was comforted by her presence; but he could not stay for long and must go back to Bordeaux. He wanted to know immediately when the child was born.

In due course he heard. Another boy. 'I am naming him Henry,' she wrote. 'You have one son Henry but this little one will be Henry Beaufort and I believe you will love him as much as you do his brother.'

He had to see her so once more he made the journey. She had lost none of her attraction and seemed more desirable than ever. She was meant to be a mother. She glowed with health and pride in her two Beaufort boys as she called them. She had never felt like this about Thomas or Blanche Swynford, and although she had been fond of the children, she had been able to leave them to the care of nurses.

'It is because these boys are your sons,' she told John. 'It is because of you that they mean so much to me.'

Reluctantly he tore himself away. The winter was passing and he would have to go into action again. Messengers kept arriving at Bordeaux with impatient messages from the Black Prince who was firmly convinced that if he had been on the scene there would be a different story to tell.

Perhaps that would have been so, thought John. He is a general; he was born to command an army. It is different with me. I believe I was meant to rule but to rule through diplomacy and thoughtful scheming. I would hold my place not with arms but with subtle actions.

A messenger from the Duke of Anjou proposed that his army should meet that of the Duke of Lancaster at Moissac and until that time there should be a truce between them.

To this John agreed with alacrity. A truce would enable him to spend time with Catherine. News came from home that the King was growing almost senile, and it seemed that he could not live very long. The Prince's health had deteriorated too; before long there must be a new King of England and it would not be an Edward.

A boy of eight or nine! He would need guidance. There would have to be a Regent. A Regent, of course, had the power of a ruler.

If there was to be a king who was a minor the natural regent would be his uncle. John knew that it was imperative for him to be in England.

He talked of this with Catherine. She understood perfectly. She would be ready to leave when he wished to go.

But he wanted her to remain for a while at Beaufort. If the situation was now as he believed it might be, he would have to come out again so he thought it was better for her to remain at Beaufort, particularly as she was once more

119

pregnant. If he were going to stay in England he would send for her; if not he would soon be with her again.

John and his army left for England. He had forgotten his arrangement to meet Anjou at Moissac.

April came. This, said the French, was a breach of faith and there was no reason why they should not march into Aquitaine.

With the exception of Bayonne and Bordeaux the whole of Aquitaine passed into the hands of the French.

The campaign had been an utter disaster.

Catherine gave birth to another boy. This was Thomas. John had two Henrys; she would have two Thomases. The joys of motherhood had settled on her and she intended to make up to Thomas and Blanche Swynford for her neglect of them when she was back in England.

In Beaufort Castle she settled down to wait for the return of John.

There was a growing tension in the streets of London. In the fields beyond Clerkenwell and Holborn, in the meadows of Marylebone and on Hampstead Health and Tyburn Fields people gathered to listen to those who had made themselves spokesmen for there was not a man or woman who was not aware of the change that was coming.

Within the City walls where merchants and their apprentices shouted the virtues of their wares as they stood beside their stalls in Cheapside under the big signs which proclaimed their trade, there were whispers. Eyes turned towards that Palace of Westminster set among the fields and marshes outside the City and they asked themselves how long the King could last.

And what then? Who would have believed a few years ago that it could have come to this.

They had had a great and glorious King but he had been seduced by a harpy; they had had a Prince who had seemed like a god come down to serve them. And what had happened? He had become a sick man who was clearly fighting now to stave off death.

The heir to the throne was a slender young boy—his father's son, possessed of the Plantagenet handsome looks but lacking the robustness which was a feature of the race; and overshadowing him was his uncle, John of Gaunt.

John of Gaunt! That was the name which was whispered in the streets and the meadows. 'He seeks to rule us,' it was murmured. 'He is waiting for his brother to die. Then he will attempt to take the crown from little Richard and there will be war.'

John of Gaunt! His very name proclaimed his foreign birth. What had he done? He had conducted an unsuccessful campaign in France which had resulted in great losses and they had paid taxes that this campaign might be carried out.

Rumour had it that he kept his mistress over there. Catherine Swynford, the wife—widow now—of one of his men. They were raising a little family of Beauforts. Three boys and a girl. And his wife the poor Queen of Castile was ignored. He had married her for her crown but before she could gain it it had to be won and they would be expected to pay for his adventures. John of Gaunt was not noted for his generalship. He was not like the hero of Crécy and Poitiers. Oh, what an ill fate for England when the great Black Prince had been stricken with sickness! The only hope for the country was that he would live a little longer, or that the King himself would not die for a while.

But the King had disappointed them. He appeared in public with that harlot Alice Perrers beside him, decked in fine satins and velvets and wearing the royal jewels. Those who remembered good Queen Philippa cursed her. No good could come of a family which flaunted its immorality, openly defying the laws of Holy Church. The King could be forgiven by some. He was old, he was senile, they said; he had once been great and England had loved him. There had rarely been a King who had been so loved as Edward the Third. Yes, they could find it in their hearts to over-look his lapse from virtue. But John of Gaunt, with his harlot Catherine Swynford, no! London did not want this man. They would not tolerate his rule.

He had returned to England after the disastrous campaign and he had been going back and forth to France for the last two years, staying in Ghent and Bruges and attempting to persuade the French to agree to a truce. On his knees almost to the French! They had come a long way from Poitiers when the Black Prince had returned with the King of France as his captive.

Sad days had come to England and at such times it was natural to look for a scapegoat. The people had looked and found one. His name was John of Gaunt.

In his Palace of Berkhamsted the Black Prince was often confined to his chamber and there he fretted about what was happening at Court.

Joan was growing more and more anxious about the state of affairs. Even her optimism was beginning to wane. She could no longer deceive herself that the Prince's health was improving. As he grew older the attacks were becoming not only more frequent but more virulent. There was one consolation. As time passed Richard was growing older. He was now nine years old; she thanked God that he was clever and had such a good mentor as Sir Simon Burley who was so obviously devoted to him.

The Prince talked to her constantly about the state of the country. His great fear—as hers was too—was what would become of Richard if his grandfather and father were to die and he become King.

'While I live,' said the Prince, 'feeble as I am, I can still look after him.'

'The people are with you.'

'Yes, the people have always been faithful. But, Joan, I fear my brother.'

'John has always been the most ambitious of you all, but I cannot believe he would harm Richard.'

'He might not try to take his place on the throne. The people would never agree to that and John knows it. What he will seek to do—as he is doing now—is to become my father's chief adviser. The Parliament consists of those who are working for him; he has agreed to tolerate Alice Perrers, even make a friend of her. My dear Joan, any who can do that is to be suspected.'

'I know. If only you were well how different everything would be.'

'Had I been well, Joan, we should never have suffered such losses in France; England would be as strong as she was in my father's heyday. I must go to Westminster. I cannot lie here and see my brother take over the government of this country.'

She knew it was no use trying to dissuade him.

'You must wait a few days,' she insisted, 'and we will try and get you ready for the ordeal.'

At length he agreed to wait and so determined was he to go that in a few days his health did improve enough for him to make the journey.

Richard was fully aware of the tensions all round him and it was particularly disturbing to know that he was concerned in them. He was very much aware of his father's anxious eyes which seemed to follow him whenever they were together. The King would make him sit by his chair or by his bed and would talk to him of the responsibilities of kingship.

It was very necessary always to keep the affection of the people. One must never forget that one was a king. Always the dignity of the throne must be preserved. The country must come first; a king must serve it even though it meant hardship and unselfish devotion.

Richard was beginning to think that kings did not have a very good time.

He broached the matter with Sir Simon Burley whom, next to his mother, he loved best in the world.

'If the life of a king is such a hard one, sacrificing all the time and doing not what he wants but what others want him to do, why do so many people want to be a king?'

'It is because of power. A king is the head of the state. He has greater power than anyone else . . .'

Richard's eyes began to shine with excitement and Simon said quickly: 'He can lose it quickly if he does not use it wisely.'

'How will he know what is wisely?'

'His conscience will tell him and also his ministers.'

'Is my grandfather wise?'

Simon was silent for a few seconds and he was conscious of Richard's awareness of the silence. Richard was very sharp. It was a good sign. He was a clever boy. He would make a good king.

'Your grandfather was the most brilliant monarch in Europe.'

'Was?' said Richard quickly. 'Was, did you say, Simon?'

'Your grandfather is now an old man. He is surrounded by people who may not be as wise as we could wish.'

'Like Alice Perrers?'

'What do you know of her?'

'I listen, Simon. I always listened. I learn more by listening and piecing the information together. Yes, I learn more that way because when you or my mother or my father tell me what it seems good for me to know, you don't tell all . . . and unless I know everything it is not always easy for very often the important bits are those which are left out.'

'My lord,' said Simon, 'I know this. You profit from your books.'

'I love my books because with them I can do well. I do not love outdoor sports in the same way because there will always be those about me, who without much effort can do better than I. We like that at which we excel.'

'We do indeed and right glad am I that you learn so quickly.'

Richard was watching his tutor intently. He knew that he was coming to the conclusion that Richard's tender years should be forgotten. It must be remembered that here was a clever boy who might within a year or so be the King of England.

He said soberly: 'The kingdom has come to a sorry state. Not so long age we were progressing to such prosperity as we had not known before but a series of mishaps befell us. The chief of those was the Black Death which carried off more than half of our people. Can you imagine what it was like when this scourge descended on us? There were not enough men left to till the fields; those who could do it demanded such high payment as it was impossible to give. Your grandfather was strong in those days. He set the country working in good order again—but we could never make up for all those we had lost. Then there was the French war—which took our men and our treasure. The people grow restive when taxes are high. They see their hard-earned money going on the battlefields of France. The King has grown old . . .'

'And,' put in Richard, 'surrounds himself with unwise counsellors.'

'We must always guard our tongues, my lord.'

'Never fear, Simon, I shall guard mine until such time as I may safely use it.'

'Your father who was a great strong man is stricken by illness. The people had looked to him as their next king. There is a great melancholy in the country because of your father's illness.'

'He is going to die, Simon.'

Simon did not answer. It was no use offering this bright boy lies.

'And when he dies and my grandfather dies . . . I shall be King.'

'That may well be some years yet. I pray God it will be.'

'Why, Simon? If my grandfather is surrounded by unwise counsellors it is better for him to die.'

'You talk too glibly of death, my lord. It is for God to decide.'

'He decided to send the Black Death so you never know what evil will come through Him.'

'We must accept what He sends as best for us. He sends great mercy too.'

'He took my brother Edward. He did that suddenly.

They were not expecting Edward to die. If he had not died *he* would have been the King.'

'We must accept God's ways,' said Simon.

'It would be better,' replied Richard, 'if we could understand them. The people want my father, do they not. Wherever he goes they shout for him. They love him dearly.'

'He is a great hero . . . a great Prince.'

'They like his name. They like Edwards.'

'There was one Edward they did not like.'

'Oh yes, my great-grandfather. They hated him and he was an Edward. Perhaps they will not mind a Richard after all.'

'My lord, my lord, a name is of no importance. When the time comes you will show them that a Richard can be the best King they have ever had.'

The boy stood up suddenly, his eyes shining. 'I will. Simon, I will.'

'God bless you,' murmured Simon.

The Black Prince was carried in his litter from Berkhamsted to London.

When the people heard that he was on his way they thronged the streets to welcome him.

He was glad he was in his litter so that they could not see how swollen his body was with the dropsy which persisted and which had killed his mother. He smiled as he acknowledged their cheers and tried to look as though he were not in pain. Indeed, the exhilaration of their affection for him comforted him so much that he felt better for it.

He first went to the King. A sorry sight. He himself had to be carried in. What have we come to the Prince asked himself. Great Edward and his mighty son, the Black Prince, two decrepit old men, their glory long past. Are these the heroes who made Frenchmen tremble at their approach? If they could see us now, they would snap their fingers at us. They would be very saucy. And they had been. They had shown what they thought of an England which had lost its mighty leaders.

The King's eyes were full of tears as he beheld his son.

'I thank God,' he said, 'that your mother is not alive to see us thus.'

'I thank God she is not alive to see who has usurped her place beside you.'

The Prince had always spoken frankly, and what had he to lose now?

'Alice is my only comfort in these sad days,' said the King.

'My lord, when comfort has to be so dearly bought it is ofttimes better to do without it.'

The King sighed and looked pathetic. 'John understands,' he said. 'He and Alice are good friends now.'

'And for a clear reason,' said the Prince. 'John it seems would be the friend of the devil if by so doing he could advance his ambition.'

'My son, let us talk of more pleasant matters.'

'We must talk of England, my lord. And that I'll grant you is not the pleasant matter it once was.'

'The old days . . . I think of them constantly. Do you know, Edward, sometimes I lie abed and I think I am young again . . . on the field. I'll never forget Crécy. Oh what joy you gave me then.'

'Past glories, my lord. They are behind us. What is to be done now? That is what I have come to ask. There are stories of bribery and corruption throughout the Court. Your leman Alice Perrers has dared to appear on the bench at Westminster and tell the judges how to act, which depends on what bribe she has received from the prisoner or his friends.'

'Alice is a clever minx,' said the King fondly.

'My lord, think back, think to those days when you were a lion among your people. You would never have allowed such anomalies then. For God's sake, Father, stop it before it is too late!'

'If you have come here to try to persuade me to give up my only comfort in life you must go away, Edward.'

'Your comfort! The whole country is appalled by your lechery.'

127

'How dare you speak to me thus. I am your King!'

'I will say what I feel. I am the heir to the throne and I will not see it sent tottering by imbecility and lechery.'

'You must leave me, Edward. I had thought you had come to comfort me.'

'There is only one comfort for you . . . so you have told me. This harlot is the one who knows how to provide it. What a confession for a great King to make! To think that you . . . you were once held up to me as a shining example of all that was great and noble in kingship . . . to think that you have come to this!'

The King was in tears. Poor senile old man! And the pain in the Prince's body was beginning to throb, and torture him unbearably.

'You must see John,' muttered the King. 'He will talk to you.'

The Prince shouted for his servants.

'Take me to my apartments,' he said. And he was thinking: No, I will not see John. I will see those who will help me to stifle John's ambitions.

The Prince summoned Sir Peter de la Mare, the Speaker of the House of Commons, to his apartments in the palace and as soon as he arrived he came immediately to the point.

'I have travelled from the country at great discomfort,' said the Prince, 'because I am suffering much disquiet at the manner in which the affairs of this country are being conducted. I am convinced that there are a few good men who deplore this state of affairs even as I do.'

'That is so, my lord.'

'You need not hesitate to speak frankly to me because what you have to say might be disloyal to members of my family,' went on the Prince. 'Speak freely. Nothing you say shall be held against you and it would seem to me that on certain matters men such as you think as I do. But let us say this: It grows late but it may not be too late.'

'Since you ask me, my lord Prince, to speak frankly, so

will I do. The country is being ruined and the chief enemy is the King's mistress. She has introduced bribery and corruption into the Court. She is an evil woman and no good can come to this country while she remains at the King's side.'

'And the Duke of Lancaster?'

De la Mare hesitated. It was one thing to speak against the King's mistress but to speak against his son was quite different.

'Come,' said the Prince, 'I have asked you to speak frankly.'

'The Duke of Lancaster has become the friend of Alice Perrers, my lord, for the purpose I am sure of gaining influence with the King.'

The Prince nodded. 'I see that we understand each other. My lord, we must act with speed. Would you be prepared to do so?'

'With you behind me, my lord, yes, I would.'

'Then you must move Parliament to act.'

'That would not be difficult. The country is restive on account of excessive taxation and when it is considered that much of what is taken from them is bestowed on Alice Perrers, they are ready to revolt.'

'Then go to it!' said the Prince. 'I see no reason why Alice Perrers should not be dismissed.'

'There is Latimer, the King's Chamberlain. He works closely for your brother. He is also responsible for the growth of bribery about the Court. I fear that nothing much can be done while he holds his position.'

'Then Latimer must be deprived of his office. Summon the Parliament and attend to these matters.'

'It means that we are going against John of Gaunt.'

'It means that you are standing with the Black Prince.'

'When they know that you are with them, my lord, methinks that will decide them.'

Sir Peter de la Mare left the Prince and went with all haste to his home that he might prepare his speech to the House of Commons.

The Prince lay on his bed. The pain had returned in full force. He was even more tormented by his thoughts.

Conflict in the family. It was always unwise, and now that the country was so weak it was a danger.

He had always known John was ambitious. What did he want?

The crown! Of course he wanted a crown. He had married Constanza of Castile for one and it was hardly likely that he would ever get it. No, his eyes were on the crown of England. And that was going to be planted firmly on the head of little Richard.

Oh God, prayed the Prince, let me live long enough to see my son safely come into his own.

Sir Peter de la Mare's speech caused an uproar in the House of Commons. He was an eloquent man which was why he had risen to his present post and he was expressing sentiments which were applauded by the majority of them—those who were not the close friends and supporters of John of Gaunt.

The Black Prince was behind them. De la Mare had made that clear. The Prince might be a sick man but he was still a power in the land.

His first attack was on the King's mistress. He wanted her banished from Court. He knew that the House was with him as regarded this woman; there was one other who must be removed—and indeed perhaps impeached—and that was the King's Chamberlain who was guilty of bribery among other misfeasances. This brought storms of applause.

The Commons was hopeful. The rot was about to be stopped. They all knew that there was one powerful man who might stand in their way. The Duke of Lancaster. But they had the backing of his elder brother. The Black Prince still lived and from his sick bed he was going to bring the country back to reason and prosperity.

* * *

Riding to his Palace of the Savoy, thinking of the welcome that awaited him there, John was a happy man. Catherine was installed as his mistress and the governess of his children. There was a nursery full now. Her own four little Beauforts as she called them—she had a daughter Joan as well as the three boys—the most loved of all the children because they were her own. Then there were Philippa and Elizabeth, Blanche's girls, and of course young Henry, his heir, and the most important of them all in the eyes of the world of course. Constanza's girl Catherine was with her mother but Swynford's son and daughter, Thomas and Blanche, had joined them now because Catherine had wanted them there, which was natural. He could never really like them because they were Swynford's he supposed, but the boy was bright and handsome and the girl attractive as was to be expected of any child of Catherine's.

He was more satisfied than he had been for some time. His triumph at home had grown since he had overcome his repugnance for Alice Perrers and had shown the King that he was ready to accept her in exchange for his confidence. From then on it had been easy. He had his friends such as Lord Latimer and other influential men in Parliament. If the King were to die and the Prince with him, and Richard became King, it would be his uncle, John of Gaunt, who would be the real ruler.

Success at home had wiped out the sour taste of defeat abroad. He never wanted to go back to Bordeaux as long as he lived.

No, what he wanted was England. He did not now want the crown of Castile, that glittering bauble which had proved to be so unattainable. He wanted what he always had wanted, the crown of England. And with a young boy on the throne and himself guiding the country's policy he would be its virtual ruler.

Once the King was dead Alice could be dismissed. That would make everything so much easier. And how long could the King live? How long the Black Prince?

As he approached the Savoy Palace he saw a crowd of men watching him and his party.

He heard the shout: 'John of Gaunt. Down with John of Gaunt. Edward, the Black Prince for ever. Banish Alice Perrers. Impeach Latimer. God bless the Black Prince.'

He spurred his horse. He hoped none of the mob was armed. He galloped past them towards the palace. They made no attempt to follow.

His elation had completely passed. The Black Prince was not dead by any means. He was making his presence felt. And he had come out into the open as the enemy of Alice Perrers and his brother.

There was nothing to be done. He must accept it. There would be revolution otherwise. He by no means shared his brother's popularity. The people had always been against him—and particularly the people of London. How he hated them—these merchants who believed because they were rich they had a right to say how the country should be ruled.

'Down with John of Gaunt.' Those words were like the tolling of a warning bell.

He knew as he rode into the palace that bad news awaited him.

It seemed that the Parliament had prevailed; the people were with them. They were called the Good Parliament and the reason was that they had succeeded in removing Latimer from office and banished Alice Perrers from the Court.

The King might weep senile tears for Alice. He might mourn the loss of Latimer but even in his feeble state he could sense the mood of the people.

'What have they done to us, John?' he mourned. 'They have taken away our friends.'

Yes, thought John, they have shown us that the Black Prince is still alive and that while he continues to live we must do as the people wish.

'What shall I do without Alice?' moaned the King.

John wanted to say: Find another whore. But he restrained himself. His strength lay in placating his father and by the look of the old man it seemed as though he would not be long for this land.

Nor would the Black Prince.

It was a waiting game, but waiting was something which ambitious men had to accept.

After his meeting with de la Mare the Black Prince had gone to the palace of Kennington. It was closer to Westminster than Berkhamsted and he was eager to be as near London as possible.

His efforts had taken great toll of his strength and Joan was beside herself with anxiety. He grew excited as he told her what he had been able to achieve. 'Now,' he said, 'I must live long enough to see Richard proclaimed as true heir to the throne.'

'None could deny that he is.'

'John is wily. I know not what is in his mind.'

'Surely he can't have plans to take the throne, to make that Henry of his Prince of Wales!'

'I do not know what goes on in his mind. I think what he wants is to rule the country and if he cannot wear a crown while he is doing so he will rule without it.'

'You mean he would take charge of Richard?'

'I think that is his idea. Jeanette, you will have to guard our boy.'

'He is not going to be King for many many years. We shall both be here to train him and guide him.'

'You were always one to deceive yourself when you felt happier doing so.'

'I was always one to believe in the good that could come to those who sought it. Remember how I married you.'

'I shall never forget that, dear Jeanette, nor could I forget the years we have had together. They have been good. They gave us our Richard. Oh my Jeanette, that boy fills my thoughts. To think that one day, ere long I know, a crown will be placed on his golden head.'

She stooped and kissed him. 'Not for many many years, I promise you.'

He sighed. It was no use trying to convince Jeanette.

He had other work to do. He must keep the Good Parliament in power. He must let all those right-thinking men know that he stood with them.

He sent for William of Wykeham, the Bishop of Winchester, who had risen from comparatively humble beginnings and who had always been a close friend of his. Wykeham was a man come to office through his brilliant mind. The Prince had always respected him and he turned to him now because he wished to muster as many trusted men as he could that he might enlist their help for his son when the time came.

Wykeham swore that he would stand by young Richard.

'I thank you, my lord Bishop,' said the Prince. 'As you see I am in a poor state, I cannot believe that many more weeks are left to me.'

The Bishop did not attempt to deny this. He believed it was true and he deplored the fact that such a great man should be so low in health and spirit. He promised to pray for the Prince and he added that he was sure that such a man as he would be received into Heaven.

The Prince replied: 'That might have been so. I have served my country and would willingly at any time have given my life for it. There was a time though, when the devil took possession of me. Limoges. I shall never get it out of my mind.'

'Many of us have one black spot on our souls, my lord. Pray for forgiveness. It may be that in recompense for the good you have done the evil will be forgiven.'

'I feel that all my prayers must be for my son. He is very young, Lord Bishop. I tremble when I contemplate his youth.'

'Burley is a good man. His mother is devoted to him. You yourself, my lord, have done him much good. Fear not for your son. The Lord will provide.'

When the Bishop had gone the Prince sank back on his

134

bed exhausted and none of the possets Joan brought him did anything to alleviate his pain.

It was obvious now that the end was near.

'Jeanette,' he said, 'my only love, the time is near now. No, it is no use hiding from the truth. It has come and we must needs face it. Send a message to my father. I would he could be here at my bedside.'

'I will send to him immediately,' she said. 'But it may be he will be too ill to come.'

'I fancy he will if he can.'

The King made all haste to reach Kennington. This was his beloved son, the child who had brought so much joy to him and Philippa in the early days of their marriage when each had been all that the other had desired. Edward the Black Prince and hero, destined to follow his father, the pride of the nation, now a sick man asking his father to come to his death bed!

What had happened to the world!

How, thought the King, have I offended God?

The tears ran down his sunken cheeks as he knelt by the bed.

The years slipped away and he was there with Philippa— dear good Philippa who had never known how to titillate his senses as Alice did; but Philippa who had been good and steady, had always stood beside him, firmly supporting him, and the people had loved her. A wonderful marriage. Yet he had sullied it. Alice had been there before Philippa had died and Philippa had known it.

Life was cruel. And we hurt most those we love best, thought the King.

And there was Joan standing there, bereft, with the strange blank look in those eyes which had once been so bright and provocative and had sent his heart pounding and wondering . . . Joan the wife of the Black Prince, royal herself, one of the sprigs from the great Plantagenet tree.

'Joan,' murmured the King, 'so it has come to this . . .'

Joan nodded, unable to speak.

She was leaning over the bed. She laid her lips on that clammy forehead and gently pushed aside the hair thick still and with a touch of gold in it. 'My dear love, the King is here.'

Edward opened his eyes. 'Father . . .'

The King buried his face in his hands and his body heaved with his sobs.

'My lord, my lord,' whispered Joan restrainingly.

'My son, my son,' moaned the King.

'He would speak with you, my lord,' said Joan. 'And the time is passing.'

Her voice broke on a sob and she turned away fearful lest the Prince should see her grief.

'Father, I must speak . . .'

'My son, speak. I listen. What you ask of me I will endeavour to do.'

'Confirm my gifts, pay my debts, Father.'

'It shall be done, my dear son.'

'And Richard . . . my boy Richard. You will protect him. He is young yet. A boy, no more. So young . . . too young. Father, promise me you will look to him.'

'I swear it,' said the King. 'He shall have my protection. Have no fear, son. Richard will be looked after. I give my word to it.'

'Jeanette . . . the boy . . .'

He was brought in, wide-eyed, pale of skin and very beautiful, such a contrast to the dying man on the bed and the poor broken one who knelt beside it . . . yet so clearly one of them.

'Richard, come here.'

Richard came to the bed.

'My lord, take his hand. Swear to me . . .'

The King took the boy's hand and said: 'I swear to you on my soul that I shall protect this boy. With my life I will protect him. He is my heir. I swear it.'

The Prince nodded, satisfied.

'Richard,' said the Prince, 'do not attempt to take away any of the gifts I have bestowed.'

'I promise, Father,' said the boy.

'You would be cursed if you did so.'

Richard looked bewildered and Joan, laying her hand on his shoulder, drew him away from the bedside.

The King was looking at her anxiously and said: 'It is time to send for the priest.'

She nodded and taking her son by the hand led him away.

The priest was with the Prince who asked forgiveness of his sins. The word Limoges kept rising to his lips.

And so he died.

The King was bewildered. His son dead and he still living! And his heir a young boy just nine years old!

He gave orders that the Prince should be buried with great ceremony and he was laid to rest in Canterbury Cathedral and above his tomb was hung his surcoat and helmet, his shield and his gauntlet that all might remember that great and glorious warrior who was known as the Black Prince.

RIOT AT THE SAVOY

THE DEATH OF the Black Prince, although expected, had brought home to men such as Peter de la Mare and William of Wykeham the precarious position in which they had placed themselves. They had succeeded in getting Alice Perrers dismissed from Court; they had put a curb on bribery; but they had only been able to do so because of the support of the Prince.

Now he was dead and the most powerful man in the country was John of Gaunt—their sworn enemy.

It was Peter de la Mare who decided on prompt action. He pointed out that there was a little time left to them before the Parliament could be dissolved and they must make full use of it.

First, agreed William of Wykeham, they must obtain the King's permission to add twelve bishops and lords to the Council; and he, William of Wykeham, would be one of them. And secondly and most important they must have Richard of Bordeaux publicly acknowledged as his heir by the King.

When this last matter was laid before the King he declared with tears in his eyes that he had sworn to his son the Black Prince to protect Richard and so would he do. Richard should be publicly acknowledged as the true heir to the throne as he undoubtedly was.

One of the selected members of the Council was Edmund de Mortimer, Earl of March, the husband of Lionel's daughter Philippa who, since Lionel was older than John of Gaunt, would come before him in the claim to the throne if Richard were to die.

Mortimer and John of Gaunt had been wary of each other for a long time. Mortimer had been behind the Black Prince in his determination to bring about reforms; his old guardian had been William of Wykeham so there was a strong tie between the two of them. Thus when the committee were selected to be close to the King and advise him, Edmund, Earl of March had been a natural choice and he with William Courtenay, Bishop of London, and William of Wykeham were the most influential of them all and every one of them was opposed to John of Gaunt and all he stood for.

The ambitions of John were made very apparent when he sought to introduce a bill to bring in the Salic law, as it was in France. If this were passed it would mean that the throne could not be inherited by a woman and John of Gaunt would come immediately behind Richard of Bordeaux in the succession.

Parliament dismissed the idea without considering it, and John was afraid to press it because of the bearing it had on his father's claim to the throne of France.

Parliament was dissolved in July—only a few weeks after the death of the Black Prince; and then the might of John of Gaunt was realized.

He had his supporters all over the country. The Londoners might detest him, but it was being said elsewhere that a child could never bring stability to the country; and it was clear that John of Gaunt—now the King's eldest living son—was going to take over the government. Therefore it was wise to stand well with him. John determined to rid himself of his enemies and the first attack came on Edmund de Mortimer who held the office of Marshal. He was ordered to proceed to Calais, and there report on the defences.

Mortimer knew that this meant he was dismissed from the King's Council, and he was certain, too, that when he reached Calais it would be easy for him to be killed. The country would not introduce the Salic law; and if he were dead there would be none to support his daughter's claim to the throne.

No, said Mortimer, I prefer to lay down my staff than my life, and solved the matter by resigning his post as Marshal which was immediately given to Lord Henry Percy, a strong supporter of John of Gaunt.

The next act was to bring a case against William of Wykeham who was accused of governing badly during the term of his Chancellorship, of embezzlement, extorting money and extracting bribes.

'I can prove all these accusations false,' he cried to his accusers. 'I need time.'

'You did not give Lord Latimer time to prove the charges against him false,' he was reminded.

John was alert, watching the mood of the people. He realized that he could not go too far with Wykeham and he declared that he should be granted time to prove his case. He was however determined to find Wykeham guilty.

When he came to stand before the Council that judgement might be passed, he was accompanied by William Courtenay, the Bishop of London, which implied that the Church was watching how one of its members was treated.

Wykeham declared that he would take his oath that never had he used funds for his advantage. The Council was not interested in oaths, was the retort, but facts.

John said: 'This man is guilty. I demand he pay the full penalty.'

Courtenay reminded him that William of Wykeham was a Bishop and therefore he could not be sentenced by a secular Court.

John was furious but he realized he could at this stage do nothing. If he had his way he would curtail the power of the Church considerably.

So the outcome of the trial was that William of Wykeham's goods should be confiscated to the Crown and the trial would be adjourned to a later date.

With the power of March and Wykeham clipped John was able to take immediate action. De la Mare was made a prisoner and Lord Latimer was released. The people of

London discussed this turn of affairs together and de la Mare became a hero. Ballad singers in the streets sang songs about him. A great resentment was growing against John of Gaunt and his friends and this was increased when Alice Peters was allowed to come back to Court.

The King was overjoyed to see her. He could not thank his dear son John enough for being so careful of his comfort.

There was no doubt that at this time John of Gaunt was the most powerful man in the country.

Then the scandal broke.

In the taverns the story was being whispered. It seemed incredible but there were so many who wanted it to be true for if it were John of Gaunt would be disqualified for ever.

Heads were close together; at first it was spoken of in whispers and then people grew bolder. The Londoners had never been noted for their fear of authority and had always regarded themselves outside the laws which must be obeyed by the rest of the country. They said what they thought and nothing was going to stop them.

John was first aware of what was happening when he came riding from Westminster to the Savoy.

'Bastard!' The name was flung at him. It was one word which meant so much.

He was soon to discover how much.

The story was that he was not the true son of King Edward and Queen Philippa. There was some mystery about his birth which had come out now through William of Wykeham who had been present at the deathbed of Good Queen Philippa and had it from her dying lips.

It appeared that while she lay in Ghent in child-bed a daughter had been born to the Queen. Now it was well known that the King longed for a son. It was true at this time he already had two, Edward and Lionel; there had been a third, though, little William who had died soon after his birth.

The King was away in the wars and Philippa wanted to

surprise him when he returned, so it was with great cha-grin that she learned the child she had borne was a girl. She had other girls and the King was devoted to them so this did not seem too great a tragedy. However, as the child lay beside her she slept and overlaid it. The child was suffocated and died.

Terrified of the King's wrath—for all knew that, great man though he was in those days, he possessed the Plantagenet temper which struck terror into all when it was aroused—she called to her a Flemish woman who had given birth to a healthy boy at the same time as she had had her child.

'Give me your child,' the Queen was reputed to have said, 'and he shall be brought up as the son of a King. He shall be educated, live in luxury and never want.'

This was too much of a temptation for the humble Flemish woman and she gave her child to the Queen—that child was known to the world as John of Gaunt.

And who would believe it? There was a good reason for believing it. The Queen had confessed on her deathbed. In her last moments she had sent for William of Wykeham and told the story to him, with the injunction that he was not to divulge it, unless there was a chance of John of Gaunt's coming to the throne.

Now the story was being allowed to seep out for John of Gaunt's ambitions were carrying him very near to the crown.

That the story would not bear scrutiny mattered not. The people wanted to believe it and they were going to. That Philippa already had two healthy sons and would not have been greatly put out by giving birth to another daughter was brushed aside. That the King, loving his sons as he did, was besottedly fond of his daughters, could be forgotten. That Philippa, the most tender of mothers, was hardly likely to overlay a child—in any case it would be the duty of the nurses to take the child when its mother wished to sleep—all this was of no importance.

The people liked the story because it was against John of Gaunt and they were going to believe it.

*   *   *

John was furious. He paced through his apartments and shouted his anger.

Catherine tried to calm him. But he would not listen to her.

'Wykeham is at the back of this!' he cried. 'He wants to destroy me.'

'It is the most stupid story I ever heard,' said Catherine.

'Stupid it undoubtedly is but it has to be disproved. Isolda would have put an end to it. Who would know better than she did? My mother would tell the world what a stupid lie it is. But they are dead . . . The fabricators of this . . . of this . . . outrage know it and that is why they bring the charge.'

'What of Wykeham? She is supposed to have made her confession to him.'

'Wykeham is my enemy.'

'Even so he is a man of the Church. He would not lie merely to harm you.'

John burst out laughing. 'You know little of the ways of men, Catherine. My enemies would do anything to ruin me.'

Catherine tried to soothe him. She wished as so many others did that the Black Prince had not died. If only he had lived there would not be all this fear and suspicion. It was a great tragedy for England that God had taken the Prince who was the natural heir to the throne and so suited to the role.

John was ambitious, she had always known it. Power was at the very essence of his being. It was one of the attributes which attracted her so vitally. The strength of him—the awareness that this man who was clearly destined for greatness had need of her.

Their children were growing up. She wanted a good future for the little Beauforts. The higher John rose the more bright would be that future. And now there was this cruel scandal. It was obviously lies and yet it was none the less hurtful for that. There were so many who would harm John if they dared.

'It is clear,' raged John. 'This is Wykeham's revenge on me. How I hate that man. How dare he! Does he think I have no power in this land?'

Catherine said: 'Have a care, John. It has always been dangerous when the Church and the State are in conflict.'

'The Church has too much power. One day I shall curb that. There was a man I met in Bruges. A certain John Wycliffe. He was raging against the power of the Church. He wants to curb it. They were saying he was a fanatic. But I am inclined to agree with him.'

'Has Wykeham publicly declared this story to be true?'

'Nay. He is too clever for that. He declares that it does not stem from him. He has said nothing. But the story is being bruited around and Wykeham is said to be the one who was at my mother's bedside when she died.'

'No one can possibly believe it,' said Catherine.

'None with good sense can.'

'You are so like your father and brothers. None could doubt even by merely glancing at you, that you are a true Plantagenet.'

'People often believe what they want to believe, Catherine, and, by God, there are many in this land who are trying to pull me down.'

'Never fear, it will soon be forgotten.'

'My dearest it will be remembered as long as men continue to hate me. There were rumours about my father and the Black Prince and they were greatly loved.'

'As you will be.'

He shook his head at her.

'Love blinds you,' he said softly. Then his rage was back.

'Wykeham has given no credence to this story so we hear, but I tell you this, I shall hate Wykeham for as long as I live and I shall have my revenge on him.'

*   *   *

At Kennington Joan was preparing her son for a very important occasion.

'You understand what this means, Richard?' she asked.

He nodded. 'The King is going to accept me formally as his heir.'

'That is right. All the highest in the land will be present. They will all pay homage to you.'

'Am I as important as that?'

'It is not you who are so important. It is the Crown. You must always remember that when people bow before you it is to the Crown to which they are paying homage.'

'Yes, I shall remember,' said Richard.

His mother kissed him fondly. She was fearful because he was so young; and he needed his father as he had never needed him before.

Sir Simon Burley who was standing by read her thoughts.

'We'll pray for him, Simon,' she said.

Excitement had put colour into Richard's cheeks. Tall, slender, with his Plantagenet colouring—golden curly hair and bright blue eyes—he was very beautiful.

The people who had lined the road to see him pass were enchanted by his youth and grace.

'God bless you, Richard of Bordeaux,' they cried.

He acknowledged their greetings with a modest charm which immediately won their hearts. The Londoners were wildly enthusiastic. Their hatred of John of Gaunt made them love him all the more.

Richard was exultant. This was the prelude to kingship. He thought there was nothing quite so exciting as the sound of the people's cheers. They expressed their love for him. They wanted him to be their next King.

'What a beautiful boy!' said the people. 'Young and lovely and innocent. There is a King in the making. God bless him.'

It was even more exciting in the House of Commons. All those solemn men—the greatest in the land, and all proclaiming him the true heir to the throne.

That was not all. Afterwards they must go to Westminster where the King was waiting for him.

Richard knelt before his grandfather and the King bade him rise that he might embrace him before the assembled company and let the whole world know that next to himself he, Richard, was the most important in the land.

Now he must sit on the right hand of the King and all his uncles were there and they must do homage to him. Uncle John of Gaunt was affable but his eyes glittered with speculation; he was ingratiating, implying that he would always be there beside him, to help him, to guide, to advise him. He had heard whispers about his uncle John; it was difficult to believe them of this splendid man who assured him of his wish to serve him. With his uncle John were his uncles Edmund and Thomas, and they too assured him of their loyalty and devotion to him. Uncle Edmund was tall and handsome; he had been abroad with John and they were good friends; they had even married sisters. Richard liked Uncle Edmund the best of all the uncles. He smiled so often and there was an air of great kindliness about him. Simon had said he was not an energetic man and thereby implied a criticism. But he was certainly pleasant to be with. Then there was Uncle Thomas, the youngest of the uncles. He was not sure of Uncle Thomas. Simon had been somewhat reticent when his name was mentioned and this Richard construed as meaning that Simon was not quite sure of him either. He did not smile as ingratiatingly as Uncle John did; nor as pleasantly and unconcernedly as Uncle Edmund. But he paid his homage just the same. He was obliged to, for the whole purpose of this occasion was to swear loyalty to the true heir to the throne.

There was one present who interested Richard more than any of the others and that was his cousin Henry, the eldest son of John of Gaunt. This was because Henry was more or less the same age as he was. He himself as a matter of fact was a few months older. He knew this because Henry had been born on the day the battle of Nájara had been won—that battle which his mother had said brought no good to anyone not even Pedro the Cruel who gained his throne through it, because he was soon after done to death

146

as he deserved to be—and it was at that battle, so his mother always declared, that the Prince's sickness began in earnest.

Richard was somewhat pleased to see that he was much taller than Henry; but in spite of the fact that he did not match up to the Plantagenet stature, Henry was sturdy and well formed; moreover he had inherited the family good looks, though he was slightly darker than most of them. His hair was more russet than gold but he had the Plantagenet features.

He too had been brought to pay homage to the future King.

The two boys regarded each other solemnly. Richard smiled slowly and Henry returned the smile.

John of Gaunt was watching the two boys. Henry knew what was in his father's mind. He is angry, thought Henry, as he always is, because *he* is not the heir to the throne.

The King took Richard to sit beside him and showed how eager he was to honour him.

He saw the notorious Alice Perrers. She was sumptuously clad and she was wearing jewels which must be worth a fortune.

She made much of him. She told him he was a beautiful boy and that he should be proud of his grandfather who was a great King.

Richard listened haughtily but he did not turn from Alice because he knew that would have offended his grandfather.

He had heard a great deal about her, for his parents had spoken of her, and so much was her conduct talked of that the servants too discussed her at great length.

Richard had heard her called a harpy and a harlot and that the King was far gone in senility to let her govern him.

I should never allow her to behave like that if I were King, thought Richard.

If I were King! It was an intoxicating thought.

And the knowledge that the old King was going to die

soon and the crown would be placed on his own golden head, set him tingling with anticipation.

Of all his enemies John of Gaunt realized that William of Wykeham was the greatest. William it was true had not confirmed the scandal about the Flemish woman's baby; he had in fact declared that such a story had not started with him. But John would not forgive him. Wykeham's fortunes had sunk very low now; his possessions had been confiscated but he could not be dismissed and sooner or later some of his Church cronies would rise and make trouble. He was not the sort of man who could be pushed aside and forgotten. The Church for one thing would not allow that.

The Church! A thorn in the side of any monarch . . . or would-be monarch!

If John ever ruled, one of the first things he would do would be to curb the power of the Church. Some of his ancestors had attempted it, the most outstanding case being that of Henry the Second and Thomas à Becket.

John had been impressed by the reformer John Wycliffe whom he had first met in Bruges. The man was a fanatic and John did not favour men of his kind; but they did share one important point of view: they both deplored the power of the Church, John Wycliffe because as he said there was only one Lord in Chief and that was God. The Pope behaved as though he were God's Deputy on Earth and in fact a god himself. He possessed too much power and in Wycliffe's opinion it should be curtailed.

John could agree whole-heartedly with this. He thought that power should be in the hands of the King and that there should be no authority over him. Kings went in fear of excommunication; the Pope had the power to harm them. That should not be.

It was for this reason that John of Gaunt was prepared to defend Wycliffe.

For some time Wycliffe had been fulminating against the Mendicant Friars, and had written a treatise against them. Their chief sin, according to him, was that they granted pardons which had to be bought with gifts to the Church.

'There is no pardon,' Wycliffe had thundered, 'that does not come from God. Spiritual good begins and ends in charity. It may not be bought or sold, as chattering priests would say. He who is rich in charity will be best heard by God be he but a mere shepherd or a worker in the fields. There could be more holiness in such a man than in Mendicant Friars, whose worst abuse is that they pretend to purify those who confess. Will a man shrink from acts of licentiousness and fraud if he believes that soon after, by the aid of a little money bestowed on a friar, an entire absolution of the sin he has committed will be obtained? There is no greater heresy than for a man to believe that he is absolutely resolved from his sins if he gives money. Think not if you give a penny to a pardoner, you will be forgiven for breaking God's commandments.

'The indulgences of the Pope, if they are what they are said to be, are a manifest blasphemy. The friars give colour to this blasphemy by saying that Christ is omnipotent and that the Pope is his plenary Vicar, and so possesses in everything, the same power as Christ in his humanity.'

It was inevitable of course that a man who went about giving voice to such opinions should soon be called upon to give an account of himself, and it was shortly after the formal recognition of Richard as the true heir that Wycliffe was cited by William Courtenay, the Bishop of London, to answer respecting his opinions and teachings.

Wycliffe arrived in London to do this and John at once invited him to come to the Savoy Palace.

There he greeted him as a friend and told him that he agreed with his view that there was too much power in the hands of the Church and he, too, would like to see it curtailed.

'You are to meet the Bishop of London and you should have no fear that you will not be able to withstand his questions. I know him well. He is a man who fears that his own power may shrink. I shall attend the meeting. Lord Percy the Earl Marshal will be present too. We shall show ourselves to be your friends before this Bishop who believes because he is the Bishop of London he has the power of a king.'

Wycliffe answered: 'I shall not be afraid to answer the questions the Bishop puts to me, my lord. I shall speak my mind and God's will be done.'

It was a cold February day when the meeting between John Wycliffe and the Bishop of London was to take place. News of the coming confrontation had spread through the City and the people were determined to witness it.

The narrow streets with their gabled houses almost meeting across the narrow road and so shutting out the light of day, were crowded with people making their way to the Cathedral. The Londoners seized on any chance to enliven their days. They would have been on the side of Wycliffe because he was clearly speaking for the people, but his patron it seemed was John of Gaunt, the man for whom they had little love. So their feelings were mixed as they crowded into the Cathedral.

Wycliffe was an impressive figure; he was of more than usual height and was simply clad in a dark robe belted at the waist and hanging to his feet. His flowing beard gave him a venerable air and the people were awed as they watched him.

At his right hand walked John of Gaunt, resplendent as always, in velvet and ermine to proclaim his royalty, a man to catch every eye, a man who must either be loved or hated; and there was no doubt which it was the people felt for him. They whispered together as they watched him. He was the man who was trying to steal the crown from that sweet innocent boy. He was the lecher who flaunted his mistress Catherine Swynford before their eyes, being seen with her on ceremonial occasions so brazenly while he deserted his poor wife whom he had married because she could become Queen of Castile; he was the base-born son of a Flemish woman—a serving wench; her station grew lower and lower as the weeks went by. He was the one who was passing himself off as the King's son.

They hated John of Gaunt; and it was bewildering that he should be Wycliffe's champion.

On the other side of Wycliffe was the Earl Marshal, Lord Percy, who had stepped into the role after John of Gaunt had rid himself of the Earl of March, because the wife of the Earl of March was the daughter of Lionel, that son of the King who was older than John of Gaunt and who had unfortunately died in Italy.

So great was the press of people in the Cathedral that Wycliffe with John of Gaunt and Lord Percy on either side of him found it difficult to make his way inside.

Lord Percy gave orders for his men to clear the crowd which they did with a certain amount of roughness. There were cries of protest as people were pushed aside and some fell and cursed the Marshal.

The mood of the people was growing sullen in a way which should have warned John of Gaunt and Percy had they given any thought to the matter.

They had forced their way through and were face to face with those who would hear the case, at the head of whom was William Courtenay, the Bishop of London.

Some might have been intimidated by the sight of John of Gaunt and the Earl Marshal standing on either side of John Wycliffe like guards come to fight his cause—not so William Courtenay. The Bishop was a man of strong principles; his intentions were good; he was kindly by nature; he was eager to do his duty; but there was a certain pride in him and he was very ready to resent what might be construed as a slight. As the fourth son of the Earl of Devon—and his mother was the daughter of the Earl of Hereford—he was highly born and did not intend any should forget it; he had had the inclination to go into the Church and in any case he was a fourth son; and because of his intellectual gifts it seemed very likely that he would rise high in his chosen profession.

The crowd pressed forward from all sides, determined after the rough treatment of the Marshal's men not to be deprived of their rights. They were sure that it was going to be as good an entertainment as a mummers' performance.

The Bishop first expressed his displeasure at the signs of rowdiness in his church. The Cathedral was open to all and people came to the holy place for refuge. He did not care to see them roughly treated in the house of God.

'Had I known, Marshal,' he said, 'what masteries you would have brought into the church, I should have stopped you from coming hither.'

Lord Percy was aghast at the rebuke; but John of Gaunt cried angrily: 'He shall keep such masteries though you say him nay.'

'We will proceed into the lady chapel,' said the Bishop ignoring the remark, 'and there the examination shall proceed.'

The crowd pressed forward. They would not be kept out. Had they heard what their Bishop had said? This was their church and this was their city and they would have none try to take any of their privileges from them.

Percy, smarting from the altercation, looked round the lady chapel and said: 'Wycliffe, sit down. You have many things to answer, and you need to repose yourself on a soft seat.'

The Bishop replied sharply: 'It is not the custom for one so cited to be seated during his answers. He must and he shall stand.'

John of Gaunt's temper burst out. He hated the Bishop; and all he stood for.

He cried in a loud voice so that all the people who were crowding round could hear: 'Lord Percy's request is not unreasonable. As for you, my lord Bishop, you have grown so proud and arrogant that I will no longer tolerate such conduct. I will put down the pride, not of you alone, but of all the prelacy in England.'

The Bishop had grown very pale. He replied in a firm voice: 'Do your worst, sir.'

'You . . . and your pride,' cried the Duke, the Plantagenet temper now unrestrained. 'You boast about your parentage. Let me tell you, they shall not be able to keep you when you are brought low. They will have enough to do to help themselves.'

'I understand you not, my lord,' said the Bishop coldly. 'My confidence is not in my parents, nor in any man else, but only in God in whom I trust, and by whose assistance I shall be bold enough to speak the truth.'

John of Gaunt turned to the Marshal and said: 'Rather than bear such things, I will drag this Bishop out of the church by his hair.'

Although he had said this to the Marshal he had spoken loudly enough for the people around him to have heard.

The shout went up. 'John of Gaunt insults our Bishop. We will not have him dishonoured in his own church.'

They were calling to the people without. 'Did you hear? John of Gaunt will drag our Bishop from his church by his hair. Come, friends. Stand together. We'll die rather than submit to tyrants.'

Great was the tumult within and without the church and fearing violence the Bishop said quietly, 'The people are in an angry mood. Follow me . . . quickly please. You must leave here at once.'

John of Gaunt, red with fury, hesitated. But he knew the anger of these people, how it quickly became dangerous. They hated him. And the few men they had with them could not stand against the mob.

There was only one thing to do and that was to forget their pride, follow the Bishop and leave the Cathedral by a side door.

After John of Gaunt and Lord Percy had slipped quietly away the people streamed into the streets. Tempers were running high but the Church was not the place in which they could give true vent to their feelings. Moreover, many of them were in agreement with John Wycliffe. For some time now there had been murmurings about the wealth and worldliness of men of the Church and that was the very thing Wycliffe was trying to stop. On the other hand John of Gaunt was hated and he was on the side of

Wycliffe. John of Gaunt had threatened to abolish the mayoralty and set up a Captain to govern the City and that Captain would be selected by the Crown. They would never allow that. Moreover he had insulted the Bishop of London and that was tantamount to insulting London.

So they were confused and because of this they were uncertain how to attack.

John went back to the Savoy Palace. Catherine had already heard that there had been trouble in St. Paul's and was very worried.

She was well aware of the mood of the people and she was constantly afraid that they would harm her lover. He laughed at the idea. No one would get the better of him, he promised her.

She said: 'There has been a mood of discontent in the streets of late.'

She had seen many a sullen look directed at herself when she rode out. She had heard insults. Not that any had dared shout them at her. They had been whispered. But nevertheless their meaning was clear.

She was anxious on account of the children, she said. 'I should be happier if I took them out of London for a while . . .'

'I must be here,' he told her.

'I know. Perhaps I will take them out and leave them in the care of their nurses. And come back to you.'

He embraced her suddenly.

'You are my comfort, Catherine,' he said.

'I know—yet I am one of the reasons why people hate you.'

'They are unreasonable. My father sports with that harlot and yet they forgive him. And you and I . . . true lovers . . . are derided.'

'I count everything worth while,' she said.

He laughed. 'I too. You are right. Take the children away . . . today . . . do not hesitate. And come back to me, Catherine.'

The very next day he was glad that she had done so. She

was clever, his Catherine. Sometimes he thought she understood the people better than he did.

The day following the scene in the Cathedral the streets were full of muttering people. John had gone by barge to the home of Sir John d'Ypres, a London merchant of great wealth who had become a great friend of the King because of his ability in financial matters. He had been knighted some years previously and the King reckoned him to be one of his most loyal subjects. Lord Percy was leaving the Marshalsea to join John at the house of the merchant.

Meanwhile the crowds were congregating in the streets. They had forgotten their doubts about Wycliffe and had concentrated all their venom on John of Gaunt.

One man had climbed a wall and was addressing the people. He could scarcely be heard above the noise.

'Who is he? A low-born Fleming . . . put into the Queen's bed when she overlaid her child. Now he wants to rule this land. Our little Prince Richard is in danger. This Lancaster will stop at nothing. He with his accomplice Percy will have us all in chains.'

Someone shouted: 'Remember the petition to Parliament to give us a Captain in place of our Mayor.'

'We'll never allow it,' shouted the people.

'Good friends, you know what this will mean. A creature of Lancaster's to take over our City. An officer of his choosing. Shall we have that?'

'Never!' shouted the people.

'Then how are we going to stop it?'

'Death to John of Gaunt,' was the cry.

'Percy has a prisoner in the Marshalsea. One of our people.'

'Then let us get him.'

That was what they needed—a plan of action.

'To the Marshalsea. We'll free the prisoner and then we'll get them. Lancaster . . . and Percy.'

The crowd rushed to the Marshalsea. Startled servants bolted the doors against them but it did not take the mob long to batter them down.

It was true. There was a prisoner there. They released him and burned the stocks in which he had been held.

'Find Percy!' cried the people. They went through the place pulling down doors and walls taking whatever seemed valuable to them. But they could not find Percy.

'He will be with his crony,' said one. 'He'll be at the Savoy.'

That was the magic word. The Savoy Palace. That was the home of the real enemy.

Soon they were at the gates of the Savoy.

One of Lancaster's retinue rode up. He was wearing the badge of Lancaster.

'What do you here?' he demanded.

'Do you serve John of Gaunt?'

'I do.'

Someone shouted: 'Here's one of them.' The knight, a certain Sir John Swynton, was dragged from his horse and the badge torn from his coat.

He was crying: 'What have I done to offend you?'

'Leave him,' shouted someone. 'He's not the one we want.'

Sir John was left bleeding on the ground and the mob passed on.

A priest rode up. 'What is the trouble? Why are you here?' he asked.

'We have come for John of Gaunt,' someone said. 'We are going to stop his giving us a Captain. We are going to make him release Peter de la Mare.'

'Peter de la Mare is a traitor,' said the priest. 'He should have been hanged long ago.'

There was a shout of rage as the priest was dragged from his horse and the mob fell on him.

Some of them had now succeeded in breaking into the Savoy. They were trying to tear down the place and many were running out with rich treasures.

'Come out, John of Gaunt,' they shouted. 'We want to give you a warm welcome, John of Gaunt.'

One of the Lancaster knights came riding to the Savoy and pulled up in time for, remembering what had happened in St. Paul's the day before and seeing the mob breaking into the Savoy, he realized what this meant. He heard the shouts of 'Come out, John of Gaunt. We have come for you, John of Gaunt.' And he knew there was murder in their hearts.

He turned his horse and rode with all speed to the house of Sir John d'Ypres where he knew his master was dining with Lord Percy.

He reached the house. He broke into the hall where they were eating dinner and had just completed the first course.

'My lord,' he cried, 'the mob is shouting for you. They have broken into the Savoy.'

John rose. He immediately saw the danger.

'They will discover we are here,' said Percy.

John nodded. 'We must leave at once.'

'Where shall you go?' asked his host.

'To Kennington,' he said. 'My sister-in-law will give us refuge. Come, there is not a moment to lose.'

Meanwhile William Courtenay, the Bishop of London, had heard the tumult in the streets, and making enquiries learned that the mob was on the march, that they had already gutted the Marshalsea and were now at the Savoy looking for John of Gaunt and their mood was murderous.

There was no time to lose. John of Gaunt was his enemy, but this was no way to deal with him. They would make a martyr of him.

With all haste he rode to the Savoy. Some of the mob were inside the palace. The noise was deafening, and he found it difficult to make himself heard.

Then a cry went up. 'The Bishop!' And there was silence.

He addressed them in a voice of thunder.

'My people. What is this I find? It grieves me. Take heed, I say. I would speak with you. Do you want to bring the wrath of God down on your heads?'

A hushed silence fell on the crowd.

'This is the season of Lent,' went on the Bishop. 'You have killed one of my priests. May God forgive you. This is a time when you should be repenting of your sins. And you add to them. Go home, and entreat God for mercy. You have need of it. This is not the way to right your wrongs.'

He rode through the crowd. There was something noble about him and his clerical vestments lent him a grandeur. He knew that one of them might have raised a hand against him and set the mood of the mob, but he showed no fear.

They were overawed. He was more than a mere man. He was their Bishop.

'Disperse quietly,' he said. 'Go to your homes and pray for forgiveness. Remember this is the season of Lent.'

He watched them.

One by one they went away.

The Bishop had quelled the riot.

THE END OF A REIGN

To return to Kennington after all the pomp and glory of the Court where he was a very important person indeed was somewhat disconcerting for young Richard. The proclamation that he was the King's heir and the banquet which had followed had given him a taste for such pleasures; and now here he was back under the care of Sir Simon Burley and Sir Guichard d'Angle who, although he was very fond of them both, did treat him as though he were a little boy.

His mother was the same; she was always afraid that something was going to happen to him. His father had always chided her for pampering him. It was different with his half-brothers, Thomas and John Holland. They liked to play rough games and were always trying out practical jokes. He was not always pleased with such horseplay and his mother's constant hovering to make sure he was not hurt.

It was not that he regretted not indulging in the sports that his elder brothers did, for he was not very interested in them. Besides Thomas and John were years older than he was; and they were wild. They took after their father, their mother said. He was the sort of man who took what he wanted and counted the cost after, whereas Richard's father had been serious, deeply concerned with doing the right thing.

'You must be like your father.' That was what he was constantly told until he grew tired of hearing how wonderful his father had been. The great hero. The Black Prince.

The tale of how he had won his spurs at Crécy and how he had brought back the French King after Poitiers were stories which grew a little tiresome, especially when they were always followed by the injunction that he must try to be like his father.

Now his half-brothers were talking about Wycliffe who was being examined by the Bishop of London in St. Paul's. Richard had heard a great deal of talk about this man John Wycliffe. He was one who had very strong views about religion and did not mind giving voice to them.

His mother was inclined to favour the man. She thought the Pope had too much power and Richard was agreeing with her now that he had tasted the sweets of coming kingship. The King was the ruler of the country, said his mother, and there should be none above him but God. The Pope set himself up as God's Deputy on Earth. God did not need a deputy, said his mother.

Richard was beginning to take an interest in what was going on in the country. After all, soon he would be ruling over it.

'The old man grows more and more feeble every day,' said Thomas Holland.

Richard admired Thomas very much. He was always so sure of himself and he had always been particularly friendly with Richard. Thomas was in fact the Earl of Kent, a title he had inherited when his father had died and which had come through his mother. Thomas made no secret of the fact that he could not wait for the old King to die. 'Then,' he had whispered to Richard, 'you will be our King.'

He made it sound very exciting. They would always be good friends, said Thomas.

'Oh yes,' Richard had cried. 'When I am King you shall be beside me.'

'I'll keep you to that,' Thomas replied.

John said he would be there too.

It was comforting to have such brothers.

'He cannot last much longer,' said Thomas. 'Poor Alice, she diverts him too much. She keeps her place by her skills and yet those very skills could hasten him to the grave. What a quandary for Alice.'

Their mother joined them. 'What is this?' she asked; she must have caught Alice's name and she did not like such matters to be discussed before Richard.

'We were talking of Wycliffe,' said Thomas with a wink at Richard.

Richard enjoyed being in the conspiracy with this man of the world. It made him feel adult. His mother began to talk of Wycliffe and how interesting it was to listen to the views of thinkers such as he was; and then suddenly they could hear the sounds of shouting coming from the river.

'Listen,' said Joan.

They were silent. There it was, growing louder.

'Something is happening in the City,' said Thomas. 'I'll swear it concerns yesterday's trouble at Wycliffe's trial.'

'The people are in revolt,' said Joan. She had turned pale. She was afraid of the people when they raised their voices and were in protest. Mobs were terrifying. Even when their causes were just they lost all sense of reason when they were massed together. There could be bloodshed.

She was thankful that Richard was here with her.

They stood by the window watching. Thomas pointed out the thread of smoke which was rising to the sky.

'They are rioting,' said Joan. 'Oh, my God, what does this mean?'

'It must be something to do with Wycliffe.'

'The people were for him, I am sure.'

'Look,' cried Richard. 'It is my uncle's barge.'

It was indeed and in it was John of Gaunt with Lord Percy, the Marshal. The speed with which the barge came along the river indicated that they were in flight.

They all ran out of the palace and down to the river steps.

As John of Gaunt leaped out of the barge, Joan seized his hand and cried: 'What news? What news?'

'There is a riot. The people have gone mad.'

'Against Wycliffe?'

'Nay. They have nothing against Wycliffe. They are threatening to kill me.'

'You are safe here,' said Joan.

How strange, thought Richard, that they should hate this uncle who looked so splendid always in his beautiful clothes. Richard could not help noticing his clothes even at a moment like this. His short tunic of rich velvet, the girdle at his waist in which was a dagger, and a purse of leather most beautifully embossed. The tippets which hung from his sleeves reached to his knees. They were most elegant and it was hard to believe that such grace could have suffered the indignity of flight from the mob.

'They hate me, Joan,' said Uncle John. 'They have made up their minds to hate me. Any crime they can think of they accuse me of. They insist on believing that I am some sort of changeling.'

'No one of any sense believes such lies,' said Joan. 'But you are distraught. Did this begin in the church?'

'It is that stiff-necked Courtenay. I'll not forget this.'

He is proud, thought Richard. He hates me to see him thus, in flight from the mob.

'Let us go in quickly,' said Joan. She is afraid, thought Richard, that they will seek him here.

If they did come he would go out to meet them. He would say: 'I am Richard of Bordeaux. I shall be your King. Hear me!' or something brave like that. And when they saw him all their anger would melt away and they would love him and shout blessings on him.

'Come along, Richard,' said his mother.

She always looked to him first and had taken him by the arm. She seemed to forget that he would soon be a king.

Later news was brought to Kennington of how the rioters had gone to the Marshalsea and sacked it. Shortly afterwards came the news that they had marched on the Savoy Palace.

John was horrified, but thankful that Catherine had had the foresight to leave with the children.

It was ironical that William Courtenay should have been

the one to stop the mob from doing more damage at the
Savoy. He must be grateful to the Bishop but even in the
midst of his relief he wished it had been someone else
whom he must thank.

It had been an ugly scene though. It showed clearly how
the resentment of the people was ready to flow over at the
slightest provocation.

Nor did the matter end there. This quarrel between the
Duke of Lancaster and the City of London could not be
allowed to fester. There must at least be some outward
sign of reconciliation. If the matter was not settled in a
satisfactory manner it would mean that at any moment
another riot such as that just experienced could take place.

Joan anxiously discussed the matter with her brother-in-
law. How she needed her strong purposeful honourable
husband beside her now! Her fears were all for Richard.
He was going to inherit a country not only impoverished
by the Black Death and the French wars but torn by
internal strife.

'You could help to bring about a reconciliation,' said
John. 'The people like you. You are the mother of the heir
whom they have taken to their hearts. There must be a
meeting between myself and the representatives of the
City. I must let them know that I wish to be their friend
and they must give an undertaking that there shall be no
more wanton destruction as that which has just occurred.'

Joan saw the point of this. She did not like the role
assigned to her but she realized it must be played for the
sake of Richard.

She sent for Sir Simon Burley whom she trusted more
than any and asked him what could be done. He saw the
point at once. There must be no more riots. It must be
made clear to the citizens of London that no encroachment
on their liberties was planned.

'Simon, you could explain this. Select two of my knights.
Go to the Mayor and talk to him. Please do this, for my
sake . . . for Richard's sake.'

Simon set out for London accompanied by Sir Aubrey de Vere and Sir Lewis Clifford.

He was received graciously but was told that London demanded the release of Peter de la Mare and William of Wykeham. They wanted to hear from the lips of the King and from his only that their conditions were acceptable.

Lancaster went with all speed to Westminster where he found the King even more feeble than when he had last seen him.

'What is this trouble?' he asked testily.

John explained.

'You shouldn't be bothered with these people, my love,' said Alice.

'I will see them for you,' replied John.

'You're my good son,' said the King. 'I do not know what I should do without you . . . and Alice.'

John was content. This John Philipot whom the Londoners had chosen for their spokesman would have a surprise when he found that instead of having an interview with the King he was faced with the Duke of Lancaster.

But John Philipot was not to be brushed aside.

He bowed and said: 'My lord, I came to see the King. My instructions are that I shall see none other.'

'The King is too ill to see you. I am acting for the King.'

A cynical smile touched the man's lips. John of Gaunt was certainly not the man to arrange the settlement of the quarrel between himself and the people of London.

'Then I will return and we will see what the citizens have to say,' he replied, and he left.

It soon became clear that the citizens were determined. They would see the King and none other.

It was at times such as this that Edward could arouse himself from the lethargy which had taken possession of him.

For a few hours he was like the old King.

He received Philipot and how different was the man's attitude towards his King from what it had been to John of Gaunt. He might be the sickly lecher, but he was still the great King under whom the country had grown rich and prosperous, who had brought home booty from France—though never the Crown. He was still Great Edward and even now that could be apparent.

He knew how to disarm Philipot; he knew how to placate the Londoners.

Of course de la Mare should have a fair trial. So also should the Bishop of Winchester. They need have no fear of that. The Mayor to be replaced by a Captain! This might have been suggested in Parliament but they could rest assured that that was something he would never give his consent to.

Philipot was overcome by that Plantagenet charm; that ability of Edward's to cast aside his royalty at the right moment and talk to a man as his equal.

Philipot assured the King that the riot had been started by a few unruly people. The City could not be blamed for that. There would always be such people.

The King agreed.

'I have never intended to cancel the City's liberties,' he assured Philipot. 'Indeed it is in my mind to extend them.'

'My lord King, I assure you that the citizens are your most devoted subjects.'

The King nodded. 'There is the matter of the Duke of Lancaster,' went on the King. 'I think those who started the riot and damaged his property and the Marshalsea should be found and punished.'

That should be done, agreed Philipot, knowing full well that they would never be found, even as the King did.

John was uneasy about the meeting. He would have preferred the King not to have seen Philipot. In any case, no culprits were brought forward and the lampoons about the Duke—chiefly referring to that changeling story—were circulated through the town and even posted up in the streets.

The King must act, said John. The Londoners were flouting him; and when they insulted his son they insulted him.

Once more the King agreed to receive a deputation. This

time it was the Mayor and the Sheriffs. He was at Sheen at this time and too ill to travel to Westminster. He was very weak and had to be propped up in a chair; he found it difficult to speak.

The citizens must understand that when they insulted his son, they insulted him, he mumbled.

They would make amends, the Mayor promised the King. They would take a candle bearing the Duke's arms and place it on the altar of the Virgin; there should be processions and the town crier should summon people to attend. This would show that the City of London and the Duke of Lancaster had buried their quarrel.

But when the ceremony was carried out it was a failure. The people refused to attend.

There was a certain amusement among those who did. Such a ceremony was usually performed in honour of the dead. Was it done subtly to suggest that they hoped Lancaster would soon be among that band?

However the people would not do honour to him.

As for John of Gaunt he saw through the insult and hated those who had arranged it. But he had to assume that the quarrel was over, because it was the only way to call a truce. And a truce there must be. There must be no more rioting. The Savoy had been saved and was hastily being repaired.

It might have been so much worse.

A great ceremony was taking place at Windsor where gathered together were the greatest nobles and all the chivalry of England.

It was to witness the ceremony of the Garter which was to be bestowed on the King's two grandsons—Richard of Bordeaux and Henry of Bolingbroke.

There were moments when the King's mind was very lucid and seemed to have reverted to its former shrewdness, and this was one of them.

These two, he told himself, will in time be the two most powerful men in England. Richard the King; Henry his cousin, son of John of Gaunt, who is the richest and most influential man in the country under the King.

Edward wanted to see them together. They were of an age, those two, and grandsons of whom a man could be proud. Richard was the elder by a few months—tall, very handsome, yet slender and delicate looking. He will grow out of that, thought Edward. The people will love him, for they admire a handsome man. And he has gracious manners and is clever with words. And Henry—rather stocky but goodly to look on. Of course the people would not care for the son of John of Gaunt as they did for the son of the Black Prince.

They had always loved Edward. He had that quality which drew people to him; and what a hero! And what a tragedy that he should die and leave this young boy to take his place. They had loved Edward as fiercely as they had hated John.

But these two boys must be friends when they grew up. He wanted that. He would have a talk with them after the ceremony.

There was little time left. Alice tried to persuade him that he was well. She tried to prove it, and he tried to pretend it was so to please her.

That affair in the Cathedral had been alarming. He thanked God Courtenay had intervened and prevented further damage. William of Wykeham was restored to his place. Alice had persuaded him and he had had him recalled. He knew that Alice, the minx, had accepted a big bribe from Wykeham, and that was why she had acted for him. It amused him really. These men of the Church were not above a bit of sly bargaining, so if Wykeham was ready to pay for favours why should people criticize Alice for taking advantage of it!

When the ceremony was over he called the two boys to him and told them that he wanted them always to be good friends.

'The Garter is the symbol of this illustrious order,' he told them. 'It is the Order of Chivalry. Never forget it. Because it has been bestowed on you, you must always be courageous and just and preserve your honour at all times. You understand me?'

They both assured him that they understood.

'Take each other's hands. There. Now you are joined in love and friendship. The time will come when I am gone and you, Richard, will wear the crown. Henry, remember, he will be your liege lord. Serve him well. And Richard, this is your good cousin. Your fathers were brothers. Proud Plantagenet blood flows through your veins. Stand together. That is where your strength will lie.'

The King was tired suddenly. But a calm had come to him. He was relieved to talk to the boys, to bring them together.

He had a feeling that he had achieved an important mission.

Now he was tired. He wanted his bed . . . and Alice.

Edward lay at Sheen Palace. It was hot in the apartment for it was the month of June.

He had known he was growing weaker and in spite of Alice's assurances that he was getting better every day he knew he was dying.

He was a sick old man. He was in his sixty-fifth year and out of those sixty-five years he had reigned for fifty-one. It was a great record.

Indeed it had been a great reign. It was only the last years that had brought him shame. Philippa had died and left him and without her he was bereft. Although to be truthful he had started with Alice before Philippa died.

Well, so are great men fallen. Their weaknesses catch up with them; and it was strange to contemplate that he, the faithful husband for so long, should have become such a slave to his senses. He knew what Alice wanted; but what a companion she had been! All through his life he had been restraining his impulses and it was only rarely that he had broken free.

Well, now here he was dying . . . great Edward, no

longer great, no longer admired, no longer loved by his people.

Just an old man—a rather loathsome old man, but still the hero of Sluys and Crécy. The shining hero who had set out to win the throne of France and had failed so miserably.

What was he leaving to his grandson? He dared not think. 'God, save Richard. It is not his fault that he is inheriting a bankrupt kingdom. Oh God, if you had not taken Edward . . .'

Ah, that was at the heart of the tragedy. Edward had died. If Edward had been in health, he would never have allowed the country to get into this state. There would not have been riots in the streets. There would not have been bribery and corruption in high places. If Edward had been strong and healthy . . . But God had seen fit to take that bulwark of strength and leave but a frail boy in his place. But he was dying now. This was the end.

There was only one priest by his bedside. He could just see him.

The priest was placing the cross in his hands and he was saying '*Jesu miserere . . .*'

He kissed the cross.

Then he was lying in his bed and he could see no one.

Slowly life was ebbing away.

Very soon after Alice came to the bedside.

He was gone, this poor doting old man was no more. This was the end of Alice.

She pulled the rings from his fingers, collected what jewels she could and left the palace.

PART TWO

RICHARD OF BORDEAUX

THE GATHERING STORM

RICHARD WAS EXULTANT. To be a ten-year-old King was surely the finest thing in the world. Tomorrow was the day of his coronation and the whole of London, the whole of the country, was eager to tell him how much he was loved.

He had come to the Tower of London, his mother beside him, and the people had thrown garlands of flowers at him; they had shouted his name. Their loyal cheers still echoed in his ears.

How they loved him! And how he loved them!

'It is the Crown they cheer,' Simon had said. 'It is the symbol of kingship.'

Oh no, he thought. They cheer me. They love me, because I am young and good to look on and they are tired of old men.

So it seemed, for it was true that they were rapturous at the sight of him. They threw kisses to him. They called him their dear little King. He was the true King, the grandson of a great King, the son of a great Prince.

'Richard!' they shouted. 'Long live Richard.'

His uncle John had been to see him. He was very quiet and serious and Richard did not quite know what he was thinking.

'I shall be with you at the coronation,' he told his nephew. 'As High Steward of England I have the right to bear the sword. I shall demand that right.'

'So should you,' replied Richard.

'And as Earl of Lincoln I have the right to carve before you at the coronation feast.'

'I know it,' answered Richard.

'And when the ceremony is over I intend to retire from Court for a while.'

Now Richard was astonished.

'Yes,' went on John, 'I have been subjected to slanderous attacks, and I think my best plan is to leave for a while. So I shall ask your permission to remain in the country for a time.'

'It is granted,' said Richard in as authoritative a voice as he could command.

John bowed his head and went on to discuss the arrangements for the coronation.

'There are many who are demanding to perform the traditional ceremonies,' he explained. 'So many claims, alas, for one post I shall have to select with care.'

'People talk of nothing but the coronation,' said Richard with delight.

'It is a very important occasion, nephew. We shall have to take care with these Londoners who are only too ready to make trouble whenever they can find an excuse to do so. The Lord Mayor wishes to serve you with a golden cup and they want some of the leading citizens to serve in the butlery.'

'I shall have no objection,' said Richard. 'They have never shown anything but kindness to me.'

John was not very pleased with that remark and was about to say something when he changed his mind.

They all must remember that I am the King now, thought Richard complacently.

'I am bringing forward young Robert de Vere, the Earl of Oxford. If you are agreeable you might permit him to act as your Chamberlain. He is quite young.'

'How old?' asked Richard.

'He must be perhaps fifteen years old. His father died some time ago when Robert de Vere was only nine. He inherited at about the same age as yourself. I have him waiting below. Would you consent to see him now?'

Richard appeared to consider. It was so enjoyable to have important men, so much his senior, asking for his consent to this and that.

Yes, he thought he could see the young Earl of Oxford now.

'Then he shall come to you. I shall introduce him and leave you together. You can give your verdict after you have seen him.'

Within a few minutes Robert de Vere, Earl of Oxford came into the room.

From the beginning Richard liked the look of him. He was good looking and it was pleasant to find that although he was older than Richard, it was not by so many years; Richard began the interview somewhat haughtily making sure that young de Vere remembered that he was the King, but his attitude changed after a few minutes because there was something so natural about the other boy that Richard felt he could be perfectly natural with him, too.

Robert de Vere told Richard he was fifteen. Richard said he wished he were. It was rather tiresome being only ten.

'Ten and a King!' said Robert. 'I was about ten when I became an Earl. But it is very different being a King.'

Robert told Richard how there were plans afoot to marry him. His guardian, Ingelran de Couci, who had been made Earl of Bedford when he had married King Edward's daughter Isabella, had been his guardian and he wanted to marry him to his daughter Philippa.

'Married!' said Richard. 'They'll be wanting to marry me to someone soon.'

'You can be sure of that. *You'll* choose your bride though. You're the King. You can do as you wish.'

It was a pleasant conversation.

'And you, you don't want to marry this Philippa?'

'I don't want to marry anybody. But if I marry her I shall have some sort of connection with you, shan't I? Her mother was your father's sister. Think of that.'

'You will be connected with my family!'

175

'That makes it a better proposition,' said Robert de Vere and they laughed together.

Richard made up his mind that he would tell his uncle that he would be very happy to make Robert his chamberlain.

A close friendship had begun.

London was determined to honour the new King. In Cheapside they had erected a castle of flowers from which ran two streams of wine. There were four turrets and on each of these stood a girl who had been chosen for her beauty and her age, which was the same as the King's. As Richard rode past on his way from the Tower, flowers and leaves made of gilded paper were thrown down at him. The procession came to a halt and the girls came down from their towers and filled golden goblets with wine which they handed to the King and his attendants. Then an angel appeared from the castle with a golden crown which she placed on the little King's head.

The crowd cheered. The people were proud of the magnificent spectacle which the Londoners had contrived, for not only did it show their loyalty but it also reminded the King of their power and that if he would rule well he must never forget the interests of his capital city.

Richard was moved with emotion and his happiness and delight was so obvious that it added to the general rejoicing.

All along the road to Westminster such pageants had been arranged and though none of these quite equalled the one of Cheapside, they were very impressive.

Crowds had gathered round the Abbey and when the procession appeared, headed by the young King with Simon walking before him, his sword bared, the cheers were deafening.

The Bishop of Rochester preached the sermon and the Archbishop of Canterbury conducted the ceremony; and as the proceedings went on, and Richard could no longer hear the cheers of the crowd, he began to grow rather tired. The Bishop seemed as though he was never going to stop and then there was the ceremony of taking off his coat and shirt while men stood holding a gold-coloured cloth around him like a tent so that none of the people gathered in the Abbey should see his body. Then he was anointed and the prayers went on and on. After that there were the coronation rituals. The crown was so heavy that it seemed to weigh down his head. Then the sceptre and the orb were put into his hands. The spurs were presented and the pallium which was heavily encrusted with jewels was put on.

He knew what he had to do. He had to walk to the altar and lay a gold purse on it, but even that was not the end. There had to be the mass and the communion after that, and he was finding it increasingly hard to keep his eyes open.

Simon was watching him anxiously. He smiled wanly at his dear guardian. 'Not much longer,' Simon seemed to be saying.

The crown was growing more and more heavy. Richard felt it would crush him; and his shoulders refused to support all his garments any longer. He felt an almost irresistible inclination to slip to the floor and go to sleep.

Simon was watching carefully and understood. Suddenly he had picked the young King up in his arms.

'All is well,' he whispered. 'We are going back to the palace now. We're going to have a rest and a nice sleep before the banquet.'

'Oh Simon . . .'

The comfort of those arms was wonderful. Richard closed his eyes while Simon walked with him through the astonished crowds and out to the litter over which a canopy of silk was held by four wardens of the Cinque Ports.

'He is but a child,' muttered Simon.

'Our dear little King is tired,' cried the people. 'Oh, he is only a boy, God bless him.'

The cheers went up. There was their little King so pretty in the arms of good Simon who clearly loved him.

As Simon pressed through the crowds who came forward for a closer look at their King, one of Richard's slippers fell off and as Simon pressed on to the litter, there was a scramble among the crowds for the King's shoe.

Richard was soon fast asleep and it seemed almost immediately Simon was at his bedside. It was time to prepare for the state banquet.

'You have had a good sleep,' said Simon fondly. 'You were tired out, my King.'

Richard sat up. He put his hands to his head. He could still feel the crown there.

'It was so heavy,' he said.

Simon nodded. 'A symbol of your responsibilities,' he commented grimly. 'But not yet. There will be many to advise you . . . perhaps too many.'

I am a King, thought Richard. I am the most important person in the country. The people love me. From henceforth I shall ride among them and they will cheer me and love me for ever. But he hoped that future ceremonies would not be quite as tiring as the coronation.

'Did I do well, Simon?' he asked—suddenly a young boy eager for his tutor's approval.

'You did very well indeed.'

'But to fall asleep when you picked me up! I don't remember coming into the palace. Then I dreamed that I could still hear the people shouting.'

'It was such a long day for you,' soothed Simon. 'I think the people loved you more for falling asleep. It touched them. They went wild with love for you when they saw me pick you up and put you in the litter. People are like that. They like very much a touch of human nature. You lost a slipper, you know.'

'What became of it?'

'It fell from your foot. There was a scramble for it. I saw one man get it and hold it up and kiss it.'

'I am so glad. He will keep it all his life as his most precious possession.'

Simon said: 'He might well sell it. It was jewelled and

doubtless could bring him more than he had comfortably in a year or two's labour.'

'Fancy,' mused Richard. 'A man would have to work for a year or two to buy a slipper which I can lose and not miss.'

'It is time to prepare for the banquet,' said Simon.

And what a banquet was that which was served in Westminster Hall. Before attending it Richard created four new earls. One of these was the youngest of his uncles, Thomas of Woodstock, whom he made Earl of Buckingham.

Seated at the High Table surrounded by all the nobility of the land, Richard thrilled with emotion—not only because he was at the center of the pageantry and had from a second son of no great importance become the most significant person in the land. It was more than that. It was the glory of kingship, of belonging to a line of kings, to be of proud Plantagenet blood, to have descended from the mighty Conqueror.

He would never be able to explain this to his Holland half-brothers; they would turn it away with a joke. Simon or his mother might make the occasion into a lesson, a recounting of further homilies as to the importance and need for service to the country.

He fancied he could explain it to his new friend Robert de Vere. He would try to at the first opportunity.

In the meantime here he was seated at the table on the dais, surrounded by the highest in the land; and at the tables on the main floor everyone was a nobleman or a person of authority.

Suddenly there was a shout through the hall. The doors were flung open and into the hall rode a knight in full armour.

The heralds cried out in ringing voices that the knight, Sir John Dymoke, had come to challenge to combat any who disputed the sovereign's right to the throne.

As Dymoke then took off his gauntlet and threw it onto the floor, there was a hushed silence through the hall. No one spoke.

The gauntlet was returned to Dymoke who repeated the challenge twice more. Each time it was greeted in silence.

There was no one in this assembly who denied the right of Richard to take the crown of England.

Richard knew what was expected of him. He took up a gold cup which was filled with wine. He drank from it and handed it to Dymoke who drank to his sovereign lord and draining the cup rode off with it.

The challenging ceremony was over and the banquet began.

In the streets of London the revelry continued. The people sang and danced and refreshed themselves from the fountains which spurted wine.

It was not every day there was a coronation.

All was well. The true King had been proclaimed. They had seen him with the crown on his head. They had heard Sir John Dymoke's challenge which none had accepted.

They had the true King of England on the throne—a boy whose youth and beauty made him particularly appealing. All the apprehension, the fear that the wicked John of Gaunt would attempt to take the crown was over.

'Long live Richard of Bordeaux, now Richard the Second of England.'

John of Gaunt realized that there was nothing to be done but submit with a good grace to the progress of events. The forces against him had been too strong and he must retreat into silence for a while; he had to convince the people that it was not his intention to take the throne from his nephew, and he now wanted them to see him in the role of chief supporter of the young King.

He had had to give way on the matter of Peter de la Mare, who was, in the eyes of the Londoners, not only a hero but a martyr. The most dangerous men were martyrs. John had long known that. And when the people clamoured for the release of Peter de la Mare, John expressed his agreement that this should take place.

He would be reconciled with Peter de la Mare, he said.

The beginning of a new reign was the time for men to forget their differences.

But how chagrined he was to learn of de la Mare's triumphant journey through London where he was welcomed with almost as much enthusiasm as had been shown to the young King.

It was a further indication of the lack of love they felt for John of Gaunt when they so fêted his bitterest enemies.

However, since it was so, John must not shut his eyes to the facts.

The King was surrounded by advisers and three days after the coronation his new Council was elected.

This had been done with great care so that every party was represented. The King's uncle Edmund headed the list; William Courtenay the Bishop of London was another; and the choice of the rest had been made so carefully that for every supporter of John of Gaunt there was one from the opposite party.

It was significant that John of Gaunt was not included. He would not show that he resented this. Nor did he very much. Edmund would do exactly as he told him and he would rather act through his brother than directly.

In the new Parliament there was a majority of members who had been in the Good Parliament which had opposed him, and Sir Peter de la Mare had been chosen as the speaker.

Of course a man such as John of Gaunt—the richest in the country and the first in importance after the King by birth—could not be ignored altogether and when an advisory committee was set up, John's name appeared at the top of the list.

This list was read out in the presence of the King, and John created a dramatic incident when, to the astonishment of all present, he rose from his seat and walked to the throne on which the young King was seated.

There was a tense silence in the House, and when John spoke all could hear clearly what he said.

'My lord King, I pray humbly that you will listen to my words. I speak out of concern not only for you as my sovereign but for your own person. The Commons have chosen me to be one of your advisers, but this I cannot accept until I have cleared myself of charges made against me. Calumnies have been uttered. These are cruel lies but they have touched my honour. Unworthy I am, but I am the son of Edward the Third and after you, my lord King, the greatest of peers of the realm. These malicious rumours which have been circulated about me if true—which God forbid—would amount to treason. My lord, until the truth were known I could do nothing. You will see that I stand to lose more by treachery than any man in England. Apart from this it would be a strange and marvellous thing if I should so far depart from the traditions of my blood. Let any man, whatever his degree, dare charge me with treason, disloyalty or any act which would bring harm to this kingdom and I will defend myself with my body.'

The members listened with amazement. It was an appealing scene, this great and magnificently attired man, kneeling to his nephew, a slender boy.

As he rose to his feet the members came forward. They were moved by their emotion. He must not go, they said. He must stay close to the King. They needed his skill and his experience.

No, replied John firmly. He needed time for reflection. He must show the country that his ambition was but to serve it.

There was protest against those who had maligned him. He smiled.

'It pleases me, my lords,' he said, 'that you have at last recognized this for what it is.'

When Alice Perrers was brought to trial John did not attempt to defend her, and stood aside while the sentence which had been delivered by the Good Parliament was confirmed.

It seemed indeed that John of Gaunt had either forgotten his ambitions or had never had them, and had just managed to incur the dislike of the people who had invented tales about him such as the one of his birth which had proved to be quite absurd.

He will stay and become an adviser of his nephew, was the opinion. He is deeply hurt by the slanders which have been circulating and wants an assurance that we believe in his good faith.

In the palace of the Savoy John talked over his future with Catherine.

'How would you like it,' he asked, 'if we were to retire to Kenilworth and live there in peace and quiet for a while?'

She stared at him incredulously.

'You cannot mean that!'

'I am considering it,' he said. 'You and I and the children . . . I could be a country gentleman . . . for a while.'

Catherine's face betrayed her joy. Then she was sceptical.

'But you would not! You *could* not . . .'

'Aye, I could. I like to see my little Beauforts growing up. I shall like to think what I can do for them. And there are the others too.'

'What has come over you? You could not leave this scene. It is your life. And you are nominated one of the King's advisers.'

'They are friendly now . . . At least Parliament is, but my enemies are there. The people are enamoured of a pretty boy. They love him dearly . . . and they may well continue to while he is a pretty boy. And the wicked uncle . . . How they hate the wicked uncle, Catherine! They tried to burn down his palace. Do you remember?'

'I shall never forget it,' she said with a shudder.

'Yes . . . I have a new role to play: the injured uncle, the honest man who will do nothing until his honour has been proved. It is a new part for me, Catherine. Not an easy one to play, but methinks I shall play it better in the country . . . away from Court. Say . . . Kenilworth . . . Leicester or another of the estates. We shall live together you and I . . . as the good squire and his lady. How like you that?'

She threw herself into his arms. 'Oh my lord, methinks I shall be the happiest woman in England.'

Richard was growing up quickly and learning that it was not all glory being a king. People did not remain enchanted for ever with their ruler simply because he was possessed of appealing youth and a handsome face.

For as long as possible the news of Edward's death had been kept from the French who would most certainly see that their old enemy had become somewhat vulnerable. The old King even when he was becoming senile and the slave of his lust was still the old warrior; his image could only die with him. But now he was dead and there was a young boy on the throne, and the truce between the two countries was coming to an end.

They were not long in showing their intentions. Fleets from France and Castile came to the very shores of England. The Isle of Wight was overrun and pillaged; they even got as far as Gravesend and the smoke of the burning town could be seen from the City of London.

It could never have happened in the old King's day, said the people.

Richard was depressed. It was not what he had looked for from kingship.

It was not to be expected that John of Gaunt would be content with the quiet life for long. A subsidy was raised for carrying on the war in France and John of Gaunt returned to public life and began to prepare a fleet for action.

He was at the coast while the ships were being made ready and Catherine was with him.

They rode out together; they inspected the ships together; he behaved with her as though she were his legal wife.

The people were aghast. Men in such positions might keep their mistresses—in fact they almost always did—but they were expected to behave with discretion. Yet John of Gaunt snapped his fingers at convention. It was as though he was telling them that he was too important to observe general rules. He did not care that they knew he had married his neglected wife for ambition. He wished to honour Catherine Swynford and so must they.

They resented this; especially as they were expected to pay taxes to help him regain the throne of Castile. He even called himself King of Castile, which was a constant reminder of his cynical approach to marriage. His poor wife was neglected and it seemed suffering from some indisposition which prevented her from bearing children. She had only one daughter, while Catherine Swynford had four bastards, all of whom were treated as though they were royal.

Who is she? they demanded of each other. No better than we are! And there she is riding out like a Duchess!

They did not actively abuse her. They were afraid of the French and the recent raids had startled them. They hoped that John of Gaunt would take his fleet across the seas and rid them of this much-feared enemy.

Any small popularity he might have gained by his behaviour at the coronation and immediately afterwards was lost when part of the fleet was defeated by the Spaniards and the rest came home having completely failed to achieve its purpose.

Then another incident occurred which set the people murmuring against him once again.

There were two squires, Robert Hauley and John Shakyl, who had leaped into prominence after the battle of Nájara. These two had captured an important nobleman, the Count of Denia, and, after the custom of the day, hoped to make a handsome sum from the adventure. It was, after all, one of the reasons why so many knights went to war and one of the most valuable perquisites of battle was what could be obtained from ransoms. And naturally the higher the rank of the captive, the greater the reward to be expected . . .

The Count had been released when his son was delivered to the two squires as a hostage; and as all that had happened ten years ago, the boy had now become a young man while the Count was still trying to raise the ransom money.

That autumn a representative of the Count had come to England with part of the ransom in the hope that this would be acceptable and his son released. The two squires, however, having kept their hostage for ten years were not going to accept less than their demand and they refused to parley with him.

It was at this point that the government stepped in and Hauley and Shakyl were ordered to surrender their hostage to the Council. After having waited ten years when they lived in expectation of a very large sum of money, the two squires, rather naturally, refused. As this was construed as contempt of the government and they were accused of making a private prison of their house, they were ordered to be sent to the Tower.

When they knew that they were to be arrested, they told their hostage, Alfonso, what was happening. He was a young man of aristocratic lineage, for Count Denia, who was also the Marquess of Villena, was related to the royal family of Castile—a fact which he never forgot and which the two squires had always respected. Alfonso had always been treated well by them and he had long since ceased to regard himself as a prisoner. He was simply a companion of the young men awaiting the day when he would return to his family.

Robert Hauley put it to him succinctly.

'Your father will not be released from the need to pay the ransom money. He will just have to pay it to the government instead of to us. Do you think this is fair? All these years you have lived with us and we have become friends. You bear us no grudge. Your father was taken in war and according to custom and on account of his rank we should have had a reward for giving him up.'

Young Alfonso saw the point of this. It was true he had not been unhappy. He had grown fond of both Robert Hauley and John Shakyl, and it seemed to him that if people in very high places were coming into the matter a higher ransom could be demanded.

'Very soon,' said Robert, 'they will come to take us.

We shall go to the Tower and you will be the prisoner of the government.'

'I would prefer to be yours,' answered Alfonso.

'Well, I have a plan,' said Robert, who was the more adventurous of the two squires. 'We shall be taken to the Tower, but why should you not come with us?'

'How could that be?' demanded John Shakyl.

'We shall tell them that Alfonso has gone. He has escaped. They will think we have hidden him. No matter. Alfonso will come with us to the Tower . . . as our serving man.'

John Shakyl burst into laughter. 'What a plan! To deceive them right under their very own noses!'

'Well, Alfonso, we cannot do it without your consent of course. What say you?'

'Will they allow you to take a servant with you?'

'It is the custom. After all we have committed no real crime and we are of good family. They must treat us well.'

'I agree,' cried Alfonso. 'It is a matter of honour. It was you two who captured my father and the ransom should be yours.'

'I knew you would see it that way, Alfonso,' cried Robert. 'Now we will prepare. You will have to adopt a slightly less haughty manner now, you know. You are not of the royal house, remember, but a humble serving man.'

To the two men and the young Alfonso the whole matter was something of a joke; and in due course they were lodged in the Tower where, as Robert had said they would be, they were treated well; but they refused to say anything about the whereabouts of their hostage.

The weeks began to pass. Alfonso enjoyed playing the part of the servant and the whole affair was an amusing adventure. But they were growing restive; and their success so far in deceiving the authorities made them grow bolder and they planned their escape. It was not so difficult. It was not as though they were regarded as important prisoners. A little wine with something in it which could be smuggled into the Tower by a bribe or two and keys taken from the pockets of a guard who had passed into a drunken stupor, and they were free.

They were detected as they passed out of the Tower and the hue and cry went up. They had not planned it that way and it was necessary to decide quickly what should be done. Robert, the most resourceful of the trio, said they must go into Sanctuary at once, otherwise they would be captured and they could be sure that if they were it would not be so easy for them to escape again.

So they went with all haste to Westminster and took sanctuary in the Abbey.

To Sir Alan Buxhull, the Constable of the Tower, who had come to his position through John of Gaunt of whom he was a staunch supporter, it was a reflection on his custodianship that prisoners could escape so easily and he determined to bring them back to the Tower; and even when he heard that they were in the Abbey he decided to follow them there and he set out with Sir Ralf Ferrers, another of John of Gaunt's men, and armed guards from the Tower.

In the Abbey he talked to them urging them to come out of Sanctuary. Shakyl eventually did emerge because he felt that their case was hopeless, and Sir Alan Buxhull had convinced him that if he would give himself up, he would merely go back to his comfortable room in the Tower and there would be no recriminations.

Robert Hauley was not so easily taken in. He was determined not to come out of Sanctuary and he said so.

'You cannot harm me here,' he said. 'I claim the sanctuary of God's House.'

'You are resisting the command of the King and his ministers,' cried Buxhull.

'They have been too avaricious and unjust,' retorted Hauley. 'We have held the hostage for nigh on ten years. Now you would take him from us.'

The Constable's patience was running out. He would not be denied. He called to his men. 'Seize him.'

Hauley attempted to fly before his pursuers and in doing so, ran into the Chapel where Mass was being celebrated.

There was confusion among the startled monks as Robert Hauley ran among them followed by the armed guards. Then one of the guards ran his sword through Hauley's body and the squire fell dying on the altar steps.

There was a hushed silence in the Abbey then. The monks were staring at the blood-stained body in horror. This was the violation of Sanctuary. The Abbey had been desecrated by murder, and the murderers were the King's servants.

The matter could not be hushed up, even when it was discovered that the serving man was the son of the Count of Denia.

He was now in the hands of the Government and John Shakyl was released from the Tower for it was hoped that the entire matter would be forgotten.

But it was not forgotten. The Bishop of London was horrified. This was more than a murder of a squire who had defied the Government. He could see in this an attempt to curtail the sanctity of the Church.

Sanctuary had been abused and therefore the laws of the Church had been violated.

There had to be scapegoats.

Sir Alan Buxhull had had no right to bring his armed guards into the Abbey. He and Sir Ralf Ferrers were the offenders. They should be deprived of their posts and made to answer for what they had done.

But they were John of Gaunt's men; and he did not wish them to be replaced. It suited him to have his supporters in important posts and that of the Constable of the Tower was a very special one.

The matter should be hushed up, said John of Gaunt. What a fuss over a foolish man who had tried to defy the King and the Government. The hostage was now in the Government's hands and the matter could be satisfactorily settled. One of the squires was free and he should have learned a lesson. As for the other, his had been a more bitter lesson; let it serve as an example to others who might try to take the law into their hands.

The Church hesitated for a while. It was not advisable to

enter into open conflict with the State. On the other hand it was equally unwise to give way. It was Courtenay, the Bishop of London, who had shown his boldness on more than one occasion who decided to take action.

In a ceremony at St. Paul's he solemnly excommunicated Sir Alan Buxhull, Sir Ralf Ferrers and all those directly or indirectly concerned in the murder.

The Bishop had openly stated that he was not including the Duke of Lancaster and the Queen Mother in the excommunication and by letting this be known he was implying that they were in measure responsible for what had happened.

It was the battle between Church and State again; and as John of Gaunt was supporting Wycliffe who wanted changes in the Church it seemed in keeping with his views that he should now be supporting one who allowed the Abbey to be defiled.

John of Gaunt had in truth had no part in the murder but as people began to take sides he threw himself into the quarrel. He wanted to go against his old enemy the Bishop of London and while, had he kept quiet, it could have been a quarrel between the Bishop and the monks against the King's Council, because of his interest in it, it became more significant.

When the Bishop was summoned to appear before the Council at Windsor he refused to attend and John was so rash as to exclaim in the presence of many who would lose no time in reporting what he had said, 'I will drag the Bishop here in spite of the ribald knaves of London.'

The quarrel had broken out afresh.

Now people were asking what had happened to all the money which had been raised for the fleet and the army. There followed an uneasy period when accounts were examined but John was able to prove that the money had been spent in a proper manner.

More serious still there was trouble brewing throughout the countryside. In the villages men talked together; they were asking themselves why they should work so hard and for so little; why they should be the slaves of their masters?

The Black Death had made them aware of their importance. There had been a time when there were not enough labourers to till the land; then they had asked for higher wages and a law had been made against them. This law had said they must work on the same terms for their masters as they had before the coming of the plague which meant even more hardship, for the cost of living had risen after the fearful scourge had passed over; so instead of being richer, as they should have been since their labour was in greater demand, they were poorer than they had been before.

It seemed to them that the masters worked everything out to their own advantage.

And now because of this war with the French which went on and on, there was a new tax—the Poll Tax which people were to pay according to their incomes. Archbishops and Dukes paid six pounds, thirteen shillings and fourpence each and an ordinary labourer was charged fourpence.

In spite of this order the money was not forthcoming and it was necessary to send collectors through the towns and villages to enforce payment.

The law was that every person over fifteen must pay.

Richard had been four years on the throne, and they had been four depressing years. At the end of them the country was in a worse condition than it had been at the death of the old King. The French were troublesome; the Scots were taking advantage of the situation; the bogey of the nation was John of Gaunt who had failed miserably in his expeditions on the Continent. There was a rustling of rebellion throughout the country and it was growing louder. Discontent was rife among the peasants. They were asking each other why it should be that men were condemned to work for others all their lives. Who decided whether a man should be a villein or a lord?

Those in high places were unaware of what was happening. They could not see the gathering storm until it burst upon them.

WAT TYLER

THERE WAS ONE man who believed so fervently that there was a great deal wrong with life as it was lived in England that he was determined to give *his* life if necessary to change it.

This was John Ball, a priest who had begun his career in the Abbey of St. Mary's in York. He had very soon found himself in conflict with the authorities because not only did he hold controversial views but he would not stop talking about them.

He had seen what had happened after the Black Death and he deplored the fact that although workers on the land had been seen to be important to the well-being of the country they continued to be treated as serfs; and when their labour was in great demand and there was every reason to suppose they might have asked a higher wage for their services, they had been completely subdued by their masters and forced to work at the same wage as they had received when there were plenty of them.

Why, he asked himself and others, should some, merely on account of where they were born, live on the fruits of other men's labours?

His watchword was:

> 'When Adam delf and Eve span
> Who was then the gentleman?'

It was his favourite theme. Had we not all come from Adam and Eve? The scriptures told us so. Why then should some of us be favoured above others?

John Ball was a born preacher. He loved to talk and took a great pleasure in expounding his views to others. He would go to the village green and the people would crowd round him to listen to his sermons. They were different from any other sermons they had ever heard. His views on the Church were similar to those of Wycliffe; but in addition to the reform of the church John Ball wanted the reform of society.

After listening to him the villeins would return to their dark hovels and their meagre fare and would think of the mansion close by in which lived the lord of the manor. He was waited on by countless servants; his table was weighed down with good things to eat. Those who served in his kitchens counted themselves fortunate, for a few crumbs from the rich man's table fell to them. And yet, argued John Ball, how had this happened? They all had the same forebears, did they not? Adam and Eve? And yet some had been born in mansions, others in dark hovels, some under a hedge maybe.

It was fascinating to listen to him and that which many had accepted before as God's will, they now questioned.

It was not long before John Ball was noticed, as anyone preaching such a doctrine must be. Moreover whenever he preached, people flocked to hear him. It was disconcerting. More than that. It was dangerous.

On Sundays he would wait until the people came out from Mass and then start preaching in the market square. He had a magnetic quality and many found it impossible to pass on. Moreover his words were so arresting. They had certainly never heard the like before.

One day he was at his usual place and was soon addressing the crowd.

'My good friends,' he cried. 'Things cannot go well in England or ever will until everything shall be in common, when there shall be neither villein nor lord, and all distinctions levelled, when the lords shall be no more masters than ourselves. How ill they have used us! And for what reason do they keep us in bondage? Are we not all descended from the same parents, Adam and Eve, and what

193

reasons can they give, why they should be more masters than ourselves—except perhaps in making us labour for them to spend. They are clothed in velvets and rich stuffs, ornamented with ermine and other furs, while we are forced to wear poor cloth. They have wines, spices and fine bread while we have only rye and the refuse of the straw; and if we drink it must be water. They have handsome seats and manors when we must brave the wind and rain in the field. And, my friends, it is from our labour that they have the wherewithal to support this pomp. What else should you lack when you lack masters? You should not lack for fields you have tilled nor houses you have built, nor cloth you have woven. Why should one man mow the earth for another?'

If John Ball was aware of strangers in the crowd who listened he gave no sign. He did not care who heard him. What he said was truth.

He would go on saying it because he believed it. No matter what befell him, he would go on telling the truth, before the King, before the Pope, before God.

But this could no longer be called the ranting of a mad priest. It was the rumblings of revolt.

John Ball was becoming a menace to security.

It wasn't long before he received a command to appear before the Archbishop of Canterbury.

Simon of Sudbury—so called because he had been born in the town of that name in Suffolk—had become Archbishop of Canterbury some four years previously. He was a staunch adherent of John of Gaunt and there could not have been a man less like the priest, John Ball. Simon was not one to allow himself to become involved in doctrines; he had been originally disturbed by the rise of John Wycliffe but preferred to forget about him particularly as John of Gaunt was inclined to favour the preacher. But Courtenay, the Bishop of London, was of a very different mettle. There was a man who was going to stand by what he believed in even if he lost his post in so doing.

Simon of Sudbury could well be without these uncomfortable men and such a one was John Ball.

The man stood before him and had the temerity to repeat what he had been saying in market squares. The Archbishop could sense the fiery fanaticism of the man and knew at once that he was dangerous. Such as John Ball should not be allowed to roam the countryside inciting people to revolution.

The Archbishop realized that it was no use admonishing him. He had already been in trouble before. People had been forbidden to attend his meetings—but that had not stopped them. He had been excommunicated, but no one—least of all John Ball—had cared very much about that.

There was only one thing to do with such a man and that was put him away where he could not preach, so the Archbishop sentenced him to a term in Maidstone prison.

Let him stay there where he could do no harm. The people would soon forget him and his dangerous doctrines.

But people did not forget John Ball. His words were remembered. When men laboured in the fields for a pittance, when they wondered where their next meal was coming from and the children were hungry, they remembered John Ball. Why should it be? they asked. They watched the rich ride by on their fine horses with their fine clothes and their attendants. Why? asked the people. How did it happen? Hadn't they all begun with Adam and Eve? Who was then the gentleman?

Resentment grew when the collectors came round for the tax. Collecting had come to be a somewhat dangerous occupation and only those would enter into it who were promised big rewards.

There was one baker of Fobbing in Essex—a man of great strength who refused to pay the tax and who so terrified the collector that he did not insist.

This baker was talked of throughout Essex and the people of Fobbing made a hero of their baker and would have followed him if he would have led them. But the baker of Fobbing had no desire but to carry on baking his bread and this he did; but he had given them an indication that resistance was not impossible.

One May day the collector called at the house of a tyler in the town of Deptford and demanded payment of the tax.

The man of the house, Walter, was close by at his work tyling a house, and two women, his wife and daughter, were alone.

The collector demanded the tax not only of the mother but of the girl, at which the woman said: 'My daughter is not yet fifteen years of age and therefore pays no tax.'

'What?' said the collector casting a lascivious eye on the girl. 'That one not fifteen!'

He approached the girl and took her chin in his hand. He forced her to look at him. She was trembling with fear. Her mother looked on with horror, for she had heard tales of how these collectors could behave and that there was no redress against them because they were working for the government and it was not easy to get men to take on the disagreeable task of collecting.

'Not fifteen! Why, she's a fine big girl. I can see that. Not fifteen. Come.' He had pulled at her gown, tearing at it so that the top part of her body was exposed.

The girl screamed. Her mother ran out of the house calling for help.

The collector laughed and seized the girl.

Within a few moments the girl's father was in the doorway. In his hand he carried the lathing hammer with which he had been working.

'Take your hands off my girl, you devil,' he cried.

The collector turned on him. He carried a knife, for collectors came well armed.

'How dare you touch my daughter,' went on the tyler.

'She's a ripe wench,' said the collector licking his lips. 'Leave us, Tyler. We'll be pleasant together and who knows I might not demand the tax off her.'

The tyler's answer was to raise his hammer and bring it down on the collector's head. In a few seconds the collector was lying on the floor, blood spurting from his body.

'He's dead,' said the girl and threw herself sobbing into her mother's arms.

The sound of the affray had spread throughout the neighbourhood and people were coming to see what had happened.

The tyler knelt beside the collector. He could see that his daughter had spoken the truth.

The man was dead.

'What'll you do?' they asked. 'You know what this means.'

'You must get away,' said his wife. 'Wat, they'll be after you. They'll refuse to believe what sort of man he was. You'll be in the wrong, they'll say. Oh, Wat, you must go away.'

Walter looked blankly ahead of him. 'What shall I do?' he said. 'Shall I run? Leave my wife, leave my family . . . run for the rest of my life.'

'You did right, Wat,' said the one man. 'I'd have done the same.'

'And I. And I.'

'A curse on the tax. A curse on the collectors. What's it for, eh?'

'To buy jewels for the rich.'

'Why should they have what we work for? Why, why, why . . .? Didn't we all come from Adam and Eve?'

'They'll never give us what we should have,' said Walter. 'I reckon the only way we'd get it is to take it.'

'Let's take it. Let's march. Let's march on London.'

Something had happened to Walter the Tyler. He had been a peaceful citizen until now. But he had killed a man for attempting to deflower his daughter and he felt no remorse. He felt only anger.

He had heard John Ball when the priest had come this way and he had agreed with what the man had said but he had never believed the words of a priest could change anything.

But why should the world go on in one way just because it had for so many years? There was much in what John

Ball had said. And no one ever got anything they didn't fight for.

Here he was at a turning-point in his life—forced to it by a tax collector.

He had killed a man and he would be discovered. Death awaited him—horrible death. But the people were watching him eagerly. They were looking to him. They were asking him to lead them.

More and more were gathering round.

Walter heard himself addressing them.

'Why should we go on as we have been? Why shouldn't we change things? The time has come. We'll march . . .'

He heard a cry go up. 'We'll march. Come on. All you people come. Fall in. Wat the Tyler is going to lead us to London.'

A fever of excitement possessed the little town of Dartford. Within a few hours after the death of the tax collector they were gathered together and ready to march. There were hundreds of them. They had snatched up anything that could be used as weapons. True these were of the most primitive kind—mostly the tools of their trades such as flails, bill hooks and plough handles. There were a few pikes. But what they lacked in weapons they made up for in the fire of their determination.

This was going to be the end of slavery. No longer would they allow the government to send its servants to their towns to take their money and dishonour their women.

News spread to the surrounding villages and from all directions men were coming in to join what they called Wat Tyler's army.

Wat had discovered in himself the gifts of leadership, which had been awakened by the sight of his daughter in the hands of the collector. He had a certain gift for oratory and the fact that this ragged army looked to him as their leader was a great inspiration.

He addressed the crowd and he was amazed at the

silence as soon as he began to speak, and the manner in which they attended to his words was gratifying.

'My friends,' he cried, 'we are going to right our wrongs. We shall not cease until we have done so. But let us not forget the man who has shown us the way to go. We have all heard his words. He has brought home to us the injustice of our lot. He has shown us that we have as much right to the good things as our masters have. I mean John Ball.'

'John Ball be a prisoner of the Archbishop, Wat,' called a man. 'He be in the Maidstone prison.'

'I know it,' answered Wat. 'So our first task is to free him.'

'To Maidstone,' cried the crowd. 'Free John Ball!'

So the march to Maidstone began. It was a distance of some twenty miles and as they passed through the villages people ran out to see them.

Marching to free John Ball. Marching to London to get their rights. It was a goodly cause and there was scarcely a man who did not want to be part of it. By the time they reached Maidstone their numbers had doubled. They were an army.

They stormed into the town of Maidstone, shouting, 'To the Jail. To the Jail. Free John Ball.'

The guards were startled to see this wild army descending upon them. 'Open the gates,' they shouted. The startled guards looked on in amazement, and did not move.

'No matter,' cried Wat. 'We'll soon break in.'

There were so many of them and they were men of muscle; their lives had been spent in hard physical labour. It was not long before the gates gave way and they were storming into the prison.

'John Ball,' they chanted. 'Where are you, John Ball? We have come to free you, John Ball.'

The terrified guards were ready to help them. They were men with a grievance too. And there was John Ball standing before them, his joy apparent on his face.

'At last, at last!' he cried. 'The day of atonement has come.'

He must hear what had happened. They told him how they had started out from Dartford under Wat the Tyler's leadership, and had gathered men on the way.

'We can gather men from all over England,' said John Ball. 'Wat, you are a fine man. You killed the tax collector and it was a righteous killing. God is with you. He has chosen you to lead these men. But it is not enough, Wat. We need more. We will arouse the whole country. There is not a villein in this land who will not join with us when he knows we are on the march.'

'How . . . ?' began Wat.

But John Ball silenced him. 'We will send messengers all over the country as far north as Durham . . . out to Essex and Suffolk, to Somerset and York. They will ride with all speed. A clarion call shall go through England. John Ball hath rung the bell.'

There had been trouble in Essex following the affair of the Fobbing baker. In that village and a few others those who refused to pay the tax had been taken to court. A priest calling himself Jack Straw had arisen to lead the people. He marched into the court and the result was that fighting broke out. The officials were no match for the mob and the court was broken up and Jack Straw's men marched through the town with the heads of officials dripping blood from the pikes on which they had been stuck.

Now the men of Essex were marching to join the men of Kent. The revolt was no longer a local matter.

The first objective was Canterbury where they might come face to face with Archbishop Simon of Sudbury, he who had sent John Ball to prison and would have let him stay there for the rest of his life if his friends had not come to rescue him.

News reached the Mayor of Canterbury that John Ball with Wat Tyler and their army of desperate peasants were marching on the town, their object being to storm the Cathedral and bring the Archbishop to justice.

The Mayor was in a panic. He was aware of what had happened in Fobbing and he was thankful that the Archbishop had gone to London. That was a mercy. He determined to do all he could to save his town.

The marchers came steadily along the Pilgrims Way and they gave a shout of triumph when they saw the grey walls of the city.

'We shall have to storm our way in,' said Wat; but this proved not to be the case.

The Mayor was waiting at the gates to welcome them, to tell them that he had every sympathy with their cause, and that he had food for them for he felt sure that was their most urgent need.

'Our most urgent need is to come face to face with the Archbishop,' replied John Ball.

'My friend, he is not in Canterbury. He left some weeks ago for London.'

There were cries of disappointment. But they were not taking the Mayor's word for it.

They partook of the food which was offered; then they searched the Cathedral and the Archbishop's palace. It was true. Their bird had flown.

'We'll find him yet,' declared Wat. 'And when we've rested a night it'll be to London.'

Joan, the Queen Mother, had been on a pilgrimage to the shrine of St. Thomas at Canterbury and was staying at a manor house near Rochester on her way back to Westminster when she heard of the peasants' rising.

She had been very uneasy lately. The King was growing up but was still very young—not yet fourteen; and she was constantly anxious about him. Each day she more deeply regretted the death of the Black Prince and often thought how much easier life would have been had he lived. She who had been so frivolous in her youth had grown very serious. She tried to guide her son. The uncles were there in the background of course. She looked more to John of Gaunt than the others; but John was so unpopular with the people and there were such evil rumours about him that she felt she must be wary. He was at this time in Scotland—for the Scots could always be relied upon to be troublesome at the most inconvenient times; Edmund was in Portugal and Thomas in the Marcher country—all on missions which she guessed would prove to be fruitless.

She had undertaken this pilgrimage to ask for St. Thomas's help; and now hearing these rumours of the peasants' activities she told her attendants that they must lose no time in getting back to London.

Travel for Joan had become something of a trial, for she had grown very fat over the last few years and riding a horse was irksome. For this reason she had had a vehicle built for herself. It was a most unusual contraption and when it passed along the roads people ran out of their houses to see it. The Queen Mother was one of the most popular members of the royal family, particularly in Kent, where she was still known as the Fair Maid of Kent, and she was the mother of the young King who, although he was not quite so rapturously received as he had been on the day he was crowned and had so appealingly lost his slipper, was still loved for his youth and beauty. Joan had never been afraid to mingle with the people and her ready smiles had kept her popularity.

Now the sight of this carriage which looked like a wagon of red and gold covered in a white hood with a curtain over it to hide the occupant from view, brought out the crowds to give a smile and a cheer for the Fair Maid, even if in truth she scarcely deserved the name, though in spite of her obesity the remains of her remarkable beauty were still apparent. Moreover although the people loathed John of Gaunt, and had little love for the other sons of the King, they had idealized the Black Prince and retained a certain affection for Joan.

Joan set out from Rochester instructing her servants that they must make every effort to reach London as soon as was possible. She sat in her carriage and made no complaint as they rattled along the roads even though the speed did not add to the comfort of travelling thus.

Then suddenly as they rattled along the carriage gave a sudden jolt and they were stationary.

'What can this be?' asked Joan anxiously.

One of her women who had been travelling with her inside the carriage lifted the curtain and looked out.

'What has happened?' the woman asked one of the guards.

'The wheels are stuck in the mud,' was the answer.

Joan heard and looked out. 'Let every man get to work,' she said. 'We *must* get to London with all speed.'

'Everything that can be done shall be done, my lady,' was the answer.

They settled down to wait. An hour passed and still they had not moved from the spot for the wheels could not be shifted from the cloying mud.

Just as Joan was wondering whether she should take one of the horses and ride to London with some of the guards she heard the shouts in the distance.

It was too late. The rioters were coming this way.

Her women were afraid. Joan sat still, her hands folded in her lap. They would know her carriage. The royal insignia of the white hart was painted on the hood; moreover it was certain that everyone had heard of this carriage and there was no other like it—and every peasant knew that it belonged to the Queen Mother.

There was a conflict between the rich and the poor and there was no doubt in Joan's mind into which category she would fall.

An army of a hundred thousand strong—if reports could be believed—was marching along this road and she was here with only a few guards and servants to protect her!

She was not one to show fear however much she felt it. She lived in a violent world where life was cheap. Her father had been murdered—judicially it was said—but murdered none the less. If her time had come, then she must face it. Her great fear was: What will become of Richard if they kill me?

Her thoughts raced on as she listened to the shouts which grew nearer and nearer. She was hardly recognizable now as the frivolous young beauty who had trifled with the affections of young Salisbury and had married Thomas Holland after he and she had become lovers, and then in widowhood had asked the Black Prince to marry her. Perhaps this all showed the strength of her character which had not been recognized when she had flirted even with the King so that there had followed that never to be forgotten garter incident.

She wanted to live chiefly because of her son who was her whole life now. But if she must die she would do so with dignity even as her father had when they had cut off his head outside the walls of Winchester.

Now she could hear the voices of the peasants. They had seen the carriage lying in the mud. They were surrounding it.

She sat tense, waiting for the moment when the curtain should be lifted and she dragged out to die.

Someone shouted: 'It's the Fair Maid of Kent. It's the King's mother. Stuck in the mud.'

There were shouts of raucous laughter.

Someone said: 'You'll need a strong arm to get those wheels out, you fine guards.'

'They look pretty in their uniform but it takes men to do a job of work.'

'Show them, friends. Show them.'

Joan sat still, her heart beating fast. The carriage jerked. A shout went up.

'There we are. You're free of the mud, fellows. There's your fine carriage.'

'Let's look inside,' said one.

' 'Tis the mother of the King.'

'What of that? All are equal now.'

The moment had come. They had freed the carriage but for what purpose? To use it themselves? She had visions of their marching into London with her carriage and her head on a pike.

And Richard . . . if he should see.

'God spare him that,' she prayed.

The curtain was drawn aside. A dirty face with a stubble of beard was thrust in.

She sat very still, her hands folded. She smiled at him with a good show of unconcern.

'Good day to you,' she said. 'I believe I have to thank you for helping to get my carriage back on the road.'

The man was bewildered for a moment. Her beauty, her royal dignity, the splendour of her garments overawed him and temporarily he forgot that all she stood for was the very reason why he and his fellows were in revolt.

The man was pushed aside and another, so like himself that Joan could not have told them apart, was looking in at her.

'Here's a very grand lady,' he said.

She rose then and went to the side of the carriage, and holding back the curtain said: 'I wish to thank you all for your good services to me.'

There was hushed silence. She was aware of the multitude surrounding the coach. She noticed the primitive weapons, the flails and the bill hooks. There were a few pikes. She thought: It is come. Let it be quick. Let me not forget my royalty. Let me die as nobly as my father did.

' 'Tis the Queen Mother herself.'

'Yes,' she answered. 'I have been to pray at the shrine of St. Thomas. I am grateful to you for making it possible for me to continue my journey.'

She saw the savage desire for revenge on some faces but they did nothing. They were waiting for an order from the leader.

The man who had looked into the coach said: 'All men are going to be equal now, lady. Each man has a right to his share of the world's goods. You're no more lady than a serving-wench to be bussed by any as takes the fancy.'

Joan had one of those inspirations which came to her now and then. One had been when she had refused to marry the man who had been chosen for her and let the Black Prince know that she would accept only him. She was cool; some might say a little wanton. But she acted on impulse.

She held out her face to the man who had spoken.

He put his lips against her cheek and kissed her.

A cheer went up. The mood of the peasants had changed. This was the Fair Maid of Kent. They had no quarrel with her. They had no quarrel with the King. He was only a boy. He was only doing as he was told. The real enemies were those such as Simon of Sudbury and John of Gaunt.

'Let us pass,' said Joan, realizing what an impression her gesture had made. It might not last. There would be some in that crowd who were thirsting for her blood. She must get away quickly. Delay could be dangerous.

Oddly enough the crowd fell back. The riders whipped up their horses. The carriage lumbered forward. A cheer went up from the crowd but Joan heard the undercurrent of growling.

But she was away. She had saved her life.

'For the love of God,' she cried, 'get to London with all speed.'

The Queen Mother's party had left the peasants' army some miles behind as it came across London Bridge and into the Tower where the King was at this time.

She burst into the King's apartment and found him in the company of several of his friends including the Earl of Oxford who had become his almost inseparable companion, and his cousin Henry of Bolingbroke who like the King was in his fifteenth year.

'There is no time to lose,' she cried. 'The peasants are marching to London. They are looting and pillaging as they go. Something must be done at once.'

Neither the King nor his friends had any solution to offer and when Joan heard that the Archbishop of Canterbury was at the Tower she sent for him at once.

Simon of Sudbury was a very old man. He was resigned to his fate for he had no doubt what it would be if he fell into the rebels' hands. He was, in their opinion, the arch-villain because he had imprisoned their hero John Ball.

206

They had murdered others; there would be no respite for him.

He came to the King and laid the seal of England on the table. He was resigning the office of Chancellor which he had held in addition to that of Archbishop.

'This is no solution,' cried Joan. 'What shall we do?'

She felt angry with these men who had nothing to offer.

'We shall have to fight them,' said Henry of Bolingbroke. 'We cannot let them come into London.'

A boy not yet fifteen. He had the right spirit, but what use was such a child!

Richard was trying to look like a king.

He said: 'I will speak to them.'

Children! thought Joan. They none of them understand.

A servant was at the door.

'The Lord Mayor asks to see you, my lord.'

Richard said: 'Send him in.'

Joan's spirits rose. Here was a man of action. William Walworth, Lord Mayor of London, who was not going to see his City decimated by a pack of rebels.

'My lord, the peasants are very close,' he said. 'We must take action against them. As soon as my lady's carriage crossed the bridge I had it drawn up and men are now putting a chain across to restrict entry.'

'Thank you, my Lord Mayor,' said Richard and Joan smiled her approval.

'These men are desperate,' said the Mayor. 'They have armed themselves with weapons of a sort. They are danger-ous but we can outwit them.'

Joan was relieved. Here at last was a man of action.

The peasant army had come to rest at Blackheath. Now that they were within a few miles of London some of the more reasonable men—leaders like Wat Tyler and John Ball—could see that destruction and bloodshed were not their ultimate goal. There were some—like the Archbishop Simon of Sudbury, who must be executed—but they wished no harm to the King. They believed that it might be possible to guide him.

'We should give the King an opportunity of listening to our grievances,' said John Ball. 'He would know nothing of them. How could he? He is only a boy. Let us send a messenger to him and ask for a meeting.'

John Ball had that special kind of magnetism which could sway a crowd. He knew and so did Wat Tyler that many of their followers were not men of ideals but thieves and vagabonds looking for easy pickings such as an adventure like this could provide.

But it was not what John Ball wanted. He wanted reforms. He was a man of God, he told them; and he did not want to see fine buildings destroyed. He wanted to preserve them for the people.

They should parley with the King and they had with them a hostage in the person of Sir John Newton. They also held his family. They had pillaged his mansion and he was their prisoner. They would now make use of him. He should go to the King with a proposition that there should be a meeting between the King and the rebel leaders.

So while the army camped at Blackheath, Sir John rode into London to the Tower. As an officer of the royal household there was no delay in admitting him; and he was soon giving the King the message.

There was a cry of protest from the King's advisers, chief of them the Earl of Salisbury and his treasurer, Sir John Hales.

Richard, though, saw in this a chance to prove himself a King. He was not afraid of his people, he said. He had never heard a voice raised against him. And if he could see these people he was sure he could convince them that he wished them well.

The Archbishop shook his head. 'You do not understand, my lord. These people are ruffians. They are intent on destruction.'

'They are my people,' said Richard with dignity.

He felt a sudden exultation. It was the sort of incident he had dreamed of; he believed that with his gentle smile and soft words he could persuade his people that they had the love and good will of their King.

Strangely enough it was his mother who thought that he might be right. She remembered vividly her own encounter with the rebels on the road and how they had cheered her—admittedly a little ironically—as they had allowed her to ride on after themselves freeing her carriage wheels from the mire.

'Let the King go,' she said. 'He will remain in the barge, and if there is any danger he can escape by the river. Do not let him go ashore if there is any possibility of their harming him. But it would be wrong to ignore this request.'

The King said: 'It is my decision, and I have decided to go.'

It was true that he was the King. He had never asserted his authority before. But he was certainly doing so now and since he spoke so authoritatively they must give way.

The barge set out. It was unfortunate that Simon of Sudbury with John Hales were members of the party— although of course their position in the country demanded they should be.

As they were rowed along the river and came in sight of the ragged army a great shout went up. There was the King himself—the beautiful fair-haired boy with the innocent smile. They would have given a cheer for him if they had not seen on either side of him the men they hated more than any, Simon of Sudbury the very Archbishop who had sent John Ball to gaol, and Treasurer Hales, the man who had collected all that money which was at the very root of their troubles.

'Give us Simon,' they chanted. 'We want Simon's head. Give us Simon.'

John Hales said; 'We cannot parley with such men. They are bent on murder.'

As if in answer to him the people began to shout.

'There's Hales. The tax collector. We want his head. We'll have his head.'

'My lord,' said the Archbishop to Richard, 'you see there is no hope of making these people see reason.'

'They will not harm me,' said Richard. 'Put me ashore.'

'My lord, they would be aboard the barge if we went to the shore. They would drag out the Archbishop and murder him. We dare not trust your royal body to them. The Queen Mother would never forgive us.'

Richard wavered. He was uncertain. He would not have been afraid of the mob. He believed they would love him. But they did hate the Archbishop. It would be cruel to hand him to them.

The royal barge turned and went back to the Tower. The shouts of derision from the banks slowly faded away.

But this was the signal. They would march on London now. They would take the City and nothing should prevent them.

William Walworth was an energetic man. He originally came from the north of England but in his youth he had been apprenticed to John Lovekyn, a wealthy merchant who dealt in salted fish and who had been very energetic in promoting trade between England and Flanders. William Walworth had learned a great deal from him; and when Lovekyn became first of all an alderman and then a sheriff and finally Lord Mayor of London, William decided to follow in his footsteps.

London had become his city; the affairs of London were his; he was proving to himself and to others that not only could he compete with his master but excel him.

He had acquired a great deal of property and was one of the richest men in the City and that was saying a good deal. There were rumours about him as there would be about all men who had been as successful as he was. It was true that he owned large areas of land in the district of Southwark on the south side of the Bridge and there were many who said that the activities which went on there should have been investigated. It was also said that William Walworth was not eager for such an investigation for there were those streets where prostitution flourished. It was even said that he had brought women from the Low Countries to inhabit his houses and that because they were fair and fleshy they were a great attraction. In any case there was no doubt that Walworth derived profit from his possession in Southwark.

He was not averse to spending some of his money in the interests of the city of which he was the leading citizen, and now he was determined to defend London against the rebels.

Meanwhile Wat Tyler with John Ball had reached Southwark and found the bridge drawn up. So they could not get into the City. But there was Southwark, and there were those prisons—the Marshalsea, the Clink, the King's Bench and the Compter. They would attack them and release the prisoners which would have the desired effect of adding to their ranks.

But so far the rioters had been led by men of principle. Now it would be a rabble of criminals.

William Walworth considered this. There would be wanton destruction, pillage and murder. But it was sometimes easier to deal with criminals than with men of ideals. There was no doubt that the cause of John Ball which some might have considered worthy, would no longer be called so.

There were traitors within the City walls. The apprentices, ever ready to join any cause which was dedicated to disorder, were already on the banks of the river shouting to the rebels on the other side. Even certain aldermen who were dissatisfied with a great deal in the rule of the country and the heavy taxation to which they had been submitted saw here a chance to reform the laws.

There were many who were ready to lower London Bridge and let the rebels in, and it was not long before they were streaming across it. Meanwhile the Aldgate had been opened and the men of Essex came in to join those of Kent. London was now at the mercy of the rebels.

The army was overseas; the King's uncles were far away; there was none to defend the King but his immediate circle. Fortunately he was in the Tower and that was a fortress which could not easily be stormed.

In any case the rebels had no quarrel with the King; they did not want to harm him. John Ball had the idea that the King might still lead a country which was given over to equality. He would be a figurehead to follow the guidance of his ministers who would all be men of the people. John Ball would be head of the Church. He did not want anarchy to reign.

But he knew that in that ragged army were men who cared little for principles and were bent on gain. They must be kept in hand. Wat Tyler was a good man. He had a righteous cause and he had only been led to rebellion because of the heavy taxes and the insults levied on his family. Wat Tyler was a man who wanted to restore peace and live in it; but to make a world where men of all ranks could retain their dignity.

That did not seem to be asking an impossibility.

That June day was one which would never be forgotten in English history. The great City of London was the scene of pillage and death. The prisons were all broken into and the convicts streamed out to join the rebels. The Priory of Clerkenwell was in flames; the Inns of Court were ransacked and documents were burned and lawyers killed. The rebels had erected a block in Cheapside and there the heads began to fall.

It was with great glee that coming down to the river's edge they saw the great palace of the Savoy.

'John of Gaunt's treasure house!' they cried; and the very name of John of Gaunt added a fresh fury in their hearts.

'To the Savoy!' they cried. 'We'll bring John of Gaunt's castle tumbling about his ears.'

'But by the bones of God that head will not be on his shoulders,' cried another.

They were at the gates of the Savoy. With the trunk of a tree which they used as a battering ram they forced open the doors and burst in.

Such richness made them pause with wonder.

'We are not thieves,' cried Wat Tyler. 'We have not come to steal. We have come to destroy those who would destroy us.'

The Savoy was ablaze. It was going to be the end of John of Gaunt's magnificence. A curse on fate which had deprived them of him. To have marched through the town with his head would have been the greatest of all triumphs.

Wat saw a man pocketing gold ornaments and thrust his sword through his heart. 'So will I deal with all thieves. By God's bones, men, do you not see? We are men with a mission, men with a purpose. Ask John Ball. He is with me in this. We are not here to steal or kill the innocent. We are here to deliver and to win it for us all.'

Fine words but what effect could they have on men who had never before seen such riches, for whom one small trinket could bring as much as they would earn in a lifetime. Moreover they had been to the cellars and there they had refreshed themselves with wine such as they had never tasted before. They who had drunk only the cheapest ale before were bemused by the wine of the rich.

They were maddened by the sight of such wealth; they were intoxicated not only with malmsey wine but with power.

Was this the end? Joan asked herself. Was the mob going to take the crown, the throne?

If only the Black Prince had lived. She could imagine how he would have dealt with these men. But it would never have happened had he lived. He would have seen revolt coming; he would never have allowed the situation to go so far. What will become of us all? she asked herself.

There they were, besieged in the Tower. Her little son who was a King. And there were only one or two brave men with them. She had great faith in Walworth, who was frantic with fury to see his city being destroyed, and he was a strong man, faithful to the King and the restoration of law and order.

But what could they do?

Poor Simon of Sudbury, he had the look of a man who knows his days are numbered. Temporarily he was safe in the Tower but unless the rebels were quickly subdued he had no hope.

The King and his mother, Salisbury, Simon of Sudbury, John Hales and a few others of the King's ministers, conferred together.

Some action had to be taken promptly and there was only one way of dealing with the situation. The rebels must be dispersed before they could be brought to order.

'How disperse them?' asked Joan.

'With promises,' said Walworth.

'What promises?'

'That what they call their wrongs shall be righted, that they shall be freed from their serfdom; that the taxes will be lifted. That is what the rebellion is about.'

'You think they will listen?'

'Men such as Ball and Wat the Tyler will. They are the leaders.'

'Then how shall we convey these promises to them?'

'I can see only one way of doing so,' said Walworth. 'There is only one to whom they will listen. The King must speak to them.'

'I will do it,' cried Richard. 'I will speak to them.'

'My lord, my lord,' said the Earl of Salisbury, 'forgive me but this is a very dangerous situation.'

'I know it well,' retorted Richard haughtily. 'I am not afraid. I am their King. It is for me to speak to them, to send them back to their homes.'

'It is too dangerous,' said Joan.

'My lady, it is a suggestion,' said Walworth. 'I can think of no other. The alternative is that we stay here besieged and how long will it take the besiegers to overrun the Tower?'

'It is a strong fortress.'

'They have broken into the prisons.'

'I *will* go,' said Richard. 'I insist. Have you forgotten I am your King? I will hear no more. I will speak to the rebels myself.'

'My lord,' said Walworth, 'your bravery moves me deeply. You are indeed the true son of your father.'

'I want to show them that I am,' said Richard.

'You understand, my son,' said Joan, 'that they could kill you. One rebel out of hand . . .'

'I know it well,' replied Richard. 'But my father faced death many times and was not deterred.'

There was no doubt that the entire company was deeply moved by this beautiful boy who showed himself to be without fear.

At length it was agreed that a messenger should be sent to Wat Tyler. The King himself was willing to see them. If they would retire to Mile End, a large field where the people gathered on holidays to enjoy open-air sports, the King would meet them there. He would listen to their grievances and would promise to consider them.

The King was excited. He would show them all that he was a boy no longer. The people had always loved him. He had enjoyed riding through this very City and they had always cheered him. It was the same in the country. They loved him. He was grandson of Great Edward, the son of the Black Prince, their King, Richard of Bordeaux as they still sometimes affectionately called him.

They would love him all the more when he promised to give them what they asked.

He said he wanted to go to his apartments. He wanted to prepare himself. He was going to pray that his mission should succeed.

When he had gone, the Queen Mother said: 'There is only one thing which will send them home and that is if he promises to give them what they want.'

'That is what the King must do,' said William Walworth.

'And how can he? Give them their freedom! Who will

215

till the fields? Who will do the menial work of the country? What must we do? Give over our manors to them!'

William Walworth faced them all smiling. He was no nobleman but he was more shrewd than any of them.

'These promises can never be carried out,' he said. 'They are quite impossible.'

'But the King is going to give them that promise.'

'He must. Indeed he must. It is the only way to bring an end to this rebellion. But remember these are only peasants, villeins. What are promises made to them?'

'I like it not,' said Joan.

'My lady, it is a matter of liking it, or an end to all that we have known in the past. It is goodbye to the wealth which men such as I have earned and which none of these rioters would have known how to earn. It is the end of your inheritance. It would doubtless be the end of your lives. This is the only way.'

'The King will speak in good faith.'

'That must be so. He is too young, too innocent, to understand. He must play his part well and he will only do so if he believes in what he is saying.'

There was a deep silence.

'My lords,' went on Walworth, addressing the Archbishop and the Treasurer, 'you must make your escape while the King is at Mile End. It is your only chance. If you can slip down the river you may be able to find a ship to take you out of the country. Whatever we are able to achieve I fear they are going to demand your lives.'

Simon of Sudbury and John Hales nodded gravely. They knew that Walworth was speaking the truth.

It was night. The King had climbed to the topmost turret that he might look down on the City.

He could see the flares, and the people massed on the banks of the river. He could hear their roistering. Many of them were drunk on the wine from the cellars of his uncle's palace of the Savoy.

A ragged army they were indeed. All the scum of the country, some of them men who had been in prison with no hope of release until the mob came—desperate men, seeking blood and revenge.

These were the men whom he would face tomorrow at Mile End. He thought what he would say to them.

'I am your King . . .'

He would not be afraid. The only thing he feared was fear. They could kill him if they would but he must not show fear. He wanted them to say: He is the true son of his father.

He looked away from that tattered army to the dark sky.

'Fathers,' he said. 'My heavenly and earthly fathers, both watch over me this coming day. Let me conduct myself like a King.'

Early on Friday morning the King was up and ready. From the turret he looked out on the rebels and could see that although some of them were making their way to Mile End others remained.

He sent a message to them, telling them that all must go to Mile End for he was about to set out to meet them there.

Then he went down and summoned the Archbishop and John Hales to him.

'My friends,' he said, 'you must take this opportunity to get away while I am at Mile End. I command you to do this.'

The Archbishop embraced him and wept because of his youth and innocence and his belief that he could with a few words put everything right.

'We shall attempt to do so, my lord,' said John Hales.

'Go, my good friends. I trust we shall meet again.'

The Archbishop murmured: 'Methinks it will not be until we meet in Heaven.'

Richard rode out. He was exultant. He felt brave and noble. There were thousands of rebels whom he had to face and he was just one boy with a carefully selected band of nobles, those who had not incurred the wrath of the people and who would be unknown to them. Sir Aubrey de Vere, the uncle of his greatest friend Robert, had volunteered for the dangerous post of sword-bearer.

And so they set out for Mile End.

There were gathered some sixty thousand of the peasant army, the head of whom were Wat the Tyler and John Ball.

Richard rode right into the midst of them, his handsome face smiling, his voice low and musical.

'My good people,' he addressed them, 'I am your King, and your lord. What is it you want? What do you wish to say to me?'

Wat Tyler answered him. 'We want freedom for ourselves, our heirs and our land. We want no longer to be called slaves and held in bondage.'

'Your wish is granted,' replied the King. 'Now will you return to your homes and the place from whence you came?'

'Ah, my lord, we want surety for what you've said. We want it signed and sealed that you will keep your word.'

'Then leave behind two or three men from each village and they shall have letters sealed with my seal, showing that the demands you have made have been granted. And in order that you may be more satisfied I will command that my banners shall be sent to every stewardship, castle-wick and corporation. You, my good people of Kent, shall have one of my banners and you also men of Essex, Sussex, Bedford, Suffolk, Cambridge, Stafford and Lincoln. I pardon you for what you have hitherto done. But you must follow my banners and return to your homes on the terms I have mentioned. Will you do this, my friends?'

'My lord, we will.'

'Then God bless you all.'

'God save the King!' the shout went up.

The King's courage had won the day at Mile End.

But all the ragged army had not gone to Mile End. There were some who had no interest in coming to terms.

What they wanted was loot. They had seen riches in London such as they had never dreamed of. If there was law and order what would become of them? The robbery and murder which they had committed would be brought against them. No. They must take what they could while they could; and there were no pickings at Mile End.

Moreover there were many who had a score to settle.

They knew that the Archbishop of Canterbury was in the Tower and with him the Lord Treasurer, John Hales, whom they blamed for imposing the hated poll tax.

They were not going to return to their homes until those men had paid the penalty which they had decided was their just reward.

The King was no longer in the Tower. They had had a respect for the King and had made no attempt to storm the Tower while he was there. But now he was at Mile End; and they were going to get the Archbishop.

The Archbishop knew that his end was near. That morning he had celebrated Mass before the King and he determined to remain in the chapel and await his fate.

He was prepared for death. He could feel it close. He knew they would never let him go.

They were not long in coming.

He knew they had broken into the Tower for he could hear the shouts and screaming coming closer and closer. They would soon discover where he was.

He was right. They were at the door of the chapel.

As they rushed, a man shouted: 'Where is the traitor to the kingdom, where is the spoiler of the commons?'

The Archbishop went forward to meet them.

'You have come to the right place, my sons,' he said. 'Here am I, the Archbishop, but I am neither a traitor nor a spoiler.'

'We have not come to bandy words,' said one of them and he gave the Archbishop a blow which knocked him down.

They seized him. They dragged him into the street. They took him to Tower Hill where a vast crowd had gathered. There they had erected a block of execution.

He tried to reason with them. 'You should not murder me, my friends. If you do so England will incur an interdict.'

'His head. His head,' chanted the crowd.

They pushed one man forward and thrust the axe into his hands.

The Archbishop saw that the man's hand trembled.

'So my son, you will do this to me?' he said.

'I must, my lord,' murmured the man.

'Tell me your name that I may know my executioner.'

'It is John Starling of Essex, my lord.'

'My son, you are more afraid than I. Have no fear. I grant you absolution for this sin, as far as I am able.'

He knelt down and laid his head upon the block, his lips moving in prayer as he did so.

John Starling raised his axe. His hands were shaking and there were eight blows before the Archbishop's head was severed from his body.

Riding back from Mile End Richard saw the heads of his Archbishop and his Treasurer being carried on poles before the mob.

The rebels had stormed the Tower while their leaders were at Mile End. Their first target was the Archbishop and the Treasurer and having despatched them for execution they turned to others.

They had found the Queen Mother among her women. These men were not of the same mood as those whom she had met on the road from Rochester. These men had one object in view—robbery, destruction, and murder if the mood took them.

And here was the Queen Mother—one of the privileged, of royal connection, and mother of the King. One man snatched at the brooch she was wearing and another tried to take the rings from her fingers.

Joan, who had been in a state of high tension since she had seen Richard set out for Mile End, could endure no more. She fell fainting into the arms of her women.

Her life was in imminent danger but one of the men

said: 'Leave her alone. She's only a woman. She's done nothing. Let her go. There are others to concern ourselves with.'

For a moment there was hesitation and then snatching the jewels she was wearing her assailants turned away.

'We must get out of the Tower,' said one of the women. 'Let us get down to the barges. Perhaps we can get away to the Wardrobe.'

Joan opened her eyes and realizing what was happening asked where the mob was. She was told that they had left this part of the Tower and it seemed that the women might be allowed to leave.

'The King will come back here . . .' began Joan.

'He will soon know, my lady, that we have gone. Come, they may change their minds.'

It was surprising how easily they could escape. No one attempted to stop them and in a short time they were in the barge on their way to the royal office which was known as the Wardrobe and which was in Carter Lane close to Baynard's Castle.

Meanwhile Henry of Bolingbroke had thought his last moment had come. He had heard the shouts against his father and he knew that the Savoy Palace was in ruins. He had heard them cursing because John of Gaunt was not in London. If he had been there they would have taken him as they had the Archbishop. He could hear the shouting of the mob and the sound of battering rams and the crunching explosions as heavy doors gave way.

It could not be long now, he knew.

Then his heart began to beat wildly. There was someone coming towards the room. He stood up very straight, waiting. He would give a good account of himself.

A man was standing in the doorway. He was dressed as a peasant and Henry believed he had come to kill him.

'My lord,' he stammered, 'you are in acute danger.'

'Who are you?'

'John Ferrours of Southwark, my lord. I serve your noble father. My lord, when they know whose son you are you will have little chance.'

'I am ready for them.'

'You will have little chance against this mob. I have come to get you to safety.'

'How so?'

'There is no time for talk. Put this cloak round your shoulders . . . Take this.' He thrust a bill hook into Henry's hand. 'We are going to run through the crowds. We must look as they do. Shout as they do. It is the only way. I shall get you down to the river. There are barges there . . . or we may have to make our way through the City. Do as I say. We may be able to deceive them.'

'I am ready,' said Henry.

He followed his saviour down the spiral staircase. They came into a courtyard where several peasants were assembled. John Ferrours joined them and shouted with them. 'No more serfdom,' he cried; and Henry joined in.

They left the Tower and were in the streets.

'All well so far,' said John Ferrours. 'But keep it up. Run. It looks as though we are bent on some mischief. Shout if anyone looks suspicious. Make sure they believe we belong to them.'

Henry was exhilarated by the adventure. It was something he would remember for the rest of his life. He had come near to death he knew and it would have been certain if he had waited in that room in the Tower. And he owed all this to this stranger, John Ferrours of Southwark.

He wanted to tell him of his gratitude. But they were still in danger.

They came along Carter Street to the Wardrobe. It was the obvious refuge.

'I shall leave you here, my lord,' said John Ferrours. 'The Queen Mother and some others who have managed to escape are here. Keep the cloak. You may need it. And remember . . . if there is danger again, the safest way is to mingle with them.'

They were let into the Wardrobe. The Queen Mother was almost hysterical with delight to see him, but she was in a state of fearful anxiety about Richard.

Henry told John Ferrours that he would never forget. He would always remember him as the man who had saved his life.

Riding back from Mile End Richard was diverted to the Wardrobe as the Tower was in the hands of the rebels. He was shocked and sickened to see the heads of the Archbishop and the Treasurer and an anger against the rebels surged up in him.

This was quickly replaced by a terrible anxiety. His mother whom he loved best in the world had been in danger. Where was she now? Had she reached the Wardrobe in safety?

'I must see if my mother is safe,' he said, forgetting kingship and the triumph he had experienced at Mile End in the fear that his mother might have suffered the fate of the Archbishop.

When he saw her white-faced, her hair in disorder, the jewels torn from her gown, he ran into her arms and for a moment they were both submerged by the intensity of their relief and happiness that the other was safe.

In the Wardrobe Richard heard what had happened. They were all overcome with depression except the irrepressible William Walworth.

'Some of the rebels have returned to their homes,' he said. 'At least we have not so many to deal with.'

There was a further conference and it was William Walworth who made them realize that they must take further action.

News had come in that Richard Imworth, Warden of the Marshalsea, who had fled to the Abbey for sanctuary when the prison had been pillaged, had been discovered there. The rebels had no respect for sanctity and Richard Imworth had been dragged from the shrine of Edward the Confessor to execution in Cheapside.

'Wat Tyler and his rebels still remain,' said Walworth. 'My lords, there must be another meeting between them and the King. Let it take place this time at Smithfield.

They must be persuaded to disband. They are not as strong as they were. After the meeting in Mile End many of them have gone back. But we still have this band of robbers, gaol breakers, men who know or care nothing for their rights except that it be the right to rob and murder.'

'Another meeting!' gasped the Queen Mother, her eyes on her son.

'I will meet them again. I know how to deal with them,' said Richard confidently.

He had changed. The adventure at Mile End had endowed him with new qualities of Kingship. Everyone in the chamber knew that he had stepped out of his boyhood and from now on he would attempt to take command.

'There is one precaution we should take,' said Walworth. 'Every man of us should wear a shirt of mail beneath his clothes.'

They were all in agreement that this should be so.

So with some sixty attendants, at the head of them William Walworth, the King rode out for that fateful meeting at Smithfield.

All that happened since that day when he had killed the tax collector could not fail to have its effect on Wat the Tyler. From a man of no importance living his life in the little town of Dartford tyling roofs for a living and going hither and thither at the command of those who employed him, he had become a leader. This army of thousands obeyed him. He was at their head. He had been a moderately modest man before; now he saw himself grown in stature.

He was as important as the King himself. More so, for the King would have to do what he, Wat the once humble tyler, told him.

It was inevitable that a little arrogance should creep into his attitude. He was a natural orator, something of which he had hitherto been unaware. For a man of no education suddenly to find himself so elevated had unbalanced him. Soon he would be Lord Tyler. John Ball should be his

Archbishop of Canterbury. As for the King he might remain as a figurehead. The boy could be guided.

It was invigorating to see how fearful the rich and powerful could be when confronted by an army even though it lacked conventional weapons. The power of the mob was great and Tyler was at its head.

It was with a lifting of spirits that he waited for the arrival of the King.

And there he was, the tall slender figure with the golden hair glistening in the sun. The King with his retinue had drawn up, with their backs to the Church of St. Bartholomew the Great.

'My Lord Mayor,' said Richard to Walworth, 'I pray you ride over to them and tell Wat Tyler I would speak with him.'

Wat immediately complied. He was smiling complacently to himself. Wat the Tyler, in conference with the King! It was like something he might have dreamed in past. Then it would have seemed wildly impossible. Not so now, Wat Tyler was on equal terms with the King.

Before he left his men, he turned to them and said: 'Do not stir from this spot until I give you a sign to do so.' He raised his hand. 'When I do this, come forward. Kill everyone but the King. Then we will put him at our head and ride through England. Thus we shall have the support of everyone when the King is our leader. He will obey us for he is young and we shall guide him.'

Then Wat spurred his horse and rode over to the King. He behaved towards Richard as though he were one of the ragged army and those about Richard were filled with resentment by the manner of this village tyler in the presence of their sovereign. How dare he behave towards the King as though he were more familiar with them than they were.

'King,' said Wat, 'do you see all those men there?'

Richard held his head high, sharing the resentment of his followers for this man's crude manners.

'I could scarcely fail to,' he replied. 'Why do you ask?'

225

'Because they are under my command and have sworn to obey me.'

'Why do they not return to their homes?' said Richard. 'That is what I wish them to do.'

'I have no intention of letting them return home,' retorted Wat. 'Letters promising our freedom were to have been given us. Where are those letters? Every demand I have made must first be satisfied.'

'It has been ordered that you have these letters,' said Richard coolly. 'Return to your companions. Bid them depart. Be peaceable and careful of yourselves for it is my determination that you shall have all I promised you.'

One of the squires beside the King had moved slightly forward and drawn his sword.

Wat's eyes were on him. 'What is in your mind?' he cried. 'Give me your sword.'

'That I will not do,' replied the squire. 'This is the King's sword and you are not worthy to touch it. You are a serf, a tyler of roofs and if we were alone you would not have dared address me as you have.'

Wat, sure of his power, very much aware of his army who at the lifting of his hand would have surged forward, cried out in rage: 'By my troth, I will not eat this day until I have had your head.'

This was too much for the Mayor. He brought his horse forward and cried: 'How dare you behave thus in the presence of your King, you scoundrel. You are impudent before your betters.'

'He is so,' said the King.

Wat was staring at the Mayor demanding: 'What affair is it of yours? What have I done to you?'

'It does not become such a stinking rascal as you are to use such language in the presence of our King.'

Walworth then drew his sword and struck Wat such a blow that he fell from his horse. Wat tried to rise but several of the King's squires had surrounded him.

At first the peasants could not see what was happening. Some even thought for a moment that the King was knighting Wat Tyler, which would not have surprised them for

226

they had begun to share Wat's own opinion of himself; and although they were against riches and titles for the nobility they would not be averse to accepting them for themselves.

But there was no doubt now. Wat was dying. Their leader was taken from them; he had gone to parley with the King and they had killed him.

'They have killed our leader!' someone shouted. 'Come let us slay the lot of them.'

In that moment Richard was inspired. It was then that he performed the most spectacular act of his life. He might have reasoned that there was little risk, for to stay where he was would be almost certain death, but he did not pause to reason. He was young; he was inexperienced in the ways of men. All he knew was that some impulse moved him.

He turned his head and cried: 'I command you all to stay where you are. Not one of you shall follow me. That is an order.'

Then he rode forward.

The ragged army was waiting to attack, but the sight of this slender and most handsome boy riding towards them, godlike, unafraid, had stunned them into silence and inaction.

He pulled up before them. He smiled at them. He cried in his rather high-pitched voice: 'My liege men, what are you about? Will you kill your King? Heed you not the death of a traitor. I will be your leader. Come follow me to the fields and what you ask you shall have.'

He sat there on his horse smiling at them. He charmed them; they could not fail to be moved by his youth and courage and beauty.

'Come,' said Richard. He turned his horse and moved away towards the fields of Clerkenwell.

They followed him.

Seeing what was happening William Walworth rode in all haste back to the City where several of the wealthy merchants had been mustering supporters. Sir Robert

Knolles, a soldier of some experience, had kept men at arms guarding his own mansion and he brought these out now to join those who would stand against the rebels. Meanwhile supporters had come in from the surrounding towns and there was a considerable force to march against the mob.

Thus while the King was leading them out of Smithfield the loyal citizens and the men at arms were riding out to attack the rebels.

Wat Tyler's body had been taken to the market place, his head cut off and stuck on a lance which Walworth carried to the scene of the battle.

To see their leader's head thus displayed robbed the ragged army of their desire to fight. Some tried to escape, some fell on their knees and begged for mercy.

There were those who would have slain them all but Richard did not wish this. He was still living in the glory of the role he had chosen for himself. Mercy suited that role. Moreover, said the wise Walworth, we shall need men to till the fields and tyle our roofs. They should be sent back to their homes, and made to realize that they would be unwise to attempt such revolt again.

So the rebels went back to their villages. And on that very day William Walworth was knighted, Archbishop Simon's head was removed from London Bridge and in its place was set up that of Wat Tyler.

That was not entirely the end. Forces were gathered together for it must be shown that it was folly to attempt to overthrow the old order. Richard was still living in the glory of that moment when he had ridden forward alone and faced the rebels. They had accepted him. He had led them away . . . to defeat. Had they ridden forward; had they killed the King and his supporters it would have been a different story. But it was the young King, a boy of fourteen, who acting on sudden impulse had made history on that day.

Now of course he saw that the men about him were

right. What the peasants had asked for was impossible. He had been horrified by the close proximity of Wat Tyler, a man who had no grace, who did not know how to behave in the presence of his King. Richard wanted no more contact with such as Wat Tyler.

Wat was dead. His head on the bridge was evidence of that and that was where it should remain, a warning to all of the fate of rebels.

But there must be more than the head of a traitor to warn them.

Accompanied by a small force and his Chief Justice, Sir Robert Resilian, Richard set out on a tour of the country and the first place to be visited was Essex, for the men of Essex had been the first to revolt.

It would only be the leaders who would be punished as an example. It had been seen through the Black Death what disaster could be produced by the loss of lives. Thousands had been involved in the peasants' revolt but they could not all be punished. So it was to be the leaders.

When the King arrived in Essex many of the people gathered about him and shouted that they had been promised freedom. Had not he himself promised their leaders?

But those leaders were no more and those that remained would soon go the way of the others when justice caught up with them.

The King replied cynically: 'Rustics you have been and are and in bondage you shall remain.'

It was betrayal. This godlike boy by his charm, beauty and courage, his seeming innocence and care for them, had deceived them. They would never trust him again. He was one of the masters. He had acted a part. Desolation came to the peasants. They should have known there was no way of escape.

It was some time before they found John Ball. He had known that he would most certainly be one of the victims. Wat had led them; but it was John Ball's words which had inspired them. It was John Ball who had rung the bell summoning them from all over the country to join the forces of freedom.

John Ball could not escape.

He had left Smithfield after the fall of Wat and had travelled as far as Coventry; but it was not possible for a man so well known as he was to remain hidden. He was betrayed and taken when he was hiding in a ruined castle.

They brought him to St. Albans where the Court was sitting and there he was quickly sentenced to the traitor's death.

Richard himself witnessed the execution of John Ball which was that most cruel of all—hung, drawn and quartered, and the four quarters of his body were then sent to be exhibited in towns where the rebels had been most strong.

A grim warning to all who might think it was possible to change the old order.

A QUEEN FROM BOHEMIA

RICHARD WAS NEARLY fifteen and there had been much talk for some time of his marriage. A King could not start too soon to get an heir; and there seemed no reason why Richard should not follow the example of his grandfather and beget a son or two.

It should not be difficult for the King of England to find a bride for, although England's position at this time was scarcely prosperous, his bride would be a Queen and it seemed likely that with a young and energetic King much of what had been lost might be regained.

John of Gaunt had returned from Scotland to find his palace in ruins; but he could congratulate himself and his nephew on the lucky escape they had all had. John saw that the last months had been some of the most difficult through which the country had ever passed; and he shuddered to think what could so easily have happened.

Richard had behaved with promptitude and bravery. He had won the admiration of many; but those of his subjects who remembered the promises he had made both at Mile End and Smithfield would have had an ideal shattered. Richard would never be really popular again.

John of Gaunt had two daughters by Blanche of Lancaster. He had been thinking for some time that it would be admirable for his nephew to marry one of them. When he put forward the suggestion it was frowned on by the Parliament and all the King's advisers. They had an excellent excuse. The relationship was too close. The pair would be first cousins. There would never be a dispensation for such a close connection.

No, the King must look elsewhere for a bride.

Some time ago an alliance with the daughter of Charles of France had been suggested but all thought of such a marriage was abandoned when there was trouble in Papal quarters following the outbreak of the Great Schism. There were two rival Popes, one holding court in Avignon, the other in Rome, each hurling accusations against the other, with threats of excommunication, and Europe was divided, France heading those who supported Clement, and England declaring for Urban.

When Wenceslaus of Bohemia denied his support to Clement this brought about a rift between his country and France with whom he had previously been on very cordial terms. Richard's ministers then saw an advantage in forming an alliance with the enemies of the King of France. Moreover, before the disagreement Charles had been seeking a match for his son with Bohemia, for Wenceslaus had a marriageable sister.

Urban, in exchange for English support, offered to speak in favour of Richard with Wenceslaus, and the uncle of the prospective bride. Primislaus, Duke of Saxony, came to England ostensibly to discuss the union but in fact to see what kind of country his niece would be marrying into.

He returned to Prague not displeased by what he saw and Richard then decided to send Sir Simon Burley to Prague so that arrangements for the marriage could go ahead; and Wenceslaus sent the Duke of Saxony back to England for the same purpose.

There was mourning in the palace at Prague because the King and Emperor Charles had that day died. He had been a great ruler if not a popular one and at such times there was bound to be change. The new ruler was Wenceslaus, Charles's son who was young and untried, but he had been brought up to know that he would one day rule. However there were changes in the air and the country's old allies, the French, were deeply involved in them.

Anne, the young sister of Wenceslaus, wondered what differences there would be. She was only fourteen years old but she had been well educated and being of bright intelligence she was not content to devote herself to needlework, distilling herbs and such feminine pursuits. Anne liked to know what was happening in the world and as she had said to her women, it could well concern her for she was informed enough to know that when the time came she would be used as a bargaining counter in a match to seal some alliance.

'It is certain to be the son of the King of France,' she often said. 'My father told me that the King of France had put out feelers for a match.'

Well, of course, it was a good proposition. She was not so foolish as to think she would be allowed to stay in her own country all her life, and she was calmly prepared.

She was by no means a beauty; but she had the freshness of youth and her long golden hair was attractive. The horned head-dress which was so fashionable in Bohemia suited her. The width of it with the horns sticking out at either side helped to widen her high forehead which was rather narrow; and her bright expression of interest in everything around her gave a vitality to her face which made up for the lack of conventional good looks.

She knew well that her father was not loved by the Germans and that he had been elected as their Emperor only because no one else was available. But it was quickly realized that he was a good and energetic ruler and as he had always made a point of being on excellent terms with the Papacy he had induced Innocent VI to bestow the Golden Bull which had settled the constitution of the Roman Germanic Empire for as long as it should exist, which was a great and beneficial achievement.

Her grandfather had been blind. He had died on the field at Crécy—fighting on the side of the French of course. The French had always been their allies and that was why it seemed almost certain to Anne that she would be given in marriage to the son of the King of that country.

All through her childhood Anne had heard stories of her grandfather—the epitome of chivalry . . . the great knight, who although blind had still insisted on going into battle led by his squires one on either side of him. He had fought gallantly at Crécy for his brother-in-law Philip of Valois against the enemy, the English who were trying to usurp the throne of France, and when he had died there he had been honoured by the Black Prince who had attached his ostrich plumes to his helmet and declared they were the greatest trophy of the day.

And then her father had come to the throne and now it was his turn to die.

Nothing seemed stable except friendship with France and loyalty to the Pope.

She was growing up. Fourteen was not very old—but neither was it young and princesses were not allowed to stay long unmarried.

Since her father's death, her mother, who had been her father's fourth wife, often talked to her seeming to forget as many did the youth of her daughter. Anne was pleased that this should be so. She hated to be treated as a child and she was as able to understand the course of State affairs as well as many older people.

So with her mother she had often discussed the Court of France, as it had seemed clear to them both in those days that would be her final destination.

But it seemed there was nothing in life which could be relied on. It was her mother who first told her of the growing strife in Papal circles. This was the beginning of a great schism. There were two Popes—one had now moved to Avignon and one was in Rome. Clement had been set up by the French but the King of Bohemia supported Urban.

It was impossible to have two Popes. It seemed that the French wanted a Pope who would work for them. This was unthinkable.

'It seems,' said Anne gravely, 'that we shall no longer

be friends with the French. An issue such as this must certainly make differences between us.'

'You are right, my daughter,' said the mother.

They looked at each other steadily assessing what it would mean.

It was not long before it became clear.

Wenceslaus sent for his sister.

'You know of this trouble concerning the Pope,' he said. 'Our old allies are against us, and any alliance with them would now be out of the question.'

'I understand that,' said Anne.

'We must stand beside our allies. Germany and Flanders are firmly with us. I am very anxious that England should be also.'

Anne had heard a little about England. The ageing King had recently died, rather sadly it seemed for he had been one of the great heroes of the age. His fame had spread far and wide; but then he had grown old and senile, some said. He had taken a low woman and set her up in such a manner as to lose the respect of all those around him. His son, the Black Prince, who had taken her grandfather's plumes at Crécy and done him honour there, and who was at that time considered the most chivalrous knight in the world, was dead. There was a new King, the grandson of Edward. He was young—a year younger than she herself. Yes, she knew something of England.

It was clear to Anne what was coming. For what other reason should her brother need to tell *her* he was seeking English friendship.

'The young King is very handsome. He is near your age. I think the English would welcome a match.'

Anne lowered her head.

Such was the fate of princesses.

An embassy had arrived in Prague. It was led by Sir Simon Burley and Sir Thomas Holland, and the purpose of this embassy was to ask for the hand of the Princess Anne for the King of England.

Anne immediately liked Sir Simon. There was something honest about him and she found the way he spoke of the King very endearing. Of the younger man who was the King's half-brother she was not so sure. He was amusing; he had charm; he was good looking, but there was a certain superficiality about him which, young as she was, she sensed.

Their main business, of course, was with her mother and her brother but they did spend a little time with her for they realized that she was a girl of quick intelligence, that her family were aware of this and that although it was expedient that the marriage should take place, at the same time the girl's preferences might have to be taken into consideration.

Her mother spoke to her about the negotiations and it was clear to Anne that she was a little anxious.

'We know so little of this country,' she said. 'It is so far away. It is true that when the old King lived it was of great account, but during the last years of his reign and the coming of the new King it has lost much of its importance.'

'Sir Simon talks much of the King. He is very young— younger than I; but he is very handsome—so says Simon Burley.'

'My dear daughter, Sir Simon wishes to go back to his masters with our agreement to the match. They are very eager for it.'

'Why are they eager?'

'That is what I should like to know. It can only be because they need us as allies.'

'And do we need them?'

'Everything has changed now we have this rift with the French. But I shall not allow you to go to England if your uncle does not bring back good reports of the place. Yes, my child, your uncle is already on his way to England.'

Anne said: 'What good care you take of me!'

'My child you are my daughter; and your marriage is of importance to the country. So much is made of male offspring, but our daughters are very often the ones who strengthen our alliances. But not for anything would I allow you to be unhappy. The King is young—as you say, younger than you. You are not without good sense. I doubt not that as he is young and so are you you could grow up together. Youth is often a good foundation for marriage.'

They embraced suddenly. They were neither of them inclined to show their emotions but on this occasion the Empress wanted Anne to know that she had her personal welfare at heart and Anne wished to imply that she realized this.

While they awaited the return from England of her great uncle, she grew to know Sir Simon and Sir Thomas Holland and talked to them often about England and her prospective husband.

'The King of England is fond of his books,' Simon told her. 'He likes music. He likes fine clothes. Yes, he is very fond of such materials and jewelled ornaments, but they must be tasteful. I was appointed his tutor by his father and I was always delighted by his love of learning.'

Anne liked what she heard of him. She would be able to talk to him, to share common interests. She was glad her prospective husband was interested in literature and music. So many kings thought of nothing but extending their power and consequently war was their main preoccupation.

From his half-brother she learned another side of his character.

'He is very good looking,' Thomas Holland told us. 'Quite the most handsome of the family. My half-brother Edward, the one who died, was not nearly so good looking as Richard. He is tall and very fair. He has what they call in England the Plantagenet look—which is fair hair and blue eyes and fair skin. Richard is a little darker than some of them. His hair is thick and yellow . . . but darkish yellow. He is very pale but when he flushes—which is often—he is pink and white. The people love him because he is young and so handsome and knows how to smile at them. He is not fond of the joust and does not indulge in it. It's strange because his father was a great jouster, so was his grandfather. His father was my stepfather you know, so I know Richard as well as most people do. He was always my mother's favourite.'

'Were you envious of him?' asked Anne.

'No. I was too old for envy. You see I was the outcome of my mother's first marriage. After my father died she became the wife of the Black Prince so it was natural that the sons she had by him were more important than we were. We accepted it. Besides we were not the sort to want the cosseting that went to the heir of the throne.'

'Is Richard serious? He is very young for such a position.'

'He is serious. Determined to be a good King. But you know how it is; he is hemmed in with advisers. It won't always be so. He's growing up. Why, he's going to have a wife.'

Thomas Holland was inclined to be indiscreet.

'His uncle, John of Gaunt, who must be the most unpopular man in England, would like to see Richard married to his daughter.'

'And Richard does not want to marry her?'

'The suggestion cannot be taken seriously. The relationship is too close. But more than that, the people would be against it . . . simply because she is John of Gaunt's daughter.'

'Is he so unpopular?'

'I think the people imagined at one time that he was scheming to take the crown. The Black Prince was ailing, so was the King . . . and John of Gaunt was very ambitious.'

'And was he really trying to take the throne from Richard?'

Thomas Holland lifted his shoulders and smiled at Anne.

'When you come to England, you will judge him for yourself. The people hate him as much as they love Richard. Richard is the son of the Black Prince and they idolize him . . . particularly now he is dead. He was the favourite of all . . . the eldest son, battle honours and all the rest.'

'I know he was at the battle of Crécy where my grandfather was killed.'

'Ah, he was on the wrong side then. He should have

been with us. But now of course your country will be with ours. Now that Richard is going to have a wife.'

Perhaps Richard was going to have a wife. But was he going to have Anne of Bohemia? Everything would depend on what reports were brought back from England.

When the Duke of Saxony returned to Bohemia, he brought rich gifts for those who served the Princess. He had found Richard a very suitable husband for his niece; and the English had fêted him and made him welcome. He had visited some of their towns; he had admired their ships; he had hunted in their forests. He believed that the marriage would be advantageous to Bohemia and what was of utmost importance the English were prepared to accept Anne without a dowry.

The Empress was a little nonplussed. They must want the marriage very much, she thought.

Yes, indeed they wanted the marriage. They were looking for the Emperor's help in their fight against the French.

Well then arrangements should go ahead. Anne should make her preparations to leave for England.

Now that the time had come she suffered qualms of apprehension. She was going to leave her mother and all her family to go among strangers. Even though she had known always that that would be her eventual fate, now that it loomed right before her it must fill her with misgivings.

Sir Simon and Sir Thomas said good-bye and the embassy returned to England.

Now she must prepare herself in earnest. It would be so strange to live in a new country. She talked of it continuously with her three sisters, Katherine, Elizabeth and Margaretha. She wondered whether there would be poets and musicians at Court. She had always enjoyed visiting Uncle Wenzel, the Duke of Brabant, for he wrote poetry himself and poets were always welcome at his Court. He was patron of the arts and consequently his Court was lively with interest for her.

Would it be like that in England, she wondered.

Katherine said that Sir Simon Burley had told them that Richard was fond of poetry, so that it surely would be.

Yes, it would be. She would persuade him to encourage the poets. They would have singing and dancing at the Court. She would make it as much like her uncle Wenzel's Court as possible. Then she would not miss her home. She would not sigh for her father's palace of Hradschin. England would be her home.

One day there were messengers at the Hradschin Palace. They had come with all speed from England, and the news they brought was disquieting.

All over England the peasants were in revolt. They were on the march and their object was to change the old system of rule. They wanted to be the masters, or at least they wanted all men to be equal. And they were succeeding. This would be the end of England as it had been known since the days of the Conqueror. It would be no place for the daughter of the Holy Roman Emperor.

The Empress shook her head emphatically.

'We will forget all about the agreement we have made with England,' she said.

But it was not long before more messengers arrived.

The revolt had been suppressed by the courage and statesmanship of the young King. All was well. The peasants had been dispersed and their ringleaders had been executed.

All was well in England reigned over by a King who was patiently awaiting the arrival of his bride.

Anne set out from Prague with the Duke and Duchess of Saxony and a retinue suitable for one of her rank.

She had said good-bye to her mother and sisters. Her brother Wenceslaus was in Brussels where he was waiting to receive her as she passed through on her way to the coast.

There were great celebrations and rejoicing in Brussels and Wencelaus talked with her frequently, always stressing the need to remember that her country looked to her to remember it. She would have the confidence of the King; she must make sure that her new country continued to be the friend of her native land.

While the party was being entertained in Brussels news was brought to the Court there of the anger of the King of France. He was not going to allow his one-time ally to marry their Princess to his enemy. They had to get to England, had they not? Had they forgotten that to do so they had to cross a perilous sea? No, he was not referring only to the weather; there were ships on those seas—his ships and they were stopping all vessels and were determined to prevent the Princess Anne reaching her bridegroom.

After much consultation her uncle, the Duke of Brabant, sent an embassy to the King of France to remonstrate with him, and to the surprise of everyone the King of France was persuaded to relent. Not, he was anxious to point out, for love of the King of England. He cared nothing that he should be without his bride. In fact it amused him that he should. But for the sake of his beloved cousin Anne, he would call in those ships which had been filled by fierce Norman sailors, and she should have safe passage to England.

It was with great relief that the party set out for the coast.

At Gravelines she met more of the noblemen of her new country for the Earls of Salisbury and Devonshire were waiting there with a guard of five hundred all carrying spears to conduct her to Calais.

It was not the best time of the year to travel, being December, and it was small wonder that it was necessary to wait for a favourable wind.

At length the sea was calm enough for them to set sail and they did so. The crossing was made in a day, which was considered a sign of divine providence, but oddly enough no sooner had Anne arrived on land than a violent wind arose. The sea immediately began to writhe in such a strange manner that it was as if some gigantic sea serpent might be lashing it with its tail.

All those who saw it declared they had never witnessed anything to compare with it. It was unlike a storm. The sea was like a cauldron; the wind was like a hurricane. Those on shore watched with horror and amazement while the ships which had carried the party across the Channel were tossed from side to side, overturned and in a short time torn apart as though they had been made of the flimsiest material.

Anne's own ship was rent into pieces and others of the fleet shared its fate.

It was the most extraordinary phenomenon and many of those who beheld it fell on their knees and prayed to God to set aside His anger.

The storm—or whatever it had been—stopped abruptly. The wind had gone; the seething waters had subsided; only the flotsam of broken vessels floating on the sea and lying on the beaches was a proof of what had happened.

There was a deep silence among the watchers. What had it meant? That it was a divine intimation no one doubted.

Was it anger at the proposed marriage? Some saw it as such, which would mean an ill omen for the King and his bride. Or was it heaven's way of saying that it was pleased by the arrival of Anne since the tragedy had taken place immediately she was brought safely to land and had the upheaval started shortly before, she and the whole party would surely have been killed.

The trouble with such omens was that there were always two constructions to be put on them and they always were. They were ill for those who wished them to be; but those who were in favour of what was taking place would always be able to turn them to good.

The journey to London had begun. Her first stop was at Canterbury where Richard's Uncle Thomas was waiting to receive her.

Anne was entranced by the sight of the beautiful city within those grey walls which was dominated by that most magnificent of cathedrals made sacred by the shrine of the great Thomas à Becket who had been murdered there two hundred years before and whose memory was as green now as it had been when he had been killed. There also was the tomb of Richard's father.

Richard's uncle Thomas, who was known as Thomas of Woodstock and was the Earl of Buckingham, had the looks of the Plantagenets, being tall, fair and handsome. He was in his mid thirties and performed the greeting with warmth and the utmost courtesy.

Anne thought him charming; she could not at that stage be expected to know that his friendliness was a façade.

Thomas of Woodstock was in fact far from the benign avuncular figure he was portraying for the Princess's benefit.

He had always resented his nephew. Thomas's life was one resentment after another. To be the youngest son was an irritation in itself. He possessed the family ambition; and it rankled that this slender effeminate boy should be the King. True he was the only remaining son of the eldest but such a boy when there were three uncles, all sons of King Edward, all grown men, experienced in the art of ruling. It was bad luck, and he resented it.

He had not wished to come to Canterbury to greet the bride. It was not his place to. John should have come. He was the eldest of the uncles. But there was at this time not a more unpopular man in England than John of Gaunt.

John had said to him: 'You must go to Canterbury to bring the bride to London. If I go who knows what would happen? The people might show their dislike of me which would not be a good start for the Princess. Edmund is abroad so it is up to you.'

Thomas agreed that this was so, not without some smug satisfaction. He was jealous of his brother and was not sorry that his unpopularity was so obvious. Moreover he harboured a special grievance against him at the moment.

John was for ever pushing his son, young Bolingbroke; he had always done so. He would have liked to bring Catherine Swynford's Beaufort bastards to the fore too, if that were possible; but that would not be tolerated. It was brazen enough to take Catherine about with him and expect people to do honour to her; but to ennoble their bastards—that would be too much even for John.

But it did not stop him as far as young Henry was concerned. Well, Henry was the son of Blanche of Lancaster—royal on both maternal and paternal sides, so it was to be expected. John fumed inwards because Henry was not heir to the throne; but he tried all the time to load his son with honours. He was already the Earl of Derby though people still called him Bolingbroke after the place where he had been born. Thomas had disliked the boy from the time—it must have been five years ago—when he had been made Knight of the Garter. He, Thomas, had hoped to be chosen, but it was like John to push everyone aside for his own advancement; and at that time he had had the ear of their father.

But there was an even greater resentment now; and that was Bolingbroke's recent marriage.

Thomas's father in an attempt to provide handsomely for him—because with so many sons there were not enough estates to go round—had arranged a brilliant marriage for him.

The bride chosen for Thomas when he had been nineteen years of age was Eleanor Bohun, the daughter of the Earl of Hereford, Essex and Northampton. Eleanor was a very rich heiress, but there was one flaw in the arrangement; she had a younger sister Mary.

For some time he and Eleanor had been trying to persuade Mary to go into a convent. Mary was a very pretty girl and mild enough, and she was very much influenced by the elder less beautiful but more forceful Eleanor. They had taken her to live in the Castle of Pleshy which was very close to one of the female branches of the Franciscans known as the Poor Clares.

Mary therefore had had ample opportunity to observe the piety of the nuns of this order; Eleanor was constantly extolling their virtues and it was clear that Mary was greatly impressed by them. Their lives were dedicated to the care of the poor and the sick.

'Ah,' Eleanor would sigh, 'I almost envy them. What beautiful lives they lead. Do you not agree, Mary?'

Mary did agree. Yes, it must be wonderful to be so virtuous. She would not greatly care to dress in that loose rough grey with the knotted girdles—four knots to represent the four vows they had taken.

'They are more becoming in God's eyes than the finest raiment,' said Eleanor sternly.

'Perhaps it is not too late for you to give up the world and join them,' suggested Mary.

Eleanor was angry. Mary was changing. She was growing up.

It was unfortunate that King Edward having given Eleanor to his son should have given the guardianship of the younger daughter to his other son, John of Gaunt. Being the guardian of heirs to rich fortunes was always a profitable matter and such guardianships were greatly sought after and given as rewards to those to whom the King owed some reward.

John of Gaunt now and then visited his ward to assure himself of her well being and for some time an idea had been brewing in his mind.

The Bohun fortune was great; there was no reason why Eleanor should have it all. He arranged, with the help of Mary's aunt, the Countess of Arundel, that the young girl should pay a visit to Arundel.

'She has all but decided to end her days with the Poor Clares,' Eleanor had explained; but it was not possible to prevent Mary's going off with her aunt for a brief visit to Arundel. 'We might have known,' Thomas had said to Eleanor afterwards. 'John is sly. He arranged this, you may be sure.'

For at Arundel Mary met the young Earl of Derby who most certainly had been told by his father that he must make himself agreeable to the young girl.

Henry obeyed. Very soon John was riding to Pleshy. By this time Thomas had gone abroad and it was to Eleanor that he broke the news.

'It seemed inevitable,' he said. 'It is charming to see

young people fall in love. Of course they are young, but I have no wish to stand in Henry's way.'

Eleanor spluttered with rage. 'You cannot mean . . . It is quite impossible. Mary . . .'

'Mary and Henry wish to marry. It is a good match for your sister.'

Eleanor was frantic. All her scheming had come to nothing. And Thomas was not there to fight with her.

'I cannot allow it. She wishes to go into a convent.'

'My dear sister, it is not for you to allow or refuse. She certainly does not wish to go into a convent. She wishes to marry and I can see no reason why there should be any resistance to such a match. *I* have none.'

It was no use raging. The objections were brushed aside by the powerful John of Gaunt. He had his way and Mary, the rich heiress, had become the wife of Henry of Bolingbroke.

When Thomas returned and heard the news he was furious. The fortune which had come to him through his wife was only half what it would have been if Mary had gone into a convent and relinquished the greater part of her share. It was true that the Bohuns were immensely rich but he would now have only half of that which he had expected.

Disgruntled as he was he must needs pretend to show friendship to his brother, and he had to pay lip service to the boy King. And now here he was paying homage to this young girl who had come to marry Richard.

She brought no dowry. That was amusing.

He wished Richard joy of her.

He set out from Canterbury with her and they turned towards London.

Outside the City she was met by a party of knights at the head of which rode her future husband.

For a few breathless moments, seated on their horses, they faced each other.

She felt a great joy at the sight of him—his fair hair hanging to his shoulders and a golden crown on his head. His fine skin was flushed with the excitement of the encounter and was delicately pink. His eyes were intensely blue; his teeth white; all that she had heard of his good looks was true.

His loose-fitting robe with its long loose sleeves which she was to learn was called a houppelande was lined with vair. The wide sleeves falling back disclosed other sleeves of the cote hardie he wore beneath it. The belt about his waist glittered with so many jewels that it was dazzling to behold; and indeed the young King's entire person scintillated.

She had been told that he loved fine clothes and that was obviously true.

But he was beautiful. He was godlike in appearance. She had never seen such a beautiful being and she loved him on sight.

As for Richard he was delighted by this fresh-faced girl with the lively eyes. If she was not exactly beautiful that was unimportant. She would admire him all the more for his good looks if she did not possess so many herself. She was smiling and her expression was one of deep interest and that she liked what she saw was clear to him. Her face was rather long though narrow; she had a long upper lip but her teeth were good. But it was her smile which was captivating; and her youth was naturally appealing. She looked a little strange in English eyes but that was because of her head-dress which was shaped rather like the horns of a cow.

However it was a happy meeting. The King and his bride were young and the people were determined to love them.

The Londoners, relieved now that their City had been saved by the prompt action of the King, were determined to show their new Queen what a splendid welcome they were capable of giving her.

The Lord Mayor and leading merchants had decked themselves in their finery and had ridden to Blackheath that they might escort her into the City, and with them came minstrels. So Anne made her triumphant entry into the City of London.

In Cheapside a pageant was awaiting her. A castle had

been erected there and from this ran fountains of wine. On the towers of the castle stood beautiful girls and as the royal pair approached they showered gilded leaves on them.

The next day Anne and Richard were married in the Chapel Royal of the Palace of Westminster.

The ceremony was followed by feasting and much revelry in the streets. The people seemed to go wild with joy. They wanted to put as far behind them as possible that fearful time when it appeared that the City would fall to the rebels.

After the marriage Richard took his bride to Windsor. They were clearly enchanted with each other. Richard loved her cool precise judgments and her knowledge of affairs which seemed incongruous in one so young and so recently come to the country. She was delighted with his good looks, his courtly manners, his love of poetry and books of all kinds. He showed her a copy of the *Romance of the Rose* which he had acquired when he was thirteen years old. He also possessed the romances of Gawain and Perceval, as well as a Bible in French.

Anne was greatly impressed; she could see that they would be happy reading together, and afterwards discussing what they had read.

She was amused by his delight in his clothes and she made him show her some of the jewel-encrusted garments of which he was so proud. She asked him to put them on and she loved to see him parade and preen before her.

He was vain of his appearance; and had cause to be, she defended him to herself. There could never have been such a handsome King.

He was fastidious in his appearance. He bathed every day to the astonishment of those about him. She sensed that they felt such a habit to be effeminate, but she liked it. He was always so fresh, so beautifully dressed.

He liked food, but it had to be delicate food. He was not a great trencherman. He picked daintily at his dishes and was enormously interested in the way they were cooked.

Chiefly though she liked to hear about the country. She

made him tell her of the peasants' revolt in all its horror. When he described how he had gone out to face the rebels she listened entranced. She could see him—so handsome, so young—facing those unkempt men. And how brave he had been.

'They could have killed you,' she said.

'I didn't think of that. I thought of my mother in the Tower and later in the Wardrobe and I was terrified of what they might do to her. I knew I had to send them home because if I did not they would kill my friends and myself too, I supposed, though I didn't think much of that. They had never showed any great animosity towards me.'

'So you dispersed them by promising to give them what they wanted. You rode to them when the tyler was killed and offered to be their leader.'

'Yes, I did that.'

She was thoughtful. 'But the promises were not kept.'

'It was impossible to keep them.'

'Yet you promised.'

'I had to promise to save London . . . to save my kingdom.'

She could see that. Anne could always see a logical point quickly. But she was uneasy because he had promised.

She came back to the subject and she wanted to know what was happening to those of the rebels who were still in prisons awaiting trial.

He said that they would suffer the reward of traitors he doubted not. Many had gone free, but it was not wise to let the people think they could rise against their rulers and then be sent home when they were defeated as though it was unimportant.

She saw that too. But she said: 'Pardon these people for me, Richard. Let it be your wedding gift to me.'

What could he do but give her her wish.

The rebels were pardoned. The people heard of this. They liked her the more for her compassion, and they were quick to respond.

Within a few months of her arrival in England she was known as Good Queen Anne.

THE END OF THE FAIR MAID
OF KENT

THE QUEEN MOTHER was feeling her age. She had grown very
fat in the last years and it was becoming an intolerable
burden to drag herself around.

She had at length become reconciled to taking second
place in her son's life. At first she had been a little jealous
of his absorption with his new Queen. Before her coming
it had always been his mother to whom he turned but in a
few months Anne had firmly taken first place in his
affections.

Well, mused Joan, that was perhaps the best thing that
could have happened. She could not but admire the new
Queen. She was a sensible girl; she loved Richard and
Richard loved her; and if he listened to Anne's advice she
could be sure it would be worth listening to.

The fact that Anne was a year older than the King was
all to the good. She was serious-minded and yet able to
share the King's pleasures. Although the people had not
been very pleased with the match in the beginning for
Anne had brought no dowry and a substantial sum had had
to be given to Bohemia from the English treasury and it
could not really be seen that any great political advantage
had been gained, Anne's good-natured smile, her ready
response to the good-will of the people together with the
freshness of her youth had gained her popularity.

The marriage had been arranged in the hope of making
an alliance with the Emperor against the French, but it
seemed that this battle for the crown of France which King

Edward had started was no nearer to its end than it had been years ago. Joan wondered whether it ever would be. The very best thing that could happen would be to make peace, to concentrate on the governing of England and forget France where so much English blood had already been spilt in battles which had proved to be useless because they had decided nothing.

Well perhaps, as the Black Prince would have said, that was a woman's point of view. But Joan believed that it was the most sensible for all that, or perhaps for that very reason.

It had seemed that every attempt on land and sea was doomed to failure. People still talked of the great victories of Edward the Third and the Black Prince but Joan knew that there was no leader at this time who was capable of such successes. The late King and his eldest son had had a rare quality and this was not apparent in anyone living at this time. Richard would never be a great fighter. She had always known that. It was something which had worried her considerably and living with one of the greatest generals of his or any age, she had recognized the necessary qualities. The Black Prince and his father were men who could arouse in their soldiers a certainty of victory just by appearing. There was no one like that today.

John of Gaunt might be the nearest, but he lacked something. Everything he entered into seemed to fail. It was not bad luck all the time. He lacked that quality which appealed to men. Edward the King and the Black Prince had been loved. John of Gaunt was loathed. Edmund of Langley was handsome and charming but he was no great soldier; nor was Thomas of Woodstock. Perhaps Bolingbroke might be one day . . . but he was young as yet and he was overshadowed by his hated father.

Joan often worried about the future. Edward would have laughed at her had he been alive. She had always been supposed to be rather frivolous. But perhaps during their marriage Edward had begun to realize that it was otherwise.

So now she must rejoice because of her son's happy marriage and graciously step back into second place.

They were uneasy times though. Richard was impressionable and quickly came under the influence of certain people.

Michael de la Pole and Richard Fitzalan were two of them. They had been selected to act as his counsellors. Now that John of Gaunt had left the country (he was still making war in Castile for since the death of Henry of Trastamare the question of the succession had risen again) there was a clear field for them and they took advantage of it.

But his greatest friend of all was Robert de Vere, the Earl of Oxford, and this friendship was so close—for the King could scarcely bear the young man out of his sight—that it was beginning to be noticed and commented on.

De Vere was of course connected with the royal family for he had married Philippa de Couci, daughter of Isabella, who was Edward the Third's eldest daughter. Thus it seemed reasonable at first that Richard and de Vere should see a great deal of each other; but as the weeks had passed their devotion had grown.

It was a sign of Anne's good sense that she did not show any jealousy of de Vere. Rather did she appear to enjoy his company; and the three of them were often together.

A wise girl, thought Joan, and remembered what she had heard of Edward the Second who had indulged in passionate friendships with men of the Court and how his wife had resented it to such an extent that she had taken up arms against him.

Yes, Joan could rejoice in the marriage. It was a good day for Richard when Anne of Bohemia became his wife.

She was often uneasy about the sons of her first marriage. They had always been rather violent. They took after their father. She could smile remembering him and the passion they had shared in their youth. Thomas Holland had been irresistible all those years ago in the Salisbury household where she was supposed to be betrothed to young Salisbury. Exciting days—carefree days when she had been quite unaware of how very reckless she had been.

It was all over now. But Thomas and John *were* reckless. Of one thing she could be certain: they would support Richard because all their hopes of advancement would come through him.

Richard was now in his eighteenth year. He was no longer a boy to be told what to do. He had selected a small coterie of friends at the head of which was Robert de Vere. De Vere was not the wisest of counsellors but it was always to his advice that Richard listened. Moreover he was inclined to act on impulse and because his temper was quick and was becoming increasingly violent, he was apt to act first and think afterwards.

There were bound to be warring factions about him and there was a great resentment towards de Vere. This was taken up by the people who blamed every reverse on the favourite. They still believed in their King; they cheered him when he rode through the streets of cities and the countryside; he looked so much the King and as yet they would find scapegoats for any action which they did not like.

John of Gaunt was back in England having come to no satisfactory conclusion regarding Castile, and about him had formed a group which was known as the Lancastrian Party. He had gone to Scotland and returned after a disastrous campaign. He had pursued the Scots who had burned their towns and villages before him so that when he arrived in them his army was without provisions. It was impossible to continue in these circumstances and the English had had to retreat back to the border.

John was blamed for lack of energy in conducting the war and the matter was brought up by the Court party in Parliament and there was a bitter discord mainly between de Vere and John.

De Vere was certain of his influence with the King and he believed that he could rid himself of this troublesome uncle who, he knew, would do everything within his power to ruin him if he had the chance.

And John of Gaunt was a very powerful man.

De Vere decided that he might be able to get rid of John of Gaunt once and for all.

The Court was at Salisbury and the King and Queen were to attend High Mass in the Cathedral there. This was going to be a very ceremonious occasion.

Robert de Vere had invited the King and Queen to sup with him before the Mass and they had repaired to his private apartments in the castle. There were but a few guests and it was a very merry party until there was a sudden interruption.

The door of the apartment was flung open and a friar whose habit showed him to be a Carmelite rushed in and threw himself at the feet of the King.

Richard was startled. 'What means this?' he cried.

The friar stammered: 'My lord, my lord. I come to warn you.'

'Speak, friar, speak,' cried Robert de Vere. 'The King commands you to say what it is you have to tell him.'

The friar lifted his eyes to the King's face. 'My lord,' he said, 'your life is in danger. There are those who plot to kill you.'

'What plot is this?' cried the King. 'And how do you know of it?'

'I know of it, my lord. I have overheard the conspirators. It is a plot with the cities of London and Coventry. They will band together and take your throne from you.'

'This man is mad,' said the King.

'No, no, my lord. It is not so.'

'Let us hear him out,' said de Vere. 'Who has made this plot? Who is at the heart of it? Tell us that.'

'It is your uncle, my lord King. Your uncle, John of Gaunt, who seeks to overthrow you and take the throne.'

'My uncle!' cried Richard.

It was significant that he believed it possible. His Uncle John of Gaunt plotting against him, trying to take the crown. Wasn't that what he had always wanted?

But they had found out in time. The friar should be rewarded. He would strike first.

'Arrest the Duke of Lancaster,' cried Richard. 'Arrest the traitor.'

One of the members of the party, Sir John Clanvowe, who was Prior of the Hospital of St. John of Jerusalem, begged the King to restrain his anger.

'My lord, my lord,' he cried, 'it would be well to find out first whether there is any truth in this friar's story.'

Anne was looking at Richard with a warning expression in her eyes; she too was advising caution.

Caution! He did not want caution. He had always known John of Gaunt had longed for the crown. He wanted that son of his to be heir to the throne. He had always wanted it.

Richard's heart called out for immediate vengeance. He wanted to show them all that he was capable of quick and firm action. He felt excited and desperately frustrated.

A kind of madness seized him. It was the old Plantagenet temper which so many of them had seen before, handed down through the generations—and it was out of control. He took off his hat and in a sudden rage threw it out of the window. The company stared at him in amazement. Then he took off his shoes and they followed the hat.

When he had done that he felt he had relieved his feelings and was much calmer.

Anne had risen and laid a hand on his arm.

'You should question this friar, Richard,' she whispered. 'We should endeavour to discover whether he speaks the truth. Demand of him that he tell you the names of those who are concerned in this.'

It was wise, of course. He knew it. He should not condemn his uncle without proof. Robert was watching him intently. Robert had planned that he would impulsively arrest John of Gaunt and hurry him off to the Tower, and have his head off his shoulders before he had time to work out some plan to show that he was innocent.

Richard had wanted to do what Robert wanted. Robert was his friend. Robert always thought of him first. He had said so.

There was a step outside the chamber and a gasp of horror when John of Gaunt himself came into the room.

'They are waiting for you, my lord,' he began. 'They wonder why you and the Queen are delayed.'

At the sight of the King's uncle, the friar seemed to fall into a frenzy.

'There is the traitor!' he cried. 'Seize him. Cut off his head. Put him to death before he kills you, my lord.'

John stared at the friar in amazement.

'What madman is this?' he demanded.

'He has just made an accusation against you,' Richard told him.

'An accusation! What accusation?'

'That you are plotting with the people of London and Coventry to kill me and take the crown.'

'Plotting! Take the crown! He is indeed a madman. Can you see the people of London joining *me* in any plot? They might like me a little better than they once did . . . but I am still hated by them. This is a madman, nephew. He should be put under restraint.'

Richard turned to the friar. 'You hear that?'

'I hear, my lord,' said the friar boldly. 'But protestations do not make innocence.'

'I would hear what this is all about,' said John.

He was told briefly. 'It is not even a clever plot,' he said. 'It is arrant nonsense. I tell you, I am innocent of any will to do you harm. I will take on any in battle who accuse me and prove myself.'

Richard, face to face with his uncle, was now completely swayed to his side. The Carmelite was lying. It was a plot he had fabricated.

Richard hated to suspect that people were plotting against his life. It unnerved him. He wanted everyone to love him as the people used to before the peasants' revolt.

Now all his fury was turned onto the friar. 'Take him away,' he cried. 'Let him be put to death. He is a traitor and a liar. There is no plot.'

The guards came forward but John held up his hand.

'My lord, this man must be questioned. He must know

the names of those he is accusing. I shall insist that this matter is sifted to the bottom. I cannot allow such accusations to be made against me and not proved false. It is clear to me that this man is only a tool of real villains.'

John was looking hard at de Vere as he spoke. The King's friend was standing very still. He looked a little uneasy and John was very much conscious of this.

'This is too important a matter to be lightly laid aside,' went on John. 'Let the friar be questioned. Let him produce his evidence. We must discover the meaning of this accusation. It may be that there is something behind it.'

'Let him be taken away,' said the King. 'This is not the end of the matter.'

Sir Simon Burley led the friar out of the apartment and at the door they were met by five knights, among them Sir John Holland the King's half-brother.

'What's afoot?' asked Holland.

Simon told him.

'A plot! To kill the King! John of Gaunt accused!' cried Holland. 'We must get to the bottom of this. We shall take charge of this matter. Give the fellow to me, good Simon.'

Simon was somewhat reluctant but he did not wish to make an enemy of the King's brother and so the Carmelite friar passed out of his hands.

His name was John Latemar and he persisted in his story. There *was* a plot to kill the King. It had been fabricated by John of Gaunt together with the leading citizens of London and Coventry. That was all he would say.

'We shall make him talk,' said Holland.

He wanted him to talk. He wanted him to incriminate John of Gaunt. He hated John of Gaunt who, he believed, was capable of plotting the murder of the King. If the King were murdered and John of Gaunt took the throne, there would be little gain for the King's half-brothers.

The fellow must be made to talk. There were means.

Holland knew of the most devilish means—such as to make even a holy friar talk.

There was something remote about this friar. He did not seem to suffer the weaknesses of ordinary men. If it occurred to them that he was suffering from madness and had a firm belief that he was speaking the truth they would not admit it. They wanted there to have been a plot. They wanted to go to the King and say: 'This John Latemar has confessed. He swears it was John of Gaunt who was plotting against the King's life.' Holland wanted John of Gaunt to lay his head upon the block—and then no more of John of Gaunt.

But no matter what vile and obscene tortures, what hideous mutilations were inflicted on the friar he would give no names.

In the streets of Salisbury people were congregating. They talked of nothing but the plot the Carmelite friar had discovered. John of Gaunt was at the heart of it. They too hated John of Gaunt. They wanted him to be proved guilty. They wanted to witness his execution. They would cheer on the day he went to the scaffold. They wanted their handsome young King to be freed of the envy of his rapacious uncle.

The tension was great as the day fixed for the enquiry drew near. People crowded into the streets, everyone eager to get a glimpse of the friar. They were taking sides. The friar was innocent, said some. He was a great man. He had warned the King although he knew he could risk his life by so doing. John of Gaunt was the villain. Had he not always been?

Sir John Holland came to the King on the morning of the day fixed for the enquiry. Richard was as usual in the company of the Queen and Robert de Vere.

'My lord brother,' he said, 'there can be no enquiry.'

Richard looked at him in astonishment.

'The friar is dead, my lord.'

'Dead! But he was not ill when he was taken away.'

'He has died since.'

The King looked at the Queen and from the Queen to

Robert. Anne had turned pale; there was real anguish in her face. Robert's expression was enigmatical.

'It was necessary to question him,' said Holland. 'He was a stubborn man.'

The King turned away and put his hand over his eyes, and Anne signed to Holland to leave them.

Sir John bowed and retired. He himself was a little uneasy. The torture administered under his direction had been savage.

When the body of the friar was examined and it was realized what had been done to him the King was overcome with horror. So was John of Gaunt. Neither Richard nor his uncle believed in that sort of torture. If men were against them they were all for the quick stroke of the sword or the axe but not that obscene and filthy torture which had been carried out on this man.

Richard wept and the Queen sent everyone away that she might comfort him as she believed only she could. Richard lay on his bed and she sat beside him stroking his hair.

' 'Tis done, 'tis done,' she said. 'There is nothing we can do now to change it. We should never have allowed your half-brother to have care of him.'

She had already discovered that there was great cruelty in John Holland.

'And to what avail!' cried Richard. 'What did we discover? Nothing.'

She tried to soothe him. She was beginning to learn a great deal not only about the men who surrounded her husband but of Richard himself.

He was weak. That she had to accept. He was not the golden god she had believed him to be when he had welcomed her to England and she had been overawed by his beauty. He needed her. She realized that more each day. He leaned on her. It was for her to protect him. And she loved him more deeply for his weakness.

*   *   *

Thomas of Woodstock came riding to Salisbury. News of the friar's outburst and his accusation against John of Gaunt had reached him.

Unceremoniously he burst into the King's chamber.

Thomas's eyes were wild as he took his sword from its sheath and brandished it before the King. Those about Richard closed in on him and Thomas cried: 'Who dares accuse my brother of treason, eh? Tell me this. Let that man stand forth and I will challenge him. Yea,' his wild eyes were fixed on Richard. 'No matter who he be. I will run him through.'

Richard was astounded. That anyone should dare speak thus of him in his presence was an insult. It was something he had never expected could be possible, even from his uncle who had always treated him as though he were a boy.

He opened his mouth to speak but he had always been a little in awe of Thomas of Woodstock. During his boyhood this big uncle had often lectured him on what he should do, and somehow the sight of him, red-faced, his eyes bulging, his sword in his hand, intimidated the King.

De Vere said: 'My lord Buckingham, this matter is over. The friar is dead. None of his accusations have been proved. The matter is at an end.'

'It is not at an end my lord if calumnies are spread about my brother. And if they continue to be I shall be at hand to defend his good name.'

Woodstock bowed and left the chamber.

Everyone who had witnessed the strange scene was astounded. The brothers had not been on such good terms. Buckingham still resented the fact that Lancaster had married his son Henry to the co-heiress of the Bohun estates.

Why then was he so concerned with his brother's reputation?

There was one construction to be put on it and Richard declared to Robert de Vere and Anne that he knew what it was.

'He loves to humiliate me. That is his motive. He wants to make me feel that I have not yet grown up and he wants to make other people believe it. I shall not forget this in a hurry,' he added. 'A plague on these uncles.'

The people of Salisbury were not going to allow the friar Latemar to be forgotten in a hurry either.

It was not long before he became a martyr.

One man came running through the streets shouting: 'I can see. I who was blind can see.'

What had happened? Crowds gathered round him.

'I touched the crate on which he was dragged through the streets. Leaves had begun to sprout from it. I touched them and lo, I could see.'

It was like touching the hem of the holy garment.

After that there was a crop of miracles. Lights were said to shine over the friar's grave. There was constant talk of the astonishing cures which were performed there. No, the friar was not going to be forgotten.

And if he was a martyr, which the miracles proved he was, then John of Gaunt was in truth plotting to murder the King, for martyrs always spoke the truth.

Robert de Vere was very much aware of the feeling which had been raised against John of Gaunt. Of course he himself was equally unpopular. Favourites always were. He was surrounded by envy, simply because he knew how to amuse the King and delight him with his company.

Richard doted on him and could deny him nothing. Robert must be watchful of Anne of course; but Anne was a wise woman; she loved the King and was in fact loved by him. She had to accept Robert and she did so with a very good grace. Just as, thought Robert slyly, he accepted her.

Richard and he were friends, devoted friends, but they had their wives of course and both of them understood this friendship which made for a harmonious household.

Richard could not do enough for Robert. When he had told him that he and Philippa could not really manage on their income, the King had laughed. He could remedy that. He could not allow his dear Robert to be poor. Robert was very soon the possessor of the town and castle of Colchester. He was also a member of the privy council and a knight of the Garter. Of course they were jealous of him. Robert expected jealousy from other nobles. But he had to be watchful in higher quarters.

The King's uncles did not like him. He had long been aware of John of Gaunt's antipathy; now of couse he had that of Thomas of Woodstock. When he had raged into the King's chamber brandishing his sword he had, it was true, been brandishing it at Richard, but he was sending more than the occasional glance in Robert's direction too.

It was unfortunate that the plot against John of Gaunt had failed. The friar was an innocent man who had been trapped into being the betrayer of the 'plot'. He had been a simple man and it had been easy to play subtly on his incredulity. Robert had banked on Richard's losing his temper and acting on impulse as he so often did. Then John of Gaunt would have been taken away and executed before enquiries were made. It had happened like that more than once.

But here he was with a failed plot and yet not entirely failed. Not while the miracles continued and they must make sure that there was no falling off of those for while they persisted feeling ran high against John of Gaunt.

Thomas Mowbray, Earl of Nottingham, another favourite of the King's though none could compare with Robert of course, was equally eager to be rid of John of Gaunt. Nor were they the only ones. They had their supporters.

He discussed the matter with Mowbray. 'This time,' he said, 'we must make sure of our man. We have agreed that it will not be difficult to get him arrested and accused. Feeling is running high. People really do believe in those miracles. He shall be summoned to a meeting of the Council at Waltham and there accused. This time he shall stand trial.'

'And you think judges would dare convict him?'

'My dear Mowbray, judges we shall choose will. They will be as anxious to see the end of him as we are.'

'And Richard?' asked Mowbray.

'Leave Richard to me.'

'He will be present, you know.'

'My dear fellow, I know how to play on Richard's fears. He is already half convinced that he should have listened to the friar. He has nightmares, dreams of the tortures. He has a very delicate mind, our King. He does not like to contemplate torture, even that of men who would be plotting against him. A nice quick stroke of the sword or the axe, that is Richard's idea of despatching his enemies. He is very suspicious of Uncle John and of Uncle Thomas. Thomas rushing in like that and flourishing his sword was playing right into our hands. Rest assured, my dear Nottingham, that this time it will be the end of John of Gaunt.'

Robert was right. It was easy to convince Richard.

'There are rumours,' he whispered to him. 'It is said that there *was* a plot and that John of Gaunt cleverly extricated himself as he has done so often before.'

'There are times when I could bring myself to believe that,' said Richard.

'There was another miracle at the friar's tomb yesterday,' went on Robert. 'My lord if treason were proved against John of Gaunt you would not hesitate . . .'

'Whoever commits treason must pay the penalty,' answered Richard firmly.

That there was some plot afoot was obvious to all who surrounded the King; and that Robert de Vere was at the heart of it seemed more than likely.

One man who was particularly suspicious was Michael de la Pole. He had become Chancellor and the King could not help being impressed by his management of affairs, for he had decreased Court expenditure considerably. His enemies had tried to bring charges of peculation against him but he had been able to rebut them. It was an absurd charge which had been brought against him. A fishmonger had accused him of taking a bribe when he, the fishmonger, was coming up for trial. This fishmonger, a certain John

Cavendish, declared that he had been told that if he paid forty pounds to the Chancellor he would get judgment in his favour. Lacking the money the fishmonger declared he had sent a present of fish, but Michael de la Pole was able to prove that he had paid for the fish and the fishmonger was condemned for defamation of character.

De la Pole was very well aware how a man's enemies could take a trivial incident, distort it and bring it against him.

He was now suspicious at the emphasis which was being placed on the so-called miracles and he guessed this meant a plot against John of Gaunt.

De la Pole was a patriotic man, and what he wanted was to bring about peace with France, for England needed peace not only beyond the seas but in England and while there was strife between the King and his uncles this could never be. Moreover it was a danger. The uncles were powerful men. It was true that John of Gaunt had distinguished himself rather by failure than success; but he was a man who must be regarded with respect. Edmund of Langley was of a milder disposition but it was very likely that he would stand with his brothers rather than his nephew; as for Thomas of Woodstock, there was a choleric man, a man ready to act rashly without fear of the consequences.

But de la Pole *did* fear the consequences, not only for himself but for England.

John of Gaunt was by no means loved by the people. In fact there was not a more unpopular man in the country—unless it was Robert de Vere. Even so if he were murdered doubtless he would become a martyr.

This plot must not be allowed to reach fruition.

At Hertford John of Gaunt received the summons to attend the Council.

He stood in the great hall with the letter in his hand, long after the messengers had retired to the kitchens to be refreshed.

Catherine found him there, and noticed at once that

264

something was wrong. Their affection had not waned with the passing of the years. She was installed here in his house as the one who meant a great deal to him. He needed Catherine and she knew it and revelled in the knowledge.

Hers was a beauty which did not diminish with age. It was true that it had changed; and instead of the flames of passion which had flared between them in their youth there now burned a steady light which was more important to him than anything else.

It astonished him more than it astonished her.

He was to her her lover and her child. She often marvelled to think of this great man and herself. Who was she, the daughter of a humble man who had managed to get a knighthood on a battlefield, the widow of another knight, a simple country woman, to be the companion of the great John of Gaunt? But such was love, and theirs was enduring.

It was a life of thrills and terrors she had chosen. She knew that he was in constant danger and when she was not with him she was full of fear for his safety. Every time a messenger arrived she was afraid he was bringing some bad news. She longed for messengers to bring her news of him but always she feared what it might be.

And the happy times were when he was with her. They were the high peaks of her life, but she knew she had to pay for them and she spent most of her days in the valleys of fear.

Recently there had been this terrible affair of the Carmelite who had brought charges against him. She thanked God that was over.

She slipped her arm through his. 'What news?' she asked fearfully.''

'A summons to the Council at Waltham.'

Her heart missed a beat.

'What is it, sweetheart?' he asked.

She answered: 'I felt as though someone was walking over my grave.'

'Ah, Catherine, you have these fears now and then, my love.'

'I fear greatly for you, John.'

'You must not. Do you doubt that I can give a good account of myself?'

'I doubt it not, but there are evil men who would do you ill. I can never trust de Vere.'

'Who does? Except the King and he is besotted. Catherine, sometimes I think my nephew is going to be my grandfather all over again. People are already comparing de Vere with Gaveston.'

'It cannot be so. What of the Queen?'

'The Queen knows of this friendship and joins in it. She appears to find de Vere's company diverting.'

Catherine shook her head. 'Their ménage does not concern me. Let them live as they will as long as you are safe. What of this summons to Waltham?'

'I must go. I shall be needed there. I am the King's first counsellor whatever de Vere may think.'

'I like it not.'

'Oh Catherine, you fear too much.'

''Methinks I love too much,' she answered.

'Nay that is something you can never do. Rest easy, sweetheart. I am as good a match for them as they for me . . . aye better.'

'That Carmelite affair . . . It could so easily have . . .'

'No, no, no. I can handle my nephew. He is a boy, nothing more . . . a weak boy.'

'Which makes it all the more easy for wicked men to handle him. There is a warning in my heart, John. You must not go to Waltham.'

He tried to soothe her. There was nothing he would rather do than stay here with her in peace. But there was no peace. His life had brought him along a strange path. Sometimes he was unworldly enough to wish that on the death of Blanche he had married Catherine. Impossible. He could well imagine what an outcry there would have been. The King's son and the widow of a man of no importance! And she had gone up in the social scale by marrying Swynford. No, he had to marry Constanza and the marriage had been a failure from the start, although it would bring him the crown of Castile one day he was sure. He and Constanza did not live together. He had done his duty and they had one daughter. There was an end of it. But his claim to Castile remained. One day he would be a king in truth.

The desire for a crown! It had haunted his life. And he might have had the crown of England too if he had been born earlier. He was born too late. That was the theme of his life. Too late.

Too late he had realized that he would have been a happier man if he had married Catherine and lived the life of a nobleman—adviser to the King yes, but not for ever dogged by this accursed ambition.

Now he had to soothe her. She was obsessed by this council at Waltham.

He talked to her a great deal—when they walked in the gardens, when they were alone indoors, when she lay beside him at night and they both marvelled in the wonder of their relationship which they knew would go on until one or the other died.

'Don't go,' were the last words she said that night but his answer was: 'I must.'

He was preparing to leave. Whatever was in store—and Catherine's apprehension had communicated itself to him—he must go.

She would watch him ride away and then she would go to the topmost tower so that she might see the last of him; and he would turn and wave to her and his heart would be sick with longing to stay with her.

But he must go. He could not say good-bye to ambition now. He could not say: I, John of Gaunt, will no longer fight for the crown of Castile. I will stay on my estates and live in comfort for the rest of my life beside my mistress.

There were sounds of arrival in the courtyard.

He hurried down to the hall. A man was there. He was talking to some of the startled guards.

'Take me at once to the Duke.'

John cried out in amazement for the man who stood there was Michael de la Pole.

'What has happened?' asked John.

De la Pole looked around him.

'Come with me,' said John, and took him to a private chamber. Catherine came in, her eyes fearful.

John took her arm and said to de la Pole, 'You may speak before Lady Swynford.'

De la Pole said: 'You must not go to Waltham.'

'Why so?'

'They are planning to arrest you before the Council and bring you to trial for plotting against the King.'

'What nonsense! They could never prove a thing against me . . . for nothing exists.'

'They will prove something, my lord Duke. They have made up their minds to prove something.'

'You mean a bench of judges . . .''

'Picked men, my lord. All your sworn enemies. De Vere failed with his Carmelite but he is determined to try again.'

Catherine had turned white and was clutching at the table to steady herself. John thought she was going to faint. She said nothing. She was too wise to attempt to advise him in the presence of others.

'There is only one thing to be done, my lord,' said de la Pole, 'and that is to feign illness.'

Then Catherine spoke. 'Yes,' she said quietly, 'yes.'

'I beg you, my lord, send a message at once,' went on de la Pole. 'You are too ill to attend the Council.'

John was silent for a moment. He could see how it would work. Speed was the answer. A quick arrest, trial and then execution before it could be realized what was happening. He must remember what had happened to another Lancaster— Earl Thomas who had been murdered in the same way as was being planned for him—and that to avenge the royal favourite Gaveston.

He said: 'My thanks to you, de la Pole, for this timely warning. I see you are right. I shall not attend the Council.'

He could not help looking at Catherine. Her eyes were shining.

It was the right decision, he knew.

De Vere was furious. The news had leaked then. He knew what was awaiting him. Illness! Bah! He did not believe it.

He raged to the King. 'This is an insult to you, my lord. He defies you. You summon him to your Council and he says, No, I prefer to make sport with my mistress. It is time John of Gaunt was taught who was master in this land.'

'He shall come,' said Richard. 'I shall insist.'

'You must, dear lord. It is the only way of showing him your power. I do declare he still regards you as the little boy—the small nephew to be bullied by his big and powerful uncles.'

'You hate him, don't you, Robert?'

'I hate all who seek to belittle my dear lord the King. But you are not going to allow it, are you, Richard? You are going to send an order to him. Illness or whatever excuses he has to offer are of no avail.'

'I am going to order him to come to the Council,' said Richard.

At Hertford Castle the summons had come.

Catherine was with him. She read it with horror.

'They are determined to destroy you,' she cried.

He took her chin in his hands and regarded her tenderly. 'But, my darling, I am determined not to be destroyed.'

'What shall you do?' she demanded.

'I must go,' he said. 'That is clear.'

'Go . . . right into that den of wolves!'

'I do not believe the King is party to a plot to kill me. He surrounds himself with men like de Vere whose great plan is to guide the King for their own advancement.

Never fear, sweet Catherine. I shall know how to deal with them.'

'But how? How, when they accuse you, when they drag you before judges who have made up their minds in advance to condemn you?'

'I shall not go to the Council. I shall see the King alone. I shall draw from him what his feelings are. Catherine, I know how to deal with him. He sways this way and that. He will be with me after a few moments, I promise you. I must attempt to make him see where he is wrong. He must understand otherwise it will be my grandfather all over again. He was bemused by his favourites. That is what is happening to Richard. It led my grandfather to the horrors of Berkeley Castle. You know what happened to him. Richard could be heading towards a similar fate. I must warn him.'

'So you will walk right into the trap.'

'The trap will not be set when I arrive. I intend to go to him with a strong escort. They shall not take me.'

There was nothing she could do to dissuade him from going and indeed, she knew that he must. Not to do so would be to defy the King and give his enemies a real complaint against him.

She was relieved that next to his skin he wore chain armour and with a strong guard he set out for Sheen where the King was at that time.

Sheen was one of Richard and Anne's favourite palaces; Anne had shown her preference for it soon after her arrival and Richard had immediately discovered that he liked it too.

It was a beautiful and impressive sight on the river's edge. John divided his escort and left half by his barge with injunctions that when and if they were summoned they should come to him without delay. With the rest he went to the palace gates. He ordered them to remain there and prevent anyone's entry or departure.

He then made his way to the King's chamber.

He was fortunate. The King was alone. He was startled to see his uncle and asked what had brought him.

'This, nephew,' said John sternly, reminding the King of the relationship between them and of his own power by the familiarity he assumed. 'I learned of the plot to murder me. It was for this reason that I refused to come to the Council.'

'Plot!' stammered Richard. 'I know of no plot . . .'

'That gratifies me,' said John. 'Not that I believed that you would be in agreement with my murder. My lord, I beg of you, listen to me. You surround yourself with evil counsellors. The country suffers. There are many who wish you well and wish England well. I am one of them. If this plot were to come to fruition, what think you would be the outcome? Bloodshed throughout England. Richard, I beg of you. Do not make this your great-grandfather's reign all over again. Think back of what happened to him. He was bemused by his favourites. You should not have favourites, Richard. Choose your friends and your ministers for the good they can do the country.'

Richard was wavering. When he listened to one side he could believe they were right and so it was with the other. There were two sides to every question and he could always see the one which had been presented to him.

Perhaps if he had been more like his father, more given to action than contemplation, he would have been able to see only one side of a problem, which would have been so much easier.

Now as he listened to his uncle he could not believe that he had been anything but a good counsellor.

He cried: 'You speak sense, my lord. I know you speak good sense.'

'Then, Richard, act on my advice. Rid yourself of these evil counsellors. Bind those to you who would do you good and ask nothing but to see the country prosper. I shall leave you now, Richard, to think of these things. And I have no intention of coming to the Council where those who call themselves your friends have planned to arrest me, try me and execute me all in the space of a few hours. No, Richard, I tell you this to your face: I shall not be there. And if you hold it against me . . . there are many who stand with me against those who plan to murder me.'

With that John bowed and walked out of the palace to his guard and so down to his barge.

The Queen Mother was aware of what was going on and was deeply disturbed by it. She could see that Richard would be deeper and deeper in trouble as the months passed if he did not bring about some reconciliation with his uncles.

She deplored his friendship with Robert de Vere, for the man had far too much influence over him. She was growing really feeble now and was disinclined to move far. She worried a great deal about her elder sons. She knew they were wild and she was distressed at the part John Holland had played in the affair of the Carmelite friar. He had always had a cruel streak and she had been aware of this. She could imagine how he would have revelled in torturing the friar and was sickened by her thoughts.

But her real concern was for Richard for what he did was of the utmost importance to the country and she lived in fear that he would, like his great-grandfather, come to a violent end. It was useless to try not to draw these parallels between the present and the past. The past in any case should be used as a lesson for the present.

She must somehow bring about a peace between Richard and his uncles. This would not be easy. Richard was highly suspicious of John of Gaunt and there was no doubt that John was going to find it hard to forgive the King's favourites who had plotted against him. But her greatest concern must be for Richard's future and she was very fearful of it.

How she wished that she could regain her old vitality. The girl who had danced so gaily through her youth with scarcely a care beyond the next excitement had become a very serious woman. It seemed to her that women had a more reasonable approach to life than men. It was the women who softened the anger of men, who could sometimes persuade them to act more reasonably in the ever worthwhile cause of peace. Queen Philippa had guided great Edward often enough; and he had listened to her. Many a poor man or woman had to be grateful to Philippa for saving them from the King's wrath. She had given the impression of being a homely woman but the good she had done might well be said to have outweighed that performed by her husband. No one would agree. But who had set up a fine weaving industry in England? Who had saved the lives of the burghers of Calais and so made that town loyal to Edward? Whereas it was impossible to know how many lives had been lost through Edward's reckless claim to the crown of France.

John of Gaunt loved Catherine Swynford. There was a clever woman. She must be to have kept John at her side all those years. She would speak to Catherine.

Sighing she ordered the carriage to be made ready and endured the jolting of her poor old bones across the rough and rutted roads.

Catherine was delighted to see her. They had always been good friends. Joan had never looked askance at her relationship with John as many did. Joan herself had had not too spotless a reputation in the days of her youth. But it was not that which affected her. It was the recognition of true love which she respected and she found it more to be admired than a contracted marriage which was loveless and made for expediency.

'My dear Catherine,' she said, 'my stay will not be long. John is not with you at this time, I hope.' She smiled. 'I know that is a matter which does not please you, my dear, but what I have to say is for you alone.'

Catherine understood perfectly, and during the few days Joan spent with her they had many talks together. Joan stayed in bed most of the time. The journey had shaken her up considerably and there was the return one to be made.

'I should not have come here,' she said, 'if I had not considered the matter of the utmost urgency. Catherine, I am afraid. I like not the way England is going.'

'Nor I.'

'These attempts on John's life . . .'

Catherine shivered.

'My dear,' went on Joan, 'I know your feelings. You are as worried as I am. There must be peace between my son and his uncles.'

'How I wish there could be.'

'It is for us to arrange it, my dear. I must leave John to you. Your word carries a great deal of weight with him.'

'I can never tell him what to do where the King is concerned.'

'You can persuade him, Catherine. He must be persuaded. He and Woodstock. Woodstock is hot-headed. John is cautious. It is for John to make the move. There *must* be a reconciliation between the King and John . . . and chiefly between de Vere and Mowbray and John.'

'My lady, they planned to murder him.'

'I know, and will plan again unless this silly quarrel is patched up.'

'I should never trust them . . . nor would John.'

'I know, but we must have a surface trust. I am sure there must be some outward show of reconciliation. If there is not there will be civil war. I feel sure of it. And that is the greatest of all tragedies.'

'I agree with all my heart.'

'Catherine, speak to John. I want him to come to Westminster and declare himself ready to forget what has happened. I want a *show* of friendship. Believe me, I know it is the only thing to save the country. Will you do it, Catherine?'

'I will do my best,' she answered. 'I know you are right. This enmity must end . . . or appear to end.'

'We shall have to be watchful, of course. But it will be an end to this plot to bring John to trial. That must be stopped. I know you can do it, and I know John will see it is the right way to act. It will come better from you, my dear. Promise me you will do it.'

''I will do what I can.'

'My dear Catherine, he loves you dearly. He listens to

274

you. He trusts you as he trusts no one else. You will do it. And tomorrow I must leave here. Oh how I dread the journey. I am getting so old now. I feel the jogging of my carriage for days after I have left it.'

'It is noble of you to come.'

'He is my son, Catherine, my little son. He is but a boy really. And these men who long for the crown do not understand that it can be more of a burden than a glory. And when the head on which it rests is young and inexperienced then that burden is a heavy one indeed.'

The next day she trundled off in her carriage and in due course she came to Sheen where she talked with Anne.

Anne was a bright girl, quick to understand. It was a pity she had been thrust into all this intrigue, thought Joan. It was a pity that de Vere had entered their married paradise like the serpent in Eden, a great pity.

But Anne had influence with the King. She did not seem to mind his pleasure in de Vere. She was a thoughtful girl, unaware that so many in her position might have been jealous. Not so Anne; she seemed contented, or perhaps she was merely clever.

Joan talked to her as she had talked to Catherine.

She feared civil war, she told Anne. This quarrel which was brewing between the King and his uncles must be stopped.

Anne agreed with her.

'There should be an end to these attempts to incriminate Lancaster. He is too powerful to be incriminated. Moreover there is no proof against him, and he is too clever to allow there to be. Woodstock is with him. And Langley would be too if it came to the point. It would be the King and his favourites on one side and Lancaster and his men on the other. Anne, Lancaster was once very unpopular. He could not venture out in London without someone shouting abuse at him. He is more popular now. Do you know why? The people have turned their hatred on de Vere. Anne, we must bring them together. It must be seen that there is no enmity between the King and his uncles.'

Anne said, 'Yes, I agree. We must do what we can to bring this about.'

'I am an old woman,' went on Joan. 'I cannot make many more of these journeys. Anne, I want to see peace in this land before I die. I want to see my son set on a fair course. You understand, I know.'

Anne did understand.

Between them, the three women worked the miracle.

At Westminster a reconciliation took place between the Duke of Lancaster and the men who shortly before had been plotting to bring him to his end.

Richard was delighted. It seemed to him that all the bickering was at an end.

'Now we are all good friends,' he said benignly.

From the turret Catherine saw her lover approaching. She went down to the courtyard to meet him. Swept up in his embrace she clung to him.

She was trembling. 'I have been terrified. I feared it was a plot.'

'No, no. The Queen Mother insisted that we profess friendship for each other and somehow she and the Queen have convinced the King that he wants it too.'

'And what does it mean? What friendship will those men ever have for you or you for them?'

'None,' he said. 'We shall be watchful of each other but at least we have declared our friendship and that has pleased the Queen Mother.'

'You will not cease to be watchful.'

Arm in arm they went into the castle.

'I have news for you,' he said. 'How soon will you be ready to leave?'

'With you? We are going away together?'

'That pleases you?'

'That for me is heaven,' she answered.

'We are going north,' he said. 'To Pontefract. It's the favourite of all my places, you know.'

'I did know and for that reason it is mine.'

'A fortress. We could hold out for months, Catherine, if any came against us. When can you be ready?'

'Tomorrow morning . . . early.'

'We will leave at dawn,' he said.

The stay in Pontefract was not long for there was trouble from the French.

The old King had died and there was a young King on the throne. This young Charles was very different from Richard. He had all the arrogance of youth and the vitality too. He made it clear from the start that there were going to be changes in his rule. He was not going to stand by and endure what he considered the insolence of the English claim to the crown of France. He was going to finish them once and for all. He was tired of hearing about the victories of Crécy and Poitiers. It was a great blot on the nation that a King of France had once been captured by that legendary figure the Black Prince and taken to England. That was something he intended to wipe out and he could only do it by achieving a victory which was as shattering to the English as that of Poitiers had been to the French. He would not be content with victories in France. He intended to carry the war into English territory. That would stop them boasting about the victories of Edward the Third and the Black Prince.

Young Charles had recently married and this had made him more than ever sure of himself. It was not exactly the commonplace fact of marriage but the manner in which his had taken place and which had shown his people that he was a man determined to have his way.

'Only the most beautiful Princess in the world will do for me,' he had brashly declared when reports were brought to him of the Bavarian Princess Isabeau. He had no intention of agreeing to a marriage before he had seen the girl. 'If her father cares to send her to me, then I shall assess her. If I do not like what I see she will return to Bavaria.'

Such an arrangement could not be entered into, was the

answer from Bavaria. They were not going to send their daughter for the King's approval.

'Then,' retorted the King, 'there will be no union between France and Bavaria. The matter is closed.'

A union with France was of great importance to Bavaria and could not be lightly thrown away. Moreover Isabeau was reckoned to be a very beautiful young girl and it was hardly likely that having seen her the young King would wish to send her away.

Isabeau herself was very confident of her charms and she wanted to go and confront this arrogant young man.

The outcome was that she went; and it was as she had predicted. When Charles saw her dusky beauty, her abundant dark hair, her languorous heavy-lashed dark eyes, her voluptuous little figure, he was completely enchanted and within a few weeks of her arrival in France the marriage was celebrated.

Now he was intent on carrying out his project to subdue England, to inflict the humiliation of making war in their own country.

The Scots could always be relied upon to rise against the English when they were in trouble. So while he was getting his fleet together at Sluys, Charles sent one of his greatest commanders, Jean de Vienne, to Scotland. The French forces were given a hearty welcome both at Leith and Dunbar and the task of harrying the English began.

From the South Richard set out with an army. John of Gaunt gathered his men together to join the King. He was able to muster a mighty force and in fact his followers made up a third of the entire army, which fact should have served as a lesson to the King that it would be unwise to antagonize his uncle. Moreover although John of Gaunt had not been successful in battle as his father and elder brother had, he had some experience of war; whereas the unwarlike Richard had little at all.

It was inevitable in gatherings of this kind that there should be certain frictions. The followers of one great lord would pick a quarrel with those of another. There were rivalries and jealousies continually cropping up. One of these occurred between the followers of Sir John Holland and Ralph, son of the Earl of Stafford, and during the mêlée one of Holland's favourite squires was killed.

John Holland was furious and swore he would be revenged on the murderers, who aware of the storm which was rising had taken refuge in sanctuary and in spite of Holland's appeal to Richard he was not allowed to have them brought to justice.

'This was a fight between two sets of men,' said Richard. 'One side was as much to blame as the other. It was just unfortunate that it was one of your squires who was killed. It could easily have been one of Stafford's.'

But John Holland was a man with a high opinion of himself and his position in relationship to the King. Had Richard forgotten he was his brother—well, half-brother. Surely some concession should be allowed to him.

He was a man of violent temper. 'Well,' he cried, 'if I cannot be given justice I will take it myself.'

He immediately set out for the quarters of young Stafford and before he had gone very far came face to face with Ralph himself, whereupon Holland drew his sword and killed him on the spot.

The Earl of Stafford was overcome with anguish and rage at the death of his son and the King was stricken with grief for young Ralph, who was about his own age and had been a favourite of his. There was an outcry. The Earl was demanding revenge.

'It seems,' said Holland, 'that when men kill all they have to do is go into sanctuary.'

He himself had sought such protection in Beverley Minster and there he remained, safe from Stafford and his followers.

This was a different matter from the death of the squire who had been struck down in a fracas between two parties. This was deliberate murder and even if Holland was the brother of the King, Stafford was going to have justice.

He went to Richard. 'My son has been murdered,' he said.

And he and the King wept together.

'My lord,' went on Stafford, 'I cannot stand aside and see this murderer go free. I want justice. This was my son and the victim of cold-blooded murder.'

Richard turned away. Anyone else yes. But his own brother! Oh, why had John been so foolish? Why couldn't he have let the matter go? Fights among squires were common enough.

The Earl of Stafford could see the King was wavering and he knew that if pressure was brought on him he would pardon Holland and that was something Stafford would not allow.

'My lord,' he said, 'if justice is not meted out in this case I and my friends will take the matter into our own hands. I beg leave to depart.'

He bowed now and went out.

Richard was distraught. What could he do?

Anne came to him and although she knew that it would greatly disturb the Queen Mother, her opinion was that John Holland should not go unpunished.

Meanwhile the expedition to Scotland was halted, and great matters could not be long delayed by such events.

The King made his decision: Holland should be banished from the country and his goods confiscated.

Joan had come to Wallingford Castle. It was restful there and she felt the need of rest. The journeys to Catherine Swynford and to the Queen had exhausted her even more than she had feared they would. There had been a certain amount of satisfaction though. They had achieved some purpose. Temporary relief perhaps but even that was important.

How she feared the future. Her life was beset by anxiety. Sometimes she thought how strange it was that it seemed to have been divided neatly down the middle. The gay careless days of abandoned pleasure and then this careworn existence. If she had married de Brocas as had at one time been suggested, would she have been spared this anxiety? It was a trial to be the mother of a King.

For the last years she had worried continuously. First over her husband's illness; then the loss of her first-born, then Richard being thrust into a position for which he was not well fitted.

There, she had admitted it. Richard had not the making of a King.

When one was old one faced realities.

She wanted peace in her family, and there was nothing but anxiety. She worried about her boys, all of them.

Messengers came to the castle. There was one from her son John and another from Richard.

She read Richard's first, and as she did so she put her hand to her fluttering heart. Trouble. She always feared it now when she saw a messenger.

A murder! John had murdered young Ralph Stafford and the Earl was insisting on vengeance. 'There is nothing to do, Mother, but to banish him. It is the only thing that will satisfy Stafford and I cannot have discord in the army now. Charles of France is threatening me. The Scots are threatening me. We must have unity. I have had to give way to Stafford. John will be banished and his goods confiscated.'

She went to a chair and sat down. She felt faint and giddy.

These turns were coming more frequently now and they followed exertion and shocks.

With trembling hands she opened John's letter.

'Richard is banishing me. I had to do this. I was not going to let Stafford's men murder mine. You must plead for me. Richard will listen to you. Dear Mother, you do not want me far away. I should be with you at this time . . .'

Her women came and found her lying back in her chair, the letters at her feet.

They got her to her bed. She was not quite sure then where she was. At times she believed she was in Bordeaux and the Prince was lying beside her. 'Limoges,' he kept murmuring in his sleep.

Something terrible had happened. She knew that. What was it? The death of young Edward? The death of the Prince?

No . . . no . . . that was in the past.

I must not lie here, she thought. I must do something. There is something that must be done. But what? But what?

There had been a messenger . . . Yes, letters. It was coming back to her. Brothers quarrelling. Richard sending John away.

'I have letters to write,' she said.

'My lady,' said her women, 'you are not fit to leave your bed.'

'There is something I have to do.'

She insisted. She could scarcely stand. The dizziness took possession of her.

'I must . . . I must do it,' she said.

She sat at her writing-table. They propped her up with cushions.

She thought of what she would say. 'Richard, he is your brother. There must not be this strife particularly in families. John will always stand beside you. He will fight for you . . .'

Yes, John would fight for the King because from the King blessings would flow.

They were ambitious, all of them. They stretched their greedy hands for lands, for riches . . . sometimes for a crown.

Why did they want a crown, these men? Did they not know that after the glorious crowning ceremony when the glittering thing was placed on their heads they spent the rest of their lives in keeping it there . . . or trying to?

'God help us all,' she murmured, 'and particularly Richard.'

She started to write.

When she had finished she sent for messengers. The letter was to be taken to the King without delay.

Then she went back to her bed. She had done her best. She had implored Richard to forgive John. Banished from the country! That could mean that he would never return.

The days passed and she grew a little better.

She waited for the return of the messenger. What was happening now? she wondered. They were going to wage war on Scotland and the French were threatening to invade England.

At such a time England needed a great Edward. A Black Prince. And all it had was Richard.

'Oh God preserve him,' she prayed. 'Give him that strength with which You graciously endowed his father. My Richard has need of it now.'

The messenger came back from the King. He sent his loving greetings to his mother, but there was nothing he could do to save John Holland.

He had murdered Ralph Stafford and must needs take his punishment. Richard wished at all times to please his mother whose loving care of him he would always remember with gratitude. But this was something he could not do . . . even for her.

She lay back on her bed. John would bitterly resent his brother's action. Trouble in the family. Where would it end?

She thought of them all . . . the uncles, John of Gaunt, a man too ambitious for comfort; Langley, well he was of not much account yet but who could say? She feared Woodstock. He had once even dared threaten Richard.

Trouble, she could see it looming. And how would Richard combat it . . . he and his young innocent Queen?

A lethargy had come over her. What could she do now?

Her days were numbered. How many were left to her? One? Two? Six?

She was ill. She was dying. She felt helpless to hold back the tide which was rising against her son. She had tried and failed.

There was no longer any point in living.

She lay back on her pillows—a tired old woman. She

thought: None would believe now that I was once the Fair Maid of Kent.

She had made her will and sent for the priest. She wished to be buried at the Church of Friars Minor at Stamford; and she wished to lie near the monument which she had had erected to Thomas Holland, her first husband. She thought fleetingly of those light-hearted days.

Then she folded her hands on her chest and lay down to wait for death.

It was not long in coming.

Her servants wrapped her in waxed swathings and placed her in a lead coffin. There she would lie until the King returned. They knew that his grief would be great.

THE FIVE LORDS APPELLANT

THE ARMY WAS on the border of Scotland and the invasion was about to begin. Richard decided to mark the occasion by creating two new Dukes. So far the only man to hold the title of Duke in the Kingdom was John of Gaunt, Duke of Lancaster. He now honoured his two younger uncles, Edmund Langley, Earl of Cambridge became the Duke of York and Thomas, Earl of Buckingham the Duke of Gloucester. Michael de la Pole was also honoured. He became the Earl of Suffolk.

Now the important matter of dealing with the Scots must go ahead. They must make it impossible for the French to use Scotland as a base; if they did the battle for England could well be lost.

The Scots with the French used their usual tactics which was to avoid a confrontation for as long as possible, luring the enemy farther and farther into the country and so lengthening their lines of communication, hoping by doing this that they would find it so difficult to feed and maintain their armies that they would at the final point suffer defeat.

There was a certain amount of friction between Richard and his uncle Lancaster. John of Gaunt wanted to push on; but Richard, thinking of his soldiers who would lack provisions, refused to allow this. It was whispered that John of Gaunt was hoping Richard would be killed in an affray and that was why he was eager to force a battle.

Richard was distraught. He kept thinking of his mother whom he knew to be very ill and he was hurt because he

285

had been unable to grant her request. If he himself alone had been involved, willingly would he have given way to her wishes. She did not understand. They came at him from all sides. Stafford, his uncle . . . the whole of them.

There was another matter which disturbed him. He loved his wife dearly. He relied on her so much. She was a perfect wife except in one respect; she had given him no children.

They were both young, and people were beginning to say, What is wrong?

There were so many problems. But the chief of course was this Scottish affair. They must not linger too long. They had to consider what arrogant Charles might do in the South, but all had agreed on one thing: The French must be made to realize that they could not use Scotland as a base.

They had pillaged the abbeys of Melrose and Newbattle; Holyrood had been sacked and part of Edinburgh burned. The Scots were in retreat; and the point had been driven home. Scotland was no place for the French to make an attack on England.

It had not been a glorious campaign; but it had achieved its purpose. They could return to the South satisfied.

When the King heard of the death of his mother he was prostrate with grief.

There was nothing Anne could do to console him.

'She died while I was in Scotland,' he cried, 'and I had refused her last request.'

'There was nothing you could do but refuse,' Anne consoled him. 'She would have known that. She was a wise woman.'

'Nevertheless she asked me and I refused her. I can never forgive myself.'

He was inconsolable. He could not forget that she had begged for her son's pardon and he had refused her.

'That was in her mind right at the end,' he mourned. 'I shall never forgive myself.'

Then he went over how they had been together in his childhood, how he had been her favourite although his elder brother Edward had been his father's, how she had taught him herself, how she had always been beside him, how devoted they had been; and it all came back to the final reproach.

She asked a boon of me and I refused her.

Impulsively he recalled John Holland. He restored his lands and granted him more. John embraced his half-brother with a show of great affection.

'I had to do it,' said Richard. 'You understand, brother, that I had to placate Stafford.'

'I understand,' said John. 'We are brothers . . . nothing can change that. Our mother would understand, Richard. She will know that we both had to act as we did.'

That was a great comfort to Richard.

Not long after his return John was married and his bride was Elizabeth, daughter of John of Gaunt. John was passionate in love and in hate, and, although Elizabeth had in fact been betrothed to the Earl of Pembroke, Holland had swept her off her feet and so far made her forget her previous vows that they had become lovers.

This had caused a great deal of trouble to her father who seeing that marriage with Pembroke was now impossible arranged to have the contract annulled and, to the great joy of his daughter and her bridegroom, they were married.

John Holland was pleased with himself. He had never yet failed, he boasted, to find a way out of his difficulties. A short time ago he had been exiled; now here he was, possessed of all the estates he had had and more, and married to the daughter of the most powerful man in the land. It was small wonder that he was delighted with the clever manner in which he had adjusted the turn of events.

Robert de Vere was decidedly unhappy because his two attempts to be rid of John of Gaunt had come to nothing. He was constantly pointing out to Richard that John of Gaunt would always try to overrule him. It had been obvious during the Scottish campaign. John of Gaunt had wanted to carry on with it; Richard had wisely decided that enough had been done.

'He did give way to my decision,' Richard pointed out. 'He did say that I was his King and he would follow me.'

'Words!' said de Vere. 'He will try to rule you and that means he will try to ruin me.'

The thought of John of Gaunt working against his beloved friend alarmed Richard.

Something would have to be done.

An opportunity occurred. It had always been the dream of John of Gaunt to gain the throne of Castile, and now that João of Avis had won the crown of Portugal in the battle of Albujarotta, he would be a worthy ally for he had his own quarrel with Castile. If Lancaster would join him they could attack the usurper of Castile and give themselves a chance of winning the crown for John and Constanza.

It was for the King and the Council to debate whether they would vote in favour of giving Lancaster the assistance he would need.

The debate did not take long. Both the enemies and friends of John of Gaunt decided that it would be good for the country for him to be out of it.

Already there had been two plots on Lancaster's life. He was too important a figure to be easily despatched and if he were killed it could well spark off a revolt in the country.

There was not a man in the Council who did not agree that this was an excellent opportunity to escape from a dangerous situation.

John of Gaunt in Castile would be removed from the political scene. That must bring a certain peace; and the Council voted for the necessary supplies to be provided.

So John prepared to leave for Castile. He was torn between two emotions—his love for Catherine Swynford and his ambition.

But this was the realization of his dream. He was going to win now. He would become the King he never could be in England. And to do it he would have to have Constanza beside him, and because of his love and ever present desire for Catherine Swynford he could feel nothing but repulsion for Constanza.

Yet he must go. Perhaps he would never return.

Catherine knew that.

He took his last farewell of her. He was taking his two daughters with him as well as his wife: Philippa, his daughter by Blanche, and Catherine, his daughter by Constanza.

If he were successful he would stay in Castile for the rest of his life. If he failed again he would return.

They spent that night together which could be their last. There was little to be said. It was life. It was fate. It had to be.

She might have wept. She might have begged him to stay or to take her with him. She knew that either would have been impossible for him.

No, she had always feared their parting would come. Now it had.

He spoke little either. What could he say? How could he explain that while he longed to feel the crown on his head yet he would never be happy again for she would not be with him?

'I'll come back one day, Catherine. Whatever happens I shall come back. Perhaps I may be able to send for you. I shall plan something, never fear.'

And she tried to smile and pretend that she believed him.

She watched him from the top of the turret as he left. She could not see him because her eyes were blinded with tears. He did not turn back.

It was symbolic of the future. She could not look into it. And for him there could be no turning back.

The threat of invasion continued. News came constantly across the Channel as to how the French were working away in their dockyards.

The young King of France was boasting of what he

would do when he conquered England. All the men should be slaughtered so that they could never make war in France again; the women and children should be taken as slaves. That would teach them to lay claim to the throne of France.

These rumours were just the sort to put heart into the English.

Were they afraid of a lot of Frenchmen? Never! They went over the old story of Crécy and Poitiers which proved, did it not, that one Englishman was worth ten Frenchmen?

Let them come! They would learn then the true state of affairs.

The Earl of Arundel was put in charge of the English fleet.

It was certainly a fine array of enemy ships which set sail from Rochelle for Sluys. Not only was it composed of French ships, but Spanish as well. It was under the command of Jean de Bucq, a Flemish admiral noted for his skill in sea warfare.

On the other hand Arundel had a reputation for sluggishness and when the French had raided the coast of Sussex—his own territory—he had been noticeably dilatory in taking action, so he seemed hardly a wise choice to take over the defence.

It was surprising therefore that he should when the occasion arose astonish everyone with his skill in handling the invaders. All through the spring he had worked indefatigably with Thomas Mowbray, Earl of Nottingham, to prepare a fleet to meet the French.

To see the magnificent armada sailing down the Channel was a sight to fill any heart with apprehension. Arundel however remained calm, watching it. Then he put his fleet into retreat trying to lure the French off course, but they would not be deceived by so obvious a ruse.

Arundel drew away waiting for the moment to attack. His archers were ready and as soon as the French were near enough they would send out a shower of those deadly weapons for which they had become renowned.

There was one enemy to which an invader might fail to

give enough attention—and that was the weather—and in particular the winds which could be encountered in the Channel and although this was unpredictable the English were more accustomed to its vagaries and could often judge beforehand what course it was about to take.

Arundel seemed to sense that the wind was going to work for him against his enemies and he was right. Up rose the wind at precisely the moment when it could be most useful to the English. The French were drifting off course. Now was the time to attack. The sky was dark with the shower of arrows which fell onto French decks; then the large ships went into the attack.

The battle was long and furious; but the French, magnificent as their vessels were, were no match for the English.

That day brought complete victory. Almost a hundred ships were captured.

Arundel had shed his slothful nature. Not content with crippling the French fleet he was determined to make it impossible for them to put another on the seas for years to come. Triumphantly he followed the remnants of the defeated armada to Sluys; he attacked it, sank some ships and crippled others, and even landed and burned the towns and villages.

After ten days during which not only did he attack the coast but helped himself to much of the treasure there, he returned to England bringing with him among other things nineteen thousand tuns of fine wine.

There was great rejoicing through the land. There had been so many disasters lately that victory was particularly sweet.

It was as though the Black Prince had been born again. England had risen out of her lethargy. She had heroes once more.

The most popular man in England was Richard Fitzalan, Earl of Arundel. He was indeed a hero for instead of taking much of the booty to himself, he decided that the people should benefit from it. Wine was very cheap in

England that summer. In the taverns people blessed Arundel and drank his health.

Richard and Robert de Vere were congratulating themselves on the manner in which John of Gaunt had been removed from the scene; but what they did not realize was that someone had stepped into his place, and Thomas of Woodstock, now Duke of Gloucester, could be as dangerous as his brother while lacking his ideals and restraint.

As uncle to the King, Gloucester regarded himself as his natural chief adviser. It was true his brother Edmund of Langley, now Duke of York, was the elder, but Edmund had never been one to push himself forward and openly showed his preference for the quiet life. Edmund was not ambitious but he would go along with his brothers if they asked him and he was more inclined to support them than his nephew who, as others did, he still regarded as a boy.

At this time Arundel, the hero of the hour, was a good man to have on one's side and Gloucester allowed his friendship with him to grow. He knew something of Arundel. A brave fighter it was true and he had shown something like genius in the recent sea battle, but Arundel, like most other men of the Court, was out for his own advancement.

Richard had taken to himself a certain dignity since the departure of Lancaster for Castile. It was time, he said to Robert de Vere, that he showed these people—and in particular his uncles—that he was their king and their ruler. They would have to realize he was no longer a boy to be guided by them.

These sentiments were heartily applauded by Robert who was well aware that he was the one whom these men would like to see removed from the King's side.

Gloucester had now taken the place of Lancaster in their minds. He was the great enemy. But neither the King nor his favourite realized that they were dealing with a very different character from John of Gaunt and that there was danger ahead.

To slight Gloucester Richard had granted Robert the

castle and lordship of Oakham together with the sheriff-dom of Rutland. This was infuriating to Gloucester because all these had belonged to his wife's ancestors and should have come his way.

Gloucester was growing more and more resentful and he was not keeping his discontent to himself.

The climax came with events in Ireland from which country urgent messages were constantly being received. The Irish were now being helped by the Scots and the Spaniards and they were determined to drive out the English colony. Action was needed. It was necessary to nominate some energetic man of high standing and ability to settle the disputes and show the Irish that the English could be as forceful within the country as on the high seas.

There was a great deal of controversy as to who would be the best man to send.

Gloucester and his friends were also complaining against Richard's Chancellor, Michael de la Pole, whom he had created Earl of Suffolk. The new Earl was disliked largely because he was not of the same high birth as those who sought to overrule him. He had the King's favour, they complained; Richard listened to him when he should have been paying attention to them. Meanwhile Suffolk's wealth was growing. He was an able man but like the rest he had to look after himself, his future and his family.

Gloucester wanted him out.

He went to see the King with the object of putting this suggestion to him.

Gloucester had never treated the King with the respect which Richard now expected. He still kept up the old attitude of the uncle talking to the nephew who was only a boy. There was little that could irritate Richard more.

Gloucester said in a hectoring way: 'Richard, there must be changes. Suffolk must go.'

'Who says so?' demanded Richard.

'*I* say so.'

'You, my lord? I have yet to learn that the Duke of Gloucester commands the King?'

'Come now, Richard. This is between us of the family—
the wise old uncle to the young nephew, you understand.'

'It so happens,' retorted Richard, 'that the nephew happens to be your King.'

'I know that full well. Have I not done homage to you
with my peers? There is unrest in the country. You must
dismiss Suffolk. The man is an upstart. Who is he? Is he
of noble birth? He has climbed to his special position
through sharp practice.'

'That is a lie,' said Richard.

'I seem to remember one John Cavendish fishmonger . . .'

'That was all cleared up. Cavendish was a rogue.'

'My dear nephew, it is not good for you to have for
your friends those who consort with fishmongers! Dismiss
this man. It is what the country and your ministers want.'

'Gloucester,' said Richard, his voice rising on a note of
anger, 'I would not dismiss the meanest varlet in my
kitchen at your bidding.'

Even Gloucester could see the Plantagenet temper rising—
and as he had had his full share of it he knew how far it
could carry them.

'You should think of my words,' he said, and bowing
went out.

Richard was fuming with rage. Robert de Vere was
close at hand. He had been listening to the interview.

'Your uncle gives himself airs,' he said. 'By God's
teeth, there is an arrogant fellow.'

'I think he's worse than Lancaster.'

'We feared Lancaster more,' Robert reminded him.

'I will show him,' cried Richard. 'Yes, I will. I will
show him he had better stop interfering with me. I shall
dissolve Parliament and we will go to Eltham and we will
stay there. See how they like that. The Parliament con-
spires against me, Robert. Why should I allow them to do
that? Yes, let us go to Eltham. We'll amuse ourselves
there.'

Richard began to laugh suddenly.

'Robert, I have an idea. How would you like to be Duke
of Ireland?'

'A Duke, Richard! Do you mean it?'

'Duke of Ireland.'

Robert was thoughtful. 'I should have to go to Ireland. That would mean leaving you . . . unless you came with me.'

'I'll tell you what we'll do, Robert. We'll make you the Duke of that country. Then perhaps you can send your deputy to sort out its troubles. Oh Robert, imagine their faces when they hear.'

They were convulsed with laughter considering it. It had soothed the King's temper. He was merry again.

Gloucester came to Eltham accompanied by Thomas Arundel—the younger brother of the naval hero—who was Bishop of Ely.

Richard wanted to refuse to see them but he thought better of that when he heard that they had not come on their own decision but had behind them the backing of the Parliament which did not like Richard's attempt to dissolve them, nor did they appreciate his leaving Westminster for Eltham.

When Gloucester and the Bishop were received by the King, they intimated that they wished to be entirely alone with him, without even the presence of the Queen and certainly not de Vere.

Richard, feeling obliged to grant this request, faced his uncle and the Bishop and haughtily asked what they wanted.

'We have come here to tell you, my lord, that the Parliament requires your presence at Westminster.'

'And shall I tell you, my lord, that I prefer to be here.'

'This is a State matter, my lord.'

'It would be well to remember it.'

Gloucester made an impatient gesture.

'Richard, I appeal to you as your uncle and one who has your welfare as deeply at heart as any. You cannot rule without your Parliament. Others have tried to do it and failed. I beg of you take heed.'

'I have never been able to rule,' cried Richard, 'except

once when the rebels were at our gates and the rest of you were cowering behind the walls of the Tower. Do you remember that, my lord?'

Gloucester did remember. That had been a terrifying time and he knew that he—like so many—had not distinguished himself by his bravery, whereas this boy—a stripling—had ridden out to face the mob. It was true. And because of that, great deeds had been expected of him. It had been his hour of glory—but alas a brief one.

Gloucester said: 'I remember it well, my lord. Who will ever forget? But you cannot live for ever on one brief spell of glory. You have a country to rule and a country is not a mob of unlettered peasants. You must listen to your Parliament. You must return to Westminster. You must not give your ear to favourites. Suffolk must go. The Parliament is demanding that.'

'It is not for them to demand.'

'Richard, I would like to remind you of what befell your great-grandfather.'

'I have heard it before.'

'Yes, but have you ever thought how easily it could happen to you? Imagine him—in his chamber of terror. They say they used a red hot poker . . .'

'Stop it!' cried Richard. 'I have heard it. I do not wish to hear it again.'

'Then remember it only as an example of what can happen to Kings who do not please their people. We shall expect you in Westminster within the next few days.'

'Get out from my sight!' shouted Richard.

Gloucester and Arundel bowed and departed.

Both Robert and the Queen tried to divert Richard, but they could not. He kept thinking of his tragic great-grandfather. That night he was awakened by nightmares. He screamed in his sleep.

It was almost as though the ghost of his great-grandfather was at his bedside warning him.

The next day he returned to Westminster. In due course, Suffolk was impeached and fined. There was a list of charges against him, among them that he had received grants from the King to which he was not entitled and that he had misappropriated funds. They were clearly trumped up that he might be banished from his office.

Richard had given way, terrified by the ghost of his great-grandfather.

The Queen had been watching events with some trepidation. Like Richard she was very wary of Gloucester and she knew that until Richard came of age one or other of the uncles would always attempt to overshadow him.

One of her favourite attendants was a Bohemian girl whom she had brought with her when she came to England. The girl was clever and, although not strikingly good looking, her vivacity made her one of the most attractive girls at Court.

Anne certainly enjoyed chatting with her. Some said that she was low born. The trouble with some people at Court was that they thought anyone who was not royal was far beneath their notice. As Anne had said to Richard —and he had agreed with her whole-heartedly in this— it was not birth that made an interesting person but character.

Robert agreed with them. He was very amusing and he enjoyed imitating some of the more pompous of the people who inhabited the Court. They could be riotously gay together. Launcecrona, the Queen's attractive attendant, was also a marvellous mimic and often Anne made her perform before the King and Robert.

Mimicry was rather a dangerous weapon. Robert said: 'Do you know the best way to defeat your enemies? It is to ridicule them.'

There was a great deal in that. So they had to be careful, and being careful had resulted in the four of them being together alone which was frowned on; but Richard had taught Anne that some of the most exciting things in life were those of which others did not approve.

Lately Anne had noticed that Robert's eyes were often on La Lancegrove as he called Launcecrona. She had seen their hands touch now and then; she had watched their lingering glances.

She thought it best to speak to Launcecrona and took the first opportunity.

'You have not forgotten, my dear,' she said, 'that Robert de Vere is married.'

'No, I had not forgotten it,' answered Launcecrona.

'And his wife happens to be a lady from a very noble family.'

'I know. Robert says that the King was determined to honour him and gave him Philippa de Couci to show his affection for him.'

'And the match was very beneficial to him. So Robert is irrevocably married.'

'My lady,' said Launcecrona, 'is anything in this life irrevocable?'

'Marriage with the royal family could well be,' said Anne, and when she saw Launcecrona's sly smile she continued to be uneasy.

It was not long after that when Launcecrona confided in the Queen that Robert was determined to put away his wife and marry her.

'How can he possibly do so?' asked the Queen.

'He says there are ways. He thinks that the King will help him.'

'The King!'

'Yes, you know how Richard loves him.'

'But on what grounds . . .'

'Robert says that grounds can be found. They are rarely together, are they? He wants Richard to write to the Pope.'

Anne was horrified. She knew that if Richard did any such thing a great many people would be displeased. There was no reason whatsoever why Robert should divorce his wife except that he had fallen in love with another woman and wanted to marry her. She doubted whether that would be considered sufficient reason for divorce.

Richard talked to her about it.

'Robert is quite determined,' he said. 'He talks of little

else. La Lancegrove is very amusing. They suit each other very well.'

'But what of his wife?'

'He asked me to do what I can with the Pope.'

'Richard . . . can you?'

'I have always told Robert that I will do anything . . . just anything for him.'

'I know, but you were not thinking of anything like this.'

'I shall do what I can for him, Anne.'

She was astounded. She had not realized the extent of Richard's devotion to his friend. Richard was watching her intently. 'I want you to do something too, Anne.'

She waited, her heart beating faster.

'I want you also to write to the Pope. I want you to tell him how important it is that there should be a dispensation, that Robert should marry Launcecrona.'

'On what grounds?' asked Anne.

'We must think of something which makes it very necessary.'

For the first time since she had come to England Anne wanted to disagree with her husband.

Before she had been eager to love him and be loved by him. She had understood how easily his temper was aroused and had determined it never should be against her.

They had been so happy together. But now he was asking her to do something of which she could not approve.

For one thing they could hold nothing against Robert's wife. It was true she and her husband saw little of each other but then it had been a marriage of convenience and as such had seemed satisfactory. If Robert had not fallen under the spell of the gay Bohemian there would never have been any question of divorce.

And they were drawing her into it. Little had she thought when the four of them had been so merry together that this would be the result.

They were all persuading her—Richard and the two lovers. Launcecrona was her attendant, her *friend*. She must do this for her.

Perhaps she was foolish. Perhaps it was a momentary weakness. Usually she liked it to stand up for her own opinions. But they were all persuading her. 'Come, Anne, what difference does it make to you? Your opinion will mean so much. Urban wants all the support he can get. He will want it from Bohemia as well as England.'

So she gave way.

How merry they were together then. Launcecrona and Robert danced round the apartment. Richard took her hand and they joined in. The four friends. Richard was contented. These were the people he loved best. He was happy with them; and he had so many cares.

It was not as though Philippa had loved her husband, Anne reasoned with herself, and Robert and Lancegrove were so happy together.

When it was known that Robert de Vere was seeking to put his wife away simply because he wanted another woman, the fury and resentment against him burned more fiercely than ever.

Was there nothing the King would not do for this man?

When the news reached Gloucester he grew pale with rage. This was an insult to his niece. How dared this fellow put aside a royal princess for the sake of a low-born Bohemian!

He would not forget this insult; but, hating Robert de Vere as he did, it was Richard whom he blamed.

He must go, he vowed secretly. He *shall* go.

The matrimonial affairs of Robert de Vere were like a spark which set off the conflagration. Since de Vere had become Duke of Ireland, it was asked, why did he not take action in that troublesome country? What was he doing lounging at Court, sporting with his concubine and the King and the Queen? There was work to be done.

'Gloucester is the enemy,' said Richard. 'I seem to be plagued by uncles. Gloucester is worse than Lancaster. Listen. You will have to make a feint of going to Ireland, Robert. We will leave London together for I shall come to

300

see you off. But you will not go to Ireland. We will march back to London surrounded by an army and there we shall denounce Gloucester as the traitor he is.'

It was a wild plan, as all Richard's plans were.

They left London and made their way to Wales where they were joined by Suffolk, Sir Robert Tresilian, the harsh judge of those peasants who had been brought to trial after the great revolt, and Alexander Neville who was the Archbishop of York and had always shown allegiance to the King in his conflict with his uncles.

They were to march on London and having made sure of the Londoners' support, summon the King's adversaries to face a charge of treason.

Richard was welcomed in London but when it was known that Gloucester, Warwick and Arundel, realizing what was happening, had gathered together a rival force and were waiting near Highgate, the Londoners changed their minds.

They were not, they declared, going to risk having their heads broken for the sake of the Duke of Ireland.

The result was that the three lords, Gloucester, Warwick and Arundel came to see the King.

Gloucester cried out that he had intended no treason against the King. It was his advisers who were making the trouble and he should rid himself of them.

Richard and his uncle faced each other, each trying to curb his anger, each wondering how far he could go.

Gloucester cried: 'We are asking for the trial of your advisers. Nothing else will satisfy the lords.'

Richard was silent. They meant Robert de Vere, de la Pole who was the Earl of Suffolk, Alexander Neville, Archbishop of York, and Robert Tresilian, the Lord Chief Justice.

There was silence in the chamber. Richard felt fear suddenly grip him. He could not get out of his mind those nightmares which had haunted him of his great-grandfather, Edward the Second. He knew his history. It had begun with him rather like this.

When those fears came on him he felt a compulsion to give way . . . or appear to give way.

He relented suddenly. Gloucester and his friends must have their way. He would agree to the parliamentary impeachment of his friends.

As soon as they had gone he despatched messengers to them all.

Escape, was his command. Get away while there is time.

The wrath of Gloucester was great when he realized that the King's favourites had escaped.

He went to Huntingdon and there was met by Henry of Bolingbroke. It was the first time the son of John of Gaunt had stepped into prominence, and none at that time—least of all Richard—was aware of the significance of this.

'By God's eyes,' cried Gloucester to Henry of Bolingbroke, 'Richard is heading for disaster. Can you see that he is setting out on the path taken by our ancestor? This man de Vere is another Gaveston. If he continues in this way he could lose him his crown.'

And if he lost his crown who then would take it?

There were lights in Gloucester's eyes, and they were reflected in those of Henry of Bolingbroke.

Richard was desolate. There was nothing but disaster everywhere he looked. The forces against him were too strong.

He wept with Anne. 'I am a King who has never been allowed to rule,' he said. 'If I had been older when I came to the throne how different everything would have been!'

She comforted him, but she knew there was little comfort to offer.

Even the people did not love them as they once had. They were fond of Richard in a way but they were not prepared to fight to keep him on the throne. As for her, she had been their mild and meek little Queen but they now blamed her for Robert de Vere's divorce for they knew that she had written to the Pope and asked him to grant it, and they would never feel the same towards her again.

There was trouble everywhere, terrible trouble. It had been foolish really to become involved in Robert's divorce and remarriage. For what had happened since? He and Launcecrona were parted.

Robert was now raising an army to fight the King's enemies.

She knew it was hopeless to pit his strength against men like Gloucester, Warwick and Arundel, the hero who had driven the French off the seas. Robert had never been noted for his military skill.

Launcecrona and she sat together talking quietly of the disasters. All the merriment was over now. They were both deadly serious.

And as they sat there the door was flung open and a groom came in.

They stared at him. The Queen rose in horror thinking the man had come to kill them. For what other reason would a groom break into the royal chamber?

Then Launcecrona gave a little cry.

'Robert!'

Robert it was, scarcely recognizable as the dandy of the past except when he spoke.

'I am in great haste,' he said. 'I have come to see the King.'

'I will get him myself,' said Anne, and left the husband and wife together for a few moments.

Richard came hurrying in. 'Robert!' he cried and they embraced. It was almost as though they were the lovers for their reunion was more poignantly loving than that of Robert and Launcecrona.

'Robert, my dear, dear friend, what brings you here?'

'Rout. Disaster! I am a fugitive, Richard.'

'And in danger!'

'Acute danger. Let me tell you quickly what happened. My men were routed by Arundel's at Radcot. My men deserted me, Richard. They had no heart to fight Arundel's men. Arundel persuaded them to desert me. There was nothing for it but flight. I only escaped by plunging into the river with my charger. I lost my baggage, my money . . . even letters of yours which I had always cherished.'

'Never mind . . . never mind now,' said Richard. 'You must get away from here.'

'Abroad. It is the only way. They are bent on bloodshed, Richard, depend upon it. They want scapegoats and they will choose those from your friends.'

'Then, my dearest, go from here with all speed. You must have money.'

'If I can get to the river I shall take boat to the Low Countries.'

'Go, go!' cried Richard. 'I beg of you. My heart goes with you.'

They gave him food and money, and did what they could to make sure he escaped undetected.

Anne was sad, looking fearfully into the future. Of only one thing could she be certain: there would be no more jolly parties for four in the royal apartments.

It was good news that Robert had escaped to Flanders. But that was not the end of the matter.

The situation had not been eased. Robert might have dodged his fate but the others remained. There was the King to be faced and he must know the truth.

Gloucester and his friends planned together.

With a gleam in his eyes Gloucester expressed the opinion that Richard was unfit to rule and should be deposed.

Arundel agreed with him.

But there was caution among the rest. Henry of Boling-broke had begun to make his presence felt. He said little, but his eyes were watchful.

He waited for the lords to say what he knew they would. The deposition of the King was too drastic.

Gloucester tried to contain his temper. They were thinking—and of course they were right—that if Richard were deposed, John of Gaunt occupied in Castile and

Edmund Duke of York too lazy to want the crown, to whom would it fall but Gloucester?

Henry of Bolingbroke was not sure that would suit him now. Richard was a weak King but his father would not wish to see his Uncle Gloucester replace Richard. Who could say what the outcome would be in Castile and if John of Gaunt had to return once more, he was the eldest living son of Edward the Third; he was the one who would be next in line. Of course there was Lionel's daughter, but she could surely be dealt with.

And if by some glorious turn of fate John of Gaunt became King, his eldest son would follow him.

No, this was surely not the moment to depose Richard. Even so Bolingbroke was on the side of the lords who had been raising their voices to save the King from his evil advisers; and he was with those who prepared to present an ultimatum to the King.

It was Christmas Day—a most uneasy one for Richard and Anne. In spite of the usual merriment, rumours had persisted; and the streets of London were filled not with merrymakers but with those who whispered together and asked what would happen next. Even the mummers had lost their zest and there was no seasonal joy in the singing of the carols.

Richard, dressed with his usual splendour, glittering with jewels, was startled when the five lords burst in on him.

They joined arms—a gesture of their solidarity—as they marched towards him, each wearing the colours of their families. Gloucester, Arundel, Warwick and the two younger men, Mowbray and Bolingbroke.

'What means this?' stammered Richard.

Gloucester was the spokesman.

'My lord,' he said, 'we have in our possession letters in your hand, captured at Radcot. These show that you sanctioned the raising of an army to make war within this realm. You have suggested that help might be procured from the King of France for which you would barter England's possessions in that land.'

Richard felt sick with fear. They had the better of him now.

'How dare you break thus into my presence . . . arm in arm as to come against me?' he demanded.

'My lord,' said Bolingbroke. 'Come to the window. Look below. See the forces gathered there.'

'You have raised an army against me!'

'We have raised an army, my lord, for your preservation and that of your realm.'

Gloucester came and stood beside them at the window.

'There below you see men determined to fight for the right,' he said, 'but this is not a tenth of those that have risen to destroy those false traitors who have given you such ill counsel.'

Richard was trembling. 'What would you have of me?' he asked in a low voice.

That you come to Westminster that you may hear in Parliament the accusations which shall be brought against those who have put this realm in danger by their wicked counsel.'

He knew that he was beaten. There was a cold rage in his heart against those five who had dared march towards him arms linked to show they stood firmly together against him.

I will have vengeance on them . . . every one of them, he promised himself. But there was nothing he could do now but obey.

'I will come to the Parliament,' he said.

That was triumph for his accusers. How he hated them. Particularly when they left Bolingbroke and Mowbray to guard him and kept their soldiers stationed outside the Tower.

He sat with his head buried in his hands. Bolingbroke was with him.

A curse on you, Cousin, he thought. This is what I would expect of John of Gaunt's son.

He clenched his fists.

'By St. John the Baptist,' he cried suddenly, 'why should I submit to this? Why should I be forced to betray my friends . . . those who have served me well . . . Who are these men to tell me what I must do? Am I not the King?'

Bolingbroke spoke very quietly. 'Richard, Cousin . . . I do not speak thus for lack of respect but to remind you of the kinship between us. You have come very near to losing your throne.'

'That is what Gloucester wants. My uncle . . . and my enemy.'

Bolingbroke did not deny that. 'I have urged him to curb his rashness,' he said. 'Richard, if you do not do what is asked of you they will depose you. They will set up a new king in your place.'

'Gloucester? He is not next in line.'

'Gloucester is here and Gloucester is strong. Listen, Richard, you must do as they wish, if you would keep your crown.'

He looked into Bolingbroke's glowing eyes. There were thoughts there which he could not read. But he knew Bolingbroke was right.

How long that night was! Richard saw clearly now what lay before him. He would have to betray his friends or lose his crown. That was the choice.

He could not lose his crown. It was a cruel and bitter choice.

The five who were known as the Lords Appellant and the Parliament known as the Merciless Parliament had forced this on him.

He vowed vengeance on the five—but he gave way.

They were terrible days that followed. The King's favourites were all declared traitors and condemned to death. Robert was safe and Suffolk managed to escape in the disguise of a Flemish poulterer; Neville was not condemned to death as he was an archbishop but he was outlawed and all his goods confiscated; Tresilian suffered the fearful death meted out to traitors and was hanged, drawn and quartered. His terrible fate did not arouse much sympathy throughout the country as his cruelty to the peasants was remembered.

When Simon Burley was arrested there was great sorrow in the royal household.

'Simon!' cried Richard to Anne. 'What has he ever done?'

Anne was stunned. She had grown very fond of Simon Burley! He it was who had come to Prague to negotiate for her marriage; she had liked him from the moment she had seen him. He had talked so appealingly of Richard and had made her look forward to seeing her new home. He had been one of their dear friends.

'I'll not allow them to harm Simon,' cried Richard.

'We must try to stop them,' Anne agreed. 'Oh Richard, we can do something.''

'Arundel always hated him. And it seems to me that on the strength of his victory at sea, Arundel feels he should rule the country.'

'It is Gloucester I fear most.'

'My own uncle,' cried Richard bitterly. 'I tell you this, Anne, it would do me much good to see his head on a lance.'

'Hush,' cautioned Anne. 'People listen. What can we do about Simon?'

'I shall tell Parliament that I'll not have him harmed. He has been my friend since childhood.'

It was all rather ineffectual talk, Anne knew; but it soothed Richard so it achieved some purpose and he needed soothing at this time.

Simon was accused of misusing power and of promoting a corrupt Court about the young King; he had raised his income in a few years from twenty to three thousand marks; it was even said that he was planning to sell Dover to the French.

It was no use protesting that this was nonsense. They were bent on his destruction.

When Gloucester with Arundel came to the Tower to

see the King, both he and Anne declared their wish that Simon Burley should be pardoned.

Anne went on her knees before Arundel and cried: 'My lord, listen to me. This man has done no harm. Or if he has it was done in innocence. He is a good man. He is my friend . . . mine and the King's. I implore you to set him free.'

Arundel was an arrogant man. He did not seem to realize that it was the Queen who knelt before him—or if he did, he enjoyed her humility.

He said: 'I have no intention of freeing Simon Burley, Madam. He must take the consequences of his actions.'

'It is unjust. It is cruel . . .' cried Anne.

Se caught at his robes but he walked on and she fell to one side.

It was unheard-of arrogance to treat the Queen so.

Richard went to the Queen and helped her to her feet.

'These men shall learn that I am the King,' he muttered.

His uncle Gloucester said in a loud voice: 'It is because we wish you to remain King that we bring these charges and are determined to see them carried out.'

There it was again, the threat. He could almost hear his great-grandfather's cries coming all the way from Berkeley Castle.

'We cannot spare Simon Burley,' said Gloucester firmly. 'Your cousin Bolingbroke has soft feeling for him too. But though he has made himself our ally I could not spare this man for him.'

A further insult, thought Richard. Not even for Henry of Bolingbroke when the Queen had gone on her knees to him!

'So you have sentenced him to the traitor's death!' cried Richard.

'He is a traitor,' retorted Gloucester.

The traitor's death. Hanged, drawn and quartered—that venerable old friend to be so treated!

'That,' said Richard determinedly, 'is something I shall not allow.'

Gloucester shrugged his shoulders. The point was that

the man was removed from the sphere of influence. How he went was not all that important. It might be advisable to give way on this point. Let Burley go by way of the axe.

He died on Tower Hill, that dear old friend.

The King and Queen were plunged into melancholy. There was nothing to be done now but mourn, and, thought the King, plan vengeance.

Thomas Arundel was made Archbishop of York in Neville's place and the government was carried on in Richard's name.

TRAGEDY AT SHEEN

As *she sat* stitching at one of her gowns in the manor of Kettlethorpe, Catherine Swynford was brooding as she often did on that period in her life which on looking back seemed so brief and so glorious.

She had been exalted then; not because she had been admired by the son of a King but because she had loved and been loved. She had believed then—and again but briefly— that the love she and John of Gaunt had borne each other was rare in the history of the world. There had been times when she had deluded herself into believing that it would go on for ever. She should have been wiser. It was true that the convent-bred girl had become the wife of an obscure knight and had lived largely away from great events. And then she had seen him. He had seemed to her like a god. John of Gaunt, the most notorious man in England, and he had been her lover.

All was over. But she would never forget; and there could never be any real contentment for her because always her thoughts would be straying back to the past with that infinite longing which would not be subdued. It imbued everything with a gentle melancholy. Yes, she accepted fate but she could never be truly happy again.

He had been good to their children. He had done what he said he would; but the fact remained that they were bastards, though bastards of royal blood. There were plenty of those about. But hers were different, she had always maintained. They had not been begotten in some hurried fumble. They had been conceived in love.

But what was the use? It was over and done.

She would never forget their last night together. There had been that terrible indecision which had obsessed him. But she had known that he would go. He had to go. He loved her, yes, but he was a man with a vision. Ambition there would always be, and he must serve it.

So now there she was, a lady of the manor, well cared for. He had seen to that. Her jewels would keep her for the rest of her life if need be. He would put their sons in high places. Even Thomas, her son by Hugh Swynford, had his niche and was with Henry of Bolingbroke. John, Henry and Thomas Beaufort would be even better provided for. She had no fears on that score.

But none of this could ease her melancholy.

She had her attendants; she lived like a lady in her manor, looking to her household, with plenty to minister to her needs. And here in the country now and then news came from Court of the young King's conflict with his uncle of Gloucester and she thought: At least John is spared those troubles.

She had heard that the young King had come near to being driven from his throne, but a year had passed since, mercifully, those troubles had blown over and he was now in control.

He had taken firm action; he had reminded those about him that he was twenty-one years old. He would have no more regencies, he said. He would rule himself.

The country had grown quieter and there had been no more disturbing rumours for some time.

So life went on—one day very like another. So will it be until the end of my days, thought Catherine. I shall grow old and if he did come back he would not know me.

But it was not to be so.

One misty November day when she had set aside her needlework because the light was so bad she was startled by the arrival of visitors.

This was a somewhat rare occurrence and always

welcomed. It was stimulating to hear news of the outside world.

She was a good housewife and there were always pies in the larder, for there were many in the household to be fed and she liked to be prepared should any travellers call and there was a constant stream of beggars to come pleading for a bite to eat and she never refused them.

She went down to the courtyard. A man leaped from his horse and as she looked at him she thought she was dreaming.

He stood still gazing at her while she stood as though rooted to the ground.

Then he said: 'Catherine. You have not changed one small bit.'

He held out his hands and they were in each other's arms.

So he was back. The world was suddenly gay. It was bleak November but it was spring to her. She was wild with joy. She called throughout the house: 'Fires must be lighted. Flesh must be roasted. The best . . . the very best. My lord has come home.

'I shall die of joy,' she told him.

'I too,' he answered.

He must look at her. He must touch her hair, her soft white skin.

'So often have I done so in my dreams,' he said.

Nothing had changed. They were the same passionate lovers as they had been when they had first met. There was so much to know. So much to learn.

They must love and they must talk. He must not go away again.

He would not, he promised her. From now on they would be together always.

'You do not know how near I came to staying, to abandoning all my hopes of Castile for your sake.'

'Ah, John, I knew,' she answered. 'But I knew too that you would go.'

'Those lonely years . . . barren of love!'

'Perhaps they will come again,' she said.

He shook his head.

'I shall never leave you again, Catherine,' he said solemnly.

'You will never cease to want a crown,' she said. 'I know you well. You love me, but ambition is there. It was born in you. You are the son of your father. He sought the crown of France . . . hopelessly it seems now, and you will always seek that of Castile.'

He smiled at her. He had much to tell her, then she would understand. He wanted news of their children. His aim was to legitimize them. Yes, he was going to do it one day. Richard would agree. He must tell her that Richard had wished him to come home, had *asked* him to come home.

'He does not trust my brother Gloucester.'

'Oh John, there will be this strife again. There was a time after you had gone when there was talk of war . . . war here in England. The barons rising against the King.'

'I know . . . I know. Since the time of John such things have been spoken of. Then there was my grandfather. Once a King is deposed, it is remembered. History can repeat itself. Never fear. Richard will stay on the throne. I think he liked me better after I had gone . . . that is he preferred me to my brother.'

'And you, John, you dreamed of a crown. You wanted a crown. And Castile . . .'

'Good news from Castile, Catherine.'

She could scarcely believe it. Castile was no longer a menace. It had come about as John said, in a most natural way. The happiest way to settle all disputes between countries was through marriage.

'I fear, Catherine, you will never see my daughters Philippa and Catherine again. Unless of course you travel to Castile and Portugal or they visit us here. Your charges are wives now, my dearest. What think you of that!'

'It seems to please you so I suppose I must be pleased.'

'I married Philippa to my ally João of Portugal. A wise

move. I was not sure that I could trust him but the alliance put a seal to that.'

'And Philippa is happy?'

'Philippa is Queen of Portugal.'

Catherine looked at him a little sadly. 'You set such store by crowns,' she said; and she thought of little Philippa and her grief when her mother had died and how she and her sister Elizabeth had been as Catherine's own children. She had loved them as dearly since they were John's.

'Philippa was never so well able to take care of herself as Elizabeth was,' she said.

John frowned and she wished she had not said that for she knew that he'd never liked Elizabeth's marriage to the King's half-brother, wild John Holland.

'The best news of all is what has happened to my daughter Catherine. She has settled the matter of the Castile succession and settled it most satisfactorily.'

'Catherine . . .'

'Your namesake, my dearest. Constanza is happy with the result and so am I. Let me tell you how it came about. The campaign was dragging on. There was trouble all about us. Constanza and I came near to being poisoned.'

She caught her breath with horror.

'These things will be,' he said lightly. 'The King of Portugal had fallen dangerously ill and it really seemed as though he were on his deathbed. Then we began to suffer the same symptoms. We kept watch and the fates be praised we found the culprit. He was trying to get rid of us.'

'He was working for Castile?' asked Catherine.

'It would seem so. However we had found the root of the trouble and it was amazing how quickly we all recovered. But such incidents sober one. I had come to the conclusion that this battle would never be satisfactorily resolved and it occurred to me that I had a daughter, Juan of Castile had a son. If they married that would settle the matter once and for all.'

'So much better than those endless wars which give victory to one side and then the other and decide nothing for more than a few weeks.'

'My wise Catherine. I put out feelers for the match. Juan was not very anxious for it, but we had a stroke of good fortune, for the Duc de Berri was looking for a wife. He wanted a young one and only a lady of nobility would do for such a noble Prince of France. He was a widower and not very young; I had no intention of giving him Catherine but I pretended to consider. And that frightened Juan. He did not want a powerful French claimant for the Castilian throne. He decided he would take Catherine for his little son, Enrique.'

'And how old is Enrique?'

'Ten. But Catherine is only fourteen. They are ideally suited.'

Catherine sighed. She herself had made a marriage of convenience with Hugh Swynford and she knew how unsatisfactory such marriages could be.

'I was very clever, Catherine. I have no intention that Catherine shall lose her right to the throne of Castile. Juan has a second son Fernando and part of the treaty is that Fernando shall remain unmarried until the match has been consummated.'

'So this matter of Castile is settled and you have ceased to long to be its King?'

'I have grown older and wiser, sweet Catherine. I tell you truthfully that all through these negotiations I said to myself: If I can settle this matter to the satisfaction of all I shall go home to my Catherine.'

'And so you did think of me while you made these plans.'

'All the time I longed for you.'

'The Duchess?' she asked quietly.

'Constanza is pleased that her daughter should be Queen of Castile. She is content, I think. She too is weary of all the conflict.'

'She knows you have come to me?'

'She knows it and she makes no protest. She is Castilian at heart. She will never be anything else. She wishes to live with her own people about her. There is no room for me in her life.'

'As soon as she became your wife she knew of my existence.'

'I could not keep it from her.'

'She knew then that your marriage to her was purely for the sake of the crown of Castile.'

'Marriages such as ours are usually for such reasons.'

'And she accepts this?'

'She must. It is life. She does not want me, Catherine. You should have no qualms. Constanza is happy now that Catherine is married to the heir of Castile. Catherine will be Queen of the Asturias. That is all she asks.'

'And for us . . .'

'Together for ever,' he said. 'We shall not be parted. You will come to Court when I am at Court.'

'You think I shall be accepted?'

'If I say you shall be, so shall you be.'

She could laugh albeit a trifle uneasily. It would not be easy, she knew. The people had never loved him. They had never liked his relationship with her. Whore, they had called her. Well, she could endure that.

She was happy again. He was home.

The last years had passed more comfortably after that period when it had seemed that civil war could break out in England. After submitting to the restrictions that had been imposed on him for a year Richard had broken free, reminded his ministers that he was past twenty-one and was determined to rule. But he did not forget how close he had been to disaster and acted with caution.

The Queen was constantly at his side. He trusted her completely. He knew that everything she said was her considered judgment as to what was best for him.

Anne had been closer to him since the enforced absence of Robert de Vere. He listened to her, took her advice and was guided by her; those who wished him well rejoiced in the Queen for she was a sobering influence.

Her great sorrow was that she was childless. Richard consoled her. He was not going to have their relationship tarnished in any way by such a consideration. They were both very young. It might well be that she would be fruitful later.

'Our lives lie before us,' he constantly told her.

'I feel that I fail you and the country,' she replied sorrowfully.

But he shook his head. 'I would not have you different in one way,' he assured her.

'I know that you love me as I love you. I know it is rare for people such as ourselves to have found this contentment. But how much more contented I could be if I had a son.'

'Then you would concern yourself more with him than with me. No, rest content as we are. I am happy while you are with me.'

'If we had a son the people would be pleased,' Anne insisted. 'It would settle the matter of the succession. So many eyes are on the throne. John of Gaunt always wanted it and so does his son, Bolingbroke.'

'Lionel's family come before them.'

'That's exactly what I say. There are too many greedy eyes on it. Gloucester . . .'

Richard's face darkened at the mention of Gloucester. He hated that uncle. He would never forgive him for the contempt and insults he had thrown at him.

Anne went on hastily: 'You see what I mean. But no matter. We have time.'

Richard went on: 'I like not Arundel's marriage.'

He was referring to the Earl of Arundel who had stood beside Gloucester in the recent trouble which still rankled bitterly. Arundel had recently married Philippa, the daughter of the Earl of March and widow of the Earl of Pembroke. This Philippa was in the line of succession through Lionel.

'Arundel had no right to marry without my consent,' went on the King angrily.

'Well, that point was made clear and he was fined four hundred marks for it.'

'It was not enough. I should have liked to annul the marriage.' Richard laughed grimly. 'He has a virago there. I wish him joy of her.'

'It is over and done,' said Anne, but she wondered whether it was. She did not trust Arundel. He with War-wick and Gloucester had worked together—no doubt still did—and it was not for the good of the King.

They often talked of Robert de Vere. Launcecrona had gone out to join him and they missed the diverting company of those two.

Richard was always hoping that Robert would come back. He knew though that if he did the trouble would flare up again. He would not be able to stop himself showering gifts on the fascinating young man and Robert would not be able to stop himself giving advice. The people would be in revolt against them.

They seemed to dislike a man having a member of his own sex for a close friend. They would compare him with Edward the Second.

Oh, great-grandfather of mine, you have a lot to answer for, thought Richard. The calumnies which people are only too ready to throw at me, the haunting dreams of the night.

There was news now and then of Robert. He had gone to Paris where he had lived for a year and been treated well which was amazing and must have been due to his excessive charm for it was certain that the Sieur de Couci, who was there, would have done everything in his power to make life uncomfortable for the son-in-law who had repudiated his daughter.

It was comforting that Michael de la Pole who had escaped at the same time was with him. They had become fast friends during their exile.

Richard talked of him constantly. When he was excited over some new garments and discussed with Anne how the jewels should be arranged on it, he would often say: 'Robert would like it this way I am sure.'

Then one day news came from France. It left Richard desolate.

Robert had fallen from his horse when out hunting the wild boar and the animal had turned on him. He was so badly gored that he had died of his wounds.

Richard shut himself away and could not be comforted even by Anne.

'Never to see him again!' he mourned. 'And they sent him away from me. Anne, I shall never, never forgive them for parting us.'

Anne murmured soothingly that he must try to put the tragedy behind him.

'I shall have his body brought home,' he said. 'He shall be buried at Earls Colne with his ancestors. It is what he would have wanted.'

Richard had thrown himself into a fever of activity after the news of Robert's death. He had at last to be reconciled to the fact that he would never see his friend again. There was no other young man whom he made quite the friend Robert had been, although he had his favourites among the younger and handsomer men of the Court. His main devotion was given to his wife and he looked to her for advice on all things. She always gave it cautiously, humbly almost. She tried to persuade him into doing what she considered the correct action rather than to voice her opinions strongly.

Life at Court had become more extravagant than ever. His passionate interest in clothes seemed to have grown rather than diminished as he grew older. He would spend a whole morning cogitating on the cut of a houppelande or cote hardie and what jewels should be used to decorate them. The toes of his shoes must always be longer than those about him and as a consequence shoe points were growing to such an extent the they extended six inches beyond the toe. A few had taken this fashion to extremes and they even wore these points so long that they had to be tied to the knees. The King loved jewels and consequently his garments were lavishly decorated with them. One of his coats was so richly embroidered with gold and precious stones that it was valued at thirty thousand marks.

Anne felt that she could only afford to be slightly less splendid. The costliness of her garments sometimes made her a little apprehensive, especially when she and Richard rode out together through the streets of cities where the poor gathered to see them.

Richard thought it pleased them. 'They like to see the splendour of our lives,' he said.

'Which,' pointed out Anne, 'could draw attention to the drabness of their own.'

He liked her sage wisdom. It made him feel safe.

There came one day in his life which he would never forget.

There had been small outbreaks of pestilence in several parts of the country but this was a fairly normal occurrence and aroused little comment.

Anne was at Sheen Palace at the time and Richard had been prodded into action to do something about the Irish question which was causing such great concern. He was well aware that some action would have to be taken and with his ministers he was discussing the possibility of taking an army to that troublesome land.

It was in the middle of these negotiations that he received news that Anne had been taken ill.

He left everything and went with all haste to Sheen. Although concerned he was not deeply so. Anne was young and healthy and this must be some minor ailment. Nevertheless he must be at her bedside to assure her of his devotion.

When he reached Sheen Palace he received a shock. He scarcely recognized the pallid figure on the bed. She smiled wanly when she saw him.

He knelt by her bed in bewildered grief.

'Anne . . . Anne . . .' he whispered. He could find nothing to say but her name.'

'Richard . . .'

He looked at her numbly.

'I am dying, Richard,' she said.

'No, no! Not you, Anne. You are going to get well. Why only a day or so ago when I left you . . . you were well. Can I not leave you for a few hours that you must cause me this terrible anxiety by falling sick. Oh it is only a minor ailment. You will be well tomorrow.'

She smiled at him and he tried to fight the cold fear which had come into his heart. It numbed him. He had not

321

thought this possible. Why should Anne, who was so young and so full of vitality . . . why should Anne die and leave him alone?

An hour passed. He would not move from her bedside, and as he watched there hope started to ebb slowly away . . . as did her life.

She *was* dying. His Anne. But how could it have been?

He questioned the doctors. What had happened? Why should she have been so struck?

'Pestilence is no respecter of rank, my lord,' said the doctors.

'What hope is there?' he demanded.

'There is always hope, my lord,' was the answer.

'Then make her well,' he cried. 'I command you. I order you . . . bring her back to me.'

They went to the sick room. He was there kneeling by her bed.

'Anne,' he cried. 'Anne, don't leave me. Speak to me, Anne.'

She said: 'Richard, my love, my king, you must look at the truth. I shall not be with you very long.'

'You shall *not* go,' he cried, clinging to her hands.

'It is not for us to decide, dear husband. You have made me very happy.'

'Anne, I cannot go on without you. I cannot *live* without you.'

'You will. You must. Oh Richard, take care. It is a rough path you must tread and I wanted to be there beside you. I wanted you to know that I was always there . . . always with you . . . no matter what happened.'

'I did know it. I do know it. That is why you must get well.'

She smiled at him slowly.

'I shall pray for you, Richard, with my dying breath I shall pray for you.'

She knew that it was time for her to pray for her own soul but she continued to pray for Richard. It was almost as though, there, lying on her deathbed she had visions of evil to come.

She lived only a few hours. Even then Richard was unprepared for her death. He seemed to have lost his speech, his awareness of anything.

He flung himself on the bed and stretched his arms over her body and silent sobs shook him.

At first he would not leave her but at length he was passive as they led him away.

He was in a daze from which he emerged to order that the most magnificent burial must be prepared for her. All the world must know how he had revered her.

Her body was brought from Sheen to St. Paul's where it was to lie in state before burial at Westminster. Richard had sent to Flanders for abundant supplies of wax for the flambeaux which would be needed in the procession. He demanded that every noble in the land should come to do honour to his Queen.

They had taken the body away. He went to the apartment in Sheen where she had died and he cried out in his anguish: 'I never want to see this place again!'

He snatched at the hangings and pulled them down. They were scarlet velvet and they lay like a pool of blood at his feet.

'I hate this room. I hate it. I hate it!' he screamed. 'She died here. Whenever I enter it I shall see her there on that bed.'

He took a dagger and slit the bedcover. Then he shouted to his attendants: 'Come here, all of you. Let us destroy this room utterly. I never want to see it again.'

He lifted a pot which stood on a small table and flung it across the room.

His attendants had appeared. They looked at this wild young man with the longish golden hair which was now ruffled and untidy. His blue eyes stared at them wildly.

'Come, you dolts. Why do you hesitate? Destroy this room. Nothing shall stand. It was this room in which my Queen died. I never want to see it again.'

He lopped savagely at the bedpost. It came away in his hands and he reeled back as the bed began to collapse.

There was nothing to do but obey the King.

The late Queen's apartments in Sheen Palace were completely destroyed that day.

Having given vent to his fury against fate Richard felt a little better.

She should have the most magnificent funeral. The whole world should know how he loved her. He summoned all the most noble of the land to come and pay homage to her as she lay in St. Paul's. There was one notable absentee, the Earl of Arundel.

When Richard heard that Arundel had not attended St. Paul's he fell into a rage against him. He wanted to arrest him but was restrained from doing so by his uncle John.

At first Richard would not listen but when John reminded him that Anne would not have wished it he was so overcome with grief that he turned away and went to his own apartments.

Arundel was an arrogant man. He was contemptuous of the King. His new wife Philippa was a forceful woman who continually reminded him of his royalty through her. She was as highly born as the King, she maintained; and she was going to make everyone remember it.

Therefore if her husband did not wish to attend the obsequies of the Queen he need not.

She and her husband decided that he should put in an appearance at the burial service at Westminster, although there was no reason why he should remain throughout. He should tell the King that he had come as summoned but had no intention of remaining and the King should therefore give him official permission to retire.

'I shall tell him that I must leave for urgent personal reasons,' said Arundel.

'That is the discreet way of doing it,' agreed his wife.

The ceremony in the Abbey had begun. Richard was melancholy, thinking of the day he had first seen Anne and how he had loved her because of her humility and grace. He could not have loved a flamboyant beauty with the same intensity.

Oh Anne, Anne, he mourned, why did you leave me? Why did I allow you to go to Sheen? We should never have parted, even for a day. I hate Sheen, Anne. And I used to love it . . . because we were there together and now . . . and now . . .

'My lord.' It was Arundel at his elbow.

Richard sprang round shaken out of his reverie and instead of the sweetly compliant face of Anne there was that of his enemy.

'For certain urgent private reasons, my lord, I crave leave to retire from the Abbey.'

'You will wait until this ceremony is over,' retorted Richard. 'You shall not insult the Queen.'

'My lord, I must leave . . .'

Richard snatched a wand which one of the vergers was carrying and with it hit Arundel across the face with such force that the blood spurted out of the wound. He then went on raining down blows on the Earl who, utterly amazed, was beaten to his knees.

There was consternation. This was defiling the holy abbey. Arundel's blood was already staining the floor.

Richard shouted: 'Arrest this man. Take him to the Tower.'

There was a hushed silence then Richard roared: 'Take him! Take him! He is my prisoner.'

Arundel was dragged away and Richard signed for the ceremony to proceed.

There was whispering of course. Many blamed Arundel but an equal number blamed the King. He was stricken with grief, they knew; but if Arundel had perfectly good reason for leaving the ceremony his wish should have been granted.

They were both at fault but the King had grief on his side.

Once more John of Gaunt came to the King.

325

'My lord,' he said, 'Arundel is in the Tower. What crime has he committed?'

'The greatest. He has insulted the Queen.'

John of Gaunt sighed. 'It is not enough to send him to the Tower, my lord. He has many powerful friends.'

'I have sent him and there he shall remain.'

'It is dangerous, my lord. You must understand that the country is full of discontent, like dry wood waiting for the flame to ignite it. I know full well that if the good Queen Anne were here she would add her voice to mine.'

'Arundel has insulted *her*.'

'Arundel deserves to be reprimanded for that. But as I tell you, he has many friends. Release him, Richard.'

'I shall do no such thing,' said Richard. 'When you went away I might have been a child. I am so no longer. My will shall be done.'

'And so it should be and so it shall be while I have a right arm to fight for it. But there should not be unnecessary unrest as there will be if you declare open warfare on Arundel. He is too influential to be slighted, Richard. I know the Queen would add her voice to mine . . . if she were here . . . if only she were here!'

Richard was ready to dissolve into tears. But his uncle was right. He knew he was right. He could almost hear Anne's voice pleading for the release of Arundel.

Within a week Arundel was a free man.

Constanza of Castile was content to live with her own attendants—men and women of her own country, for she had never been able to get on with the English. She had lived quietly at Hatfield knowing that her husband would visit her but rarely and then only for the sake of appearances.

They had not lived together for some years. She had sensed his repulsion and it offended her dignity that she, a Princess of the House of Castile—the true Queen she had always maintained—should have to accept the fact that her husband preferred his mistress and was going to spend every spare moment he had with her.

Constanza was very much aware of her royalty and although she certainly did not want John or any man in her bed, she deplored the manner in which he made no attempt to keep his relationship with Catherine Swynford a secret.

She had to admit that Catherine was discreet. She never flaunted her position. She behaved with more decorum than many a more nobly born woman might have done who found herself in a similar position. But the fact remained that John insisted on Catherine's being with him at every function he attended; and people were accepting her. The King received her; in fact he seemed to have a fondness for her, and Constanza had to admit that Catherine was possessed of a certain charm which had been utterly denied her.

It was not surprising in the circumstances that she preferred to live quietly in the country where she could be surrounded by her own people, where she could eat the dishes of her native land and wear those clothes which the women of her own country all enjoyed making for her.

It was a life of quietness and meditation for she had always been deeply religious.

In the early spring of that year when the Queen had died, Constanza began to feel a certain lethargy creep over her.

She had never taken a great deal of exercise but spent most of her time either in meditation and prayer or sitting with her attendants sewing for the poor; and since her daughter Catherine had married the heir to Castile it seemed as though she had no great reason for living. Those about her noticed that she grew more frail every day.

They were not really surprised when one day when they went to call her she told them that she was feeling too unwell to rise.

Within the week she was dead.

John of Gaunt was free, and his feelings were mingled. He was relieved that he should not have to see Constanza again. Her existence had been a continual reproach to him. On the other hand it placed him in a quandary as far as Catherine was concerned.

He had always maintained that if he were free he would marry Catherine, yet he had to consider what such a marriage would mean to him.

Catherine was beautiful still; she was discreet and he loved her dearly. He had never glanced at another woman seriously since he had known her. But on the other hand she was not of the nobility and their relationship had been far from discreet so that the whole country knew that she had been his mistress.

Could he marry her? Would it be an act of unprecedented folly to do so?

A man in his position must consider these matters.

In any case nothing could be done until after a suitable period and he rather welcomed the need to go to Aquitaine to take charge of his duties there.

So he sailed away and he vowed to himself that he would look facts squarely in the face and when he returned he would have the solution.

The months began to pass and he found life in Bordeaux intolerable. All the time he was longing to be with Catherine. He wondered what she was thinking. He fancied that she was resigned, telling herself that what she had always longed for could never come to pass.

He reviewed his life. His ambition had availed him little. All the wishing in the world could not make him King of England. And who in his right senses would want such an unenviable lot? The people had never liked him; they would never have accepted him. To rule, a King must have his people's love and approval.

The only happy times he had known were with Catherine. That was not quite true. He had been happy with Blanche. Theirs had been a good union. But it had not equalled his relationship with Catherine. There could never be anything to rival that.

He came back to England at the end of the year 1395.

Richard had returned from Ireland where he had conducted a not unsuccessful campaign. It seemed the Irish had been so overwhelmed by Richard's magnificent array and general

328

splendour that they had made no resistance. However the expedition had been costly in money if not in lives.

Flushed with success and feeling his power as a ruler, Richard was not inclined to give a very warm welcome to his uncle.

John left Court quickly and went at once to Kettlethorpe in Lincolnshire.

Catherine was about the business of her household when the herald arrived. She recognized his livery at once—the blue and the grey and the Lancastrian arms embroidered on his tabard.

Her heart beat uncertainly. He was coming. She had waited long for him and she had tried to convince herself that she would never see him again. It was true he had talked to her of what he would do if he were free—but did she believe him? Did she not know that some project must present itself, some thing which would further his ambitions. How could he possibly marry a woman such as herself who had been criticized by so many for what would be termed her loose behaviour?

No, it had been pleasant talk, lovers' talk of what should be, when it was believed it was impossible.

She went swiftly about the house giving orders here and there.

'Make ready, my lord Duke of Lancaster will soon be with us.'

She stood in the hall waiting to greet him—alone. First she must see him alone.

He strode towards her, looking a little older than when she had last seen him. There were flecks of white in his tawny gold hair and new lines about his fine Plantagenet eyes. He was no longer young. He was fifty-five years of age and she was only ten years younger. They had first been lovers twenty years before.

'Catherine,' he cried, taking her hands. He held them firmly in his and looked into her face. 'As beautiful as ever,' he said.

She laughed and shook her head but he just drew her to him and held her fast.

'Never to be parted again,' he said, 'for such time as is left to us.'

'My lord . . .' she began.

'Nay,' he said, 'call me husband for I am going to marry you, Catherine.'

She felt dizzy with joy; but even then she would not believe it.

She answered: 'My lord, have you thought . . .'

'Of nothing else,' he said, 'since Constanza died.'

'It is not possible.'

'I will show you how possible. All we need is a priest.'

'You are sure?'

'Never more sure of anything. What is it, Catherine?' He had seized her shoulders and drawn back to look at her more intently. 'Is this marriage distasteful to you?'

She laughed in the way he remembered so well.

'It is something I sometimes dreamed of.'

'Then you need dream no more.'

'It is wrong,' she said.

'It is right,' he answered.

'Our children . . .'

'Our Beauforts shall be my legitimate children. Catherine, will you marry me?'

'Never have I done anything in my life with a thousandth part of the joy with which I shall do that.'

'So it is settled. We will lose no time. From this day forth, my love, you are my Duchess of Lancaster.'

Anne was dead and Richard would mourn her for the rest of his life, but he was reminded by his ministers that he was a King and must marry.

Gloucester was back at Court, suave and placating, trying to pretend that there had never been any trouble between him and the King. He would know of course that Richard was one never to forget a slight; all the same Gloucester's mind was so full of plans that he was not going to let a little matter like the King's enmity come between him and his ambition.

It was Gloucester who broached the matter of the King's marriage.

It had been suggested to him, the King replied, but at the time he could think of nothing but his adored Queen Anne and the thought of replacing her did not appeal to him.

'I understand, my dear nephew,' said Gloucester, but Richard looked at him contemptuously. How could Gloucester understand? Married to the not very attractive Eleanor Bohun for the great fortune she could bring him! How could Gloucester compare his marriage with the bliss Richard and Anne had shared.

'The fact is,' went on Gloucester, 'you should choose a bride and I am of the opinion that the people would like someone from our own country.'

'Tell me whom?' asked Richard.

'My daughter Anne is recently widowed as you know. Poor Stafford! He was young to die. My daughter is beautiful and experienced. She is royal . . . as royal as you yourself. You share the same grandfather. I can think of no better match.'

'I can think of none more likely to cause complaint,' retorted Richard.

'And why so? Anne is a very desirable young lady, I can tell you.'

'She happens to be my first cousin. The blood tie is far too close.'

'Bah! Popes can help very much in such instances. All we have to do is make it worthwhile.'

'I consider the tie too close.'

'Oh my dear nephew, you have yet to grow up.'

There could be nothing more maddening than this persistence that he was a boy and unable to arrange his own affairs as well as those of the country.

'Do you realize,' he said, 'that I am thirty years of age?'

'Oh not yet . . .'

'I shall soon be thirty and if I were not I would have you remember that I am the King.'

It was true what his brother John said, thought Gloucester, he and the King could not be together for more than a few minutes before a storm arose.

Richard went on: 'I have already discussed this matter of my marriage with those whom it concerns.'

'Your happiness concerns me as a subject and as your uncle.'

'Then you will be very pleased that I have found a wife.'

Gloucester's brow darkened.

'Who . . . may I ask?'

'You may. I have chosen the daughter of the King of France. It has always been my ambition to bring about a peaceful settlement of these continental affrays in France which absorb our wealth and bring us little gain. This marriage will please both the King and myself. It will make us friends.'

'The eldest daughter of the King of France is but seven years of age . . . if that.'

'An enchanting child, they tell me.'

'You need a *wife* . . .'

'It is what I intend to have.'

'This child is far too young. Why even in five or six years' time she will scarcely have reached the proper age for a wife.'

'Every day will remedy the deficiency in her age. Moreover her youth is one of my reasons for choosing her. I wish her to be educated here and brought up in our ways. I want her to be English in manners and customs and her way of thinking. That is what the people will like. As for myself I am not so old that I cannot wait for her.'

Gloucester asked leave to retire. He was fuming with rage which he could not keep to himself much longer.

So the King had already entered into negotiations to marry Isabella of Valois, daughter of the King of France.

THE LITTLE ISABELLA

THERE HAD BEEN an air of great excitement in the Hotel de St. Pol ever since the embassy had arrived from England; and there was none more aware of this than the little girl who was the cause of it.

Isabelle de Valois, although but eight years old, was very much aware of her beauty and importance. She was clever too and had always believed that as the daughter of the King of France a bright future lay ahead of her.

'Many people will want to marry me,' she told her maids who clustered around her, dressing her in soft silk gowns and curling her beautiful dark hair. 'I wonder who will be the lucky one?'

They smiled at her; secretly they said: 'The Lady Isabelle has a good conceit of herself. She is too pretty, that one. But she will have her own way, that is a certainty.'

If Isabelle had heard them, she would have agreed. Yes, certainly she had a good conceit of herself. Why not? Was she not very pretty? Were her little ways not quite fascinating? Was she not alert of mind? And in addition to all this she was the daughter of the King of France.

Life at the Hotel de St. Pol circulated about her. Her mother, who was beautiful—Isabelle was very like her— doted on her child. So did her father. He and his Court were at the Louvre, but he often slipped over to the Hotel de St. Pol to see his family. She looked forward to his visits, but there was a strangeness about him and some- times he disappeared and was not at the Louvre and although she was told he was travelling about the country there was something in the looks of the people which made her wonder what he was really doing. Lately she had discovered that he suffered from some mysterious illness which attacked him now and then, so that he acted in a strange manner and had to be hidden away.

Her mother was gay and beautiful; she liked to dance and surround herself with admirers. Isabelle thought that her mother must have a very pleasant life . . . much better than her father who was always surrounded by dull ministers and had his bouts of illness to contend with.

Then came this exciting day when the English embassy arrived in Paris. Her attendants talked of nothing else. She listened avidly. It was sometimes better to listen than to ask questions for grown-up people always seemed to have so much they wanted to hold back and to question them made them cautious. So she listened.

'They say the streets of Paris are crowded with them.'

'There are at least five hundred.'

'It is rare that we have the English in Paris!'

'No, but it is where they would like to be.'

'I doubt it not. Well, this should put a stop to this foolish war.'

'Who knows? They are lodged near the Croix du Tiroir, I have heard.'

'Yes, there and all the streets close by.'

'It won't be long now.'

No, thought Isabelle, it won't be long. She was right. The very day after the conversation her father came to the Hotel de St. Pol. Her mother was with him and they summoned their daughter to them.

Isabelle had been well schooled in correct behaviour, and with grace and charm she knelt before her father.

His eyes were soft at the sight of her. She was such a beautiful child and it was sad that one so young must leave her home.

He raised her up and seating himself drew her close to him. She studied him, fascinated as she always was by the strangeness in his eyes. Sometimes they looked wild as though he were seeing things which were invisible to others. Today however, they were less wild. He was looking at her and seeing her and, she guessed, thinking how beautiful she was.

'Daughter,' he said, 'the time has come for you to leave us. Your mother and I have decided that it is best for you. We do not want to lose you, but . . .'

She nodded gravely. She looked at her mother who was said to be the most beautiful woman in France, and people said that she, Isabelle, closely resembled the Queen.

'All Princesses leave their homes in time. Many of them then become great ladies.'

Her eyes widened. She would enjoy being a great lady she was sure.

'The King of England wants to marry you.'

'I shall wear a crown,' she said, and she pictured herself with the golden circlet on her flowing dark hair. She would look very like her mother then.

'It means you will go to England.'

'When shall I go?' she asked.

Her mother said: 'That is a matter which we shall have to decide when we have consulted with the English. We shall miss you sorely, Isabelle.'

'Yes, my lady, and I shall miss you.'

It was amazing, thought the King, how very calm the child was. One might have expected tears. But Isabelle was thinking of her golden crown rather than the parting with her parents.

Of course, she was very young.

'The King of England has sent his ambassadors to us,' said her father. 'You understand, my child, that there has been great conflict between our countries.'

'Yes,' said Isabelle. 'The King of England wants your crown.'

'This King—the one who will be your husband—is different from his father and his grandfather. He is a lover of peace. When you are married to him that will be a reason for keeping the peace. He will not wish to fight against his own father.'

'Shall you be his father then?'

'His father-in-law as they call it.'

'And I shall be the Queen.'

The King looked at his wife and said: 'I think the English could be brought in now. She is very composed and will know how to behave.'

She watched with wonder as the men came in. They looked very splendid and one of them came forward and knelt before her.

'Madam,' he said, 'if it please God, you shall be our lady and our Queen.'

There was a moment's silence. Her parents were watching her.

Then she said: 'Sir, if it please God and my lord father that I be Queen of England, I shall be pleased thereat, for I have been told that I shall then be a great lady. Pray rise that I may conduct you to my mother.'

Queen Isabeau was beaming with pride and pleasure. Her daughter was indeed a credit to her and her upbringing. The English could not fail to be impressed.

Richard was gratified. He was to have the little Isabelle as his bride and this delighted him. He had to have a wife and there was no one who could take Anne's place in his heart; but it would please him to have this little girl—who was charming by all accounts—and to bring her up in the English tradition. In due course she would be his wife and perhaps by that time he would be prepared to live with her.

He had never been greatly attracted by women. It was true he had been devoted to Anne; but Anne had been a beloved companion, a helpmeet, one whom he could trust absolutely. That was different; and perhaps it explained why the idea of a child wife with whom there could be no physical relationship for some years appealed to him.

He sent word to his uncles, Lancaster and Gloucester. They were to accompany him with their wives to France. The foremost men in the country—among them Arundel—received the same summons.

The Countess of Arundel was thoughtful when she heard that she was to prepare to go to France with her husband for the King's marriage.

'Richard will have summoned all the most noble in the land,' she said.

'He will want to make a display,' replied her husband. 'You know what he is. He will expect us all to dazzle the French.'

'Lancaster will be there, of course.'

'My dear, Lancaster could not fail to be there. He is the leading noble, second only to the King.'

'And,' went on the Countess, 'if Richard has summoned the wives as well, can that mean *that woman* will be there?'

'Richard accepts her.'

'Richard!' spat out the Countess. 'He is very foolish sometimes.'

'Sometimes?' replied Arundel with a laugh. 'Often times, I would say.'

'And never more so if he invites that woman to attend the ceremony.'

'Lancaster married her.'

'After she had been his mistress for how long was it . . . for twenty years?'

'It shows his regard for her.'

'And his lack of regard for the rest of us! I shall show her no friendship. In fact I shall refuse to speak to her.'

'You will arouse Lancaster's wrath if you do.'

'Lancaster! What of Lancaster? Whatever he touches he fails in. He only settled the Castile question by marrying his daughter to the heir. I take little count of Lancaster.'

'Perhaps I take more, my dear. He is a very powerful man.'

'And are we not powerful? Were you not the victor of the sea battle off Margate which crippled the French and made England safe for the English? As for myself I am descended from royalty and not very far from the throne. I can tell you this, husband, I shall have nothing whatsoever to do with that woman.'

'Lancaster is also near the throne, my dear. Let us remember that.'

'I remember this. I will not have anything to do with that woman Lancaster has made his wife. Lancaster should be ashamed to bring her with him. Who is she, anyway? A low-born slut. Daughter of a knight, they say. A Flemish knight. Knighted on the battlefield. And when she was married to Hugh Swynford . . . some country hobbledehoy . . . she was Lancaster's mistress and has a string of bastards to prove it.'

'You are right, my dear. You are indeed right. But let us remember the power of Lancaster.'

'You may remember,' said the forceful Countess. 'I shall never allow that woman to come near me.'

Richard was happier than he had been since the death of Anne. He could feel really excited about the ceremonies which lay ahead. They should be lavish in the extreme and there was nothing that pleased him more than accumulating a sparkling wardrobe. He spent hours with his tailors. It became a matter of burning importance whether a girdle should be decorated with rubies or sapphires. At the same time he could be pleased at the prospect. A marriage with France could bring nothing but good.

Peace! That was what he had always wanted. If only his grandfather and father had been of like mind so much hardship might have been avoided. No, it was a much happier state of affairs to have a wedding rather than a battle—and wiser too.

He was at Eltham—a palace he dearly loved. There he could enjoy the clean Kentish air and from the royal apartments which were almost one hundred feet above sea level he could look out from the turrets across the moat and the fields to the walls of the city and see the dome of St. Paul's reaching for the sky.

Here they were gathered together. Lancaster had arrived with his new Duchess, a very beautiful woman—no longer young, but then nor was Lancaster—and she was one who would remain beautiful until she died.

Richard had met her before and had liked her from the first. It was ridiculous for people to compare her with Alice Perrers—that harpy who had tarnished his grandfather's reputation in the last years of his life. Catherine Swynford was discreet, well mannered, all that he would ask from a lady of his Court; and he trusted she would be a good influence on Lancaster, which he was sure she would.

Catherine herself was feeling a little disturbed. It was the first great occasion which she had attended as the Duchess of Lancaster, for although John had often taken her with him to ceremonies, they had never before been such as this.

The King received her courteously and told her that it pleased him that she should be a member of the party. He told her about his little bride and how he wanted the ladies of the Court to be especially gentle with her.

'She is only a child,' he said. 'But, I hear, very self-possessed. I want her to like us and our English ways.'

'My lord, I shall be delighted to do what I can to make her feel at home. I know something of children. I have several of my own and I was in charge of the Duke's children when they were young.'

'I know it,' said the King. 'And I know this too. They love you well. We will talk more of this later.'

Richard had rarely seen his uncle John so pleased with him. It was, of course, because of the way he had received his wife.

John was watchful, Richard noticed with amusement. It would go ill with any who attempted to slight his Duchess.

The Duchess of Gloucester and the Countess of Arundel came to pay their respects to the King.

He disliked both of them. The Duchess of Gloucester, Eleanor Bohun, was not a very attractive woman, most unlike her sister, whom John had married to his son Bolingbroke. Poor girl, she had died about the same time as Anne had. Worn out with childbearing they said—and only in her twenties. None could say that of his beloved

Anne. It was a pity though that they had not had even one child.

Richard had seen Eleanor Bohun's eyes on him when he was chatting with the Duchess of Lancaster. She had been disapproving. There was nothing Richard disliked more than people disapproving of him. He had had enough of that already to last him a lifetime.

And there was the Countess of Arundel—another disagreeable woman and one whom he disliked heartily. For one thing she should never have married Arundel without his consent. And she gave herself too many airs and graces because she was descended from his uncle Lionel.

He was cool to them both.

They turned away. A pity they had to come with the party, thought Richard. But of course he could not tell two of the most important men in the country that he would prefer not to receive their wives.

Richard noticed it happen and he was not the only one. The Duchess of Gloucester and the Countess of Arundel were standing close to the Duchess of Lancaster, and Catherine had turned to them. Some words were spoken, but the two women looked right past her.

The Countess of Arundel said in a very loud voice which could be heard distinctly: 'Is it not strange—the people who come to Court in these times. I have always maintained that harlots should be kept in their own quarters.'

The Duchess of Lancaster had turned and was speaking to someone else as though she had either not heard the words or could not imagine that they applied to her.

The Duke, who had heard, went swiftly to her side. There was a moment when all watching thought some trouble might break out.

If it had been Gloucester instead of Lancaster there could have been violence; but John of Gaunt had always been one to think before he acted.

He could not in any case challenge the two women to a duel.

He put his arm through that of his Duchess. Like her he was pretending that what had been said did not concern them; and at the same time he was showing all that this lady was his Duchess and he was going to see that she was treated as such.

Richard watching thought: Lancaster will not forget this. Both Gloucester and Arundel should beware.

The royal party crossed to Calais.

Gloucester was fuming. He scarcely listened to his wife's complaints about the presence of the Duchess of Lancaster.

He had wanted his daughter to be the Queen of England.

He was making a great deal of trouble, for in his usual overbearing bullying manner he did not hesitate to make his opinions known.

Peace with France! France was a rich country. There was much treasure there. They had a right to it. They were going to give all that away, were they? For what reason? So that they could bring a little girl to England who was too young to be a wife to the King. It was all such nonsense and he for one was against it.

Richard was afraid that his uncle would offend the French and to quieten him he said that if he would keep the peace he should have fifty thousand nobles when he returned home and his son Humphrey should be created Earl of Rochester. This offer was so wildly generous that Gloucester was first amazed and then placated and ceased to make trouble.

Meanwhile there was a distinct coolness between Lancaster and Gloucester and Arundel. Lancaster saw that his wife was treated with respect by all others; and although some of them would have liked to show their disapproval they dared not.

The time had arrived when Richard was to come face to face with Charles of France. The enemies were to become friends and tents had been set up in a field outside Calais as the scene of their ceremonial meeting.

Four hundred English knights and as many French, all in glittering armour, stood with their swords drawn making two ranks through which the Kings with their attendants should pass. On either side of Richard were his uncles Lancaster and Gloucester and on either side of the King of France were the Dukes of Berri and Burgundy, the uncles of the French King.

Richard felt a glimmer of amusement which he could have shared with Anne or with Robert de Vere had they been with him. For it was ironical that both the Kings of France and England, coming to the throne when they were very young, should both have been plagued by uncles.

There was a shout of jubilation from the assembled knights as the two Kings with bared heads met and embraced.

Then the King of France took Richard by the hand and the two French Dukes took the two English ones also by the hand and they entered the tent of the French King.

Inside the tent the Dukes of Orleans and Bourbon were waiting to receive the party. They fell to their knees and remained there until bidden to rise by the Kings. Wines and comfits were served by the Dukes who knelt as they proffered the boxes and goblets to their Kings.

After this the whole company assembled for dinner, the two Kings seated at the high table alone with the rest of the company below them.

The King of France declared his pleasure in the alliance and said he was only sorry that the bride was not older.

'My good father-in-law,' replied Richard, 'the age of our wife pleases us right well. We pay not great attention respecting age as we value your love, for we shall now be strongly united and no one in Christendom can in any way harm us now.'

The King of France expressed his gratification at what had been brought about; and then the moment had come for the little bride to appear.

She came into the tent accompanied by a company of highly born French ladies among whom was the Lady de Couci.

Richard looked with delight at his little bride. She was all that had been said of her. She was dainty, beautiful, bright-eyed and she charmed him completely. He could not hide his pleasure in her. Her father had gone to her and taken her by the hand.

He led her to Richard who in turn took her hand and kissed it. They smiled at each other and it was clear that she liked him as much as he liked her.

The ceremony of handing over the bride being completed there was no reason for delay.

A magnificent litter had been prepared to carry the little Queen to Calais; and she left behind all her attendants with the exception of the Lady de Couci and attended by the Duchesses of Lancaster and Gloucester she prepared to make her journey into the town of Calais.

A few days later the marriage was celebrated in the Church of St. Nicholas, the Archbishop of Canterbury having come to Calais to officiate.

Isabelle was delighted. She had noticed that they had changed her name slightly giving her the English version Isabella. That amused her. Everyone was delighted with her, and she thought Richard the most wonderful husband a girl could have. His hair glistened like gold and he looked so beautiful in his crown. When he spoke to her his voice was soft and gentle and he was always smiling as though he thought her very amusing and he showed in a hundred ways that he was delighted to have her as his bride. She was already fond of the Lady de Couci and she had taken a great fancy to the Duchess of Lancaster. She liked beautiful people. She dislike the Duchess of Gloucester who was ugly and she did not like the Countess of Arundel. She sensed that they were trying to be unkind to the Duchess of Lancaster and without knowing what they could have quarrelled about—for she was sure they had quarrelled—she was on the side of the Duchess of Lancaster.

It was all very exciting. The marriage, the celebrations, the meeting once more with the King and Queen of France at St. Omer before boarding the ship and crossing the Channel to her new country.

She stood on deck with Richard beside her and he pointed out to her the white cliffs of Dover.

'There is the castle,' he said. 'Mine and yours now.'

He said she was a brave girl. She had shed no tears for her old home. Why was that?

She answered promptly: 'Because I am going to like my new one better.'

He laughed. 'Do you know,' he said, 'I thought I should have to comfort a homesick little girl. But not my Isabella.'

She put her hand in his. 'This will be my home,' she said; and there was a deep satisfaction in her voice for she believed that they were going to indulge her in her new country even more than they had in her old.

She was enchanted by Dover Castle; and the next day they went on to Rochester. In a short time they reached the palace of Eltham and there the nobles who had come to France said farewell and went their own ways.

She took the hand of the Duchess of Lancaster and said: 'I shall see you again.'

'I am sure of it,' answered the Duchess.

'It will be soon,' replied the little Queen. She spoke with assurance. She knew she only had to make her wishes known to her adoring husband and they would be granted.

How she enjoyed riding into London where the people came out to marvel at her. 'The dearest little queen that ever was!' 'Why she is but a baby.' 'What a little beauty!'

She smiled at them and enchanted them and afterwards she and Richard were alone together. He liked to look at the clothes she had brought with her. He was delighted by their richness and so was she. There was a beautiful robe and a mantle to go with it. It was of red velvet embossed with golden birds perched on branches of emeralds and diamonds. The robe was trimmed with miniver and the mantle lined with ermine.

'I never saw such elegance!' cried the King.

He showed her one of his surcoats which glittered so much that it dazzled her.

She clapped her hands with joy at the sight of it. 'I never saw jewels sparkle so!' she cried.

'Ah, but it lacks the elegance of your robe and mantle, Isabella. You French have a style which we lack.' He held up another of her robes which was of murray-mezereon and pearl roses. 'Enchanting,' he cried.

Then he took her hand and danced with her round the chamber.

'My little Queen, I am going to have the greatest pleasure in choosing the most beautiful clothes for you to delight us in.'

She laughed with him.

She was so happy. She was sorry for everyone who was not the Queen of England—and that was everyone else in the world, she reminded herself.

It was decided that Windsor was the best place for her to live. Apartments were prepared for her and these were so sumptuous that those about the little Queen declared they had never seen such magnificence. It was on the King's orders. His great pleasure was in delighting his little Queen.

He could not be with her all the time of course, but he was a constant visitor to the castle and when she heard his approach she would fly down to the great hall and fling herself into his arms. He was her beautiful King, and she was his pet, his darling. She would hurry him to the stables that she might show him her new horse—a gift from him of course. He must watch her ride, so they must go into the forest together. He must tell her stories of the forest, of Herne the Hunter who had hanged himself on one of the oaks because he had committed some sin and feared he would be condemned to die. She listened intently, she loved the stories, the more gruesome the better. She said she would like to come face to face with the Hunter.

'Never say that, little one,' cried Richard. 'It would mean that you were to die.'

And how pleasant it was to see his deep concern at the thought of losing her!

She was as avid as ever at listening. Once she said to him: 'Do you wish I were older so that I could be a real wife to you?'

She had overheard something of that nature, it was certain.

'No,' he cried vehemently. 'I want you just as you are.'

And as that was just what she had wanted to hear she was content.

She was very happy at Windsor. She had to do lessons, of course, but that was no hardship to her; she was bright and liked to amaze her teachers with her cleverness.

She delighted in the rich garments she wore. Richard used to spend hours with her and the seamstresses saying how her clothes should be cut and how embroidered.

He would clasp his hands together in an ecstasy of delight when she paraded before him in her fine garments. She liked to ride out with him and see the people crowd round and marvel at her.

'The little darling!' they would cry.

Richard would pretend to be jealous. 'By St. John the Baptist,' he would cry, 'I'll swear they will depose me and make you their ruler.'

It was an enchanted life and she thought it would go on for ever. She could not be expected to know of the rumbling discontent which was brewing around her.

She was crowned with great pomp and ceremony at Westminster by the Archbishop of Canterbury and that seemed the very pinnacle of glory.

At Windsor she was put in charge of the Lady de Couci, a lively woman, the second wife of the Lord de Couci whom he had married after the death of that Isbella who was the daughter of Edward the Third and therefore aunt to the King.

There was little the Lady de Couci enjoyed as much as lavish spending and consequently the little Queen's household was run on somewhat extravagant lines.

The Duchess of Lancaster, for whom the little Queen had taken a great fancy, visited Windsor and they were very happy occasions. But the most frequent visitor was the King who so often rode out to Windsor and there they would play music together, dance a measure and he would read to her, sitting in the window-seat with her curled up beside him.

He was eager for her comfort. When the winter set in there must be fur-lined garments for her and fur covers for her bed. He could not have his little darling uncomfortable. As she so loved pageants he constantly contrived them for her.

They lived very lavishly. She had brought a good dowry with her from France but even that would not last indefinitely.

THE KING'S REVENGE

The Duke of Gloucester was fuming in secret. He was often with those other discontented people, the Earl of Arundel and the Earl of Warwick.

It seemed to Gloucester that everything was going against him; Arundel and Warwick were almost equally disgruntled. Arundel was prodded by his Countess who continued incensed by the acceptance of Catherine Swynford at Court and Warwick because a case in which he was involved with the Earl of Nottingham concerning some land had been decided against him.

Gloucester was intent on action. He could see himself being displaced and denied that goal on which he had set his heart. What he wanted more than anything was to step into the King's shoes. But how could this be? There were too many ahead of him.

He had been against the French marriage, and the only joy in that for him was that the Queen was too young to provide an heir. Richard was now on very good terms with Lancaster. Not only had he accepted the Duchess at Court and given her access to the Queen who had grown very fond of her, but he had legitimized all the Beaufort bastards.

Of the two eldest sons John Beaufort was made Earl of Somerset and Richard promised that he should in due course come to the office of Admiral. Henry, who had shown signs of more than average cleverness, was to go into the Church. He was only in his teens as yet but as

soon as possible a bishopric should be foun.
Richard had assured his uncle that the other
should receive like honours when the time came.

This was very gratifying to Lancaster who had se.
into a happy life of maturity. He was behind the King but
was discreet enough not to impose too much of his will.

If only Gloucester had been the same.

But Gloucester was bent on mischief. How much longer,
he demanded, was the country going to accept Richard's
ineffectual rule? He had made this peace with France and
saddled himself with a child who could not produce an heir
for years; he had frittered away her dowry. He was useless
and the sooner he was deposed and someone else wore the
crown the better.

The King had named Roger de Mortimer, Earl of March,
as his heir if he should die without a child of his own body
to follow him, and Roger, who was a son of Philippa the
daughter of Lionel who was the second son of Edward the
Third coming after the Black Prince, was accepted generally as the next in line of succession.

Thomas who could never wait patiently for events to
happen sought out Roger to sound him, for it seemed to
him that Roger would make a good figure-head.

It was a great mistake, he quickly realized.

Roger was a young man who had been brought up to
believe that he owed his first loyalty to the crown. He was
heavily committed to Ireland for Richard had some time
before appointed him lord lieutenant of that turbulent country.

He was twenty years old, idealistic, eager to prove
himself and when Gloucester told him what he had in mind
he was not only astounded but horrified.

'My dear Roger,' said Gloucester, 'you are heir to the
throne. Depend upon it, we cannot wait for the time to
come when it shall fall naturally to you.'

Roger was bewildered. 'What does this mean?' he asked.

The boy was a simpleton, thought Gloucester. Was it
not obvious?

'An army would follow you,' persisted Gloucester. 'You
are beloved of the people. They are weary of Richard's

..eble rule. His extravagances must be stemmed or the country will suffer.'

Roger still said nothing; he was too bewildered for speech. What was Gloucester suggesting? Revolution? War? And against the King!

'An army would rally to your banner. We should secure the King and his French wife and they would be kept in confinement till Richard agreed to resign his crown. We should have to seize my brothers Lancaster and York. But that should not be difficult. You are so pale. Why so? I tell you this plan cannot fail.'

'This . . . this is treason!' stammered Mortimer.

Gloucester seized his arms and glared into his face.

'You mean you would not join us?'

'I would not take up arms against the King. That is treason.'

Gloucester then realized that he had made one of the biggest blunders of his life. If Roger de Mortimer reported what he had suggested that would be the end of him.

'By God,' he said, 'you are a man who does not know what is good for him.'

'I know, my lord Gloucester, that no good could come to me if I were a traitor to the King.'

Gloucester's hand was on his sword. Kill him. It was the only way. He had betrayed his schemes to this young man and if he went to the King . . .

Still, Richard could not be victorious. There was too much against him.

'You shall not whisper a word of this to any,' cried Gloucester.

'Heads would fall if I did,' replied Roger.

'Aye. And yours would not be too safe.'

'I have spoken no treason.'

'There would be those to say you had shared in the plot.'

The young man was disturbed. There was no doubt about that.

'Listen to me,' said Gloucester. 'You are not with us. But it will go ill for you as with us if you breathe a word of what I have said to you.'

Roger understood that. He was thoughtful and Gloucester went on: 'Say nothing of what you have heard. It is the best way.'

Roger nodded. Of course it was the best way. It was the only way.

And shortly he would be leaving for Ireland.

They were uneasy days before he left. Gloucester was no more relieved to see him leave than Roger was to go.

So there was a plot afoot to take his crown from him. Richard knew it. Rumour was rife throughout London and the countryside. Gloucester was determined to stir up the people against him. They were whispering about him. He was enamoured of the little girl who was his Queen, they said. Why had he chosen a child? It was because he had no love for women. He was like his great-grandfather Edward the Second. Everyone remembered how he had surrounded himself with men favourites, pampered them, wasted the country's money on them. Richard had spent money so extravagantly that the royal coffers were fast emptying. They had all witnessed the lavish manner in which he spent on his Queen. His table was filled with rich foods when there were many going hungry.

This was no way to rule.

Gloucester was fomenting trouble, and Richard knew why. There was something else. Why had Roger de Mortimer been so eager to get back to Ireland? What had Gloucester proposed to him?

Richard could guess.

There had been a time when there had been an attempt to depose him; and the head of that rebellion had been Gloucester, Arundel, Warwick and his cousin Bolingbroke with Thomas Mowbray.

Richard was never one to forget an insult and he would remember that five as long as he lived. Now it seemed that three of them had banded together—Gloucester, Warwick and Arundel; and those were the three he intended to deal with.

Having had experience of rebellion he was not going to make the same mistakes again. Then he had been a boy; now he was a man who knew how to rule. He was going to strike first before they could.

He came to London and with him was his troop of archers. The Lord Mayor of London, Richard Whittington, viewed the troops who filled the streets with some apprehension, and gave secret orders that the London trained bands should be ready for action.

Richard's operations began by summoning a meeting of Parliament which would bring all the nobles to London and he sent special invitations to Gloucester, Warwick and Arundel to dine with him at the house of the Bishop of Exeter in Temple Bar.

Gloucester was not without his spies, nor was Arundel. Neither of them liked the sound of that invitation. Moreover they knew that Richard had his archers in London.

Gloucester sent word from his castle of Pleshy that he was too ill to attend. Arundel sent no word but all the same he returned to his castle at Reigate and put it in a state of siege.

Warwick, failing to realize the true position, arrived at Temple Bar.

The King received him graciously and talked of domestic matters so that Warwick had no idea that anything unusual was happening.

They sat drinking wine and talking in desultory fashion of the Parliament which was to assemble shortly.

Then suddenly Richard rose and called to his guards. Warwick was on his feet wondering what the change in the King's attitude could mean.

'You are under arrest,' he said.

'My lord . . .' stammered Warwick.

'I know of your plots,' Richard told him. 'You had better admit that you were planning with Gloucester and Arundel to come against me.'

'It is false . . .' stammered Warwick unconvincingly.

'Let him be taken to the Tower,' said Richard. 'He will tell us all in time I doubt not.'

The protesting Warwick was taken away.

That takes care of Warwick, said Richard to himself. Now for Arundel.

Arundel was skulking in Reigate, but Richard did not want to take up arms and go out to his castle to get him, which would be to declare open warfare. The best plan was to lure him to London and once there he could easily be put under arrest.

Richard sent for Thomas Arundel, now Archbishop of Canterbury, and when the Archbishop arrived Richard told him that he had a request to make.

'I wish the Earl, your brother, to come to me here in London, and you must bring him to me.'

The Archbishop looked startled. He did not know yet that Warwick had been arrested but he was filled with alarm by the King's words.

'My lord,' he said, 'would he not come more readily at your bidding than mine?'

'I think he has some notion that I am displeased with him. I have requested him to dine with me but he does not answer my invitation.'

'My brother must have some reason, my lord. He must be sick.'

'I think he needs a little assurance and that will come best from you. I promise this—by St. John the Baptist I swear it—if he will come to me of his own accord no harm shall come to him. But I wish him to come peacefully. You understand, my lord Archbishop, I do not wish to go to his castle and take him. All I wish is to have speech with him. Persuade him to come in peace.'

'He must have heard some warning . . .'

'My lord Archbishop, you know how these things happen. Go to him. Persuade him. I have sworn, have I not?'

The Archbishop then said that he would go to his brother, which he did.

The Earl was pleased to see his brother but alarmed when he heard the cause of his visit.

'He has heard some rumour,' said the Earl. 'He wishes me some harm.'

'He has sworn by St. John the Baptist that no harm shall befall you.'

'Nevertheless I would not trust him.'

'Come, brother. You should return to London with me. If you do not come you will anger the King. He will come here to get you and he has a troop of archers with him.'

'But why should he come to take me unless he wishes me ill?'

'Because he is young and is still new to power. He asked for obedience. Give it to him and he is your friend. I tell you he has sworn not to harm you.'

At length the Earl was persuaded and he returned to London with his brother where the two spent the night at Lambeth.

The next day they were rowed across the river in the Archbishop's barge to Westminster where the brothers said good-bye to each other and the Archbishop was rowed back to Lambeth.

The Earl was taken to the King's chamber where Richard was in conversation with several of his ministers and when he saw who had come he merely looked at him, giving no welcome. Arundel felt his confidence ebbing away.

The traitor! thought Richard. You were one of those who hurried my dear friend, Simon Burley, to the scaffold. There shall be no mercy for you now. Anne wept for Burley . . . she pleaded for him on her knees. My dear sweet Queen, who never harmed any. And you spurned her! You turned away from her pleas. By St. John the Baptist, Arundel, there shall be no mercy for you now.

'Take my lord Arundel away,' he cried.

So they took him to the Tower and later to the Isle of Wight where, Richard said, he was to be held a prisoner until Parliament met.

That, said the King, accounts for two of them.

Two of the enemies were where he wanted them; there remained the third and most dangerous of them all.

It was beginning to grow dark when the King with an armed guard set out for Pleshy in Essex, Gloucester's favourite residence.

All through the night they rode. There had been a light rain falling but as they came in sight of the magnificent Pleshy towers the sun came out. It was a strong fortress that castle with thick walls and moat surrounding it.

The King had left the larger part of his force hidden in a thicket with instructions to come to him at a given signal.

Richard hoped that Gloucester had not yet heard of the arrests of Warwick and Arundel. If so he would be preparing himself for a siege and in such a fortress he could hold out for a long time.

The sound of the approaching party had brought the guards to their posts and because it was a small party no suspicion was raised. Richard was exultant when he heard the shout of 'The King!' And the portcullis was immediately raised.

Gloucester came quickly to welcome his nephew. It was clear that he had heard nothing.

Richard shouted: 'Prepare to leave at once. You are to return with me to London.'

'My lord . . . for what purpose?'

'Oh just a little matter for our good . . . yours and mine. You will learn in time. Now I and my men are hungry; we would eat before setting out.'

While food was served, Gloucester was growing more and more uneasy.

When they had finished eating the King expressed his wish to leave at once. The horses were waiting and Richard and his uncle rode out side by side.

'What a fine morning!' cried Richard. He felt exultant. Everything was working out neatly as he had planned it. It had been a simple matter to catch them in the net. He had made Arundel his prisoner through a trick but he cared nothing for that. He was ready to achieve his ends no matter by what means. He thought of Robert de Vere driven from his country; he thought of his good friend Simon Burley hunted to his death; he thought of Anne on her knees pleading for the life of their beloved friend. Oh, he had much to avenge, and he was going to do it.

He chatted in a seemingly light-hearted manner to his uncle. He wished him to come up for this sitting of Parliament. There were certain matters which had to be discussed and naturally he did not want this done without the attendance of his uncle.

Gloucester who had been apprehensive at the sudden appearance of the King felt a little better. He had feared that news of his plotting might have come to the King's ears but Richard's manner, which was so affable, was lulling his fears. Therefore he was startled when as they were passing a thicket a party of armed men rode out at the head of whom was the Earl of Nottingham.

The Earl rode straight up to the Duke and laying a hand on his shoulder cried: 'My lord Duke you are under arrest. In the name of the King.'

The Duke turned angrily on the Earl. Smiling the King rode on.

'My lord,' cried Gloucester. 'My lord King! Richard! This fellow is seized with madness. I beg you, nephew, come back.'

But Richard rode on; and Gloucester then realized that he was the victim of a plot. He should have realized this when the King came to Pleshy. He should have discovered his business before he meekly rode out with him.

He was silent for a while—all his bombast seemed to have deserted him.

The King was out of sight and he realized that they were not making for London but for the coast.

'Where are you taking me?' he demanded.

'The King's orders are that you shall be taken to Calais,' was the answer.

'To Calais! For what purpose? How dare you treat me

thus? By God's ear, Nottingham, you will be sorry for this. What have I done to merit such treatment?'

'That you will be able to answer better than any, my lord Duke,' was the cynical answer.

Excitement was high in the City of London. The Earl of Arundel was to be brought to trial. It was not so long ago that he had been the hero of the country, when he had beaten the French in such a spectacular fashion that he had made the seas safe for England and saved the country from threatened invasion. And now here he was to be tried as a traitor.

With great dignity, clad in his scarlet cloak and hood, he came before the assembled Parliament, walking calmly through the ranks of archers.

He was aware of his enemies ranged round him, like dogs straining for the kill. The chief of these was the Duke of Lancaster who was the High Steward for this day; and with him was his son Henry of Bolingbroke.

There would be little mercy shown him this day, thought Arundel.

John of Gaunt gave the order for the charges against the Earl to be read out. Arundel listened to the list of his crimes, the most damning of which was of course his recent activities which were summed up as having taken up arms with the Duke of Gloucester and the Earl of Warwick against the King.

Arundel had little hope. He knew his days were numbered. He had heard that his brother, the Archbishop, was to be impeached. They would not kill him, of course, he being a member of the Church, but his career would be at an end. He would doubtless be banished from England, but his life would be left to him.

He spoke in a loud clear voice declaring that what had been done was with no ill intent against the King's person. It was all for the benefit of the King and the country.

He was aware of Lancaster's eyes upon him. Lancaster would be remembering the way he, Arundel, and his wife had slighted Catherine Swynford. He could imagine that Lancaster had avowed revenge for that slight on his wife and Arundel would pay for it.

'You are a traitor,' cried Lancaster.

'You lie,' retorted the Earl. 'I was never traitor to the King. I was pardoned when I was accused before.'

'Why should you have needed pardon if you were not guilty?' demanded Lancaster.

'To put a stop to malicious accusations by those who did not love me or the King but were my implacable enemies. You were one of them. You have more reason to ask pardon than I have.' He turned to face the assembly. 'You are gathered together,' he went on, 'but not to do justice.'

Bolingbroke had risen and demanded: 'Did you when we first drew together, when there was first talk of an insurrection say that the best method was to seize the person of the King?'

'I never entertained a thought for my sovereign that was not intended to serve him well.'

Richard cried out then. 'Once you said to me that Sir Simon Burley deserved death and I made answer that I saw no reason why he did. And yet you and your friends killed that good man.'

Richard was momentarily overcome by emotion at the thought of the man he had loved and whom the Queen had loved and pleaded for.

Everyone knew then that Arundel would pay the price not only for plotting against the King but for his part in the murder of the King's friend and tutor.

Lancaster in due course pronounced the sentence.

'I, John, Steward of England, adjudge thee Richard Fitzalan, Earl of Arundel, a traitor and condemn you to be hanged, drawn and quartered . . .'

There was a deep silence. This was the most barbarous sentence known in the land. Arundel heard it without changing his expression. Then it was seen that the verdict had already been decided on before the trial had begun for Lancaster went on: 'The King, our sovereign lord, of his mercy and favour has remitted all other parts of the sentence but the last and you shall lose only your head.'

There was no reason for delay. The Earl was immediately taken to Tower Hill, but to reach this spot he must pass through the streets of London and there the crowds came out to watch him. There was an awed silence. This was Arundel, the hero of the great sea battle, the man they had cheered and called their saviour. And here he was walking to his death with, as they said, no more shrinking or changing of colour than if he were going to a banquet.

He stood boldly by the block and turning to the executioner he said: 'I forgive you for what you are about to do. And this I ask you. Do not torment me further. Strike off my head in one blow.'

Arundel then ran his fingers along the edge of the axe.

'It is sharp,' he said. 'Let it be quick.'

He laid his head on the block and at one blow his head was severed from his body.

After the Channel crossing and his incarceration in the Castle of Calais, Gloucester had lost something of his arrogance. He realized that he was in a desperate position. The King was no longer a boy to be told to do this and that; he was clearly capable of acting with guile and his ruse to capture his wily uncle had succeeded. Gloucester knew too that Arundel and Warwick had both been taken.

What next? Gloucester asked himself.

The King would never have the courage to kill him. After all he was his own uncle. Lancaster would never allow it. His brother had no love for him but no royal Duke liked to see another destroyed.

He would come out of this. He must; and then he would have to act very cautiously for some time.

The castle was a grim fortress built mainly for defence, though he was housed comfortably enough there; but each morning when he woke he wondered what the day would bring.

He was not kept long in suspense. Sir William Rickhill,

who was a justice of the Common Pleas, arrived from England and he told Gloucester that he had come to question him and take a statement from him.

Gloucester was almost relieved. It was better for something to happen than to go on in this state of suspense.

Sir William Rickhill was surprised when he came face to face with the Duke. He knew of his bombastic manner and how in the past he had behaved with great arrogance as though he were the King, instead of his nephew.

He found a changed man. Even Gloucester's ruddy complexion had turned sallow and there was an anxious brooding in his eyes. He was clearly a very worried man.

He talked freely to Sir William. He admitted that he had held the King in restraint ten years before and had threatened to depose him. It was no use trying to pretend otherwise for Richard knew this was true. Yes, it could be said that he had looked upon his nephew as a boy and had not shown him the respect a subject should show to his King. He could only beg the King's pardon.

Rickhill returned to England and Gloucester tried to settle himself to wait patiently for the verdict.

There was no news from England. Each day Gloucester looked from the castle window of his apartment which was well guarded by his jailers, out over the stormy sea awaiting the arrival of the King's messengers.

They would come. He would be pardoned. The King could not put his uncle to death.

He had a new servant, a man named John Halle who told him that he had once served the Earl of Nottingham.

There was something sly about the man and often Gloucester would find his eyes on him as though there was some plan forming in his head. Gloucester was indeed changing since he concerned himself with the mood of servants. Not that there was anything to complain of in Halle. He was subservient enough. And there was another named William Serle who admitted that he had once served in the King's chamber.

Gloucester asked John Halle why they were here. The answer was that they had been sent.

'We but obey the orders that are given us, my lord Duke,' said William Serle.

One day John Halle came to the Duke and told him that he was to prepare himself to leave the castle.

Gloucester cried out in his joy. He was going home. Of course Richard could not hold out for long against his own uncle. His brothers Lancaster and York might not exactly love him, but they would remember that they were the sons of the same royal father. Families should stand together and that was of particular importance if they were royal.

He was ready. Waiting for him was a small band of guards—among them were Halle and Serle to escort him, as he supposed, to the coast.

In the midst of them he rode out of the castle, but to his dismay instead of going to the shore where he had expected a ship would be waiting for them, they went into the town of Calais.

'Where are we going?' he demanded.

It was William Serle who answered: 'To a new lodging for you, my lord Duke.'

'A new lodging! Here in Calais?'

They had pulled up before an inn. Gloucester looked up at the sign swinging over the door. The Prince's Inn. It looked an ill-kept place.

'I like this not,' said Gloucester. 'Why do you bring me here?'

'My lord Duke, you should not ask us. We but obey the orders that are given.'

'I do not understand . . .'

They took him inside. It was dark and gloomy. An evil ill-smelling place.

He turned to leave but he was surrounded by the guards.

'Have you the room ready?' said William Serle who seemed to be their leader.

An unkempt man in a filthy jerkin appeared out of the dimness.

'All ready, good sirs,' he answered.

'Then to it,' said Serle.

'I shall not ascend those stairs,' cried Gloucester.

'My lord Duke, we have orders.'

They were pressing round him so that it was clear he must obey.

A door was opened, he was led forward. He stood in the middle of a room on the floor of which was a pallet. The closeness of the place and the rank odour nauseated him.

'Take me out of here,' he shouted.

Serle sadly shook his head.

'It won't be long, my lord Duke. I can promise you that. But I'm just doing as I'm told.'

The men who had brought him here were outside the room. Serle stepped back. The door was shut and he was alone.

He had never felt such despair in his life. On whose orders had he been brought here? On Richard's? What did they intend to do with him? To leave him here, to starve him to death, to go away and forget him?

He sat down on the pallet. He buried his face in his hands. He wanted to shut out the sight of this evil room.

He could sense the doom all around him. He would never escape. They had brought him here to die.

But why? Why? Why had they not despatched him in the castle? Some evil fate was intended for him, he felt sure.

He could hear the rats in a corner of the room. One of them ran across close to him . . . boldly looking at him with baleful eyes.

'Oh God,' he prayed, 'get me out of here. I'll do anything . . . but get me out of here.'

Then he thought back over his life, of his anger because he was the youngest of his father's sons, of all his dreams and longing for power. And it had brought him to this!

Did Lancaster know? He was his brother. Did York know? Edmund had always been the quiet one, never seeking power, living in the shadows. He had hardly ever thought of Edmund in the last years. It seemed Edmund was perhaps the wisest of them all. And Lancaster had lost his fire lately. Who would ever have believed that the ambitious John of Gaunt would have been content to live quietly with his low-born wife.

And that this could happen to me! He wanted to scream, to shout to them to come and let him out. He knew it was useless.

Instinct told him that he had been brought to this room to die. Now he was praying silently: 'Let it be soon, oh Lord. Let it come quickly.'

He seemed to have sunk into a stupor. The darkness was closing in on him. He thought: At night the rats will come out.

He felt numb and he could only pray: 'Oh Lord, let it come soon!'

It seemed as though his prayer was about to be answered. He heard footsteps on the stairs—quiet stealthy footsteps. The door was being opened quietly, slowly. There were men in the room. He recognized William Serle.

He stood up and as he did so he was seized.

They were carrying something. He did not know what it was. It looked like feather-beds.

God had answered his prayers. It was happening quickly. He was thrown face downwards onto the pallet and the feather-beds were placed on top of him.

They were held firmly down on him. There was no air. He could not breathe.

So died the proud Duke of Gloucester.

Richard congratulated himself on his prompt action. The three main protagonists were all taken care of. Only one of them lived—the Earl of Warwick—and he had never been the menace that the other two had presented. Warwick had been drawn into the conspiracy almost against his will. At his trial he had confessed to his guilt and had implored the King's pardon. There was no point in sending him to his death. There had been enough death already and after the manner of the people, death was the accolade of saintliness. They were even saying that miracles were being performed on Arundel's grave now.

No, let Warwick be sentenced to forfeiture and imprisonment for life. He had been sent to the Isle of Man where he would be under the control of the governor there, William le Scrope, who was not the man to show much leniency to a self-confessed traitor to the King.

With Arundel dead and Warwick imprisoned and Gloucester dying rather mysteriously in Calais there remained only one thing to be done. Gloucester's body must be brought to England and given decent burial.

There were rumours about the cause of his death for at the time of his arrest Gloucester had been a healthy man. Richard wanted no martyrdom for this far from saintly uncle.

He sent for one of the priests that he might give him personal instructions as to how his uncle's body was to be dealt with.

The priest came to the King and when they faced each other Richard was struck with amazement, for the priest was so like himself that had they been dressed in similar clothes it would scarcely have been possible to tell them apart.

'Who are you?' asked Richard.

'Richard Maudelyn at your service, my lord.'

Richard said: 'I am struck with amazement. It must be obvious to you that we resemble each other very closely.'

The priest smiled. 'My lord, all my life I have been told that I bear a close resemblance to you.'

'It is remarkable,' Richard smiled. 'There must be some blood tie.'

'I have often thought so, my lord.'

'Your parents . . .'

'My parents are dead, sir.'

'I wonder . . .'

'It is possible, my lord.'

Richard was thoughtful. His father had been a faithful husband but Richard knew that he had at least one illegitimate son, who had been born before he married. Richard Maudelyn was about ten years older than he was. It was possible.

'I am so overwhelmed by this unusual resemblance,' said the King, 'that I forgot the reason why I sent for you.

364

You know that the Duke of Gloucester has died in Calais. I want you to see that his body is taken to his widow for burial in Westminster Abbey.'

'It shall be done, my lord.'

'And, Richard Maudelyn, when it is done, I would have you wait on me again.'

'Thank you, my lord.'

Richard had taken such a fancy to his double that he gave him a post in his household.

They became great friends and everyone was startled by the resemblance. Richard Maudelyn's voice was even like the King's and he could with the utmost ease give an impersonation of his master which was indistinguishable to many of his courtiers.

Richard was amused and liked to play little tricks on them, changing clothes with Maudelyn. Sometimes they did not let people into the deception, and Richard began to realize that Maudelyn could often take his place. He had even ridden through the city and acknowledged the greetings of the people.

It occurred to Richard and those close to him that there might come a time when this strange quirk of fate could be put to good use.

Thomas Mowbray was uneasy. It was true that as Earl of Nottingham he had helped bring Warwick, Arundel and Gloucester to justice and for his services he had been created Duke of Norfolk. The King though had shown himself to be one who would not easily forget an insult. And Mowbray, though now Duke of Norfolk, had been one of the five who had confronted Richard on that memorable occasion years ago. The King had had his revenge on three of them. Two remained, himself and Bolingbroke, now Duke of Hereford.

Norfolk remembered the King's outburst against Arundel when he reminded him of his implacable and relentless pursuit of Simon Burley. To bring it up after all those years showed how it had rankled. Richard was one who would never forget an injury; and it was logical to assume that that occasion when the five lords had faced him and made him their prisoner, was something which would remain in his memory. And he would want revenge on all five.

There was one other who had been present on that occasion—one of the five—and that was Bolingbroke.

One day when Norfolk was travelling between Brentford and London he met Hereford. They stopped at an inn and drank some ale and during their conversation Norfolk broached the subject which had been uppermost in his mind.

'Do you think,' he said, 'that the King is ever going to forget that you and I were each one of the five Lords Appellant?'

'My dear Norfolk,' replied Hereford, 'that happened years ago.'

'But the King is not one to forget and forgive.'

'The matter is over and done with.'

'What of Gloucester? What of Warwick and Arundel?'

'They plotted recently. We have our pardons.'

'What are you proposing?' asked Hereford.

'That we should consider this matter very carefully. We have our enemies. They could be advising the King to take action against us.'

'You are suggesting that *we* take some action?'

'I would suggest you think of it, my lord.'

Hereford was thoughtful. He was wary of Norfolk who had had too many honours bestowed on him and was becoming too powerful.

He decided to see his father, tell him what had happened and ask his advice.

Lancaster was at Ely House in Holborn with his Duchess and it was here that his son came to see him.

He had aged considerably in the last years, but there was a serenity about him which he had lacked before. He was undoubtedly happy in his marriage and Catherine was assiduous in her care of him.

She welcomed Henry warmly but at the same time she

was uneasy and when she heard why he had come her apprehension increased.

It had seemed terrible to her that Gloucester and Arundel should have died as they did. She had little cause to love them, it was true; it was their wives who had done everything they could to discomfort her. They were spiteful women but she bore no rancour towards them. They did not know the happiness she did; and she would never cease to be proud of the fact that John had flouted them all for her sake.

And now Henry's coming meant trouble.

He recounted what Norfolk had said.

'What should be done?' he asked his father.

'You stand well with the King,' replied Lancaster. 'But who can say that Norfolk's words and your reply were not overheard. It may well be that someone has already carried an account of them to Richard. Words can be misconstrued and this could be dangerous. My son, there is one thing you must do with all speed, and that is to go to the King and tell him of this conversation between you and Norfolk.'

Henry nodded. 'I think it is the wisest course of action,' he agreed. 'I will go to him at once before he can hear another account of it.'

'Go with all speed,' advised Lancaster.

He stood with Catherine watching his son ride away.

'We live in dangerous times,' he said.

Catherine shuddered.

'There is no need to fear for me,' he went on, smiling tenderly at her. 'I have learned my lessons well, Catherine, and I think Henry is learning his.'

She was unsure. Henry she knew had a burning ambition which was to possess the crown. John had been plagued by the same deep feelings; but looking back she could see that he had lacked that certain ruthless determination which she sometimes glimpsed in Henry.

Once again she was set wondering how it would all end.

The King listened to what Hereford had to tell him. He had always been wary of this cousin of his, and a little jealous of him too. Henry was popular with the people. He was rich and powerful. He was the father of four sons and two daughters and the eldest was known as young Harry of Monmouth because of the place of his birth. He was now some ten years old and a sturdy, bright boy of whom anyone could be proud. It was true Hereford's wife had died, but he had a fine family.

There was one thing which Richard could not forget—and Norfolk had been right in this—Hereford and Norfolk had once stood with those three who had been brought to justice. Yes, they had been pardoned, but Richard could not forget.

Now he regarded his cousin through narrowed eyes and he said: 'I wish to hear Norfolk's version of this tale. For that reason, you will remain here under restraint until he is brought to us.'

Henry was nothing loth. He was sure his father had been right when he had advised him to tell the King exactly what had been said.

The meeting took place before the Parliament at Oswestry where Hereford in the presence of the King accused Norfolk of making traitorous suggestions to him.

'You are false and disloyal to the King,' he announced. 'You are an enemy of this realm.'

'You are a liar,' retorted Norfolk. 'You are the false and disloyal traitor.'

Richard was bemused. He did not know what to believe. That these two hated each other was clear. For what reason? How much truth was there in Hereford's accusations and Norfolk's denials and counter-accusations?

Richard placed them both under arrest while he considered how best to deal with them.

What was behind this quarrel between these two powerful men? Richard kept reminding himself that they had been two of the five lords who had come against him ten years before.

Hereford was now accusing Norfolk of receiving eight

thousand nobles to pay the soldiers who were guarding Calais and not using the money for the purpose for which it was intended but putting it to his own use.

Norfolk refuted the accusation with vehemence. He swore he had not appropriated the money, but he had used it all in the defence of Calais.

Richard sent for them once more and advised them to forget their differences; but the two men declared that they would never do this and the only thing that would satisfy them would be for them to meet in single combat.

Richard considered this. It would probably mean death for one of them; and the other might not come well out of the affray. Perhaps it was not a bad idea. They had been against him once; who knew when they would be again? It was not such a bad notion to let them destroy themselves in a petty personal quarrel.

There should be this combat. The people would enjoy it and it was always a good idea to give them lavish entertainment when they were restive.

The contest was to be held at Coventry and it was to be a very splendid occasion. Richard had ordered that a very luxurious pavilion be erected for him and his Court. Lancaster had another—equally magnificent—put up for him and his family.

Hereford had ordered a special suit of armour for the occasion and this was supplied by his friend, the Duke of Milan. Not to be outdone Norfolk sent to Germany for his for everyone knew that the Milanese and the Germans were expert armourers and it was a matter of opinion who was the better.

The day of the tournament arrived and all through the previous day people had been arriving to take their places in order to ensure a good view.

There was a gasp of delight when Hereford appeared mounted on a white horse very elaborately caparisoned with green and blue velvet embroidered with swans and antelopes in gold.

The ceremony began with the Marshal's demanding who he was.

'I am Henry of Lancaster, Duke of Hereford,' was the reply, 'which am come hither to challenge Thomas Mowbray, Duke of Norfolk, as traitor unto God, the King, the realm and to me.'

'Do you swear upon the Holy Ghost that your quarrel be just?' asked the Marshal.

'I do,' cried Hereford in a loud ringing voice as he sheathed his sword and dropped his visor; and crossing himself and taking his lance in his hand he moved forward.

Norfolk then appeared, his charger caparisoned with equal splendour in red velvet embroidered with lions and mulberry trees.

He gave the same assurance and cried out: 'God aid him that hath the right.'

All was ready now for the signal to begin.

Richard had been waiting for this moment. He had made up his mind before his arrival at the field. He did not trust either of these two; they had come against him once, they would do so again. It was true one might kill the other but there would still be one left. He had come to the conclusion that here was a heaven-sent chance to rid himself of the two of them.

He had allowed the preparations for combat to continue because he knew that the people would have been angry if it had been cancelled. Now they had seen the splendours and had witnessed the arrival of the two protagonists; and although they were not going to see the actual combat, they would have the thrill of being present at the dénouement.

It was a dramatic moment as Hereford and Norfolk, lances ready, were about to move forward. Then Richard rose in his seat and threw down his staff. This was a sign to call an immediate halt to the proceedings.

The heralds gave the traditional shout of 'Ho! Ho!' while the crowd waited, tense with excitement. Richard ordered that the Dukes should give up their lances and return to their places.

It was then announced that the King wished to discuss the

case of this quarrel with his Council and they would retire to the royal pavilion to do so. Meanwhile all must wait for their decision as to whether the combat should go on.

It was two hours later when the decision was given.

The King and his Council had come to the conclusion that no good purpose could be served by this combat. It was not a matter of which man could acquit himself best in the lists, but which was a traitor to the King and the realm; and as neither of them had assured the King of his loyalty and he lacked trust in either, he was going to send them into exile, Norfolk for life and Hereford for ten years.

There was a great sigh in the crowd and then a deathly silence.

The horror of the two men was apparent. Exile! It was the most dreaded word. And why should the King have given such stern sentences? One thing was clear. He was very uneasy and he saw something more in this than a petty quarrel between two proud men.

During the time of their exile they were not to see each other or to communicate in any way.

There was a great deal of murmuring among the crowd as it dispersed. It had been robbed of one excitement but another perhaps even greater had replaced it. They had little sympathy for Norfolk; he was not popular but Hereford was one of their heroes. He had lost his wife recently—a young and beautiful woman; he had a family the eldest of which was a bright boy known as Harry of Monmouth. They could not understand why both men should be punished. Surely Hereford had done the right thing in disclosing what Norfolk had said to him.

It was all very mysterious. But not to Richard. There had been five knights who had come against him and this would mark his vengeance on them all. Hereford had given him the opportunity when he had made his complaints against Norfolk.

Fifteen days in which to settle affairs and leave the country!

It was a drastic sentence and clearly showed the spite in Richard's nature.

He did not wish to see either of them again, he said. Let them look to their affairs and be gone.

Hereford rode to Leicester Castle to see his father. John of Gaunt had aged considerably. When he had heard the news he could scarcely believe it. His son, Henry, who was the hope of the Lancastrian cause, to be sent into exile! There could not have been a greater blow.

He embraced him with great sorrow.

'My son,' he cried, 'what does this mean?'

'It's Richard's revenge,' said Henry. 'He has never really forgiven me.'

'But because of that stupid affair . . . I blame myself for advising you to go to him.'

'It was the only thing. Norfolk was up to some trick I know. He was trying to destroy me.'

John nodded. Henry was wise and he was dedicated to one purpose. He wanted the crown as John had once wanted it; but Henry was more subtle than his father. He worked with more caution and with a more ruthless determination.

' 'Tis done,' said John. 'We must make the best of it. One thing we must make certain of. When I die my estates must not be forfeited to the crown but must go where they belong . . . to you.'

'I pray you do not talk of death.'

'Sometimes I feel it close. Do not mention this to Catherine. She watches over me like a mother with an ailing child. I would not have her distressed.'

'You have many years left to you.'

'My son, you say what you think I should like to hear. It may be that I shall not die for years but we must make my estates secure. Richard must swear that they shall not be forfeit to the crown, for if you are not here to claim them and are still living in banishment he could take them.'

'Do you think he will agree?'

'He is going to agree,' said John. 'Before you leave, you and I shall visit him.'

'Do you think he will see me? He has told me to leave in fifteen days. Two of them have already passed.'

'He will see me and you will be with me,' said John with a flash of his old spirit. 'Never fear, he will grant this. I shall see to it. His position is not such a happy one as he could wish. The people have great regard for you, Henry, and for young Harry too. That boy has a way of winning hearts.'

'The King is never seen without his bodyguard of Cheshire archers. It seems as though he fears attack.'

'It is unwise of him for they do not make the people love him. They have an evil reputation, those archers. They behave as if they are at war. They are like soldiers pillaging the enemy's towns and villages as they march through our own. But these are the King's own subjects. They rape and murder and are not brought to account. The King will not be loved for his archers.'

'Richard is a fool, Father. One of these days he will be brought face to face with his folly.' Henry's eyes glowed with determination as he said that.

'Take care, my son,' warned John of Gaunt. 'Do nothing until you are ready. Await the opportunity.'

'Aye,' said Henry. 'You must trust me to do that.'

'And what of the children?'

'I want you and Catherine to take the three eldest.'

'Indeed we shall. Harry is at Court, is he not?'

'Yes, I have sent for him,' said Henry, 'but he has not yet come.'

John looked grave. 'We must see the King,' he said. 'And what of Humphrey and the girls?'

'My friend, Hugh Waterton, is taking them. He will care for them and I have asked that they attend Mass each day to pray for the repose of their mother's soul.'

Catherine joined them. Her beautiful eyes were uneasy; she knew how upset John was at the banishment of his son; and she feared that Henry might make trouble while he was on the Continent and that John would become embroiled in it.

But she was happy at the prospect of having his grandsons in her care. She liked the boys, particularly Harry who was the brightest of them all. She was also relieved that John was getting older and no longer felt the inclination to take an active part in the troubles of the kingdom.

She was apprehensive though when John said he was going to accompany Henry to Eltham to see the King.

'For what purpose?' she asked.

He explained about the necessity to get the King's agreement regarding his estates. She was depressed, for she knew that the question of the estates would only arise on John's death.

'He'll be back long before there is any problem about the estates,' she said rather angrily.

John pressed her hand and said no more on the subject; but when Henry rode out he went with him.

Richard received them at Eltham Palace. He could hardly turn his uncle away, particularly as John had supported him and had been for some time reckoned as his principal adviser.

'This is a sorry matter,' said John. 'And one it is hard to understand.'

'It is clear to me,' replied Richard shortly; and John saw that it would be unwise to anger him.

'I am saying farewell to my son,' said John.

'His time here is growing short,' replied Richard coldly.

'And there are one or two points which I want to clear up before he goes. I am sure you will understand my concern, for you will wish to be just to your cousin and to me.'

'It is always my desire to administer justice,' retorted Richard.

'Then, my lord, I want your undertaking that in the event of my dying during my son's absence, my estates will pass to him and not be forfeited to the Crown.'

Richard waved his hand. 'That request is granted,' he said. Then he added: 'Why Uncle, you have many years left to you.'

'So I trust,' answered John of Gaunt.

'My father will care for my elder sons,' said Henry. 'Thomas and John are on their way to Leicester now. He will take Harry back with him.'

Richard shook his head and regarded his cousin coolly.

'Nay, nay,' he said. 'Not young Harry. I have grown fond of the lad.'

John saw the stricken look in his son's eyes.

'My lord, his place is with his grandfather. He will be his guardian during my absence.'

'I have decided to be his guardian . . . for a while,' said the King.

'You mean . . .'

Richard was smiling gently. 'I mean, cousin, that I love the boy so well that I would have him at Court. He shall have his duties there and you need have no fear for him.'

He was making his meaning clear. No, Richard did not trust his cousin. He was holding young Harry of Monmouth as a hostage for his father's good behaviour.

There was nothing more to be said. Henry took his farewell of the King and his father rode with him to the coast.

'You see what this means,' said Henry. 'Harry is to be a hostage.'

'Richard grows wily . . . at last,' answered his father. 'You will have to be careful, Henry.'

'I intend to take the greatest care,' was the answer.

'At least we made him swear that my estates shall not be forfeited to the Crown; and that was what we came to do.'

'And to take Harry away.'

'Do not fret about Harry. I tell you this, there is a boy who will know how to take care of himself.'

Henry agreed with that.

At the coast he and his father took a sad farewell of each other and Henry set sail for banishment and France.

The loss of his eldest son whom he had looked on as the hope of the house of Lancaster had a marked effect on John of Gaunt. Richard had, out of compassion to him, shortened the length of exile from ten to six years. But six years! mourned John. Shall I ever see my son again?

He loved his children, all of them. His Beaufort boys as he called them delighted him because they had a look of Catherine; but Henry his first-born son, his heir, royal Henry, had been the one on whom all his hopes were fixed.

Richard was a failure. He had seen that for a long time. Richard was feckless and extravagant. He cared far too much for fine clothes and lavish displays. He gathered the wrong people about him. He had a talent for taking the wrong action—for instance marrying a child who could not be a wife to him for years. Was ever such a piece of folly committed by a King who needed an heir?

Richard's power could not last. He could see that as clearly as he could see anything. Richard would go. And Henry was in exile.

This was particularly significant at this time because news had come from Ireland that Roger de Mortimer, Earl of March and Richard's heir, had been slain in the fighting at Kells.

The crown was perilously in danger of falling from Richard's head. And who should wear it next?

If only Henry were here! Henry should take the crown. Life was ironical. How he, John of Gaunt, had yearned for that very crown; and it had been denied him, although he had found crowns for his daughters and it might have been that the most coveted of all could have gone to his son.

Life was bitter. Henry at this moment—this significant, this most fateful moment—was in exile.

He brooded a great deal on Henry's exile. He thought of young Harry whom the King kept at his side. Catherine busied herself with the others—delighted to have children to care for again. She was watchful of him but she was growing more and more anxious every day.

There came a time when John took to his bed and Catherine knew that he must indeed be falling ill to agree to do this. He lay there, his eyes closed, and Catherine was filled with a terrible fear.

He made her sit beside him and took her hand.

'These have been happy years,' he said, 'these we have had together.'

'There are many left to us,' she said firmly.

He smiled at her. 'It is not like you to hide your face from the truth, Catherine,' he said.

'You are not going to die. You are too great a man to die.'

'And where is the logic in that? Greatness has nothing to do with death. One thing is certain—I shall die. As for my greatness that is not such a certainty. I have failed so often, Catherine.'

'We have been happy,' she reminded him. 'You have just said so. To achieve happiness . . . is that not what we all seek, and to achieve it . . . that is the true success.'

'You talk like a woman . . . you always did,' he told her fondly.

'Perhaps it is no bad way to talk.'

She sat beside him holding his hand. He slept a great deal and when she looked at his face, so pale, so still, she felt a great desolation touch her for he looked as though he were already dead.

'Oh John,' she whispered, 'don't leave me. Now . . . we have come together . . . after all these years. Don't leave me . . .'

He opened his eyes and said: 'There is trouble coming, Catherine. Richard cannot last. And then . . . and then . . .'

'Don't think of it, it distresses you.'

'And then,' he said, 'what of Henry . . . ? Henry banished . . . Henry should be here. It is Henry's place . . .'

'Let it take care of itself . . .' she said. 'Rest now. It is not for you to worry.'

'It is true,' he murmured. 'I shall be gone . . . There is no peace, Catherine, for those who see the crown within their reach and yet cannot quite attain it.'

'Rest. To please me. It matters nothing . . . now.'

But it mattered still to him, she could see. He had

longed for the crown. He would be happy if he could see Richard deposed and his son Henry reigning in his stead.

'It is what Richard feared,' he murmured. 'That is why he sent him away . . .'

She sat long by his bed. She would not leave him because she knew that there was not much time left.

John of Gaunt was dead. It was like the passing of an age.

Catherine was desolate. It was the end of life for her. Since she had first met him years before, he had dominated her thoughts. He had raised her to become his Duchess and that filled her with exultation, not because he had placed her specially high but because it showed his esteem for her. Their children had been legitimized and would play a big part in the country's affairs. All that had filled her with pride but now she could feel nothing but this utter desolation.

They had taken his body to the Carmelite in Fleet Street where it would lie until burial.

In accordance with the wishes he had expressed in his will he was buried in St. Paul's Cathedral by the side of his first wife the Duchess Blanche. The funeral was a ceremonial occasion and Richard was present, expressing deep sorrow at the loss of this uncle who had played such an important part in his life.

THE RETURN OF
BOLINGBROKE

EDMUND OF LANGLEY, Duke of York, who had lived very quietly for so long, much preferring to shrug off all responsibilities and enjoy life on his country estates, had been commanded to come to see the King and was in a state of some concern.

Richard received him with affection and explained the reason for the summons.

'Well, Uncle,' said Richard, 'you see me in the throes of great preparation. I am going to show the people of Ireland that I have had enough of their disobediences. I am going to avenge Mortimer's death. You will preside over my government during my absence.'

Langley was disconcerted and uneasy, but he saw at once that protest was useless so with his usual nonchalance he accepted what he must.

'There is one matter of which I would speak with you, my lord,' he said.

'Could it possibly concern Lancaster's estates?' asked Richard.

Edmund Duke of York said that it did.

'You have not come to reproach me, Uncle?' said Richard. 'I see you so rarely. Must there be conflict between us when we do meet?'

'Not conflict, I trust,' replied York. 'I merely wish to say that I hope what I have heard regarding the estates is not true.'

'I have a feeling, Uncle, that it may well be true.'

'Not that you have taken them! I understood from my brother that you had sworn they should not be forfeit.'

'Your brother is dead, Uncle of York. The heir to these estates is in exile and will remain there for some years yet. Why should the Lancastrian estates be passed to an exile?'

'Because he is the true heir to those estates and you gave your word that they should not be forfeited to the crown.'

'You have stayed in the country overlong, Uncle. It does me good to see you here. But I like it not when you tell your King how he should rule his kingdom.'

The Duke was aghast. What had happened to his nephew since he had last seen him? Where was the young man who had sought to rule his kingdom well? Richard was not only arrogant but foolish. Did he not realize the importance of this matter of the Lancaster estates?

Henry was in exile it was true. But how long would he remain there if he found that the King had broken his word to his father? Might not Henry retaliate by breaking his word to the King?

The country was not as peaceful as he might well believe it was. There was trouble brewing and if he was going to behave in this manner Richard was going to foment it.

He took a step towards the King and at that moment one of the hounds which had been lying in the corner of the room sprang up and bared its teeth at Edmund.

Richard laughed. 'Come here, Math.' The dog went to him, placed its feet on his shoulders and began to lick his face.

'He was not going to harm me, Math. You would not have forgiven him would you, if he had?'

He patted the dog's head, and grinned at his uncle.

'My faithful friend,' he said. 'He will defend me with his life. Let any come against me and Math will make short work of him.'

The King sat down. Edmund remained standing. Richard said: 'This is my favourite hound, my Math. He is a royal dog. He serves none but the King. He likes me to wear my crown. Do you not, Math? How excited you become when you see that bauble on my head. Has it struck you, Uncle, that dogs have an extra sense which we lack? They will not go to haunted places. They bristle, they draw back, they bare their teeth. Sometimes I think they are aware of coming events. What say you?'

It was Richard's way of telling Edmund that the matter of the Lancaster estates was to be discussed no more.

Edmund asked for leave to retire and it was graciously given.

The little Queen was restive. It was so long since she had seen the King. She lived for his visits. She thought he was the most handsome man in the world; and they always had such fun together. He would ask her how she was getting on at her lessons with a certain mock severity which would have them laughing so much that there would be tears in their eyes. Then they would talk about clothes and he would bring in the musicians so that they could dance together.

Once he had played a trick on her and sent Richard Maudelyn to her. She was proud of the fact that she had quickly discovered him not to be her King, although she had had to admit that Richard Maudelyn played the part well.

She was a little anxious because she fancied Richard was concerned about something. She did get scraps of information mostly by listening to servants. She knew that there had been a big quarrel between John of Gaunt's son and the Duke of Norfolk and that Richard had sent them both into exile.

Much nearer home so that it concerned her more was the departure of the Lady de Couci. It seemed that she had been spending too much money and behaving as though she were the Queen Mother.

Well, perhaps she had. Isabella did not greatly regret her going. She had a new governess who was the wife of the Earl of March, a sad woman at the time—very different from Lady de Couci—because she had just lost her husband who had been killed in Ireland.

Oh, if only Richard would come to see her! She would sulk a little when he did come. It had been such a long time.

Every night she prayed: 'Oh God, let him come tomorrow.' But God took no notice of her prayers.

But finally they were answered. She was at her lessons with her new governess when she heard the sounds of arrival; and throwing aside her books she dashed down to the great hall and there he was—handsome, fair hair glistening in the sunlight, standing there looking about him for his little Queen.

She flung herself at him. 'Richard! Richard! Are you indeed here?'

'It would seem so. Is this the way to greet your King? Would you suffocate him?'

'I would hold him so fast that he could never get away.'

'Methinks he would be happy if you could do that.'

'Richard . . . Richard how long you have been!'

'Affairs of state, sweet lady.'

'I hate affairs of state.'

'I am often in agreement with you.'

'I thought Kings sat on thrones with their Queens beside them and went riding out and the people cheered them . . . and they were always together.'

'It rarely happens so. But here I am. Now tell me, how have you been faring?'

Arm in arm they went into the castle.

She said: 'Feasts must be prepared. I must command them to roast the finest deer.'

'I think they will do it for me, and leave you to be with me, little Queen.'

'Yes, mayhap they will and I would not lose one moment with you. How long shall you stay?'

He stroked her hair. 'I leave today, dearest. I broke the journey just to see you.'

'No!'

'I fear so, my little one. I am going to Ireland.'

'Is it because of the Earl of March?'

He nodded.

'And when will you come back?'

'Soon and then straight to you.'

'Lady de Couci has gone.'

'Does it grieve you?'

'No.'

'She gave herself airs. She thought she was the Queen. Did you know she kept three goldsmiths, three cutlers, three furriers all at my expense.'

'I must cost you a lot of money.'

'The Exchequer groans under your extravagance.'

She laughed and nestled close to him.

'I am glad,' she said. 'It will stop you forgetting me.'

'Do you think I should ever do that?'

She threw her arms about his neck.

'What, preparing to suffocate me again! They say a King's life is always in danger. It would seem so.'

'Don't say it! Don't say it!' she cried, putting her hands over his mouth. He took them and kissed them.

'Shall I tell you about Math?'

'Oh yes, yes.'

'He is such a naughty dog. When he sees me in my crown he leaps with excitement. Do you know I do not believe he would love me half as much if I were not the King.'

'I would love you always.'

'My dearest and most faithful Queen. Will you always love me then, Isabella?'

She nodded gravely. Then she was laughing. 'I pray you do not think you can deceive me by sending Richard Maudelyn to me again.'

'Nay. I learned my lessons there.'

'Richard, must you go today?'

'I must.'

'Ireland is so far away.'

'As soon as I am back I shall come to you.'

'Promise me that.'

'I swear it.'

Then she said: 'Let us forget now that you are going to leave me. Let us be happy while we can.'

So they were merry together, both pretending to forget that parting was imminent.

They went to Mass together in Windsor Church and on leaving took wine and comfits at the door.

There he must say his last farewell to her. He picked her up in his arms and kissed her again and again. She clung to him.

'Richard, don't go. Richard, stay.'

'My little love,' he said, 'people watch us. We must remember, must we not, that we are the King and Queen? Adieu, my sweetest, until we meet again.'

Then he released himself and turned away to hide his emotion.

Henry of Bolingbroke was brooding in Paris. He had good friends with him—all Richard's enemies. There was Thomas Arundel the Archbishop of Canterbury and the young Earl of Arundel who still talked fiercely of avenging his father. Agents from England had been coming back and forth with news of the people's discontent with Richard and now Henry had a grievance. The King had broken his promise. Solemnly he had sworn that the Lancaster estates should not be forfeited to the crown and immediately on the death of John of Gaunt this had been done. If the King could break *his* promise that released Bolingbroke from his.

Henry was going to England. He was going to take the crown from Richard, but he must act cautiously. He could have gathered together an army in France but the English would not wish to see foreigners on their soil and his cause would be lost before it started. What Henry wanted was an English army fighting to replace a weak king by a strong one.

The moment had come. Richard was in Ireland, and Edmund of Langley, Duke of York, a pleasant good man but completely lacking the ability to rule, was in charge of the government. Edmund had been retired from Court life and living in the country for some years. Moreover Richard had appointed to serve with him some of the most unpopular men in England: the Earl of Wiltshire, William Scrope, Sir William Bagot, Sir John Bushy and Sir Henry Green.

Henry laid his plans with care. He had good reason for returning and he would come only with a few friends at the head of whom would be the Archbishop and the Earl of Arundel. He did not land in the South but in the Lancastrian stronghold of Yorkshire and made his way to Pontefract Castle.

When it was heard that Henry was in England and that he had sworn that his only aim was to regain his estates many flocked to his banner. Few men of property approved of the confiscation of estates by the crown and they were ready to help Henry regain his.

But the people were ripe for rebellion. Edmund of Langley hearing that Henry had now amassed a considerable army and was marching south went to meet him. There was no battle but Edmund Langley was no strategist and men began deserting from his army which fell back to Bristol. But the people of Bristol were not for the King and they seized the Earl of Wiltshire, Sir Henry Green and Sir John Bushy and executed them because they said they were the King's evil counsellors. Thus when Henry came into Bristol the first thing he saw was the heads of these men on the city walls. He himself was greeted with cheers wherever he went.

When the news was brought to Richard in Ireland that Henry had landed and had placed himself at the head of an army, he was mad with fury.

He sent for Harry of Monmouth and contemplated what he would do with the boy.

If he could catch his father, he told him, he should die a death which should make a noise as far as Turkey.

Young Harry did not flinch. Richard looked at him through narrowed eyes. A hostage! Yet Henry of Bolingbroke had not cared that his son was in the King's possession.

He could not harm the boy. He had spoken truth when

he had said he was fond of him. It was not the fault of Harry of Monmouth that his father was a traitor.

'Take the boy away,' he said. 'Make him my prisoner. Let him be placed in Trim Castle and kept there until I say what shall become of him.'

So young Harry of Monmouth was taken to the Irish castle and there held prisoner while Richard made his plans to leave for England.

He was full of hope when he landed at Milford Haven. 'We shall show this traitor what happens to his like,' he declared, and he gave himself up to the pleasure of what he would do when Bolingbroke was in his hands.

Alas, when he arrived in England he found there were few who were ready to rally to his banner; and those who had been with him in Ireland had little heart for the fight.

It was alarming. They were all stealing away from him. Only a few remained. Where was the army he needed to subdue Bolingbroke? What had happened? Why had they all deserted him?

What could he do? He summoned two whom he trusted— the Dukes of Exeter and Surrey—and told them they must go to his cousin and ask what his intentions were. If as he said he merely wished for the return of the Lancaster estates, they must discuss this matter.

The two Dukes rode off to Chester but when they arrived at Henry's stronghold he ordered them to join his forces and they immediately declared themselves willing to do this, for they believed that Richard's was a lost cause.

Richard was desolate for there seemed to be no way out of this morass into which he had so suddenly fallen. He could only wander from castle to castle with the very smallest band of faithful followers, knowing well that he could not continue in that way. From Conway to Caernarvon and from Caernarvon to Beaumaris and then back to Conway; and there the Earl of Northumberland, acting as Henry's emissary, came to see him.

'What would you have of me, traitor?' demanded Richard.

'I come from the Duke of Hereford, my lord.'

'I know it well—traitor from traitor.'

'We are no traitors, my lord. The Duke of Hereford does not mean to seize the throne. He merely wishes to escort you to London so that a Parliament may be held to deal with your evil counsellors through whose advice you have misgoverned the realm.'

Richard said with dignity: 'I will meet my cousin.' Indeed he knew he had no alternative.

'I will conduct you to the castle of Flint, my lord, where he awaits your coming.'

'Then let us go,' said Richard.

Flint Castle was a formidable looking fortress—square with a large round tower at each corner and a keep of great size and strength detached from the main building and joined to it by a drawbridge. This tower was the donjon of the castle.

It was dusk when they arrived and being exhausted by the journey Richard soon slept and did not awaken until the morning.

He sat up in his bed wondering for a moment where he was. Then the memory of the previous day came to him. It seemed like a nightmare but the more wakeful he became the more real he realized it to be.

It was undignified. It was demeaning. He would never forget this. Once his cousin was in his power he would lose no time in bringing about his end; and it would be in no delicate manner either.

He rose and went to hear Mass in the castle chapel and as he came out he heard the sounds of marching.

His spirits rose. His friends were coming to rescue him. He had known the nightmare could not persist.

'I want to go to the tower,' he said. 'I wish to see what is happening outside the castle.'

He went and when he looked down on that army gathered there he knew it was the end for him. Hereford's men were surrounding the castle; and he recognized among them some on whose loyalty he had believed he could rely.

He covered his face with his hands; he wanted to shut out the sight.

One of his guards spoke to him. 'My lord,' he said, 'the Duke of Hereford will be here after dinner.'

'I shall have much to say to him when we meet,' replied Richard grimly.

He saw the sly smile on the face of the guard and he thought: By St. John the Baptist, how has this come about? Such a short while ago I was their King and they trembled at my word. Then I went to Ireland and now that I am back, everything is changed.

How quickly men who had once shown respect could delight in betraying their contempt. But there were a few friends left to him.

Yes, there were some who had not torn off the badge of the White Hart.

He went to the chamber where a table was laid for dinner. He turned to those who still wore their badges and said: 'Kind friends and loyal gentlemen, sit down with me and eat for you are in peril of death for your fidelity to me.'

'Aye,' cried one of the guards, 'you should all eat well. For soon your heads will be off and how will you eat then?'

'My friends,' said the King, 'heed not these oafs. Their time will come, I promise you.'

And what alarmed him most was the lack of concern on the faces of these men. It was clear that they did not believe him.

After the meal he made his way to that chamber where he was to receive his cousin.

He had commanded that a chair be placed for him which should act as a throne. He was the King, he would remind them. This was not denied him and he went to it and seated himself and there awaited the coming of his enemy.

Henry came before him as a subject to his King. He bowed and knelt. Richard took his hand and bade him rise. It did not seem that he was the vanquished one and the man who knelt before him the conqueror.

'My lord and sovereign King,' said Henry, 'I have come back before my time.'

'Why do you come thus, cousin?' asked Richard.

'I have come to seek the restitution of my lands and heritage.'

'I am ready to accomplish your will so that you may enjoy all that is yours without exception.'

'There is one other matter,' went on Henry. 'The common report of your people is that you have governed them badly for twenty years. They are not content therewith. If it pleases you, I will help you to govern better.'

The Archbishop then asked leave to speak, and when this was granted he told the King that his rule could no longer be tolerated and that he must abdicate.

Richard had expected this. He knew that the soft words of his cousin could be set aside. Here he was his cousin's prisoner and Henry of Bolingbroke, Duke of Hereford and Lancaster, had an army behind him, while Richard's followers had deserted him.

What was a King without an army when his enemies came against him?

He was a prisoner in his cousin's hands and no good could come of denying it.

He faced Henry and said meekly: 'Fair cousin, since it pleases you it pleases me.'

They began the journey to London. They had given him a miserable little horse to ride and when they reached Chester Richard was a prisoner in his own castle and the one who was set to guard him was the young Earl of Arundel who bore him a grudge for the murder of his father.

But when I reach London, thought Richard, it will be different. The people of London will rally to me. Everything will be changed then.

Alas it was not so. He soon realized that London had rejected him and had transferred its allegiance to Henry.

They took him to the Tower and there he remained while Henry went to St. Paul's to pay respect to the tombs of his father and his mother. The people liked the sentiment he showed at these tombs and they came into the streets to cheer him.

Henry was moving cautiously. He was determined that Richard must abdicate of his own free will. He did not want it to be said that he had driven him from the throne. That Richard was a weak ruler all must admit; and that England needed a strong king was equally obvious. But it must come about as Henry wished.

He wanted it to be known that Richard, who was still the King, must be treated with respect and every effort must be made for his comfort. He even ordered that his dogs should be brought to him. All must know that Henry was a just man and would only take the crown if it was seen that Richard could no longer wear it.

He was with the guards in the chamber when the hound Math was brought in.

It was then that the strange thing happened for Math came bounding towards the King but before he reached him, he stopped suddenly. Then he turned away from Richard and went to Henry and placing his feet on his shoulders licked his face.

There was great astonishment in the chamber for the dog had previously paid little attention to any but the King.

Henry was the first to speak. 'What does this mean?' he asked. 'Is this not your dog?'

'Like others,' said Richard, 'he was mine, but, you see, even my dog knows which side he should be on.'

It was uncanny. The guards talked of it. It was a sign.

Nothing could have convinced them more than that strange act of the dog that Richard's reign was over, and that of Henry of Bolingbroke had begun.

PONTEFRACT

THEY HAD GIVEN him the clothes of a foreigner that he might not be recognized as they took him down the river. He was not sure of his destination. He felt numbed and at times he was certain that he would wake up and find he had been the victim of a nightmare that had seemed to go on for weeks. At Gravesend they alighted and went by road to Leeds Castle in Kent.

A prisoner, he the King! No, no longer the King—plain Richard of Bordeaux. He would never forget those last days in the Tower. Gloomy days, with the rain pelting against the grey walls and the darkness of despair in the fortress.

For the last time he had worn his royal robes, but he was not allowed to sit on the throne. He had gone there only to give it up.

How they had shamed him! They had kept him standing while they read out the long list of his deficiencies. And then had come the degrading moment when he had taken off his crown and handed it to Bolingbroke.

Oh fool that I was! he had thought. I had him in my power once. I exiled him. I should have destroyed him then.

And Bolingbroke was now Henry the Fourth of England. It was the end. He had failed and it had all happened too quickly for him. He had not seen the danger until it was right upon him.

Leeds was one of the most beautiful castles in England standing as it did on two islands connected by a double drawbridge, but Richard was in no mood to admire his surroundings. He could see nothing but that terrible scene in the great hall at Westminster when he had meekly handed over his birthright to his cousin.

It was all over now. This was the end. Pictures from the past filled his mind. He remembered so well the anxious looks in his mother's eyes. She had feared for him from the moment she knew he was destined to become a king. He thought of his great father and wondered what he would feel if he could look down on what was happening to his son.

He must not brood on these things; of what then could he think? Of the present? He shivered. The future? What hope was there in life for him?

They did not leave him long at Leeds. They did not tell him where they were taking him, but he knew that he was riding North. Ah yes, to some Lancastrian stronghold of his cousin-enemy. First they kept him at Pickering and after that at Knaresborough and finally they came to the Castle of Pontefract.

It was built on a rock and the high wall was flanked by seven towers. The moat on the western side was deep. He had visited Pontefract before and had heard of the dungeons there. There was at least one he knew which could only be entered through a trap door. Prisoners were lowered and left there to die.

What did they intend to do with him? The fact that he had been taken to this grim fortress of Pontefract could be significant.

It was deep winter now and the weather bitterly cold. There were snowdrifts about the castle walls. From one of the towers Richard could look down on the town and he could see the guards who were stationed about the castle. There were always guards; when one group went off duty another took its place. It was heartening in a way because it meant that his enemies feared there might be an attempt to rescue him.

He let himself dream. This nightmare would pass. He would be back again. He would be King; men would bow before him; he would ride to Windsor and his dear little Isabella.

Isabella, Isabella, he murmured, what do you know of this?

Poor sweet child! She was growing up now. She would hear news and her sweet heart would be torn with grief.

He must write to her. Perhaps they would send her to him. She was too young to be suspected of subtlety. She was but a child. She would be faithful to him in his adversity. Unlike Math. When he thought of that incident it struck him as uncanny. It had unnerved him more than anything that had gone before. Looking back, he saw that in that moment when Math had turned from him to Henry he had known it was the end.

Dear, sweet Isabella! She would never turn from him.

They allowed him writing materials. With mingling pleasure and pain he took up his pen.

'My mistress and my consort, cursed be the man who has separated us. I am dying of grief because of it. Since I am robbed of the joy of being with you, I suffer such pain and am near despair . . . And it is no marvel when I from such a height have fallen so low, and lose my joy, my solace and my consort.'

'Sweet child,' he murmured. 'What will become of you? What will become of us both?'

They had set Sir Thomas Swynford to guard him. Trust Henry to make sure that those on whom he could rely should be given positions of trust. Swynford was the son of Henry's stepmother, Catherine of Lancaster, and as all his possessions had come to him through Lancaster he would serve the Lancastrian cause with all his heart because it was his own.

But he, Richard, had been good to Catherine. Had he not, on his uncle's urgent request, legitimized the children they had had? The Beauforts were now the recognized legitimate sons of John of Gaunt. Surely they should be grateful for that. But it was natural that they should support their half-brother.

He did not like Thomas Swynford. He fancied the man took pleasure in humiliating him.

He talked to him now and then almost condescendingly and showed no respect for one who had once been a king.

Once Richard said to him: 'I was a good friend to you and your mother, Thomas Swynford.'

Thomas Swynford replied: 'You thought it well to please the man you called your mighty uncle.'

'There were times when John of Gaunt felt it advisable to please me. Why do you say the man I call my uncle?'

'Because many say now that he was not your uncle because you were not the son of the Black Prince.'

'None would believe such a lie.'

'Some do. There is a priest who is so like you that men say he must be your brother.'

'Richard Maudelyn! He bears a resemblance to me but who has said that he is my brother. How could that be?'

'Your mother was a lady much given to gaiety. The Black Prince was a man who suffered from much sickness. There were some handsome priests in the Court of Bordeaux.'

'You lie! How dare you utter such foul slander against my mother.'

Thomas Swynford gave a mock bow. 'My apologies. You asked for truth and I gave it to you. I tell you this is what is being said. There is a priest who is so like you that he must be your brother . . . your half-brother that is.'

'These are lies put about by my cousin.'

'I must warn you it is unwise to slander the King. That is treason.'

'Then, Thomas Swynford, you should at this moment be condemned to the traitor's death.'

'How forgetful you are! You are no longer a king, Richard. You are less than the least of us.'

He was in despair. There was nothing he could do. He must accept this slander. He was powerless.

394

Where was Isabella now? What was she thinking? Sad little Queen. And even sadder Richard.

Cold despair had settled on him. Was there not one man in the kingdom who was his friend? Was he doomed to stay here, his cousin's prisoner, until he died?

One day one of the guards contrived to be alone with him and the words he said sent wild hope soaring through Richard's heart.

'My lord King, you have your friends . . .'

A great gladness came to him. He was not entirely forgotten then.

'Whence came you?' asked Richard. 'And what do you know?'

'I am to tell you that all will be well. Ere long the traitor Bolingbroke will be no more.'

'Whom do you serve?'

'My lord, your brother, the Duke of Exeter, who is stripped of that title and is now known as the Earl of Huntingdon.'

His half-brother, John Holland! He could have wept with joy. John would help him. Of course he would. He was their mother's son. How he and his brother had teased him when he was a boy; how they had indulged in rough horseplay and practical jokes and their mother had reprimanded them. 'Remember Richard is but a boy yet.'

They had laughed at him, joked with him, tried to teach him their rough games . . . but they had loved him.

'Are you sure of this?' he asked.

'My lord, I serve the Duke your brother and he would have you be prepared and not lose hope.'

'Who is with us?'

'Your half-brother and his nephew, the Earl of Kent, with Thomas le Despenser, your nephew, the Earl of Rutland, and others. It is a simple plan, my lord, but simple plans are most likely to succeed. Bolingbroke is holding a tournament at Windsor. Our party will go there with carts of harness and armour for the tournament it will be believed. Then we shall choose our moment, overpower the guards, kill Bolingbroke and his son, Henry of Monmouth, and restore you to your throne.'

'Oh God, bless them. My good brother, my good friends.'

'We shall succeed, my lord. But there is one thing you must know. The people will want to see you, and it will take time to release you from this place. It may be that they will have to fight their way through to you.'

'Are there other good and faithful friends like yourself in the castle?'

'There are a few, my lord. But I am wary of trusting them.'

'I thank you. I shall not forget you when I come back to my own.'

'I thank you, my lord. What I must warn you of is this. You may hear that the King is marching at the head of his troops, and you will scent treachery. My lord it will not be so. It will be part of the plan. Richard Maudelyn will take your place. He will show himself as yourself. The people will see him and will believe that you have indeed escaped from your captors.'

Richard started to laugh; and stopped himself. It was hysterical laughter and he saw the fear it inspired in the loyal guard.

'My lord, we must be discreet. I was to tell you this that you might hold yourself in readiness. Give up your despair, my lord. The day will soon be here.'

'My good man, you have given me new life. I should have known my brother John would not forget me. Nor would my brother Thomas had he lived. Others are with me too. So I am no longer alone.'

'My lord, I beg of you, give no sign of your elation. It is imperative to our success that the matter is of the utmost secrecy. Everything depends on our success at Windsor.'

'Aye. But it shall come to pass. I shall march to London and before me the head of Bolingbroke will be held aloft on a lance.'

'I pray God it may be so. I must leave you now, my

lord. I beg of you to hide your joy. Continue in your melancholy. It is necessary, I do assure you.'

'I understand. My joy shall remain hidden in my heart.'

He lay down to sleep and he dreamed he was marching to Isabella. Where was she now, his little Queen? He imagined her joy when she heard that he was coming to her. She would be waiting on the battlements of the castle where they would have taken her. She would run to meet him. They would cling together and laugh and make merry.

Isabella was desperately unhappy. She knew that Richard was in danger and that the traitor Bolingbroke had taken his crown. If they would only let her go to him. If she could only speak to him, hear from his own lips what had happened, she could have borne it. But to remain in ignorance, a prisoner of the man who called himself the King, it was unbearable.

They had moved her to Sonning-hill and here she must see the badges of the usurper on all the servants and the men who guarded her.

Henry was the King now, she was told. Richard had abdicated in his favour. Richard no longer deserved to be King nor wished to be, for he had willingly given over his crown to his cousin.

'It is lies . . . lies!' she sobbed. 'I do not believe it. I will never believe it.'

If only she could know what was happening. She had grown up in these last months. She was no longer a pampered child. She was a desperate woman.

What joy was hers when Richard's half-brother arrived at the castle. John Holland, wild adventurer that he was, was sure of success.

He had taken the place with the utmost ease from those who made an effort to defend it. Henry had never thought Sonning need be heavily protected. True it contained the Queen but the Queen was a child and had never been regarded of great importance.

John Holland knelt before her and kissed her hand.

'Rest assured, my lady, that soon you will be restored to the King. Soon the usurper will be no more.'

'Oh, how happy you have made me! I have been so miserable. Dear, dear Richard! Shall I see him soon?'

'Ere long, my lady.'

She clasped her hands together. 'I hate it here. I have heard so little of Richard. Tell me . . . is he well?'

'You will soon see for yourself and I doubt not he will be bounding with good health when he has you beside him.'

'I hate Bolingbroke. He is a wicked cruel traitor to Richard. They wear his badges here. I am going to order them to remove them at once. They must tear them off and replace them with those of the white hart.'

'That will be a good start,' said John Holland smiling.

Richard's supporters were meeting at Kingston in readiness for the attack on Windsor. At this time there was need for the utmost secrecy.

The Earl of Rutland, son of the Duke of York, who had promised support for the coup did not arrive with his men and notice was sent to him to remind him of his obligations.

When Rutland received the notice he was with his father and the Duke of York was amazed at his son's demeanour.

'What news?' he asked.

Rutland hesitated. His father was a meek and kindly man and they had always been on terms of great affection.

He said: 'It is a reminder that I am to join my friends. We are going to put Richard back on the throne.'

The Duke stared at his son in horror. '*You* are involved in this!'

'My lord father, Richard is the true King.'

'There is no hope of reinstating him.'

'He is the son of the Black Prince, my grandfather's eldest son. My cousin Henry is not the true heir.'

'The battle is over. Richard is deposed. He will never hold the throne. Henry is strong. He is recognized as the King. The people want him. They will never take Richard back. You must not join with these men, my son. If you do you will lose your head and soon too. I am going to save you from that.'

Rutland stared at his father in horror. He had betrayed his friends, he knew. Although Edmund Langley, Duke of York, had never had the wild ambition of his brothers he was determined on this. It was no use supporting a lost cause and his nephew Henry was the man to take the throne in place of Richard.

He had to save his son though and he was thinking quickly.

'You are a dead man, my son, if you do not act promptly. Henry must be warned. There must be no more bloodshed. There will be revolt throughout the country. Under Henry we have a chance of peace and prosperity. I shall show this letter to Henry—unless you show it to him before me. Go with all speed to Windsor. Tell Henry that Richard's supporters are rising against him. Tell him of the plot to kill him while he lies unsuspecting at Windsor. Go now . . . as fast as you can. I tell you this: I shall follow you. My task will be to tell the King of this so he is certain to know. But I want you to be there before me. Do you understand?'

Rutland looked into his father's earnest eyes. Never before had he seen him so determined.

'I will do as you say,' he said. 'I see that you are right.'

Henry received the news from Rutland with calm. His prompt action confirmed to all about him that he could be relied upon to take charge of events with the resourcefulness of a true leader.

With his sons beside him he left Windsor and made for London. Within a few hours he had mustered an army.

Meanwhile John Holland had left Kingston for Windsor. The little Queen rode with him. He talked to her of how they would take Richard from his prison and set him on the throne again.

She was beautiful with the glow in her cheeks and the

shine in her eyes. She had never known such excitement. Everything will be worth while, she told herself, when I see him again.

John Holland was so sure. She believed him. Richard had talked to her often about this half-brother of his. He had always loved him; and she would love him ever after.

'I wonder what he will say when he sees me riding with you,' she said. 'What a surprise for him.'

'It will make his joy complete,' Holland told her.

They had come close to Cirencester and here they were to join up with friends.

When Isabella saw him riding at the head of the party she felt almost faint with joy. There he was, his fair hair blowing in the wind; his blue eyes alight with excitement.

She rode up to him.

'Richard. Richard, I am here . . .'

He turned to her. Her heart seemed to turn to stone; the pain of disappointment was unbearable, for the figure riding at the head of the troops was not Richard. It was the priest who looked so like him.

She did not hear the words of consternation; she was not aware of the numb terror that was all about her. She did not even hear the words: 'Bolingbroke is on the march. He has mustered a great army to come against us.' But she was conscious of a sudden despair.

It was all over. They did not harm her. She was too young to be taken seriously. Moreover she was the daughter of the King of France and Henry of Bolingbroke was a cautious man.

She was hurried away from the scene of the battle to Havering atte Bower and there she was to be placed under restraint until it was decided what should be done with her.

News reached her now and then. Richard had never escaped from his prison in Pontefract. The priest had once more impersonated him. It had been of no avail. The poor priest had lost his head for his part in the farce. John Holland was dead too. He had escaped from Bolingbroke's forces but was captured at Pleshy by the Countess of Hereford, the sister of the Earl of Arundel. She had him beheaded without any delay and his head was stuck on a lance on the walls of Pleshy Castle.

Isabella wept and talked constantly of Richard. At least he was not dead and while he lived she would never give up hope of joining him.

Now all she could do was wait in Havering and pray and hope that one day she would be with her husband.

King Henry was uneasy. There would be no safety for him while Richard lived.

He had always said that if there was any attempt to put Richard on the throne he would have to be removed. How?

If only he would die! It would have been better if he had escaped. Then he might have been killed in battle; but now he lay a prisoner in Pontefract fretting away his days; and the people who lived nearby were aware that he was there. They would look for the light in the tower and shiver as they passed by.

'There lies one who was once a king,' they said, and there was pity in their eyes and voices.

Henry decreed that there should be a curfew at dusk and no person from the town should venture out when the bell had rung. The guards must be watchful.

There was no peace for the new King of England while Richard lived.

Thomas Swynford knew that, and he was eager to serve his mother's stepson well. All his good had come from the house of Lancaster. His mother's marriage to the mighty Duke had changed their lives.

Who had he been but Thomas Swynford—son of a humble squire . . . until his mother became the wife of the Duke of Lancaster?

He would like to show his gratitude to the man whom he daringly referred to as his brother.

Henry knew it. Thomas Swynford was to be trusted.

Thomas Swynford knew that Henry could have no peace while Richard lived.

There must be no bloody murder, though. Murdered men became martyrs. Richard must never be allowed to become one.

But Richard must not live.

How gloomy it was in the castle of Pontefract; how the winds howled about those walls. How long the winter was!

Richard lay listless on his pallet. His coat was stained. His golden hair was matted, his beard uncombed.

In the past he had cared so much for his appearance; how he had loved fine clothes, jewels, perfumed unguents, good wine, good food, gracious living.

But now . . . There was nothing now. There were no fine jewels nor sumptuous materials. His meat was often tainted, his bread mouldy.

Thomas Swynford was always there, watching him sardonically; the son of a squire now the master of the son of a great prince.

'And you expect me to eat this?' Richard had demanded.

'Why not?' was the answer. 'It is good enough.'

'Would *you* eat it?'

'I am not the King's prisoner.'

He could not eat. He felt faint from hunger but the food they brought him only sickened him.

'You must eat or you will die,' said Thomas Swynford.

'I will die then,' replied Richard.

Thomas Swynford said nothing and continued to serve the tainted meat.

Richard was often light-headed. His thoughts would slip away into the past. That was comfort, for the past was so much easier to live in than the present.

But there was a nightmare which haunted him. His great-grandfather, Edward the Second, had been treated thus. So must he have lain in a castle prison. And one night they had come to him . . .

Richard could not bear to think of it. What if they

should remember and say as it was with Edward so shall it be with Richard?

Pontefract instead of Berkeley . . . Richard in place of Edward.

'Oh God, let me die first,' he prayed.

He was so weak now. He could scarcely raise himself. He ate nothing. He did not want food now. He could only lie still and drift from the past to the present and when he was most lucid he remembered what they had done to his great-grandfather.

If one wish could be granted me now, he thought, I know what it would be. Death.

It was a wild night on the 14th of February. No one was about. Even if the curfew had not kept people in the weather would.

Thomas Swynford came stealthily into the room. He knew it could not be long now. His prisoner had eaten nothing for many a day. He was fast fading away.

How the wind howled as though for a soul in torment!

It cannot be long now, thought Thomas Swynford. To-day . . . tomorrow . . . I shall be sending my news to the King.

He tiptoed to the pallet. There he lay, the once handsome King, the proud Plantagenet.

The last wish of Richard of Bordeaux had been granted.

He was dead, and the throne was safe for Henry of Bolingbroke.

ABOUT THE AUTHOR

Jean Plaidy, who is Victoria Holt, resides in England.
This is her fifteenth novel for Fawcett and the tenth
book in the Plantagenet saga.